FOREVER EVERGREEN

E. M. LANGSTON

For my grandparents, Paul and Annelies Squeri
For all the summers at the lake
Please don't read chapter 18

TRIGGER WARNINGS

While I personally believe tropes and trigger warnings to be spoilers, I do understand that for some they are necessary. I also recognize that by writing about college age characters I attract a younger audience, however please note that this book is intended for readers 18+ for the following reasons:

Alcohol & Drug Use
Anxiety & Anxiety Attacks
Addiction
Firearms (for safety and recreation)
Hit-and-Run
Preterm Labor resulting in Child Death
Sexual Acts Detailed on the Page

PROLOGUE

"I SHOULD HAVE ABORTED YOU WHEN I HAD THE CHANCE." —LAUREL

Jensen Fisher tapped her leg anxiously as she stared up at the clock. A quick glance around the room told her she wasn't alone. Everyone was counting down the final two minutes of their last class before being set free. But for Jensen, the final bell felt the opposite of freeing. To her, freedom was the feeling she got when she dove into a crisp, chlorinated pool. It was the ache of working her muscles in a way that had become second nature. It was the rush she felt when she tore through the glass surface and the stretch of her fingertips as she reached for the wall. The two minutes it took for her to swim a 200 meter free were exhilarating. And the feeling of touching the wall first and seeing her name at the top of the leaderboard was a high she chased time and time again. Those two minutes always seemed to fly by, and yet the two minutes she had left of class dragged on.

She'd been in denial for weeks, still waking up at 5:00 a.m. every morning to swim despite the season ending nearly a month ago. She ended the competition season by announcing her retirement, but hadn't yet come to terms with the reality of that choice. The impending ring of the final bell felt like it was announcing the end of everything she'd worked for. Her swim that morning could've marked the last time she'd ever dive into an olympic sized pool–the last time she'd push her body to its limit and feel that rush.

The bell rang while she was recalling that morning's swim, kicking herself for not giving it just a bit more. She clocked herself at just over two minutes which meant that after two years of trying, she'd never be as good as she was when she made the Olympic team at sixteen. It was hard to accept that she'd already peaked. It felt wrong to walk away and leave her goal forever unfinished.

Jensen walked toward her dorm in a daze. All around her yearbooks were being signed, people were wrapping each other in tight hugs, tears were being spilled, and plans were being made. She heard whispers about an end of the year party for the seniors, but ignored them. No one but Lucy would think to invite her anyway. And why would they? None of them really knew her, they only knew *of* her. She was either *'that swimmer girl'* or *'Lucy's friend'* to her peers. Even amongst the swim team Jensen had always been in a league of her own.

In a last minute decision, she veered away from the dorms and headed across campus toward the pool.

Two hours later, with her shoulders hunched from exhaustion, she pushed open the door to her dorm and was hit with a wall of sound. Lucy was lying on her bed blasting a summer playlist she'd had on repeat for the past three weeks.

Lucy, a second generation Chinese-American, was Jensen's complete opposite. She was totally popular, always disorganized, and had an edge that was enviable. Somehow she even managed to make their drab blue and gray uniforms look cool. She was head-banging to "The Boys of Summer" by The Ataris. And by the mess that was usually silky black hair, she'd been doing so for a while.

Jensen crossed the room and turned the speaker down, triggering Lucy to stop head banging and twist around to face her. Her almond shaped eyes immediately crinkled into a smile. "You're back!" Lucy screamed, her ears still ringing from the volume. "Where were you? You were supposed to be back two hours ago." Then, noticing Jensen's wet hair and the athletic bag flung over her shoulder, she rolled her eyes. "Never mind, I already know where you were. Did you at least beat your time?"

"No, not even close." She dropped her bag defeatedly and plopped down on her bed, before finally taking in their room. Lucy had done a lot in the two hours Jensen had been at the pool. Five large suitcases were stacked neatly at the foot of her bed along with two boxes. The twinkle lights, posters, and pictures had already been taken down.

"Sorry," Lucy said as she fell back onto her bed. She let out a long yawn and burrowed into her pillow. "Look, I'm gonna get some shut eye so I'm not exhausted tonight. Wake me up in an hour so I have time to get ready?"

"Sure, no problem." Jensen said, setting an alarm on her phone.

"I still think you should come with me," Lucy said through a yawn.

"Thanks for the invite but you know parties aren't really my scene."

"Yeah, but I'm selfish and I know I'll have more fun if you're there."

When Jensen refused again, Lucy pulled up her blanket and was asleep in minutes.

Jensen spent the next hour packing. By the time she woke Lucy up she'd shoved everything into a large suitcase

"Can you come sit on this?" she asked Lucy, who was stretched out like a cat on her bed. She answered with a groan then rolled off the bed and sprawled her entire body across the top of Jensen's luggage, her black satin fringe falling in front of her eyes. Blowing the bangs out of her face, she watched Jensen tug at the zipper, but the bag refused to close.

"That didn't help at all. You're too light," Jensen said. "Switch places with me."

"How is that gonna help?" Lucy asked, sliding off the suitcase.

Jensen rolled her eyes and situated herself atop the bag. She was a good fifty pounds heavier than Lucy but because she was also a foot taller they could usually share clothes. As if proving her point, the bag sunk a little under her weight.

Unfortunately, they still didn't have any luck getting it to close. Jensen sighed and moved to the floor next to Lucy.

"What do you have in here, anyway?" Lucy asked, unzipping the part Jensen had successfully gotten to stay closed. When she opened it she gasped. "Why are you packing all your uniforms?"

"All I own is uniforms," Jensen said. Lucy, of course, knew this. After all, she was the one who supplied Jensens with count-less outfits, for everything from picnic dates, to fancy dinners, to her graduation dress. It all came from Lucy's closet.

"Seriously?" Lucy pulled out a stack of uniforms. "We're graduating tomorrow. That means no uniforms for the rest of our lives." She threw a pile of plaid skirts and collared shirts at the door. "And you're not packing these!" She pulled out a stack of knee-skin swimsuits.

"Those are nostalgic." Jensen yanked the pile of team suits out of Lucy's hands before she could discard them with the rest of her belongings, and laid them on her bed to repack once Lucy was done tearing her bag apart. "Besides, you can't expect me to go all summer without a bathing suit and those were crazy expensive."

"You can afford new ones," Lucy said, still purging items.

"Preferably ones that flatter you and don't make you look like a deranged salamander."

"Okay, I admit that one is pretty bad," Jensen conceded. "But some of these are cute."

Lucy leveled a stare at her that said '*you're delusional,*' then continued throwing the contents of the luggage into the pile against the door until she'd discarded every item of St. Timothy's College Prep paraphernalia.

"What am I supposed to wear all summer without all my stuff?"

Lucy pointed at her five large suitcases. "You're taking those."

Jensen glanced at the pile of luggage and was about to argue but Lucy didn't let her. "Everything is promotional gear or stuff from the sample closet and you know how my mom is. Even if I wanted to, she won't let me wear any of it once I get back to New York. It's all from last season."

Lucy's mom, Annie St. Claire was a designer and according to her, Lucy was a direct representation of the brand. It would be a travesty for her to be spotted wearing anything but the newest trends. So Lucy, who loved old movies, never listened to music that came out after 2010, and had a secret closet at home full of vintage pieces had a whole celebrity persona that was a lie. Lucia St. Claire, sweetheart of the fashion world and daughter of A-list actor Vincent St. Claire, was adored by millions of people who were being sold a lie. Jensen felt lucky to be one of the few who knew the real Lucy.

Jensen pulled her friend into a tight hug. "Thank you. I'm not sure how much of it will fit me, but–"

"You always say that, but it's summer, and shorts and baby-T's look great on you. And besides, you should take every opportunity you can to show off your abs." She pinched Jensen's waist, causing her to squirm away.

After makeup, three outfit changes and yanking a brush through the rats nest her hair had become, Lucy left for the end of year party. Once alone, Jensen stepped up to the window and looked out over the campus. She was only eleven when she first arrived there. Back then it had been terrifying to be taken from everything she knew and thrust into the competitive world of academia.

But she owed a lot to her school: her best friends–Lucy and Eric, her swimming career, and her acceptance into Stanford. Smiling to herself, she realized she was going to miss it. At some point in the past seven years what used to feel like a cage had become her home. It was everything that was waiting for her outside that felt incredibly daunting.

Just as she was spiraling into thoughts of college and the future, Eric's picture lit up the screen. His blond hair and brown eyes stared up at her and she smiled in response to his startling good looks as she swiped to answer the video call.

He was sitting in his car. "Hey–just got to the hotel for dinner with my parents. How's packing going?"

"Just about done." Jensen scanned the phone across the room so he could see the bare walls, and packed bags. "I wish I could come."

"You could have if you hadn't put off packing until the last day of school. It's so unlike you. I've been packed for a week."

"We still have lunch tomorrow after graduation," she reminded him. "I can't wait! I've missed your mom." She'd been counting down the days until she got to see Katrina again.

"I'll tell her you said that. I've got to go or I'll be late for dinner."

"Okay." As soon as she hung up with Eric, she went back to reminiscing. She thought back to meeting Lucy on the first day of school. They were roommates, and Lucy wasted no time introducing her to Eric. Lucy and Eric had known each other their entire lives, having grown up in the same neighborhood in New York. Eric attended their brother-school, St. Christopher, right down the street. For the past seven years Jensen had spent every long weekend, school break, and summer vacation at one of their houses in Manhattan.

Eric, the best friend, was one of Jensen's favorite people in the whole world, but Eric, the boyfriend, was a development she was still adjusting to. About a year ago, he'd started to catch feelings. She tried to ignore it at first, finding it hard to see him as anything other than a friend. If it was meant to be she wouldn't have to convince herself, right?

When Jensen was little, she always imagined she'd find an uncomplicated love like that of her grandparents. She used to act out weddings with her neighbors and fantasize about her own happily ever after. But she'd grown up a lot since then.

There were a lot of different ways to love someone. Maybe she never craved his touch the way you read about in books, but he was exactly what she needed. Eric was steady. He was there for her after she'd lost her grandparents. He comforted her and kept her grounded, which was everything to someone who was desperate for stability.

When they were both accepted to Stanford, she took it as a sign. They were already such good friends and they fit seamlessly into each other's lives. So when he asked, she said yes, and over the past three months their relationship had progressed. Jensen had given Eric all her firsts.

The following day at their graduation Jensen and Lucy walked the stage in the morning while Eric and his parents sat in the front row in the seats reserved for the school's most prestigious donors. They received their diplomas, posed for pictures, then found Eric. Jensen bent down to where he was sitting and gave him a quick kiss. Then, when it was his turn to walk, Lucy and Jensen jumped up and screamed at the top of their lungs, trying to embarrass him. Katrina shook her head at them but when they retook their seats she reached over and squeezed Jensen's hand, smiling.

At lunch, Eric's parents shared stories about their college days. They'd met at Harvard while in Medical School and were hopeful that Eric and Jensen would follow in their footsteps after Stanford. Eric knew he wanted to be a surgeon like them, but Jensen was still undecided about which medical field she would enter. She had never considered a career in medicine but since she didn't have a plan of her own, it made sense for her to go along with Eric's.

Just as lunch was winding down, Eric's dad, John, asked Jensen if she would be driving back with them to New York. She hesitated a few seconds too long because Lucy's mom offered a ride in the chopper. "Actually, I was hoping you'd drop me off at LaGuardia on your way home."

"The airport?" Katrina asked. "Where on earth are you going?"

"Mom, didn't I tell you last night?" Eric put his arm around Jensen, "She's going to California."

After her grandparents died, a few months ago, Jensen inherited their home in Atherton, California. It was her childhood home, where she'd lived until she went away to school. She'd planned to move back in with her grandparents while attending Stanford. But with them gone, she wasn't sure if she wanted to live in their big empty house alone. Selling it was an option, but before she made that decision, she wanted to go through their belongings.

"It's long overdue," she said. "The house has been sitting empty for months now. I need to sort through everything and decide if I'm going to sell."

"Are you going alone?" Katrina asked, rightfully concerned. "Are you sure it's safe?"

Jensen refused to lie but she made sure not to answer in any definite terms. "I have a locksmith scheduled to come tomorrow, and I've already updated all the alarm passwords. Besides, she doesn't know I'll be there."

The 'she' Jensen was referring to was her mother, Laurel. Katrina had met her once when she, John, and Eric had flown to California with Jensen after her grandparents died. Despite forgoing a funeral, she was required to be present for the reading of the will. Thankfully, Katrina accompanied her. Jensen was eighteen, overwhelmed, and desperate to have a proper adult by her side. Therefore, Katrina was with Jensen at her house in Atherton when Laurel arrived.

Katrina and Jensen were sitting at the large dining room table. Jensen was fidgeting and Katrina reached out and gave her hand a reassuring squeeze. The man across the table from them was familiar, he was a friend of her grandfathers. "My name's Gregory," he reminded her, "I was one of your grandparent's lawyers and I'm the executor of their will."

He told Jensen she would gain access to her inheritance in three to six months. He also reminded her that her trust was already accessible since she'd recently turned eighteen. Then Gregory told her that she was the sole beneficiary of her grandparents' will and read off a long list of their assets. As he finished reading the list of investment proper-ties, Jensen felt the rise of panic. How did anyone expect her to manage everything on her own?

Katrina, noticing her distress, began asking questions about prop-erty management companies and liquidating assets. Then she got the contact information for their financial advisor. Jensen zoned out while they talked, thankful to have Katrina there.

It was while she was letting Katrina do the talking that the front door to the house slammed open. Jensen immediately put her guard up, pretty sure she knew who was barging in. When Laurel turned the corner into the dining room, her suspicions were confirmed.

Laurel was a shell of a person. Jensen must've gotten her height from her father because Laurel wouldn't even reach her shoulders. She looked smaller than she actually was because she was so skinny. She was wearing a low cut top and Jensen stared at her collar bones jutting out from her chest. Her hair could've been the same golden brown as Jensen's, but it was so greasy it was hard to tell. Her eyes were red rimmed. A product of grief from losing both her parents or a side effect of whatever drug she was on. Maybe both.

"Jenny, baby, is that you?" She rushed to her side and wrapped her bony fingers around her daughter's upper arm. Jensen held on even tighter to Katrina's hand. "Baby, it's me. It's your mom. Wow, look at how grown up you are." Laurel smelled like sickeningly sweet perfume applied heavily to try and mask the smell of smoke, but failing.

"Aren't you going to stop them from doing this to me, baby?" she pleaded. "It has to be a mistake. How could they leave me with nothing, right? I'm their only child. You'll help me sort this out, won't you, my sweet girl? It's not like you need all of it, anyway. You're still just a kid."

Gregory interjected. "I told you after you barged into my office that you need to keep your distance during these proceedings."

"I wasn't talking to you, was I?" she snapped, her voice full of venom. She reached across the table and grabbed a handful of documents. She shredded them and threw them back on the table. "This is my house. I grew up here. It's the only home I've ever known." Her voice quivered. Then she pulled out a matchbook. "These papers are bullshit." She lit a match and tossed it on the stack of remaining documents, setting them on fire.

"Are you crazy?" Gregory cried, smothering the small flame with the sleeve of his sport coat. He glared at Laurel. "You could have burned the house down."

"If I can't live here, no one should." She turned her attention back

to Jensen, her sugar-sweet tone back once again, "Jenny, my sweet, sweet girl. I've missed you so much."

"Jensen?" Katrina pulled Jensen's attention away from the woman pawing at her arm. "Is this woman truly your mother?"

She tried to say yes, but her voice caught in her throat. The way Laurel kept calling her Jenny like she was still a little girl made her feel like one. No one had called her that since her mom went to prison. To her horror, a tear threatened to roll down her cheek.

"Would you like me to ask her to leave?" Katrina whispered as her eyes searched Jensen's. She responded with a minuscule nod, but Katrina saw it and a moment later, she was addressing Laurel. She cleared her throat, "Excuse me, please remove your hands from Jensen. Then, perhaps you can give me your contact information and we can schedule a time to speak when emotions aren't running so high."

As Katrina finished speaking, Laurel's gaze slowly shifted in her direction. She had been so fixated on Jensen, she only now noticed the woman sitting beside her. Her eyes fell to Jensen's hand, still gripping Katrina's, and narrowed.

"Who the fuck are you?" She practically spat in Katrina's face.

"Jensen is like a daughter to me. I only want what's best for her, as I'm sure you do," Katrina tried to reason, but they both realized too late that it was the wrong thing to say.

"Like a daughter to you?" Laurel repeated. "She IS my fucking daughter and I haven't been able to see her in years. You should be the one to leave." Her voice grew loud and aggressive. "Yeah! You should leave! You're not her mother. Get the fuck out of my house. Get out! I am her mom. Get out! Get the fuck out!" She screamed in Katrina's face, getting more agitated as she went. Jensen looked at Gregory for help, but he was across the room on his phone. Laurel reached across Jensen as if to yank Katrina out of her chair, but Jensen stood between them.

Somehow, she found her voice. "Mom!" She was tempted to call her Laurel, but she knew that wouldn't go over well. "I don't even have the money yet. It's going to take months before I have access to it. We can talk about it later, but I can't help you right now." Jensen had no intention of enabling her, but she didn't know how else to calm her down.

"A few months? I don't have a few months, I'm hard up right now. I need it now. Don't you have some way to help me? Come on, baby."

"We support Jensen financially. She doesn't have money of her own," Katrina lied smoothly, coming to her rescue. Jensen hoped her mother didn't know about the half-a-million-dollar trust she recently received. She must've been oblivious to it because her attention shifted back to Katrina.

"Spot me a couple hundred? Just to get me by until the money comes through and then Jenny and I can work out my share."

"That isn't happening," Katrina said. Her patience had snapped. There was an undercurrent of anger in her voice and she was speaking through her teeth. "If I have anything to say about it, Jensen will not be giving you a dime of that money."

Laurel smacked her. The sound of her hand hitting Katrina's cheek rang out through the room. Jensen lost the last drop of pity she had for her mother. She was trying to be understanding. Laurel was grieving and self-medicating her pain away, but with that slap she saw red.

"Don't touch her!" Jensen shoved her mother away from Katrina. "I'm never giving you anything. How dare you? I hate you!" Tears fell freely down her cheeks. She wanted to keep screaming at her, but she stopped when sirens drowned out her voice.

Seconds later, Gregory led two officers into the house and pointed at Laurel. Jensen told an officer what happened and when he asked if she wanted to press charges for breaking and entering, she said, "Yes."

The officer pulled Laurel's hands behind her back and slipped on a pair of handcuffs. He read Laurel her rights. She wasn't listening. She was busy screaming at Jensen. "You little bitch.! You spoiled bitch! I should have aborted you when I had the chance! When my mother told me to, I should have listened. I wish you never existed! You're ruining my life!" She kept screaming until an officer guided her into the back seat of a police cruiser.

Gregory talked to Katrina, assuring her not to worry about the damaged documents. He'd already filed the originals, and he had copies. One officer lingered to ask more questions. Katrina held an ice pack to her cheek as she answered them.

Eric and John arrived back at the house as the last officer was leaving. Eric, seeing Jensen rattled, rushed to her side and wrapped her up in his arms. He held her tight while Katrina filled them in on what happened. Eric held onto Jensen as they made their way to the airport and during the entire flight home. He became her anchor, the only thing keeping her from drifting into the sea of sorrow that felt like it was going to drown her.

Jensen hadn't been back to California since that day, and it wasn't until she was sitting in the airport that she began to worry about what she was about to walk into. Laurel only stayed in jail for a few days before Jensen dropped the charges. Katrina tried to talk her out of it, but she felt guilty for being the one responsible for her mom's imprisonment. Out of respect for Jensen, Katrina agreed to drop the assault charges as well.

Jensen paid a fortune for Laurel to spend three months in an extensive rehab center. Katrina told her it wouldn't work, rehab only helped people who wanted to change. Jensen paid for it anyway.

Three months had passed since then.

Jensen had access to all the accounts.

Laurel was out of rehab.

And Jensen was returning to California.

1

"LONG TIME NO SEE" —ANDREW

Jensen planned to stay in California for a week or two, but after three days of sorting through her grandparent's belongings, it was clear it was going to be a much bigger project than she anticipated. It made her uncomfortable to discard items that were once dear to her grandparents, but she had no use for them.

On the fourth day, she found a file-a-fax in the kitchen and called all her grandparent's friends to ask if anyone wanted anything. Even after setting things aside for them and taking three carloads of clothes to a charity in East Palo Alto, she'd barely made a dent. Eric was spending a month in Spain with his parents and at the rate she was going he'd be back to New York before her, and he hadn't even left yet.

While piling shoes into a large cardboard box to bring to the donation center she pulled a shoe box down from the top shelf and was instantly suspicious. The box was heavier than she expected. Curious about what her grandmother was hiding in the back corner of the closet, she opened it.

The box was full of letters all addressed *To Jenny, From Laurel*. The oldest one dated back eight years. Jensen combed through them, confirming her mother's name on the upper left corner of every envelope, but she stopped when she brushed past a photo.

Flipping back to the picture, she pulled it out. Her breath hitched and she felt like she was being thrust back in time as she looked at the family smiling up at her. The heavy, cardstock photo was of a family all donning cozy knit sweaters and warm flannels. It was a holiday card, and despite the photo being slightly grainy and several years old, there was no mistaking them.

Lydia and Patrick Reese and their kids, Andrew, Grayson, and Nicole, looked exactly like they did the last time she'd seen them, seven years ago before she'd left for school. Jensen looked at each person carefully, feeling a rush of memories come back to her. Long hot summers, night swims in their backyard, and bike riding in the street. The Reeses lived next door for her entire childhood. She was two years younger than the twins, Nicole and Grayson, and four years younger than Andrew. Lydia was the mom she always wished she had. She was so kind and easily accepted Jensen into their family. She used to spend more time at their house than her own.

On the backside of the card Jensen was delighted to find a hand-written note from Lydia.

Jensen,

I hope school is treating you well. We have seriously missed your presence in our home these past few months. Our family feels incomplete without you. I hope you know that I truly consider you another daughter and if you ever need a place

to call home, you will always have one with us. I love you.
      Merry Christmas,
      Lydia.

Shuffling through the box she found a stack of six more Christmas cards from the Reeses, most recently from the past December. Quickly finding the next oldest card, she glanced at the photo. Patrick Reese was absent from this card and it triggered a horrible memory.

Returning home after her first year away at school, Jensen couldn't wait to see her second family. She didn't get to come home for the winter holiday. Gran and Gramps came to visit her at school instead. They'd spent Christmas together in the city. She picked out souvenirs for each member of the Reese family, and couldn't wait to hand them out. Gran had offered to bring them back after Christmas, but she wanted to do it herself.

Impatiently, she waited for Nicole to come over. She must've known she was home. Nicole had likely been asking for updates on Jensen's arrival all month.

When she didn't come over after an hour, Jensen decided she couldn't wait any longer and she ran next door. She tried to walk in the front door like she used to, but it was locked. Weird. The door was always unlocked. Mr. Reese's car was in the driveway, so she knew someone must be home. She banged on the door and pushed her face up against the window that looked into the entryway. Finally, a woman she didn't recognize answered. Confused, she asked for Nicole, hoping the mystery woman would know where she was. Her heart jumped in relief when she saw Patrick walk up behind the woman, but her hopes plummeted when he reached out and wrapped an arm around her. He was holding the stranger the same way he used to hold Lydia. Jensen wore her confusion across her face, and Patrick looked down at her sympathetically. He explained that he and Lydia were no longer married. She and the kids moved away a few months ago. That night, Jensen cried harder than she ever had before. It felt like she'd lost a piece of herself that day.

She looked closely at the second card for signs of sadness on any of their faces. But, like so many pictures, everything was hidden behind their smiles. The only sign that anything had changed was Patrick's absence.

Flipping the card over, she read the next note from Lydia.

Jensen,

I can't believe it has been a year and a half since we've seen you. I hope you're well. I'm sure you know by now that we've had quite a tough year. The kids would love a call from you, especially Nicole. I hope we hear from you soon. As always, we miss you. Forever we love you.

Merry Christmas,

Lydia.

There was a new man in the next picture, next to an extremely pregnant Lydia. She was beaming and cradling her belly. The card read *Merry Christmas from the Alton-Reese Family.*

Under the photo were the names: Joe, Lydia, Andrew, Grayson, Nicole, and Baby Dustin coming soon.

Jensen flipped it over and the note on the back was short but to the point.

Jensen,

Our family is growing, but you will never be

replaced. I hope you never feel like it is too late to reach out. I will always consider you a part of our family. Merry Christmas.
Love,
Lydia.

Lydia was holding the baby boy, Dustin, in the fourth picture. She flipped over the card and read.

Jensen,
I can't believe that you're already a teenager and you're in high school! These are such big milestones. I wish I got to be a part of them. I called your gran to check in recently and she said you were already swimming for your high school's varsity team. We're so incredibly proud of you. I miss you and I love you.
Merry Christmas,
Lydia.

As she read her anger grew. Gran could've easily read the messages to her over the phone when they arrived. What business did she have hiding them? If Jensen had received them years ago, she wouldn't have lost touch with the Reeses. She'd always assumed they'd forgotten about her when they moved.

She read the fifth card next. The note was the longest by far. Lydia's cursive was scrunched together to fit on the back, making it hard to read.

Jensen,

I know you probably have so many new friends in Connecticut and according to your gran you don't spend much time in California anymore, but I was hoping this coming summer you'll consider coming to visit. We have a house right on Lake Evergreen and I know you would love it here. You could swim every day. I'll mention the invitation to your gran as well. I do hope we get to see you soon. It's been too long. Merry Christmas.

With love,

Lydia.

Picking up the next card, she was surprised to see that Lydia was pregnant again. Next to her, Andrew had the same cocky smile that had once triggered her first crush. He was four years older than her, good-looking, athletic, and even as a child he had a magnetic pull that drew everyone in. Nicole looked as wild and carefree as she remembered her. Then there was Grayson. He was a constant presence in her childhood, but only in the background of her memories. He liked it that way, always allowing his siblings to get the attention. But there was no way he flew under the radar anymore. Not with that crooked, laid-back smile and those piercing blue eyes.

She couldn't seem to take her eyes off him. Apparently he'd had a growth spurt between the previous year and this one. In the other cards, he blended in, but now, he stood out. Andrew probably refused to stand next to him, Jensen thought with a laugh. It would make their height difference too obvious.

She flipped the sixth card over and read.

Jensen,

Nicole spotted you in some fashion designer's Instagram story a few weeks ago. She was freaking out when she realized it was you. We all were. Wow, you've grown into a gorgeous young woman. I still remember you as a little girl. You are so grown up now. I hope life is treating you well. Merry Christmas!

Love,

Lydia.

P.S. Congrats on your record-breaking swim. I must've watched that clip of you winning 100 times. I love seeing you thrive.

The last card was from six months ago, just before her grandparents died. Lydia's husband, Joe, was sitting with the young boy, Dustin, on his lap. Lydia was next to him with a baby in her arms. The card said her name was Julia. Behind them, Andrew, Nicole, and Grayson were kneeling. Unlike the other pictures, this one was candid. They were all laughing at something with their eyes closed and mouths gaping open. And even though they all looked different from how she remembered them, she felt the energy of their laughter pouring out of the photo and wished she was there with them.

She read the last note.

Jensen,

Congrats on getting into Stanford! I am so proud of you. I've asked a few times now for *your address at school or your cell phone number, but I get the feeling your gran wouldn't like me to be in touch with you beyond these cards. I'm sorry if my notes have ever made you feel like I'm crossing a line. I've always wanted you to know that I'm in your corner. I love you and I miss you so, so much.*

Merry Christmas,
Lydia.

Once she finished reading all seven cards, Jensen placed them back in the shoebox and ran downstairs. She tossed the box onto the counter. Then, flipped through her gran's file-a-fax, looking for Lydia's number.

She found a small off-white card with her information on it and, not entirely sure what she planned to do next, she pocketed it. By the time she convinced herself to pick up the phone, it was already past midnight so she'd have to wait.

By morning, she'd gone over every scenario that could play out. She'd even planned what she would say if the call went to voicemail.

"Alton residence, this is Joe," Lydia's new husband said into the receiver. The phone number must've been for the landline. She didn't know people had those anymore.

"Hello, hi, I um ..." she stumbled over her words, "This is Jensen. I'm looking for Lydia. It's Jensen Fisher," she clarified.

"Who is it?" someone asked in the background.

With his voice muffled, like he was covering the phone, she heard Joe say, "A girl calling for your mom. She says her name is Jensen Fisher. Isn't that the name of your old ... Hey!"

Andrew yanked the receiver out of his step dad's hand, "Well, damn. Fish, is it really you?"

The old nickname triggered something, and a huge grin spread across Jensen's face. How did she forget they used to call her that? Andrew started it back when they swam for the Menlo Swim Club together. Jensen was an above-average swimmer, so she practiced with the older kids. Andrew used to say she only beat him because she was part fish. It was fitting considering her last name and soon everyone at the swim club began calling her that.

"Andrew?"

"Long time no see! What has it been, seven, eight years? How've you been?"

"I've been good. Just getting ready to start college in the fall."

"Damn. Our little Fish is all grown up now, huh?"

"And not exactly little anymore," she laughed.

"Oh yeah, you shot up, didn't you? I bet you can turn at the flags now?"

She rolled her eyes. She heard that all the time. "I don't even swim backstroke anymore."

"Yeah, I know, but what are you now, like six feet?"

"Six-two. How'd you know that?"

"I've been following you online for years. You've become a hell of a swimmer."

"You have?" She was tempted to open her accounts and scroll through her long list of followers to find him.

She wasn't really one for social media. But between her swimming career and being best friends with Lucy, who had a massive social media presence, her face had become well known on the internet. She hadn't even noticed that Andrew followed her. She wondered if anyone else in his family had been keeping tabs.

"Andrew, who's on the phone?" she heard Lydia ask. "Joe said the call was for me."

"It's Fish," he told her.

"Jensen?" she asked, then into the phone she asked again, "Jensen?" and her voice wobbled.

"Hi Lydia," Jensen's voice came out in a whisper.

Lydia sniffed into the phone, and before she could burst into tears Jensen jumped in with, "I'm sorry it's taken me so long to call. I've missed you."

"Oh Jensen, I've missed you so much. How are you, Honey? Are you staying with your grandparents for the summer?"

"No. Gran died back in February from complications after a respiratory infection and Gramps passed away a few days later from a heart attack." She had explained her grandparents' passing so many times that it came out like a well-rehearsed line. "I'm at their house now, cleaning it out."

"Oh Honey, I'm so sorry to hear that. Are you there by yourself? You shouldn't be doing that alone. Do you need help?"

"It's okay. I'm used to doing things by myself. It doesn't bother me anymore."

"I know we haven't talked in a long time and I'm nearly a stranger to you now," Lydia said, "but I would feel better if you'd let me come help you."

"Lydia, you aren't a stranger to me," Jensen reassured her. "That's actually why I'm calling. When I was going through Gran's stuff, I found the cards you sent me. I didn't know that you'd been writing to me all this time. I feel awful that I never responded, and we lost touch."

"Oh, Honey, don't blame yourself for that. You were so young when you went away to school. Besides, I had a feeling you weren't receiving them. I should've tried harder to get in touch. I'm the one who's sorry."

"Don't be." She hesitated before gaining the courage to

follow through with the real reason for the call. "I guess I was just wondering if your offer still stands?"

"My offer?" Lydia asked.

"To come visit?" She squeaked out nervously.

"You want to come visit?" The excitement in Lydia's voice brought a huge smile to her face. "Yes, of course! You're always welcome here."

"She's coming here? When?" Andrew asked in the background.

"Andrew, you are twenty-two years old," Lydia hissed. "Why are you still interrupting my phone conversations like you did when you were five?"

"Is she coming here?" was his only response.

"I don't know. She hasn't given me an answer yet because *someone* interrupted." Jensen imagined the annoyed look Lydia was shooting at him, and it made her laugh.

"Is tomorrow too soon?" Jensen asked.

"Tomorrow is perfect."

She wrote down the address on a piece of scratch paper so she could put it in her GPS. Then left it on the counter and went upstairs to pack.

2

"DON'T ACT LIKE YOU'VE NEVER SEEN LEGS BEFORE." —ANDREW

Packing turned out to be unnecessary, since all five of Lucy's bags were still in the garage where Jensen had dumped them when she arrived. She just needed a few things. Finding a small yellow vintage suitcase that once belonged to her gran, she loaded it up with her toiletries and a few other essentials. Instead of wasting time sorting through all of Lucy's stuff, she threw the bags in her grandpa's car, she could look through them when she got the chance. The boxy suitcase looked out of place in the backseat beside Lucy's matching set of Louis Vuitton luggage.

During the long drive, Jensen called Eric to wish him luck in his golf tournament, but she didn't tell him about her change of plans. She was only going to be at the Reese's house for the weekend and she already knew what he'd say. He'd be annoyed that she was putting off packing the house. And if she needed a break, he'd expect her to be spending the weekend with him. It was hard to explain that the Reeses were like family, despite her never mentioning them.

She called Lucy after getting off the phone with Eric and spent nearly the rest of the five-hour drive informing her where she was going and who the Reeses were, but the call dropped mid-conversation. In her attempts to call her back, she accidentally swiped up and closed her maps. Normally she would turn around and seek out service but the one lane road she was on made a u-turn impossible.

She stayed on the narrow, winding highway and tried not to panic. There were vast evergreens to her left and a winding river to her right. The drive brought her under a mountain railroad bridge and through two separate stone tunnels built into the sides of the mountain. When she popped out of the second tunnel the river was gone and all that remained were endless trees. She was in the middle of nowhere, the only sign of civilization was a single sign that read: Welcome to Lake Evergreen. Out her driver's side window, through the trees, she saw a glimpse of sparkling blue water.

She knew she was in the right place, but it felt like she would never reach her destination. She was driving her grandpa's Escalade and unfortunately she never took the time to figure out the GPS system in the car. Instead, she'd opted to use the maps on her phone, a decision she regretted now.

At the first turnout she got out of the car and stared at the lake. Why hadn't she put the address in her phone? Instead, she'd left it on the counter in Atherton where it was of no use to her. Pacing back and forth she went over her options. She could continue on until she got enough service to call Lydia and ask for the address again, or she could turn around. That made the most sense. What was she even doing there in the first place? She was supposed to be working on the house. She kicked a rock at a tree, frustrated, then stomped back to her car. Her mind was made up, she was turning around. But first she needed to figure out how to get back to civilization. A knock on her passenger side window had her jumping and banging her head on the roof of the car.

A guy on a dirt bike, wearing a full-face helmet, cringed as she rubbed the top of her head. He said something, but she couldn't hear him over the rumble of his bike. He flipped a switch, and the bike went silent. Then he pulled his helmet off and asked again, "Do you need help?"

The window muffled his voice, so she rolled it down an inch. "Do you know this area?" She tried to hide the tremble in her voice. "I think I'm lost."

"Where are you trying to go?" he asked.

"I don't know the address," she admitted, feeling stupid and irresponsible, which was a new feeling for her.

"Well, that's a dilemma." He chuckled. "Is it in town? Because if so, you're still a ways off."

"No, I don't think so, I'm pretty sure their house is on the lake."

"Well, what are their names, maybe I know them?"

"The Reeses."

"Seriously?" Of course he knew them; it was a small town, and he looked like he was around their age. "I just came from there. You're not far. It's on the left-hand side a few minutes down."

She groaned, embarrassed to have to ask, "Do you happen to have their address?"

"Why don't I just show you the way?"

He tried to kick-start his bike a few times, but it only offered a few pitiful mutters. After several unsuccessful attempts, he bowed his head in defeat. He looked back at Jensen through the window and pointed to the passenger seat. "How 'bout a ride?"

"Sure?" Her answer didn't sound convincing, even to her own ears. Letting a stranger into her car went against everything she'd ever been taught, especially in the middle of nowhere and without witnesses. She'd seen enough murder documentaries, this was how good people died.

Maybe it was the fact that he knew the Reeses, maybe it was his innocent, boyish face, but for whatever reason, she unlocked her door.

He climbed into the car, leaving his bike on the side of the road. Sitting so close, Jensen got a better look at the amount of dirt and grease that speckled his hands, arms, and even his hairline. The black specks disappeared into his thick dark hair. He smiled, and it was open and friendly. Thick dark lashes framed his green eyes, making them pop next to his caramel skin. Just as she noticed them, a lock of hair fell in front of one of his eyes. He swiped the hair back with one grease-covered hand and it left another black smudge on his forehead. Noticing Jensen eyeing his dirty hands, he said, "I've been working on the bike all morning." He glanced at the lonely motorcycle in the side mirror. "Clearly, I still have some work to do." He laid his hands on his lap, careful not to touch anything in the spotless car. "I'm Brent by the way."

"Jensen. Nice to meet you." And it was nice. She was immediately comfortable with Brent and felt silly for worrying about letting him in her car.

"So? Grayson or Andrew?" he asked.

"Excuse me?"

"Sorry. Who are you going over to see? My guess is Andrew, Grayson doesn't really go for summer-timers."

"Oh, both of them."

"Both?" He lifted an eyebrow and shot her a mischievous smile.

"Not like that. Gross, neither. I'm here to see everyone. I'm staying with the Reeses."

"Huh," Weird, he thought. Grayson didn't say anything. "You're gonna want to slow down. It's just up here. If you blink, you'll miss it." He pointed to the left. Carved into a tree, just before a narrow dirt road, was the name Lakeview Ct.

The road wound through the thick forest until suddenly they emerged from the trees and Jensen had to slam on her brakes because a basketball rolled in front of her car. The paved cul-du-sac led to three separate driveways. Faded lines of a basketball court were painted onto the street. It wasn't regulation size, but there was a hoop on either end and four guys were in the middle of a game. Andrew sat on a porch watching. She recognized him immediately even though the last time she saw him he was fifteen, and she was only eleven. He looked like an older version of the teenager she remembered. She suddenly wondered how different she must've looked to them. The last time they'd seen her, she hadn't hit her growth spurt yet or even puberty.

"This is where I get out. It's the one in the middle," Brent pointed. "The blue one." But she would have known which house, even without his help or Andrew sitting on the porch. Everything about it screamed Lydia. The houses on either side were dull neutral colors that lacked personality, but the house in the middle was a bright powder blue with white trim. A chipped white railing wrapped around the large porch, which was littered with handpainted pots, all bursting with flowers. But all of that was secondary to what truly transfixed her. The tangle of vines that overwhelmed the house were impossible to ignore. Long leafy vines with thousands of yellow flowers wrapped around the porch and along parts of the roof. They snaked up the front of the house and wrapped around the sides, embracing it in a hug.

Brent climbed out of the car and ran over to the guys playing basketball. He pointed and everyone turned to look at Jensen. She didn't notice. She was mesmerized by the idyllic house.

There was a tap on her window, making her jump. Turning, she found Andrew looking down at her. She hadn't even noticed him walking over. He had the same short brown hair, bright blue eyes and that adorable dimple that made her swoon when she was younger. All the stress from the long drive melted off her with one raise of his brow. She rushed to fling open her door, climbed out of the car, and without hesitation pulled Andrew into a hug. She was momentarily surprised by how solid his body was, not that of an adolescent boy anymore. It had been years and they had both changed a lot, but it felt like just yesterday they were hugging goodbye as she left for school.

"Hey, Fish!"

"Hi," she released him only for a second before she hugged him again. She didn't care about the group of guys watching them embrace. He chuckled and squeezed her tight. They held onto each other for longer than was socially acceptable, and when she finally pulled away from him, it was with a giddy smile on her face which made him smile too.

"How've you been?" he asked. Then before she could respond he directed his focus to his friends. "Guys, make yourselves useful and grab her bags. They're going up to Nicole's room." His friends each grabbed a suitcase, heading inside without introductions and without giving her a chance to explain that she didn't need them all.

Andrew was the last to grab a bag, leaving only one for Jensen to carry. He headed toward the house, but before he went inside, he stopped on the porch and looked back. He looked past her to Grayson, who she hadn't noticed yet. He was standing at half court. "Oh yeah, I forgot to tell you," Andrew hollered to his brother, "Fish is staying here for a bit. Pick your jaw up off the floor, put your tongue back in your mouth, and don't act like you've never seen legs before. Come help the girl." Then his gaze flicked over to her and her long legs, which suddenly felt very exposed in her white dress and he winked before disappearing into the house.

When Brent had climbed out of the black Escalade with the

dark tinted windows and told Grayson that some girl named Jensen was there, he had thought his best friend was messing with him. Somehow, Brent had learned about Grayson's childhood crush on his neighbor and he was screwing with him. He had to be.

A girl stepped out of the car and threw herself at Andrew. That was nothing new. Girls always threw themselves at his brother. But that familiar golden hair had him hoping that maybe Brent wasn't messing with him at all.

But what would Jensen Fisher be doing there?

His eyes drifted down the defined muscles of her back. Then, down her mile-long legs. She was still hugging Andrew, and for the first time in years he was envious of his brother.

When they finally broke apart, he got a look at her face. He felt like he could collapse to his knees right there. She looked entirely the same and yet completely different from the girl he once loved. There was no doubt in his mind that it was her; only Jensen Fisher could make him feel so entirely helpless. Thankfully, he didn't fall to his knees. He didn't do anything. He just stood there frozen in the middle of the basketball court as all his friends responded to something Andrew said and went to help.

Then Andrew said his name, but he didn't hear whatever insult his big brother threw at him. Distracted was an understatement. Grayson couldn't tear his eyes away from her. She was gorgeous. Tall and thin, but clearly strong. When she looked at him, her eyes widened slightly and then they softened as she smiled.

"Hi Grayson," she said, when he finally figured out how to move his feet toward her. And he nearly stumbled at the sound of his name on her lips. Perfect lips, he noted. Her voice was wispy and feminine and he loved the way it sounded.

He had to find words. "Hey. You still go by Fish? Or is it just Jensen now?" His voice was deep. She felt the timber of it from her fingertips, down to her toes, and in other places that she refused to acknowledge.

"Either is fine." She pushed a lock of hair behind her ear nervously. "Call me whatever you want." Why was she so nervous? She'd just thrown herself at his brother.

Fish was what he called her as a little kid, but she definitely wasn't a kid anymore. "What about, Jen?" He asked and the way his deep voice was hushed for only her to hear made it sound like a secret.

Something about his whispered words and the way his eyes lingered as they ran down her body made her feel more like an adult than she ever had before. Standing in front of Grayson, she felt beautiful.

"Jen is fine." No one had called her that in her entire life, but coming from Grayson, she liked the way it sounded.

Grayson was leaner than Andrew but there was a subtle strength about him and a confidence in how he held himself. He had broad shoulders and long limbs, much like Jensen's. When they were kids, he was always gawky and awkward, but he'd grown into himself and his sturdy legs and defined chest made his height attractive.

When he was little, his brown curls were ridiculous. They'd mellowed out since she'd last seen him, just curling up at the ends. He smiled at her and she felt herself respond with one in return.

Realizing they'd been staring at each other for two exceptionally long seconds, breaking eye contact simultaneously. Jensen glanced toward the house and Grayson turned his attention to her backseat, where he pulled out the last suitcase, the yellow one that used to belong to Gran.

"So, what are you doing here?" he asked at the same time that she asked, "What, seven years doesn't warrant a hug?"

Grayson wanted nothing more than to hug her, but his head

was so foggy he'd forgotten how to act. He whipped around with a broad grin on his face, dropping the yellow suitcase and opening his arms wide for her to fall into them like she did with Andrew. The yellow suitcase hit the ground and popped open. All her things poured onto the ground. Makeup rolled down the driveway, toiletries scattered in every direction, and her pile of bras and underwear spilled out.

Grayson's eyes went wide, "Oh shit, I'm sorry," he said, dropping to his knees. He picked up a white thong, and Jensen quickly yanked it out of his hands. "It's fine, I've got this," she said, her face heating. Grayson did *not* just touch her underwear.

He chuckled and got up. Then he walked down the driveway to grab the makeup that rolled away. Meanwhile, Jensen quickly stuffed the bras and panties into her suitcase. When Grayson got back he dropped the makeup into the bag, then bent down to help her collect the rest of her things.

It took far longer than it should to cram everything back into the suitcase thanks to her hasty, disorganized packing. She had haphazardly thrown in everything she might need. There were loose bobby pins and Q-Tips all over the driveway.

"So, how have you been? It seems like it's been forever," Grayson said.

"It has been forever," she agreed, looking up at him as he put a handful of tampons into their box. "What are you doing?" It came out more accusatory than she planned. She snatched the box from him, mortified. "Why would you ...? I mean, what are you ...?" She struggled to get out a clear sentence. She went to an all girls school, she didn't know how to talk to boys, which was embarrassingly clear by how frazzled she was.

Grayson snatched the box back and filled it with the tampons he was still holding. He placed the full box in front of Jensen and she fell out of her crouched position and onto her butt, running her fingers through her hair. "Wow, I'm so embarrassed." Her cheeks heated, turning pink.

"Just be glad you're not alone. I'm the one who busted your bag open and then picked up your underwear ..." Just thinking about that tiny scrap of lace and what it must've looked like on her made his head feel fuzzy again. *Damn it*, he adjusted his pants. He didn't have to deal with that issue the last time he saw her.

"Oh my God, stop it! Don't talk about it! Don't even think about it!" She hid behind her hands.

"I'm not sure I'll be able to stop thinking about it," he mumbled. Then, trying to ease her embarrassment he added, "It's okay you know, it's not like I've never seen a thong before."

There he went. He said it. *Thong*. Jensen's face heated further. Turning it around on him, she asked, "Your sister's, right?"

"What? No." He choked on his laugh and started coughing. The problem in his pants dissipated quickly at the mention of his twin sister.

"You've never seen Nicole's underwear when you do your laundry? It never gets accidentally mixed in? I haven't seen her in years, but I bet she's got some naughty–"

"Oh my God, please stop talking about my sister!" He groaned, trying not to allow the mental picture she was painting to enter his mind. "Just ... Stop."

"So you can dish it but you can't take it?" She bumped her shoulder into his with a laugh. "So, nothing's changed?"

He let his eyes wander down the entire length of her body. "From the looks of it, everything's changed," he answered with a return bump to her shoulder. He left his bare arm pressed up against hers.

There was a cord of tension between them that kept Jensen from pulling away despite knowing that she should. She was too aware of the amount of his skin touching her. It wasn't until she thought about the last boy she touched, Eric, that she jumped back, "I'm sorry, I'm so awkward." She reached for a handshake, trying to make the situation less weird. "Should we start over?"

Grayson latched the suitcase and stood in one smooth motion. "A little embarrassment is good sometimes." He grabbed her outstretched hand and helped her up. "Come on, I'll show you your room. I assume you're gonna be sharing with Nicole." She tried to tell herself that the tingles lingering where he'd touched her were just nerves. She'd never had such a visceral response to anyone. Grabbing her purse from the driver's seat, she followed Grayson into the house.

The second they walked in the door, Jensen's eyes found Lydia, who rushed over but didn't embrace her immediately. She held Jensen at arm's length and spent ten long seconds taking her in. Then, she beamed and whispered, "Still as golden as ever," before pulling her into the tightest hug Jensen had ever received.

Lydia was an eclectic person, with frizzy brown hair bunched atop her head, drawing attention to her wacky earrings. She always donned an apron covered in sod, paint, or flour. She rarely wore shoes, often made up songs about mundane tasks as she was doing them, and perhaps the oddest of all, she had always believed she could see people's auras.

Lydia didn't make a big deal out of it. But she always used to tell Jensen she was special because hers was gold. As a child, Jensen used to love it when she'd tell her about it. It made her feel like she was destined for greatness. Despite her mother going to prison and her grandparents sending her away, she was still special.

Not sure if she believed the whole aura thing anymore like when she was a kid, Jensen still felt special knowing that after all this time, in Lydia's eyes, her light hadn't dimmed.

"Oh honey, how are you? How was the drive? I'm so glad

you're here. We've all missed you so much," Lydia said in her ear as she squeezed her tight.

"I'm good, the drive was long, but it wasn't bad," Jensen replied after Lydia released her.

"You know, besides the part where her navigation lost service, and she threw a tantrum on the side of the road," Brent said from a doorway across the room.

"I was not throwing a tantrum," she replied, sending Brent a look of betrayal. She didn't know he had seen that. No wonder he'd stopped to see if she needed help; he likely thought she was losing her mind.

"If I hadn't shown up, you would have been in tears within two minutes. I saved the day. I'm pretty sure that makes me your hero."

Andrew smacked the back of Brent's head as Grayson warned, "She's off limits."

"Oh, I don't think he was hitting on me," Jensen said on Brent's behalf.

"He was," came a chorus from everyone in the room, including Lydia.

"Oh, well, I have a boyfriend," she said, but her words got drowned out by the stampede coming down the hall.

Two boys came running around the corner and nearly ran her over. Behind them, panting and slobbering, was a golden retriever. When the dog saw a new friend, he leapt up on her, nearly sweeping her off her feet. A little girl came toddling in next and Lydia scooped her up into her arms. Jensen recognized the younger boy and the toddler from the Christmas cards.

The other boy was small but he looked older than the other kids, maybe ten or eleven?

"Avery," Lydia addressed the boy, "Can you bring Oreo-Hotdog outside?"

"Sorry, he got away from me."

"No problem sweetie," Lydia said, as the dog started dragging the boy down the hall. "You know we don't mind him being here. Let's just put him out for a few minutes while Jensen settles in."

"Okay," the boy said. He turned to Jensen and apologized, then he released the collar and chased the dog outside.

Lydia didn't seem fazed by the chaos, she just nodded towards her daughter in her arms, "Jensen, this is Julia. Julia is fourteen months, and Dustin, who just followed Avery out, is also mine. He's four."

"Nice to meet you, Julia." She said to the toddler, not knowing what was proper when introducing oneself to a baby. Could one-year-olds even talk yet?

The child smiled widely and held up a hand in a wave. Lydia beamed at her daughter as if her waving was equivalent to breaking the world record in the 800 meter free.

Someone, likely Dustin, started crying outside. Lydia directed Grayson to show Jensen to Nicole's room, then said they'd catch up in a bit as she made her way toward the wailing.

Grayson led the way upstairs.

"Who was the boy with the glasses?" she asked him.

"That's Avery. He lives with his brother Davis next door. Davis works a ton, so Avery spends a lot of his time here."

So, Avery was the new her. She wondered how long it had taken them to replace her. Was she just the first in a line of strays Lydia had taken in? Maybe she wasn't as special to them as she thought.

"Avery always has Oreo-Hotdog or some other animal with him," Grayson continued. "They're practically raising their own zoo over there. Davis can't stand it, but he can't say no to the kid either."

They ran into Andrew on the stairs. He tried to slip past, but Grayson put an arm out to stop him. "You knew she was coming," he accused his brother. "Why the hell didn't you say anything?"

"Hey man, I just found out yesterday. Besides, I knew it'd be a good surprise."

"Please tell me you at least had the forethought to tell Nicole." Grayson couldn't imagine what his twin's reaction was going to be. She hadn't taken it well when Jensen left for school. Hopefully, she'd be happy to see their old friend, but Grayson knew her better than anyone and he doubted the reunion would go over well. Nicole had an uncanny ability to hold a grudge.

"Nah man, she's in for a surprise too," Andrew said as he ducked under Grayson's arm just as a door slammed upstairs. As Andrew passed Jensen he whispered an ominous, "Good luck."

"What the hell, Grayson? Why did your boys just put some girl's shit in my room?" Nicole stood, with her arms crossed at the top of the stairs. Despite just seeing her in all the Christmas pictures, her appearance still shocked Jensen. She and Grayson used to look so similar when they were kids, but now it was hard to tell they were even related, let alone twins. It was like Grayson took all the height and there was none left for Nicole. She was around the same height as Lucy, but unlike Lucy, Nicole was not a toothpick. Her waist was fairly small, but her hips and chest were ample, giving her Marilyn-Monroe-esque curves that Jensen could only describe as sexy. Nicole seemed to know it too because her clothes showed off her best assets. Her short black shorts were high-waisted, making her waist look tiny. The top buttons on her shirt were undone, revealing a good amount of cleavage. On her shirt, across her chest, was the handle @Nicole-ReesesPieces. She had a full face of flawless makeup and her hair cascaded over her shoulders in faded pink waves.

Jensen took two steps up so Nicole could see her behind Grayson. She smiled as their eyes met but it quickly morphed into a frown at the look of disdain on her old friend's face. Nicole gave her a quick once-over before looking back at Grayson. "Who the hell thought it was a good idea to invite this Blair fucking Waldorf wannabee into our house?"

"Nicole, you remember Jensen, right?" He knew she did, but he was hoping she would catch the warning in his tone and back the hell off.

"I'm not sharing a room with her for the entire fucking summer."

"I'm only staying for the weekend," Jensen interjected, trying to ease the tension.

"You packed five bags for one weekend?" Nicole scoffed, "Excessive, no?"

Under her scrutiny, Jensen felt small and out of place. She regretted throwing Lucy's bags in her car. She regretted calling Lydia and making the ridiculous trip out there at all.

Nicole pushed past Grayson on the stairs. She stood in front of Jensen, two steps above her so they were almost eye to eye. "Nice dress, by the way. What was it? Four ... Five hundred dollars? Totally practical for the lake." And without giving her a chance to respond, Nicole rushed down the stairs.

Looking down at the white Vineyard Vines sundress she'd thrown on that morning, she couldn't see what was wrong with it. She'd worn it at the beach last summer and had gotten several compliments. Plus, Nicole was majorly over exaggerating, it was definitely closer to two hundred dollars.

At school, no one judged her based on her clothes. Even after class and on weekends, they had to abide by a strict dress code. And when they went off campus, Lucy always picked out her outfits.

"Don't listen to her. You look great." Grayson's eyes lingered where her fingers nervously pinched the hem of her dress.

"I don't want to put anyone out. I don't mind staying at a hotel."

"You clearly haven't been to town yet. We don't have a hotel. There is a bed-and-breakfast, but it's usually full in the summer. There are also cabins on the West Shore, but they're a twenty-minute drive from here. Besides, you shouldn't worry about Nicole. She'll calm down. She just doesn't like when things are sprung on her."

Jensen conceded his point, and followed him the rest of the way up the stairs to Nicole's room. She stood in the doorway and watched Grayson continue into the room next door. He closed the door, and she turned back to examine Nicole's space.

It felt intrusive to look around without Nicole present. It wasn't that Jensen was above sharing a room. She shared with Lucy for seven years, but that was different. This was very much Nicole's space, and she was encroaching on it. Three of her suitcases layed haphazardly across the bed. Two more sat on the floor. They weren't small suitcases either, holding Lucy's entire wardrobe from the past year. The bags overwhelmed the small room.

Jensen found a trundle under the bed and pulled it out. Then she tucked three suitcases under the bed and stacked the other two in the corner. She felt incredibly stupid for how high-maintenance she must've looked and decided it was best to keep her stuff packed all weekend in order to stay out of Nicole's way as much as possible.

Last time they saw each other, Jensen lived in t-shirts and cutoffs. Her gran used to have to fight with her to run a brush through her hair. Finding herself reflected in the vanity across the room, she examined her long hair. She'd straightened it that morning because it was so rare she had the opportunity. Her hair was usually tucked under a swim cap or soaking wet, but she'd put in effort that morning because she wanted to feel good about herself. One snide comment and a judgmental look from Nicole and her confidence crumbled.

She looked around the room of the girl she used to know. The pictures on the walls were of strangers. They used to share everything, including friends, but she didn't recognize the girl smiling back at her in the photos.

There was an easel in the corner. At least she still painted. There wasn't any evidence of her work and Jensen didn't dare snoop through her stuff, but she remembered the handle Nicole had on her shirt.

She sat on the swivel chair at the vanity and pulled out her phone. Opening Instagram she typed @nicolereesespieces into the search bar. Finding her account was easy, but she found it hard to accept that the person who just called her a Blair Waldorf wannabe was the same artist who'd created the incredible pieces she scrolled through. There were tons of hyper-realistic charcoal drawings of different people. Interspersed were a few of the most beautiful landscapes Jensen has ever seen; mountains, lakes, sunsets, and trees that reached the sky. She wondered how something so enchanting could come from someone so harsh?

She reminded herself that she was not the only one whose entire life changed all those years ago. Nicole's parents divorced, and she lost her best friend, too. She was forced to move away from everyone she knew to this middle-of-nowhere town. Along the way, they veered in different directions. Nicole must have coped by forming hard edges around herself while Jensen coped by becoming invisible.

She needed to talk to Lucy. She was the one Jensen went to for advice. She pulled up her favorites list and clicked Lucy's name where it sat at the top, but the call went to voicemail. She knew Lucy wouldn't check her messages, so she opened their texts and left a voice memo. She figured Lucy would get a kick out of it when she got around to checking her phone.

"Ok so, I'm here and I'm pretty sure I'm literally in the middle of nowhere. The roads are dirt and there aren't even proper street signs. I'm feeling disillusioned. It might have something to do with the fact that I'm taller than Andrew now. Ugh. Not that I'm still into him, but seriously, why do I have to pass up every guy I've ever liked? Oh well, at least he's nice to me. Nicole, meanwhile, called me Blair Waldorf and insulted my white Nantucket dress from last summer. Also, she's freaking gorgeous and totally scary. I may need to sleep with one eye open. As for Grayson, I'm not positive yet, but I'm fairly certain he's already undressed me with his eyes. These people are crazy. What am I doing here?"

She sent the absurdly long message and then typed out a few follow-up texts.

If you call and I don't answer, it might have something to do with the multiple signs for bears, falling rocks, and flash floods.

Also, I'm pretty sure Mt. Lassen is an active volcano and, according to Smokey the Bear, its peak wildfire season.

Here's hoping I don't die.

Love Ya!

3

"YOU CAN'T REASON WITH A FOUR-YEAR-OLD."
—LYDIA

The upstairs hall was narrow. Pictures adorned the walls in mismatched frames. The biggest one was of Andrew, Grayson, and Nicole a few years ago in front of the Golden Gate Bridge. Next to it was a more recent shot of the whole family on a boat.

The more Jensen looked, the more she noticed reoccurring themes. Andrew was always in athletic gear, including an orange Boise State football jersey. Nicole's style seemed to be ever-changing, but the one constant was the way her clothes hugged her curves, accentuating her best features. But, while his siblings displayed who they were blatantly through their style, Grayson was harder to figure out. There weren't any pictures of him playing sports, and his style didn't seem to have changed since they were kids. In every picture, he had on simple shorts and a t-shirt like he'd been wearing in the driveway. There was a photo of him with a group of guys, all wearing staff shirts, but it was impossible to tell where they worked.

She was still examining it when Grayson appeared at the top of the stairs. He leaned in and looked at the photo over her shoulder. "What are you doing?"

"I just realized," she answered, trying not to react to his closeness, "I don't think I've ever printed out a picture and framed it in my whole life. I wish I had thought to do that before I went away to school."

"Which picture would you have framed?"

"Probably one of the four of us," she answered.

"Come here," he led her down the stairs into an office. Once inside he took a frame off the desk and handed it to her. Sure enough, there they were, all four of them: Andrew, Grayson, Nicole, and Jensen. It was the last week of the last summer she'd spent in California. They were at the Menlo Swim Club in their team suits, sitting on the diving platform. Nicole and Jensen had their arms wrapped around each other so tightly their cheeks were smashed together. Andrew and Grayson were smiling with their arms around each other, too. They were all so young and innocent, unaware that soon all their lives would change forever.

"Do you want to see my favorite?" Grayson asked, but he was already leading her to the living room, to a mantle scattered with frames. He took one down and handed it to her. It was a picture of the two of them sitting in the Reese's backyard, their feet were in the pool and they were eating chocolate-covered bananas. It was the summer after she'd finished second grade. Their mouths were covered in chocolate and they were both wearing huge smiles. Jensen's smile was showing off two missing front teeth.

"We were so messy."

"No, we were so happy," Grayson corrected, and he was right. It was before life felt so complicated.

They made their way to the back deck giving Jensen her first uninterrupted view of the lake. Lake Evergreen was a bowl, surrounded by mountains on all sides. There was a long penin-sula that reached out to the middle of the lake. And everything from the shoreline, to the peninsula, to the mountains in the distance were all covered in the lake's namesake, evergreens. Directly in front of the house, there was a long wooden dock with a speedboat parked beside it. The boat bobbed in the restless water and Jensen found herself hoping the water would be calmer in the morning.

As if reading her mind, Grayson said, "It's a great swimming lake. In the mornings the surface is like glass. It doesn't usually get choppy like this until the wind picks up in the late afternoon."

Lydia hollered that dinner was ready and everyone rushed to the kitchen and filled their plates before heading back out to the porch's long picnic table. Jensen waited until everyone had their food before serving herself. Then, she found a seat on the end next to Andrew and across from Dustin. There was no sign of Nicole, but no one commented on her absence.

Dustin mumbled, "Jensen, bensen, densen, pensen, wensen."

"What is he doing?" she asked no one in particular.

"Dustin has a thing about rhyming," Andrew explained. "He doesn't like words that don't rhyme with anything."

"Sorry," Jensen said to Dustin, "nothing rhymes with my name."

"Mine either," he pouted.

"But Jensen has two names," Andrew told his little brother. "In our family, we call her Fish."

Dustin smiled, "I like Fish better, it rhymes with wish."

"You're right, it does," Lydia said from down the table.

"Can I have two names too?" Dustin asked.

"Sure," Grayson said, joining the conversation. "You want your nickname to be Dust?"

"No, I want it to be Billy."

They all laughed. "Why Billy?" Andrew asked.

"It has so many cool rhymes. It even rhymes with willy," he giggled.

Dustin's laughter was infectious. It had everyone at the table smiling. "Why not Dusty? That makes more sense as a nickname for Dustin," Jensen tried to reason.

He pondered this. "But it doesn't rhyme with willy."

"But there's trusty and rusty, and lots of other good words." She smiled, sure she'd won their debate.

"But those aren't funny words," Grayson argued.

"Why does it have to be funny? Doesn't it just have to rhyme?" she asked.

"Billy and Grayson are right," Andrew put in. "The rhymes are always better when they're funny. Billy is a better nickname."

"But ..."

"Jensen, you can't reason with a four-year-old," Lydia cut in.

"I wasn't trying to reason with a four-year-old." She looked pointedly at Grayson and Andrew. "I was trying to reason with the two adults who just agreed with the four-year-old."

"There's no use trying to reason with them either," Lydia chuckled. "Believe me."

The conversation moved on and Jensen turned her attention to her food. It was surreal to be sitting with the Reeses, listening to them laugh and joke like no time had passed. Halfway through the meal, Lydia said, "Jensen, I want to hear all about swimming."

She finished chewing before asking, "What about it?"

"I heard a rumor that you were being recruited to swim for Stanford?" Lydia posed her statement as a question, searching for confirmation.

"Actually," Jensen glanced around the table to find all eyes on her. "I turned down the scholarship. I've retired."

"I thought that was just a rumor. What do you mean you're retired?" Andrew asked in disbelief.

"I'll still be going to Stanford. I just won't be swimming."

Confused looks shot around the table. She dropped her gaze back to her plate and tried to explain, "I know myself. When I swim, I put everything into it. I don't make space in my life for anything else. It's all-consuming. I am going to be pre-med at Stanford and I can't afford the distraction."

"You're going to be pre-med?" Grayson asked, his tone entirely disbelieving. "Aren't you afraid of needles?" The question was rhetorical. The entire Reese family knew about her fear.

"That was a long time ago," she lied. It's something Eric didn't know, hence his urging for her to become a surgeon. "I have a plan. I'll do my undergraduate years at Stanford and then apply to Harvard for medical school. If I spend the next few years swimming, I won't be able to keep up with school. I don't want to lessen my load and fall behind. Besides, swimming was always just for fun. It's not part of the plan."

"Who cares if it's not part of the plan? Then change the plan!" Andrew said, raising his voice. "Do you know what some people would give to have a fraction of your natural talent? Even at ten-years-old, anyone who watched you swim could tell it's what you were born to do."

"Maybe I don't want my future dictated by what other people want me to do."

Andrew stood abruptly, causing his chair to fall backwards. "Don't give me that bullshit."

"Language!" Lydia hollered, but Andrew didn't even glance her way.

He planted his hands on the table and leaned across it towards Jensen. "Medical school is a cop-out. You're selling your-self short and spitting in the face of every athlete who wishes they could be where you are. You were in the Olympics when you were sixteen, for fuck's sake. If you quit, you're a waste of talent."

Jensen cringed at his blunt, unforgiving words. "I qualified tenth, and I didn't even make it to the final," she pitifully tried to defend herself.

"You were in the Olympics!" He was yelling now.

"Andrew," Lydia bit out his name and gave him a stern look. "That's enough. Jensen is an adult and capable of making her own decisions. It's not your place to tell her what she should or should not be doing."

Andrew just shook his head, disappointment written across his face. He left his half-eaten dinner and stormed into the house.

Joe scooted over on the bench, whispering so only Jensen could hear. "If it were up to Andrew, he would have never quit football. That choice was taken from him. He doesn't understand the decision you're making, but he'll calm down."

"I need to make the choice that's best for my future. There's no success in swimming, not unless I become the next Michael Phelps."

"I think that depends on your definition of success. Be careful comparing yourself to others."

"That's the opposite of what my private school preached to me for the past seven years."

"Well, I went to private school, too. And tried out the whole Stanford thing."

"You're an Alumnus?"

"Not really. I only lasted three semesters."

"You dropped out?"

"I did," he confirmed, smiling at the disbelieving look on her face. "Spent a lot of time up here at the lake after that. It's a good place to think. I'd sit in my boat on the water all day thinking about what came next for me. It really helped me figure some things out. You know, if you find yourself at a crossroads, I would encourage you to stay a bit longer than just the weekend. There's something about the air up here. It really helps clear your mind of everything except what's important."

As Jensen mulled over Joe's words, Davis and Avery, the next-door neighbors, came over and helped themselves to food from the kitchen. She searched for anywhere to look except at Davis. It was hard not to gawk. He was covered in tattoos which spanned both his arms, only leaving a long menacing scar ink free. The scar ran all the way up his left arm, up his neck, over his left temple and disappeared under his baseball hat. Jensen couldn't stop staring at him. She knew she was being rude but his alarming appearance made her nervous and when he joined the table, taking Andrew's abandoned seat across from her, she feigned exhaustion and excused herself.

Lying in bed that night, Jensen went over what Joe said to her at dinner and wondered if it was obvious to everyone that she was at a crossroads in her life. She'd been trying not to let it show how much she was going to miss swimming, but there was no hiding it from the Reeses.

The decision to quit wasn't one she'd made lightly. It had been the death of her grandparents that cemented her choice. She'd missed out on so much time with them, instead putting everything into swimming. She spent her summers training and competing rather than going home to visit. So many nights she'd meant to call and check-in but she was too tired after practice. She'd let swimming consume all her time, realizing too late that it was the people in her life she should have prioritized. With Lucy going to Columbia in the fall, nearly three-thousand-miles away, it felt like Eric was all she had left. She was holding onto him with both hands, scared of letting go. She couldn't regret putting him first.

The room was dark and quiet when Jensen woke up. She'd fallen asleep early, still on East Coast time. Sitting up, she searched around for her phone. Once it was in hand, she turned the light towards the bed next to her and found it empty.

She made her way downstairs, wondering if Nicole slept on the couch but the living room was empty too. About to head back upstairs, she was startled by a noise in the kitchen. "Hello?" she whispered into the dark room.

"Fish?" Andrew asked as she entered the kitchen. He was pulling a bowl out of an upper cabinet and when she walked in, he took a second one down and placed it beside his.

"Hi," Jensen waved awkwardly, hoping he wasn't still upset with her.

Andrew placed two bowls and spoons on the table. Then he retrieved a gallon of milk and a box of cereal. She stared at the box of cereal and grimaced.

"How is that considered food?" she asked, eyeing the rainbow-colored box of sugar-coated, marshmallowy diabetes. Andrew chuckled and poured some for each of them. He did the same with the milk.

Jensen sat at the table and Andrew took the chair directly next to hers. He'd already taken a few spoonfuls when he noticed she wasn't eating. "If you don't eat it fast, it gets soggy and gross."

"It already looks gross," she whispered. "Look at my milk," she faked a gag. "It's turning gray from the dye on the marshmallows."

"Just try it," he bumped her with his leg. "I promise if you hate it, I will buy you a box of healthy cereal tomorrow."

"Fine," she took a spoonful with exactly three pieces of cereal on it, poured off as much of the gray milk as possible, then took a bite.

"It doesn't count if you don't try a marshmallow with it," Andrew said through his chewing.

Begrudgingly, she spooned out a bright blue marshmallow and popped it in her mouth. "Happy?" she asked.

He laughed and nudged her again. "You like it, don't you?"

"That doesn't mean I should put this junk in my body," she said as she took another bite.

"Spoken like a true athlete. It doesn't sound to me like you're retired."

"Just because I'm retired doesn't mean I should start eating like shit."

"Well, I eat this *shit* all the time and it hasn't had any negative effects on me." He flexed and rubbed his hand over his abs. "It can't be that bad for you."

"God, could you be any more full of yourself?" Jensen huffed out a laugh and looked away.

He smiled deviously. It was a smile she knew well from when they were kids. He hadn't changed. He was still confident, and he was still a shameless flirt.

He used to make her swoon just by paying attention to her. Now, she kept her head on her shoulders and her eyes on her cereal. She didn't crave his attention the way she had as a child, besides, she had a boyfriend. Thinking about Eric and how he would feel about her sitting in the dark kitchen alone with Andrew, she stood, abandoning her uneaten snack. She walked to the other side of the kitchen and took a banana from the fruit bowl, watching Andrew finish the rest of her cereal.

Jensen thought about her childhood crush. She had once been so infatuated with him, despite being too young to know what infatuation was. Even after she had moved away, she used to think of him often. But in all her daydreams, he had always stayed that cute fifteen-year-old boy she knew. Jensen stared at the stubble on his jaw. He wasn't boyish at all. He was broad and sculpted. His voice was deep. He was a man, and next to him, she felt like a child.

"Are you just gonna stand over there and watch me eat?" he asked, and she nodded, continuing to stare awkwardly.

A few minutes later they headed upstairs quietly so they wouldn't wake Dustin or Julia. Once in front of Nicole's door, Andrew stopped. The hallway was narrow, causing him to stand close. "A group of us are going out on the boat tomorrow around seven. Do you wanna come?"

"Boats aren't–" She was interrupted by the creak of a door opening.

Grayson peaked his head out his bedroom door. "What are you guys doing?" he hissed at them.

"Midnight snack," Andrew held up the banana he grabbed on the way out of the kitchen. "And I was just asking Fish if she wants to come out on the boat with us tomorrow."

"Change of plans; I can't go tomorrow." Grayson said, "I told Phil I'd pick up a shift. He's short on help this summer." He was sleepy and confused. His hair, which normally flopped in his eyes, was a mess of curls.

"Fish, you'll still come, right?" Andrew asked her.

"I don't really do boats," she said. "Sorry, I think I'll pass."

"You guys are both killjoys," Andrew walked down the hall towards his room. "Night Fish," he called back to her.

"Goodnight," she whispered back.

Turning to Grayson, she asked, "You have a job? Where do you work?" She thought back to the picture of him in a staff shirt.

Grayson yawned. "Jen, it's three in the morning. Can we talk about this when the sun's up?"

"Oh, yeah, sorry," she giggled. The sound was so unexpected that she closed her mouth quickly.

"Goodnight," he said, closing his door.

But she wasn't ready to say goodnight. Instead, she felt an urge to ask him for the hug he still owed her from earlier. Without realizing what she was doing, she heard herself say, "Wait!" And to her horror, Grayson stopped the door an inch before it latched.

Was he dreaming or did she just say 'wait?' He pushed the door open. Instead of poking his head out like before, he swung the door wide. He raised his eyebrows curiously, but Jensen didn't notice his look of surprise because she was no longer looking at his face.

There was so much more to look at. She was left speechless, staring at Grayson in nothing but a pair of boxer briefs that didn't leave nearly enough to the imagination. He wasn't flexing or doing anything in particular to draw attention to his chest, but it seemed to be where her eyes lingered, until they drifted downward.

Was she checking him out? he wondered, looking down at himself. Her eyes seem to be plastered to his stomach.

His skin had a golden tan and Jensen was eating it up. His stomach was flat and there was a small trail of hair that she followed with her eyes until it dipped into his waistband. She looked lower, and Grayson saw the blood rush to her cheeks. There was no hiding that she was staring right at his cock. The thought made blood rush there and he could feel himself hardening. He cleared his throat, trying to pull her attention away from his growing member. Jensen, realizing she'd spent entirely too long checking him out, forced herself to look up.

He tried to conjure up images of gruesome things to get control of himself. Thankfully, Jensen didn't notice the pained look on his face as he forced his body to relax.

Slowly, after a long silence, Jensen met his gaze. Grayson's eyes were alight with curiosity and mischief. The look sent her mind spinning. "What's up?" he finally asked with a crooked smile.

"What?" she squeaked. "Nothing, I mean ... what?" She shook her head, trying to form a coherent sentence. But her focus was on not letting her eyes roam.

How was it possible? Was the girl of his dreams seriously rattled by *him*? She was aggressively staring him in the eyes, as if scared to let her gaze drift.

"I'm pretty sure you said 'wait.'" He was toying with her now, wondering if she could be wound any tighter. He leaned against his door frame in the most casual way he could manage despite the semi he was sporting.

He was smiling at her casually, as if he wasn't standing there in nothing but his boxers after she blatantly looked at his crotch. Just thinking about it made her face feel warm again.

"No, I don't think I said anything," she denied. She lifted her hands to feel how hot her cheeks were, sure that in Grayson's eyes, she must've looked insane.

Her denial made him chuckle and he whispered, "You're funny." She didn't feel funny, she felt ridiculous. Why was she acting like she'd never spoken to a boy before, let alone seen one half naked? She and Eric had slept together a few times. There was no excuse for why she was responding to Grayson that way. Maybe she was over-tired? Maybe she needed a good night's sleep, so the tingly feeling would go away.

"Ok, bye. I mean, goodnight," she said as she turned for the door to Nicole's room.

"Sweet dreams," he whispered, making her look back at him, which caused her to crash into the bedroom door. She scrambled to find the handle, turned it hastily, and threw herself into the room. '*Sweet dreams?*' she thought to herself, *who says that?* Leaning against the inside of the door, she took a deep breath.

She couldn't breathe properly in the hallway. The air had been too thick.

Once her heart calmed down, she sat on the bed and made herself think about her boyfriend. Out of respect for Eric, she needed to make it clear to Grayson *and* Andrew, and possibly Brent, that she was not available or interested. When she eventually told Eric about how she'd spent the weekend, she needed to be able to tell him he had nothing to worry about and it had to be the truth.

The next morning Jensen was sitting on the couch reading a book when someone snatched it out of her hands. Andrew was standing over her, shirtless, in board shorts and sandals. She noticed immediately that despite his muscles, she had significantly less reaction to seeing him shirtless than she did Grayson. "You sure you don't want to come with us?" he asked. "We're going wakeboarding." She looked out the window at the lake. There was a group of guys she didn't recognize on the dock.

"No, thanks." She faked a smile.

"Suit yourself," he shrugged. "But just so you know, you're missing out." He stood there for a few more seconds hoping she would change her mind. When she didn't, he shook his head slowly, disappointed. He backed out of the room, keeping his eyes on her until he was outside.

As he jogged out to the dock, Jensen stood and walked to the window. She watched as he dived off the end and swam out to the boat. He drove it up to the dock where his friends loaded boards, skis, and a cooler before climbing aboard. Just before they pulled away, Andrew looked towards the house. Jensen jumped behind the curtain so he wouldn't see her watching.

"What are you doing?" a small voice asked from behind her. Jensen peeked out from behind the curtain and found Dustin looking at her quizzically.

"Hiding in a curtain," she answered.

"Who's it?"

"What?" she asked, confused.

"Who are you playing Hide-and-Seek with? And who's it?" he clarified.

"Oh!" A lightbulb clicked on in her head. "You are."

"I'm it?" he asked, delighted. "I didn't even know I was playing." That's how Jensen ended up playing a two-and-a-half-hour game of hide-and-go-seek with Dustin that Saturday morning.

4

"THERE'S NOTHING LIKE SUMMERS AT THE
LAKE." —BRENT

"What does Eric think of all this?" Lucy asked after Jensen finished describing her encounters with both Grayson and Andrew the day before.

"I haven't talked to him since yesterday," Jensen admitted. "It's not like he needs a play-by-play of what's happening."

"He might want to know that his girlfriend is getting reacquainted with the hot guys from her past."

"First of all, I never said they were hot. And second of all, I don't think he'd care. Eric's not the jealous type."

"How would you know?" Lucy challenged, "Who's he ever had to be jealous of?"

"You think I should tell him?"

"He's your boyfriend, Jensen! You're supposed to want to tell him everything."

"I do. I just want to tell you more."

"Everything except that," Lucy laughed. "God, if he knew half the shit you say to me, he'd dump your ass. Listen, I've got to go." But before hanging up, she added, "I'm hanging out with him tomorrow. Please call him so I don't have to keep this from him. I hate being in the middle."

"I will," Jensen promised.

Ten minutes later, after weighing the pros and cons of calling him, she sucked it up and dialed. Eric picked up immediately.

"Hey, I was just thinking about calling you," he answered. "I miss you. How's your weekend going?"

"It's been good–" she started to say, but Eric was still talking.

"I shot a sixty-eight and qualified to play again tomorrow. And last night my dad let me join him at a medical conference where he was lecturing. They had all these amazing speakers. I know I've always said I want to go into general surgery, so I'll be well-rounded. But I got to talking to the keynote speaker and he was a cardiovascular surgeon. He really got me. He told me I would be a good fit for Cardio. Can you believe that? I've been doing research and I think it's a viable option."

"That's great!" She said, playing the role of supportive girl-friend well. "But, hey! Who really knows? By the time we get to med school, you may decide you want to work in plastics."

"Plastics?" he scoffed, "You don't know me at all if you think I'd even entertain the idea of plastics."

"Relax, it was a joke."

"Good," Eric said, then continued to talk about his weekend for another ten minutes before finally asking, "How's your weekend going?"

"Not nearly as exciting as yours. I'm spending my weekend connecting with my old neighbors."

"Oh, that's cool. How's the house clean-out going?"

"Pretty slow. I'm not even there right now. The old neighbors have a lake house. I'm spending the weekend here. I needed to get away for a few days."

"Bummer. Sounds like you won't be finished on time to come with us to Barcelona?"

"I told you, not this year. I need to get the house dealt with before school starts."

"Next summer, wherever we go, you're coming with us. And of course you're coming skiing in Aspen with us over Christmas."

"I wouldn't miss it!" Her voice rang with excitement but outwardly she cringed.

She'd been skiing a handful of times but it was never very fun. At first she hadn't enjoyed herself because she was stuck on the bunny slopes with a private instructor while Eric and Lucy were off hitting black diamonds. She picked it up quickly but the circumstances didn't change. Even with the ability to move to a steeper mountain, Jensen refused. Falling on a bunny slope hurt plenty, if she were to wipe out on a black diamond it could result in a career ending injury. There was a reason Leon, her swim coach, warned her away from extreme sports. So, while her friends glided across the slopes effortlessly, Jensen spent most of the day sitting in the snow, freezing her ass off, or sitting in the lodge, bored and lonely.

She listened to Eric ramble on about all the plans he had for them, plans for the coming school year and beyond that. He was leaving for Spain soon, so she endured his rambling, knowing they wouldn't be able to talk much while he was gone. There would soon be a nine-hour time difference between them.

Admittedly, she felt better after their call. She'd told him about staying with the Reeses and he didn't get upset or jealous at all. He never even mentioned that she'd missed his golf tournament.

She let out a long breath and relaxed the shoulders she hadn't realized were so tense, then dug through her suitcase to find Lucy's least revealing bathing suit. She settled on a navy one-piece that cut incredibly high on her hips. It felt like half her ass was hanging out and she was thankful that she had nothing to brag about in the chest department or she'd be falling out of the top, too. She didn't pack a swim cap, so she threw her hair into a ponytail and ran downstairs where Lydia directed her to the towel closet.

The dock wobbled as she ran across it. At the end, she kicked off her sandals and dove in without hesitation. She swam out to the closest buoy and looked out across the lake. There were two boats on the water. No one else was on the shore or in the shallows besides her. She had the vast expanse of water all to herself. She swam to the cove five houses down, then turned and swam back.

When she returned to the dock, she turned and kicked off of it, continuing to swim laps until her arms and legs were screaming. She didn't stop when Andrew pulled up, despite the boat's wake rippling through the water.

Andrew and his friends unloaded the boat, and out of the corner of his eye he watched her swim. He'd been right to yell at her yesterday, anyone with that much talent couldn't just quit. His friends left but Andrew stayed on the dock. Jensen knew he was watching her, but she didn't stop. She pushed herself, only quitting when the wind picked up and the waves became too choppy to get any productive strokes in.

When she hauled herself out of the water, Andrew had already gone inside.

She collapsed on the dock, breathing in through her nose, out through her mouth, trying to catch her breath. Once the wheezing from the strenuous swim had subsided, she dried off and checked her phone. It was just after three. She dragged herself up to the house, her legs singing with each step up the slight incline.

She stopped in the kitchen to guzzle two large glasses of water, then headed upstairs, desperate for a shower. When Lydia called out that dinner was ready, she rushed downstairs. Unlike yesterday, she didn't wait for everyone else to get food. Instead, she planted herself second in line, behind Andrew, and filled her entire plate. Two chicken breasts, three heaping piles of roasted asparagus, a scoop of red potatoes, and a scoop of rice.

"A little hungry, Jen?" Grayson asked, coming up behind her.

"She's gotta be starving after that training swim I just witnessed," Andrew answered on her behalf.

"That wasn't training. That was a normal swim." She argued as the three of them sat together at the end of the long picnic table on the porch. "I may not be competing, but I still like to swim every day."

"You can tell yourself whatever you want, but I know what I saw. You were in perfect form and you had your stopwatch open on your phone?" Andrew pointed out.

Jensen shrugged one shoulder. "Old habits, I guess," she replied between bites as she scarfed down her food.

When Lydia excused herself to help the kids get ready for bed, Jensen excused herself too. She'd been up since 2:00 a.m., so as soon as her head hit the pillow she was asleep.

On Sunday, she woke up with the sun, ready to get back in the water. It was only sixty degrees out and the water was cold, but not unbearable. She swam for two hours and by the time she went back inside, Lydia was pulling out pans to start making breakfast.

"Good morning, Honey."

"Good morning. Are you the first one up?" Jensen asked.

"The little ones are awake too. They're watching a show."

"Do you need help with breakfast?"

"I would love that," Lydia smiled.

"Okay," Jensen replied. "Let me just throw something on over my suit." Before leaving the kitchen, she added a warning, "Oh, and just so you know, I've never cooked anything in my life, so I probably won't be much help."

"I'll start you off with something easy," Lydia chuckled.

Five minutes later, back in the kitchen, Lydia cracked eggs

into a frying pan and handed Jensen a spatula. "Just keep the eggs moving so they cook evenly," she explained, unfazed by the horrified look on Jensen's face. She stirred the eggs, but they fluffed up a lot faster than she expected them too.

"Am I doing this right?" she panicked.

Lydia turned down the heat, reassuring her, "Don't worry, it's hard to ruin scrambled eggs. You've got this!" Then, trying to ease her mind she asked, "So, what are your plans for the summer? Joe told me he thinks you should stay and I agree. One weekend isn't enough time to make up for the last seven years."

Jensen hadn't seriously considered Joe's offer, but she wondered if she should. "I'll think about it," she said.

Lydia spent the next few minutes talking about her kids. She bragged about Nicole's art and how she planned to move to New York at the end of the summer. She told Jensen that Grayson was majoring in environmental science. He'd become passionate about forestry and conservation after they moved to the heart of the Sierra Nevadas.

Lake Evergreen was so remote that the high school didn't offer regular sports. There weren't enough students and only one neighboring school in the larger town of Tanglewood to compete against. Instead, the local high school offered wilderness days a few times a year for the entire school. They did things like backpacking through Lassen State Park and they took weeklong ski trips to Shasta. Grayson had been mountain biking, snowshoeing, sailing, and cross-country skiing all before leaving for college. He loved adventure and new experiences, something he didn't know about himself when he was younger.

Unfortunately, the lack of sports was a deal breaker for Andrew. He'd refused to move somewhere that didn't give him the opportunity to play football competitively. Instead, he lived with his dad after the divorce, only visiting the lake during the summer. His choice paid off. He got into Boise State. They began recruiting him when he was still a sophomore in high school.

"Andrew loved playing football," Lydia explained, "but he hurt his knee right before his senior season." According to Lydia, the accident was a blessing and a curse. Before, he always skated by with the lowest possible grades to be eligible to play but last year he really turned things around. He changed his major to finance and started taking school more seriously. He was leaving just after the 4th of July to start working at his dad's company.

Jensen tried to imagine how hard it must have been for Andrew when the doctors told him he couldn't play anymore, but she couldn't.

"I just hope that wherever he ends up, he finds his happiness," Lydia said. "School was never his thing. He got antsy sitting behind a desk all day. I hate to think of him going into a career that'll stick him behind one again, crunching numbers and resenting the choices he made that led him there." Lydia looked past Jensen and smiled at her son, who'd just walked in. "Grayson is the smarty-pants of the bunch," she joked.

"Not as smart as Jen. Stanford didn't want me." He didn't sound jaded, just matter-of-fact. He walked to the fridge to fill a glass of water as Jensen turned to face him.

He was glistening with sweat. His shirt was clinging to his stomach and his hair was damp. She shouldn't have found his sweat covered body sexy, but she couldn't pull her eyes away. As he stood next to her gulping down water, she stared at his throat and wondered what it would be like to lick the side of his neck. The thought was so unexpected that she let out a barely audible squeak.

Grayson gave her a curious look.

"You applied to Stanford?" she asked, trying to act nonchalant.

"Of course. We always said we were all going to."

She was surprised he remembered that. The four of them, Andrew, Nicole, Grayson, and Jensen, made a pact that they'd all go together. They swore it to each other the night before she left for boarding school. That way, after they graduated they'd be together again.

"You didn't get in?" She couldn't imagine how she got into a school that he didn't. He was always the smarter one.

"Nah. I go to UC Santa Cruz."

Andrew came into the kitchen and threw an arm around Jensen's shoulder like it was the most natural thing in the world. But it wasn't natural. It was awkward, mainly because of their height difference. "You're coming out on the boat with us today," he announced before scrunching up his nose at the smell wafting out of the pan. He looked down at the eggs Jensen was still stirring. "What's that?"

"Scrambled eggs?"

"And Mom always says you can't mess up eggs," he said, bewildered before taking the pan off the stove and tossing the contents into the garbage. "Guess she was wrong."

Jensen looked to Lydia for help, but she was glancing toward the playroom where Julia had just started crying. So instead Jensen turned her pleading eyes to Grayson.

"We'll fix breakfast. You go get ready," he encouraged. "You don't have to wakeboard if you don't want to. But, you should come out with us."

"Okay," she agreed hesitantly. She'd been sailing with Eric and his family before and it was actually pretty fun. A speedboat couldn't be that different.

They ate a quick breakfast with Lydia and the kids before walking down to the lake. Brent and Nicole had already brought the boat to the dock and were waiting for them.

"Are you guys serious right now?" Nicole directed the question to her brothers. "If she takes one step on this boat, I'm out."

"Nicole, chill out. Don't make a scene." Grayson's voice came out calm, but he knew his words would bite at her.

His twin took it personally when he took anyone's side but hers. When they were kids, she and Grayson were incredibly close. Nicole always had the bigger personality and strong opinions about everything. Meanwhile, Grayson was quiet and more reserved. It made sense that he'd back her up. In high school, and even more so in recent years since moving away for college, he was less willing to play the role of Nicole's sidekick. "You need to deal with whatever's got you so pissed off and give Jen a chance."

"Hey, you've got this," he heard Brent whisper to Nicole. He had his hands on her shoulders like he was giving her a pep talk. Grayson was glad his best friend had the patience to deal with her attitude right then because he didn't. Plus, he felt an overwhelming need to defend Jensen.

"Don't let her being here stop you from having a good time. Don't let her have that kind of power over you." Brent was whispering, but Nicole's response was drowned out by the music blasting from the overhead speakers as soon as Andrew turned the key in the ignition.

Jensen joined Grayson and Andrew at the front of the boat, trying to give Brent and Nicole privacy to finish their conversation.

"Don't worry about her," Grayson urged.

"Half the time she doesn't even know why she's pissed off," Andrew added. "That's just Nicole. She always holds a grudge."

"But I never did anything for her to hold a grudge over?" Jensen said. "It's not like it was my choice to go away to school. I was sent away."

"Hey guys," Brent approached cautiously. The tension surrounding their small boat was palpable. "Nicole is going to take the first run. She's got some aggression she needs to work out."

Andrew and Grayson both chuckled and Jensen peeked over her shoulder at the back of the boat. Nicole had shed her clothes, revealing a black bikini and, sure enough, her curves were everything Jensen thought they would be. She had always been envious of curves. She had a very specific body type which was great for swimming and she usually loved her body; it was strong and got the job done. Stacked up next to Nicole's, however, it was obvious that she lacked certain *assets*.

Nicole buckled a lifejacket over her top and then clipped her feet onto a board.

Andrew stopped the boat and handed Jensen an orange flag. "Sit at the back and as soon as she goes down, you hold this up," he instructed. "Keep it in the air until she's back on the boat. Think you can handle that?"

She nodded and took the seat Nicole was sitting in moments ago. Andrew started up the boat and as soon as the rope went taut, Nicole stood easily atop the water. She glided on the surface effortlessly, zig-zagging back and forth before catching the boat's wake. She jumped the inside wake and within seconds, she was back, jumping the outer wake to line up in the middle.

"She's incredible," Jensen said, more to herself than anyone else.

Brent slid onto the bench next to her. "She's a beast, huh?" He admired her out on the water. "Is she a pain in the ass? Yes. But she's also a major badass."

"Do you know why she hates me?" Jensen asked, still dwelling on Nicole's harsh words.

"No, she hasn't said anything. But that's Nicole. She keeps everything inside. I'd just give it time."

"Great, time is the one thing I don't have. I leave tomorrow."

"Well, then, what does it matter if she hates you?" he challenged. "You're leaving anyway."

"We used to be best friends," Jensen answered under her breath, the words were more for herself than for Brent.

She watched Nicole jump another wake and add a 180-degree spin. When she landed it, she beamed. Jensen saw her old best friend out there on the water. Her smile stretched from ear to ear. She was chalked full of adrenaline and showing off. Jensen longed to feel as carefree as Nicole was right then. Even when she was swimming, which she loved, it had been years since she'd done it just for fun. Andrew was right, she was tracking every swim. It was all about breath control, perfecting her form, or beating her time.

Nicole glanced briefly at Jensen, then looked away just as fast. She whipped to the left and hit the wake, flinging her entire body into the air, flipping the board over in a wide arch. The edge of the board clipped the opposite wake and yanked her from the rope.

Jensen held up the orange flag and momentarily panicked. Nicole went down hard. But no one else seemed to be concerned by her wipeout. Brent told Andrew to circle around and Jensen watched Nicole bob in the water a ways back. When they pulled up beside her, she was cracking up. She smacked both hands on the top of the water in excitement. "Did you see that? I was *this* close." She held her thumb and pointer finger an inch apart.

Brent helped her back into the boat. "That backside one-eighty was clean." He offered her a high-five. "And the amount of airtime you had on that side flip was crazy. I give it a week and you'll have it down."

Nicole detached herself from her board and wrung out her hair. Then she placed the board on the upper bar next to the speakers and Brent pulled down a slightly larger one.

The boys each took turns wakeboarding and Jensen continued manning the flag, watching them in awe.

After a few runs, Brent sidled up to her. He'd spent all his time with Nicole and she'd made a point of staying far away from Jensen. He held out a helmet to her. "Show us what you've got."

"I think this is more of a spectator sport for me," she responded.

"Just a quick lesson. I'll teach you how to stand."

"I really can't," she said. "I'm a competitive swimmer and I'm not supposed to do anything that puts my body at risk." She really hoped Grayson and Andrew didn't overhear and contradict her excuse.

"Hold up! They expect you to refrain from anything that could get you hurt? Even in the summer?" Brent looked aghast. "That's a bullshit rule if I've ever heard one. How do you have any fun?"

"Swimming is how I have fun." She tried to sound convincing, but hadn't she just been thinking, while watching Nicole, that it hadn't been fun in awhile. Swimming wasn't fun, it was necessary. It was how she coped. What did she do for fun?

"I mean, unless you're an Olympic swimmer, it shouldn't be all you do. Even if you are that good, there's more to life."

She didn't tell him she was *that* good. "I guess I've never really considered what I'm missing out on," she admitted, just as Grayson sat down beside her.

"What do you do with your friends?" Brent inquired further.

"I've never had many friends. The two friends I have were under as much pressure as me. Our school was competitive and all-consuming. Sometimes on weekends, we'd go to New York and walk around the city. Mostly, I just went along with whatever they had going on. Lots of golf and watching people walk runways."

Brent scoffed at that answer. "You know what I think?" He didn't give her a chance to answer. "It sounds like you've spent your entire life on the sidelines." He looked at Grayson, "I think we need to take her under our wing this summer. We can teach her how to actually live her life instead of letting it happen around her." He turned to Jensen, excitedly, "We can teach you how to wakeboard and parasail. We'll show you the best hiking trails, and we're definitely putting you on a dirt bike."

"That sounds great in theory, but I'm leaving tomorrow morning," she reminded him.

"When will you be back?" Brent's excitement didn't fade.

Jensen hesitated, unsure how to answer.

"Historically speaking, she'll probably disappear and we won't see her again for about seven years," Nicole interjected from across the boat.

"Or I could not disappear this time. I could come back next weekend, or I could even stay," Jensen spit out without thinking about what she was saying.

As soon as she said it, she felt a spark of excitement. There was no reason the Reeses couldn't be a part of her life again. They could stay in touch. She could even visit again before school started.

Nicole rolled her eyes at the idea, but Grayson smiled. "You're thinking about staying?" And there was something akin to hope in the way he said it that sucked her in. She stared into his eyes. They were so blue they became the lake and she wanted to swim in them. They sparkled like the sun off the water, full of excitement at the prospect of her staying.

She was about to correct him, but she was lost in the way he was looking at her. Why not stay longer? Lucy would understand and Eric would be in Barcelona for the next month anyway. Jensen thought about Brent's offer to teach her how to live, and that flutter of excitement returned. If she was really done swimming competitively, then why not? She was being presented with the opportunity to have fun, something she was realizing she'd forgotten how to do. It felt like it was exactly what she needed.

She had to deal with her mom, clean out her grandparent's house, and get ready for school, but she didn't want to do any of that. For the first time in years, what she wanted to do was outweighing what she should do.

"You don't think your parents will mind, do you?" She asked, looking to Grayson for an answer.

"Of course they won't. Mom will be thrilled. You could stay until school starts. There's nothing like summer at the lake." He offered her a crooked smile that gave her stomach a little jolt.

"I don't know about the entire summer, but I could probably stay for a week or two," she reasoned.

"You'll end up staying longer," Brent said matter-of-factly. "It's the lake. It will draw you in with its siren song, like it does to all of us. It's why I'll never leave and why these guys," he nodded towards Andrew and Grayson, "keep coming back every summer."

"It's true," Grayson said, looking out across the water.

"We can even hook her up with a job," Brent added. "We need help at The Marina anyway and you haven't truly lived until you've had your first job."

"What makes you think I've never had a job before?" She tried not to sound as offended as she felt. Brent just met her. Did she really come across as that privileged?

"It's obvious."

Damn. She hated that she gave that impression. When did she become the type of person she used to hate? No wonder Nicole took one look and judged her. Apparently, she was wearing her wealth like it was a pair of satin gloves she couldn't remove.

"It's just a part-time position and it'll be super easy. Brent and I both work there." Grayson explained, trying to keep his cool. He hadn't let himself consider the possibility of her staying longer. If Brent was successful in convincing her to work with them he'd get to spend every day with her. He owed his best friend big time. When he'd told him at work yesterday about his childhood crush, he was expecting to be mocked. Instead, Brent was playing the role of the ultimate wingman.

Jensen knew that if she refused, she'd be labeling herself as an outsider, too privileged to work. Hesitantly, she agreed. "Okay."

"Yes!" Grayson and Brent celebrated, high-fiving each other.

"What's going on over there?" Andrew called out from where he was driving.

"Jen's staying," Grayson hollered and Nicole's face fell at the news.

"Wait! How am I supposed to work at a marina when I know nothing about boats? What should I do to prepare? Aren't there *boat words* I should know?"

"Boat words?" They laughed.

"There are boating words, aren't there?" She'd heard Eric say words like jib and starboard when they'd gone sailing.

"You'll be fine," Andrew assured her. "Lots of local kids work there and half of them don't know shit-all about boats."

She found this hard to believe. They lived on a lake, after all. Surely they knew more than she did. "Or ... Grayson could go over the words with me this afternoon," she rationalized. "I'm not really a learn-as-you-go type of person. I prefer to go into things already knowledgeable."

"What do you want? Boat flashcards?" Grayson teased.

"That would be great."

"I was joking."

Even if he was joking, flashcards weren't a bad idea, but she wouldn't embarrass herself by asking for his help again.

That night she searched: *boating words and phrases,* and found a glossary of nautical terms. She wasn't wrong, there were boating words, hundreds of them. Copying each one down, she separated them into two piles, novice and advanced. She went through the novice stack first.

AFT: the back of the ship (can also be called the stern)

BOW: the front of the ship

PORT: the left side of the boat when facing the bow

STARBOARD: the right side of the boat when facing the bow

MAST: the upright post generally carrying a sail

She stayed up late memorizing a stack of flashcards. However, she still felt uneasy about the job. Grayson and Brent weren't giving her much time to stress about it. According to them, she started in the morning.

She tossed and turned all night, worried about what the next day would bring.

5

"OUT OF SIGHT, OUT OF MIND." —JENSEN

Jensen dug into Lucy's suitcase in search of work-appropriate clothes, regretting letting Lucy discard all her collared shirts. Eventually she settled on a pair of high waisted black shorts and a crop top. There were plenty of bikinis in Lucy's luggage, but she cringed at the lack of fabric on them. She tossed them aside and dug through another bag until she found a sporty two-piece with a black racer-back top and boy-shorts. The tags were still on, which wasn't a surprise since Lucy rarely swam.

Grayson was waiting for her when she headed down for breakfast. "Phil just called," he said when she entered the kitchen. "He needs me to come in a half hour early." He handed her a cup of coffee and a muffin. "That means we're already late."

They rushed out the door, waving goodbye to Lydia, Julia, and Dustin, who were sitting at the table eating breakfast.

"Good luck," Lydia called out.

The drive to The Marina took about fifteen minutes. Jensen picked at her muffin and tried not to stress while reciting the boat words in her head.

There was a short, middle-aged man waiting for them when they got to the parking lot. As soon as Grayson exited the car, the man filled him in on the problem. "The McKinnon's boat isn't shifting. It's idling just outside the buoys. Their boat has a mechanical cable shift, so it's probably just a broken linkage, but it could be the transmission. I tried to walk them through how to shift manually over the radio, but they weren't getting it. Can you take a jet-ski out and bring them back to the harbor?"

After agreeing to fix the problem, Grayson led Jensen to the shore. "That was Phil," he said while they walked, "he owns The Marina."

Jensen was only partially listening, because her mind was spinning. "So much for not needing to know anything about boats," she said, accusatorially. "I didn't understand half of what you guys were just saying. What am I supposed to do if I'm asked to fix something? I've never even driven a boat."

Her wide-eyed panic was cute but also worrisome. Grayson wanted her to enjoy working there and he knew she wouldn't if she spent the entire day anxious and stressed.

"You won't be asked to fix anything," he explained as he led her to a pop-up tent. There was a counter with a cash register atop it, a mini fridge tucked in the corner, and a wall full of life-jackets. "Just hang out here for a bit." He looked behind him and saw Reed entering the tent. Oh, great. He had hoped she'd be shadowing Brent or Hawk.

Reed was a great guy and one of Andrew's close friends, but he wouldn't take the time to teach Jensen anything, that was for sure. Reed usually only worked at The Marina when there was an emergency or if they were short handed. The guy could get more done in a day than five people, and he knew his shit, but he wasn't particularly patient with new employees. "Don't worry, you're going to be great," Grayson said. "And I'll be back as soon as I get this all sorted out. If you have questions, ask Reed."

His words didn't ease her worries, but fortunately his abs did. She realized this a second later when he pulled off his shirt, effectively distracting her from her panicked state. Grayson was spectacular. Every time she saw him shirtless, she carved out a place in her mind to store the memory. How soft his skin looked when he opened his door in only his boxers the other night. The way his abs were tight and flexed after wake-boarding yesterday, glistening with lake water and sweat. And now, just casually standing before her with his defined chest and flat stomach, which showed a shadow of the six-pack she'd seen the day before. Her heart skipped a beat as she took in the V that dipped into his shorts, but she didn't dare let her eyes wander lower. She learned that lesson already. Maybe she had a medical condition, one where her eyes acted like magnets to his bare skin. Maybe it was just something she'd have to learn to live with. His chest, illuminated by that golden tan, was triggering her disorder.

He ran the short distance to the shore to a group of jet-skis. She watched as he sprayed on sunscreen, then pulled a ball cap over his head, making wisps of curls stick out in a cute, messy way. He bent down, grabbed a life-jacket and pushed the jet-ski into the lake. As he guided it out, she sighed at his long legs and the way his swim shorts hug his backside.

"You know you have a little drool," Brent announced, coming up next to her. She jumped and prayed her reddening face wouldn't give her away. She was so distracted she hadn't even heard him enter the tent.

"I wasn't watching him. I mean, I was, but just so I can learn, you know, for my job." She tried to explain, but even she knew she didn't sound convincing. "And I wasn't drooling."

"It's totally cool if you were. I mean, I don't swing that way, but even I can acknowledge that my boy is fine."

She felt herself turning even redder. "What exactly do you want, Brent?"

"Oh nothing, I was just stopping in to say hi before I have to go gas up the boats."

"Okay, you said it. You can go now," she said, trying to get rid of him quickly, mortified that he'd caught her ogling Grayson.

He took a few steps away. "Just one piece of advice," he added. "Don't let other girls catch you looking at him that way, or your summer is gonna be significantly less fun. Local girls can get a bit territorial about summer-timers coming here and fishing in their lake, if you know what I mean."

"I'm not fishing for anything," she argued, but she couldn't rid herself of the little green monster on her shoulder whispering, *"What other girls?"*

"Suuure," he smirked. "Our secret." And he winked.

It was the wink that did it. She picked up the closest thing, a facial sunscreen stick, and threw it at him. She missed by a yard, which made him laugh even more boisterously. He continued laughing the entire way down the dock.

Jensen spent the rest of the morning in the pop-up tent, while Grayson was dealing with the McKinnons' boat.

Reed introduced himself and bragged, "I'm the most qualified to teach you about the job." And yet, he didn't actually teach her anything. He showed her the cash register but left to help with an emergency without training her first. A family came in to rent a boat and when she didn't know what to do she had to call for help. Reed ran in, did it for her and ran out again without any explanation. She felt like she was in the way rather than actually helping.

By lunchtime, she was contemplating quitting. The only productive thing she'd done all day was organize the lifejackets by size. That was mostly for her own benefit, because she liked things tidy.

When she headed back to the tent after eating her lunch, she was ready to tell Reed the job wasn't for her, but he wasn't there. Instead, Grayson was sitting on the counter smiling at her and she couldn't get the words out. So she went back to her spot behind the counter and when the next group came in to rent a boat, she shot a *'help me'* look at him.

"You've got this, Jen," he encouraged with a squeeze to her arm. She liked how the nickname easily rolled off his tongue. Jen felt like a new person, someone entirely different from Jensen.

Grayson pulled out a rental packet, like Reed had done earlier and showed her how to have the man fill it out and where to sign it. "I'll go make sure Brent has the boat ready to go," he said once she was set, then he jogged down to the dock, leaving her alone with the customers.

Once the packet was filled out, she checked their ID's, even though she was not really sure what she was looking for. They looked legit, so she handed them back and smiled. After making sure she got enough life jackets for the entire group, she asked, "Would you like any water sports equipment?"

"We'll take a knee-board," the oldest man said just as Grayson reentered the tent.

Jensen looked at the rack of skis and wakeboards behind her. "A knee-board?" she asked, hoping Grayson would jump to her aid. But he was too busy flipping through the rental contract, making sure it was filled out correctly, to hear the exchange.

She cleared her throat, uncomfortably. "I'm sorry. It looks like we don't have any knee-boards left." Grayson's head snapped up, confused.

"There are like three knee-boards behind you," the customer said.

"Here, let me get that for you." Grayson detached a board from the rack. From the back, it looked exactly like a wakeboard, but when he placed it on the counter, she saw knee pads instead of footholds.

Grayson directed the family over to dock two, where Brent was readying their boat. When he returned, Jensen was laying her forehead on the counter. "That was so embarrassing," she groaned.

"Sorry," Grayson sympathized. "I didn't know you were really that clueless about this stuff."

"This is my first time at a lake. In Connecticut, I went sailing once on the ocean but there weren't any water sports involved."

"You know, maybe the flashcards weren't a bad idea."

"I made them last night, and they were no help at all."

"Well, why don't I teach you right now? If by the end of our shift you're still worried about it, I'll help you with your flashcards."

"Seriously?"

Grayson nodded and walked over to the equipment rack. He pointed out each item as he explained, "We offer a wide variety of equipment here: boats, jet skis, paddle boards, and sports equipment, like skis, wakeboards, knee-boards, tubes, and rafts."

She nodded, making a mental note of everything. He kept explaining policies and procedures as they walked out to dock one. He climbed aboard a boat and motioned for her to join him.

"I think maybe I should just watch the cash register," she said nervously. But, when she turned around she saw that Reed was already at the counter.

"I don't have to drive it, do I?" she asked, following Grayson onto the boat.

"Not this time, but I'll teach you soon, so pay attention."

She spent the rest of her shift shadowing Grayson. It went by quickly and before she knew it, they were off.

When they got back to the house, they both rushed upstairs to change. They were planning on meeting Brent at the meadow. After changing out of their work clothes Jensen knocked on Grayson's door to see if he was ready to go. He swung his door open and waved her in. She proceeded cautiously, not sure of proper protocol when entering a guy's room. At school, they weren't allowed in the boy's dorms and vice versa.

It wasn't that she was nervous about being alone with Grayson, it was just rare to be so entirely unsupervised with a guy that wasn't Eric. Jensen reminded herself that Grayson was only staying at the lake for the summer. He'd been living in a college dorm for the past two years. To him, this freedom was normal. Inviting her in probably felt like no big deal to him. She was the one overreacting, like a child. She took a deep breath and stepped into his space.

When they were kids, Grayson's room had shelves displaying his many LEGO creations. He used to spend hours in his room building with those little blocks. He had bins of LEGOs under his bed, and he didn't care when she and Nicole would tease him tirelessly that he was too old for them.

There weren't any LEGOs adorning his walls anymore, just two paintings. There was a guitar in the corner and she approached it asking, "Do you play?"

"Nah," he smiled, "A few summers back, I asked Davis or Brent to teach me, but they never had time. I tried teaching myself, but it wasn't as easy as I thought it would be."

She looked at his bookcase, mostly school books with a few science fiction titles mixed in. Then she wandered over to a tank next to his bed and examined the lizard inside. It was missing a leg. "I found her on my run this morning," Grayson explained. "She's hurt so I'm planning on giving her to Avery."

"What's her name?" she asked.

"I was thinking Lizzy," Grayson shrugged.

Jensen looked at him flatly. "You guys came up with the stupidest nickname for me, but you couldn't come up with anything more creative for your lizard than Lizzy?"

"I knew you didn't like being called Fish anymore. I could tell by your reaction when Andrew said it yesterday."

"It's not that I don't like it, it's just that I don't feel like that girl anymore. Fish was someone you guys used to know. It's been seven years. Besides, what kind of girl wants to be called Fish?" she asked.

"You used to love it. And, the nickname fits. You come alive in the water."

He remembered what it used to be like to swim alongside her. He would be in the middle of a race and he'd get distracted watching her. It was impossible not to. His arms and legs would be aching, he'd be panting, and praying he'd touch the wall soon. Meanwhile, she'd fly past like it was nothing. When she would reach the wall, she always had the biggest smile on her face, like she'd just created magic. And the thing was, she had. He'd watched it happen.

"When you swim, you become someone else entirely. I've never seen anything like it." He stepped closer to her. "You shouldn't be ashamed of the connection you have to the water. You should be proud of it." Another step closer. "I see the way you look out at the lake. People live their entire lives looking for that kind of connection." He was looking for that kind of connection. Standing so close to her, he wondered if he'd finally found it. She felt like his own personal gravity.

They stood face to face, and he could feel the warmth of her breath. He wanted to lean in. He wanted to sweep her into the story he was writing for them in his head.

Her phone rang, cracking through the tension. They both realized how close they were standing and took a step back in unison.

"Answer it," he encouraged, already making his way to the door. "I'm gonna go grab some food." He left her in his room, needing a few seconds to regroup. He'd come too close to kissing her. What if he moved too fast and totally freaked her out? He had to remember it had been seven years. He needed to get to know her again and stop thinking with his cock. Not an easy task when she was traipsing around in those tiny shorts showing off her mile-long legs.

Jensen pulled out her phone just as Grayson closed the door behind him. Eric was requesting a video chat. She was still buzzing with Grayson's words and the electric air that lingered in the room. She wanted to bask in it, and forget about everything else. But that wasn't her real life and she needed to talk to Eric to bring her back down to earth. She shook her head, took a deep breath and swiped to answer his call. It took a few seconds to connect.

When the image was clear, she had to hold back her laugh. "What are you wearing?" He had on a pair of glasses with surgical magnifiers attached to the lenses.

"They're called loupes. I thought you'd get a kick out of them. I was just practicing with them." He shot her a perfectly straight all-white smile.

"You're such a nerd," she joked. In reality, Eric was the opposite of a nerd. He was the captain of the golf and lacrosse teams at school. Girls always used to ask her about him before they started dating.

"Just you wait! When we're in med school and everyone is struggling with their loupes, I'll already be an expert." He shot her a joking smolder. "If you're nice, I might let you practice with them, too."

"Is struggling with loupes a common problem?" she asked.

"I don't know, but it won't be a problem for me, that's for sure."

Grayson walked in, holding a plate piled high with two sandwiches and fruit. He offered her one and she took it with her free hand, still holding her phone in the other. "Are you off the phone yet?" he asked.

"No," she held her phone up so they could see each other. "Eric, this is Grayson, one of my old neighbors that I was telling you about. Grayson, this is my boyfriend, Eric."

Grayson nearly choked on his bite of sandwich. He had just been contemplating kissing her, and she had a boyfriend? It didn't line up. Why was she so easily convinced to spend the summer at the lake? And why hadn't she mentioned him at all? He would have cataloged that information for sure. He regained his composure and swallowed. "Hey man, nice to meet you."

"Yeah, you too," Eric's voice has lost its laughter, and he sounded unconvincing. "What are you guys doing?" he asked.

"We're just having lunch. Then meeting up with some people at a meadow," Jensen told him.

"What meadow?" Eric asked. "Where are you?"

"Still at the lake house. Remember I told you I'd be here all weekend."

"It's Monday."

"Yeah well I'm thinking about staying a few extra days."

"You'll still get the house done though, right?"

"Yeah of course." She could tell Eric was starting to get frustrated and she didn't want to argue with him in front of Grayson. He wouldn't understand why she was shucking her responsibilities, it was so unlike her. "You know what," she said, "let me go to the other room." She stood and started to leave.

Grayson knew he should give them privacy, but he followed her into the hall anyway. Screw it, he was curious. Was that Jen's type? Because if so, he didn't stand a chance with her. '*Shut up,*' he told himself, trying to shake the thought out of his mind. She was taken, and that meant nothing could happen. He tried to wrap his head around the idea of just being *friends*, but it was a hard pill to swallow.

Grayson watched her walk into the hall, where she nearly crashed into a shirtless Andrew.

"Fish, just who I was looking for," his brother announced. "Grayson says you're coming with us to the meadow."

"Who's that now?" Eric asked.

Andrew's eyes darted to her screen. He plucked her phone out of her hand. "Who are you?" Then to Jensen, he asked, "Fish, who is this tool? Please tell me this isn't your type." He looked at Eric with the same disgusted look he had when he saw Jensen's ruined eggs that morning.

"I'm Eric, Jensen's boyfriend. Who are you?" Eric snapped out, and even though she couldn't see him, she could hear the sharp bite of annoyance in his voice.

She yanked the phone out of Andrew's hand before he was able to say more. "Sorry about that," she apologized lamely. "Andrew's another old neighbor. He's actually a nice guy." She shot him a *'you better be nice'* glare. "He was just messing around."

Andrew shook his head and mouthed, *'no I wasn't.'* Then he looked at Grayson and whispered, "Did she just call us neighbors? I think that's a level below friends. That hurts."

Then, Andrew added loud enough for Eric to hear, "Who is this guy? He literally stinks of trust fund."

Jensen muted her phone and hissed, "In case you guys forgot, *I* am a trust fund kid, and *you* used to be too."

"Yeah, but we're not anymore and you don't count. We know you," Grayson countered. "You're more than your money."

"Well, so is Eric. You guys don't even know him." She unmuted herself and gave Eric apologetic eyes through the phone. "Can we talk tomorrow?" she asked. "We were just heading out. There are people waiting for us."

"Seriously, Jensen? No, we can't talk tomorrow. I'll be on a plane to Barcelona. Did you forget? I've been talking about it for months."

Shit, she cringed. It's not that she forgot about Eric's trip, it'd been at the forefront of her mind for weeks. Without thinking, she said, "Eric, I'm so sorry. It's been such a crazy weekend and I guess I forgot. You know how it goes ... out of sight, out of mind."

Grayson and Andrew both cringed, and she knew she'd said the wrong thing. She played her words back in her mind and immediately regretted them. She sounded like what she'd really forgotten about was him. "That sounded bad." She said apologetically. "You know I miss you, right?"

Eric sighed, "I miss you too. I'll let you go and I'll call you from Spain as soon as I get a chance."

She was about to hang up when he added, "Hold up a second, Jensen. Mom and Dad want to say hi."

His parents appeared on the screen behind him. They were all smiles. "Hi sweetie," Katrina sang. "Eric told us you're coming with us to Aspen this Christmas. We're so excited to have you join us."

"I can't wait," she smiled. "Thanks so much for inviting me."

Aspen for Christmas. Grayson tried to process that. Their relationship had to be serious. She clearly knew his parents well if she was planning on spending the holidays with them.

"Of course, of course," John bellowed. "We wish you could join us this summer. We could still get you a flight and you could meet us there."

He felt his heart sink into his stomach at the thought of her leaving before he really got the chance to cement himself back in her life.

She looked over and made eye contact with him. "I think I'm good where I'm at," she said into the phone and he let out a long, relieved breath. "It's been a long time since I've spent a summer in California. I want to be here. Listen, I've got to go, but I can't wait to see you guys at orientation."

"Two more months till Stanford," Eric added.

They were going to school together? Of course they were, they were the perfect couple. He could see that already. But, if that were true, then what was with the magnetic pull yanking him into her orbit?

"I'm sure it'll go by fast," Jensen said to Eric.

As soon as she hung up the phone, Grayson asked, "So, what's the deal with your boyfriend?"

"Real subtle man," Andrew clapped him on the back.

"The deal? You mean why was he wearing those ridiculous glasses? He's going to be a surgeon. He was practicing with them."

"He's in med school? How old is he?" Grayson asked.

"No, we're the same age. We've known each other since we were eleven. We're going to Stanford together, pre-med. He comes from a family full of surgeons and we plan to continue the legacy."

"So, he's the reason you quit swimming?" Andrew said accusatorially "I knew I didn't like him."

"So you can follow 'doctor boy' to medical school?" Grayson added, teaming up on her.

She didn't know how to respond, so she just rolled her eyes. Did Eric play a part in her decision to quit swimming? Yes. Would she be pre-med if it weren't for him? Probably not.

But, instead of letting herself overthink it too much, she turned the conversation on its head, glaring at Andrew. "Taking my phone from me was not cool. You distracted me and totally made me look like an idiot in front of my boyfriend. Now he thinks I forgot about him."

"To be fair, you did, kind of, forget about him," Grayson countered, not able to hold his tongue.

"It's not that I forgot. It's just that things with Eric can get really intense. Sometimes I need a break."

"Sounds like a super fun relationship," Andrew intoned.

She was about to defend Eric, but an alert on her phone cut her off. She looked down at the device in her hand and saw that it was the alarm system at the house in Atherton.

"What's that for?" Andrew asked, looking over her shoulder at her phone screen. Grayson was on her other side, also peering at the security message currently lighting up her phone.

She swiped open the security app and there was a warning. She could either disable the alarm or authorities would be called. There was a one-minute countdown running at the top of the screen. She clicked over and opened the app that was attached to the house's exterior cameras. She already knew who was trying to break into the house, and it was probably best if she dealt with Laurel herself.

She looked at her mom through the doorbell camera. Laurel was saying something, but the service was poor. Her voice came through choppy and robotic. Jensen could see her face clearly, though.

She'd probably end up regretting it, but she clicked back over to the alarm app and, with two seconds left in the countdown, she put in her code and disabled the alarm. Laurel was still her mother, and she'd already had cops take her away once that year.

"Why'd you do that? She's totally trying to get into your house. You're just gonna let her walk in?" Andrew asked.

"Don't be an idiot Andrew, didn't you see the resemblance? I'm pretty sure that was her mom," Grayson explained.

"I'm not letting her get away with anything. I'm going down there."

"Now?" Grayson asked.

"Yes, right now."

6

"YOU'RE NOT THE ONLY ONE WHO'S CHANGED." —GRAYSON

"You guys don't need to come with me," Jensen said when Andrew slid into her driver's seat and Grayson hopped into the back.

"Just drop it, Fish. We're coming," Andrew replied.

"You shouldn't go alone," Grayson argued. "None of us have work tomorrow, so we can even stay the night. Besides, our dad still lives next door. It'll be a good excuse to see him. It's been a while."

"Shit Grayson, you don't really want to see Dad, do you?" Andrew groaned. "We can check on Jensen's house and come right back to the lake. He doesn't even need to know we're there."

Jensen eyed Andrew curiously. She'd assumed he was close with his dad since he lived with him throughout high school and would soon be working for him. She wanted to ask about it, but Grayson was faster. "Seriously, what is your issue with Dad lately?"

"It's nothing, I just don't want to hear him lecture me again about how I'm wasting my summer away. He wanted me to start work right after graduation, you know, and I refused. It's bad enough I have to start the day after the 4th of July."

"That's bullshit and you know it. Dad's been lecturing us forever. It's what he does. I don't understand why you're suddenly listening to him. Now you're avoiding him as much as Nicole does? What gives?"

"Just drop it Grayson, it doesn't concern you," Andrew argued.

"'*It doesn't concern you*' is a hell of a lot different than '*it's nothing.*' At least be honest," Grayson retorted.

"Well, this is going to be a fun drive," Jensen mumbled under her breath. To her surprise, the rest of the drive was fine. Once the tension from their argument dissipated, they turned up the music and the mood in the car shifted. They spent the time joking, laughing, and reminiscing.

When they finally arrived in Atherton, the sun was setting. Exhausted after her first day of work, and the five-hour drive, Jensen longed for her bed. Unfortunately, Laurel was a problem that wasn't going away. She had to be dealt with first.

Andrew pulled the car into the driveway and silence fell over them as they stared up at the house. All the lights were on, but the house was quiet.

"I know I should have asked this sooner ..." Grayson broke the silence. "But, what should we expect when we see her?" He didn't have any memories of Laurel. He wasn't even sure if he'd ever met her.

"I don't know. The last time I saw her, she was threatening to burn down the house. We had to call the cops. But that was months ago. She's been in rehab since then. Maybe she's clean and stable and I'm making this into a bigger deal than I should."

"A stable person doesn't break into someone's house," Andrew retorted as they got out of the car and stood together in the driveway. Grayson elbowed him. "Ouch. Damn, what was that for?" he hissed. "You're the one who told me to be honest."

Jensen took a deep breath. Readying herself for whatever she was about to walk into.

Hopefully Laurel was sober, but what would she do if her mother was clean? The subject of the inheritance still needed to be addressed. Katrina told Laurel she would never see one penny of that money, but would Jensen be able to stand firm if her mom really was getting better?

It was a terrible thought, but part of her felt like it would be simpler if she was still using. It would make it a lot easier to deny her and walk away. She buried that thought quickly, knowing that wasn't really what she wanted.

Grayson walked up to her and whispered, "You okay?"

She wasn't sure how she was feeling so instead of responding she reached down and grabbed his hand. He refused to let himself read too much into it. She just needed a friend, so he squeezed tightly.

Jensen led the way up the path to the front door. When they stepped under the overhang, Andrew cut in front of them and asked for the code. Jensen gave him the six-digit pin, and he keyed it in. There was a faint sound of a lock unlatching followed by a green light on the alarm box.

Andrew reached out for the knob and entered the house first with Grayson and Jensen right on his heels. They could hear the echo of their footsteps on the entryway tile, but Jensen also heard noise coming from the kitchen. "Hello?" she called out.

It wasn't a voice that called to them, it was a soft whimper that led them to her. Laurel was sitting on one of the leather bar stools. She was hunched over the white marble counter, crying into her hands. They entered the kitchen from behind her, and Jensen dropped Grayson's hand before moving closer, her steps slowing, like she was approaching a scared animal.

"Mom?" she whispered and Laurel's back stiffened. She picked up her head slowly and swiveled on the chair to look at her daughter. Their eyes locked and Jensen released the breath she'd been holding. Her eyes went wide. Laurel looked like an entirely different person from three months ago. Her complexion had cleared, her sharp features were rounding out, and while she was still incredibly skinny, she no longer looked like she was caving in on herself.

Jensen wasn't sure what to think. Laurel looked so much better, but, Andrew was right, a stable person wouldn't be breaking into the house.

"Jenny, what are you doing here?"

"What am I doing here? This is my house. What are you doing here?" Her reply came out sharper than she intended.

"It's not what it looks like." Laurel's defensive tone drew Jensen's attention to what she was hiding. She scrambled to cover the contraband on the counter, but she was too late. They had already seen the small bag of pills.

"I can't believe you! What was the point of rehab? I didn't really expect you to change but to relapse so quickly ... How long have you been out, a week?"

"I promise it's not what it looks like. I was just experiencing a low moment. But I stopped myself. I came to my senses, and I called my sponsor. She's on her way here now. It was just a moment of weakness. I came home to pick up some stuff. I've stopped by a few times, but you're never here. I had no way of getting a hold of you. I wasn't even sure if you were back in California or if you were staying on the East Coast. I needed to get in, so I tried using my old pin for the alarm. I thought maybe I put it in wrong since I haven't used it in a while so I tried the old combinations I knew. Then, when I got in I found this," Laurel reached behind her and pulled out the box of letters from Gran's closet.

Not knowing what else to do, Jensen reached out and took them from her.

"I found them sitting on the counter."

Jensen remembered bringing the box downstairs and placing it next to the phone when she called Lydia to invite herself to the lake. She had been so excited to see those cards from the Reeses that she had ignored the rest of its contents. Now, she remembered the letters from Laurel.

"You can't imagine how upset I was to find out that every letter I've ever written you went unopened. No wonder we don't have a relationship. You never knew I wanted one."

Jensen heard her words, but she was scared to believe them. After all, she had been told her whole life about Laurel's manipulations. Was Laurel doing just that, manipulating her, using the letters as a ploy to get money. Or, was there truth behind her words? Either option terrified her.

"Please say something?" Laurel begged.

"You said you were coming to pick up some of your things?" Jensen needed her to clarify. "What things?"

"I came for clothes, some makeup, and some mail I need for a court appointment. Then, I found the letters. It was so upsetting. I was trying to deal with it and then I went into my room and found an old stash I had hidden a long time ago. I've been sitting here trying to talk myself down. It's difficult for me to see those letters unopened. It just sent me spiraling. I need you to take them. Please. Promise me you'll read them."

Jensen looked down at the box she was holding. Her hands were shaking. Grayson, noticing her unease, swiftly slid his hands under hers and took the box from her. "This is a lot to digest right now," he said. "Why don't we take the box home with us and you can read them when you're ready?"

Jensen nodded. His plan sounded a lot more reasonable than trying to read through them right then. She wasn't sure what to expect from the letters but she knew she wasn't comfortable reading them with an audience.

"Home?" Laurel asked, "Where's home? I thought you were living here?"

"She's staying with us ..." Andrew said, but he stopped himself before giving away any more information.

"Wait, did you say that you have a room here? How come I never knew that?" As far as Jensen knew, her grandparents had not seen Laurel since she left for prison.

"Of course. I've lived here nearly my entire life. After I got out of jail, I spent a year at a halfway house and then I was on my own for a few months, but that didn't last long. Other than that, I've always lived here."

Jensen felt like such an idiot for not figuring it out sooner. "You were in jail for how many years?" she asked, needing to confirm her suspicion.

"It's not something I really like to talk about." Laurel averted her eyes.

"You got out while I was in the fifth grade, didn't you?" she asked, ignoring Laurel's discomfort.

"Yes," her mother answered after some consideration. "I was in from the time you were three until you were ten."

"So you've lived here the entire time I was away at school and they supported you all these years?"

Laurel nodded.

"Holy shit." Jensen turned and made a break for the door. "I need a minute," she called, rushing outside into the warm night air.

She placed her hands on her head and tried to take deep breaths as she paced up and down the driveway, like she did before a big race. Only this time, she couldn't breathe for an entirely different reason. After a few seconds, Grayson and Andrew came after her.

"Did I miss something?" Andrew asked, "because from where I was standing, that conversation felt pretty damn civil compared to what I was expecting to walk into."

"Don't be an idiot. Don't you get it?" Grayson spelled it out for him. "All those years that Jen was away at school, she clearly didn't know her mom was around."

"It's more than that." Jensen let her words fly out, unfiltered. "They didn't send me to school for my benefit. It was for theirs. I begged them to let me go to school in California. Then, I would have been able to come home and see you guys on the weekends. My mom had gone to a private school close by. I didn't understand why I couldn't. California has some incredible schools that could have given me the same education as I received at St. Timothy's. Still, they sent me to a school on the opposite side of the country. They forced me to live over three thousand miles away from everyone I loved just so they could keep her their dirty little secret. Everything they've done has been to keep me away from her. They never gave me a choice. What if I wanted her in my life? No one ever asked me. They stole my chance to have a mom in my life, and took away my right to decide whether I wanted to forgive her. And even if they were trying to protect me, they could have made her leave and then I could have stayed. She's the reason I was never invited home for the holidays. Because she was here, and they didn't want me around her. She's the reason everything I loved was taken away from me."

Jensen's mind was spinning. "I bet that's why Gran hid your mom's cards too," she said, looking at Grayson. "She tried to erase anything that connected me to Laurel or to this house. She wanted to make sure I never had a reason to want to come home. There were always excuses why I shouldn't come back and I never argued because without you guys, there was nothing pulling me home. I thought you guys had forgotten about me.

They chose her over me time and time again, and I didn't even realize it was happening. They took care of her and enabled her, by pushing me away and making me feel invisible."

Grayson couldn't process how anyone could ever make her feel that way. He wanted to tell her he saw her. He had always seen her. To him, she was like the sun, impossible to ignore because she lit up every room she entered. For her to feel invisible was unfathomable.

"I can't believe I constantly made excuses for them," she continued ranting. "I said they were too old to travel, or that I *wanted* to spend the holidays with my friends. I told myself it didn't matter, but of course it mattered. It always mattered!"

"It sounds like you're more upset at your grandparents than you are at your mom," Grayson reasoned. He was upset with them too, for keeping her away for so long and the way they'd made her feel.

"Of course I'm mad at them!" she fumed. "But they're dead, so I can't be mad at them." She knew she was raising her voice, but she couldn't help it. It had been years since she let her emotions spill over the edge. "They left me with all this shit to deal with and all these unanswered questions and this stupid box of letters." She yanked the box out of Grayson's hands and threw it on the ground like a child.

Then, after a few heaving breaths, she knelt down and gathered the letters back into the box. Grayson and Andrew knelt to help her.

"You don't need to help me."

"Hey, it's cool." Grayson grabbed a handful of letters and shuffled them around, so they sat in a neat stack. "At least this time it's just paper and not your underwear, am I right?"

She let out a weak laugh, but even that didn't help relieve the tension in her shoulders.

"Did she say anything to you after I ran out?" Jensen asked, belatedly realizing that she just left her emotionally unstable mother in the house with access to drugs.

"She wanted to come after you, but we told her not to. Then she asked if we were leaving and we told her no."

"But that doesn't mean we can't leave. If you need to get out of here," Andrew said, and Grayson shot him a look.

"I don't need to leave," Jensen said.

"What do you need?" Grayson asked.

"We could break some stuff," Andrew offered.

"I need to swim," she said with so much conviction in her voice, she probably sounded like an addict herself. But sometimes it felt like she had an obsessive need to be in the water. To feel her muscles working, her heart pounding and her breathing gradually growing heavy. To feel the initial rush of diving in and then the control as she moved through the water in the practiced motion she knew so well. She wondered briefly if the Menlo Swim Club was open, but before she could ask, she was interrupted by a car pulling into the driveway.

The woman that stepped out of the pristine sedan was in a pressed suit. "I'm Wendy," she introduced herself, approaching with an outstretched hand. She shook each of their hands and they all exchanged names. When Jensen gave her name she saw recognition flash across Wendy's face.

"You must be Laurel's daughter," she smiled. "I'm her sponsor. She's told me so much about you. Is she inside?" Jensen relaxed a little, thankful that Laurel wasn't lying about having called her.

Jensen nodded but didn't make a move toward the door.

"Are you coming in?" Wendy asked, looking at Jensen.

"You go ahead," Andrew answered for her. "We'll be back in the morning." Then he looked to Jensen for confirmation. "Right?"

"Yeah, go ahead," she smiled, remembering her manners.

"She's in the kitchen. It's on your right when you walk in. We'll be back tomorrow."

Wendy nodded, thanked them, then made her way into the house.

Jensen turned to Grayson, who gave her a reassuring smile, then to Andrew. He was pointing a thumb over his shoulder at the house next door. "Dad isn't good for much, but he does have a pool."

As Jensen snuck into the house to grab a swimsuit, she heard Laurel and Wendy in the living room talking. She headed to the second staircase in the back of the house so she could avoid being seen. When she got to the upstairs hall, she went to her room, but as she placed her hand on the doorknob, she paused and looked down the hall at all the closed doors. Rooms she hadn't bothered cleaning yet because she thought they were just generic guest rooms, the maid's quarters, and Gramps's study.

She hesitated for only a moment. Then, tiptoed down the hall. She opened the first door she came to and sure enough, it was a guest room, as generic as she expected it to be. The bed was made and there were no signs that anyone had been there recently.

Opening the next door, she knew she'd find Gramps's study exactly as she remembered it. As soon as she stepped inside she was taken aback by how overwhelmingly it smelled like him. The scent of tobacco tinged with cinnamon flooded her with emotions. She both missed him immensely and felt guilty that she didn't miss him more. She knew she should, but her grandparents hadn't been a part of her daily life in a long time.

She stepped out of the study, and before getting too emotional, walked across the hall to what Gran always referred to as the maid's quarters. The room should've been empty. The woman who used to take care of the house moved out months

ago. Jensen turned the handle and stepped into a room that was
bursting with personality and chaos.

There was stuff everywhere. Art on the walls, laundry on the
floor, and little knick-knacks on top of the dresser. She stepped
up to the dresser and examined the pieces, but there didn't seem
to be any rhyme or reason to them. There was a hot wheel still
in the packaging, a rubber duck with a blue mohawk, and a
polaroid camera with a stack of pictures under it. The room was
so different from the rest of the house. It was undeniably
Laurel's space and clearly had been for quite some time.

On the bed was an old photo album with printed pictures
tucked into plastic sleeves. It was lying open. Flipping through
it, Jensen quickly realized the photos were all of her when she
was little. There were pictures of Laurel holding her in the
hospital with tears in her eyes. There were dozens of photos of
the two of them together when she was an infant and toddler.
Laurel didn't look the way Jensen had always pictured her. She
looked happy and healthy and so incredibly young. Laurel was a
teen mom and by the looks of it, a great one. Jensen was so
young when she'd gone to prison that she didn't have any clear
memories of her. The image she'd always had in her head was
the way Laurel looked the one time Jensen saw her after she
got out.

Jensen had been in fifth grade and Laurel had tried to take
her out of school, planning to take her away. Her behavior was
so erratic and emotional. She was pale and far skinnier than the
girl in the pictures who looked happy and full of life.

She placed the album back on the bed, opened to the same
page. On her way out, she closed the door as quietly as possible
and rushed back to her own room. Grabbing her bag from the
corner where she'd tossed it only a few days ago, Jensen put on
one of the racer-back swimsuits that Lucy nearly threw away. It
was red, white, and blue and said USA in the upper right corner.

It was one of the practice suits issued to her for the Olympic team.

She tucked her clothes into the bag and carried it downstairs. Laurel called out from the other room, "Jenny, is that you?"

"Yes, I was just grabbing something from my room."

"I want to talk to you."

"I can't right now," she placed her hand on the doorknob, "I have to go."

"Can we talk tomorrow?" Laurel's voice grew louder as she approached.

"Sure, that's fine."

"You promise?"

When Jensen turned around, she was right behind her. "Fine," she agreed, just to avoid a confrontation. Then she stepped outside and closed the door.

Grayson and Andrew were waiting next door by the back gate. Andrew whistled when he saw her and she rolled her eyes, used to people making fun of her team suit. She didn't mind. She wore it with pride and confidence, she had worked her ass off for it.

"What? You look cool," Andrew chuckled. "That whistle wasn't sarcastic, it was appreciative."

"You're such an idiot." Grayson punched him in the shoulder, but he couldn't help but agree with his brother as he admired how fierce she looked.

Jensen didn't spare them another thought, approaching the pool, she gave it her full attention. Standing on the edge, she stretched her shoulders and legs. Then, she dove in, gliding underwater for a long stretch. When she surfaced, it was with a clearer head.

She swam her worries away for a long while. When she finally took a break, she looked up to find Andrew and Grayson sitting at the opposite wall. They'd changed into their suits, but neither of them were swimming. Instead they dangled their feet in the water as they watched her.

"Do either of you want to race?" she asked.

They looked at each other, then simultaneously back at her shaking their heads. "No offense, Fish," Andrew said, "but you're a bit intimidating in the water. I'm not sure our egos can take it."

"Come on, please," she begged. "I'll even swim backstroke."

Grayson slid into the water and nodded. "Fine, but don't laugh. I already know you're gonna win, and I don't think I can take it if you also laugh at me."

"Deal," she grinned widely as they lined up next to each other on the wall. They agreed on two laps and after Andrew's countdown Jensen darted off of the wall and Grayson swam after her. He knew he was doomed, so he stopped just before he finished the first lap. When Jensen turned at the wall, he waited for her and pounced. He landed on top of her, dunking her entire body underwater. They wrestled for a few seconds before they both came up for air, sputtering. While she was catching her breath, he quickly touched the wall and then swam to the other side.

"No fair, you totally cheated."

"I don't remember any rules being established. Besides, when did I say I'd play fair?"

"You've always been all about the rules."

"News flash, Jen, you're not the only one who's changed."

She splashed him, and their laughter drowned out the sound of the back door sliding open. All three of them jumped when they heard Patrick Reese say, "Andrew? Grayson? Is that you?"

Grayson turned with a smile, "Hey Dad." But Andrew's back stiffened.

"Hello, son," Patrick replied to Grayson, but his eyes were on

Andrew, whose back was still to him. He walked up to his son and addressed him with a stern voice. Far harsher than how he spoke to Grayson. "You haven't been answering my calls. We have things to discuss."

Grayson's eyes darted back and forth between them. Andrew's face had gone white as a sheet. "Not here," he responded between clenched teeth, his voice lacking the confidence he usually exuded.

He followed his dad inside and after the door shut behind them, Jensen looked to Grayson for answers.

"I knew there was something weird going on. Something's been off with him since the beginning of summer. Obviously, Dad knows. Has he said anything to you?"

Jensen didn't have a chance to answer because a second later, Andrew was storming out of the house, slamming the sliding door behind him. He threw two towels down on a lounge chair and announced, "We're leaving."

They quickly climbed out of the pool and wrapped themselves up in the oversized towels. "Hold up a second," Grayson called out, but Andrew didn't stop walking.

"Get dressed. I'll wait for you guys in the car."

Grayson and Jensen looked at each other as Andrew stormed out, slamming the gate behind him.

They hastily got dressed, and Jensen scooped up the box of letters before following Andrew. When she reached to open the gate, Grayson put his hand over hers and stopped her. "Jen, wait," he said, holding her there. She turned to look at him. He was standing so close that even in the dark she could make out his features.

"What?" she whispered.

He didn't want to pour his heart out and make it weird between them. But what she said had been eating at him all night. He had to say something or he'd regret it. "I just wanted to say before we go ... you're not invisible. You've never been invisible. Not to me."

She was taken aback by his words. She wanted to get lost in them, but too soon, Grayson was pulling the gate open. They made their way to the car. The ride back to the lake was silent and tense. Grayson and Andrew didn't say anything to each other.

So much had happened in the last few hours. Jensen's mind could have been on any number of things: the realization that Laurel had been living in that house for years, whatever Andrew was going through that was seriously upsetting him, or the box of letters on the seat beside her. Instead, she kept replaying the words Grayson said to her on the side of the house. She wasn't invisible. She smiled to herself and felt seen.

7

"DON'T BE SO SENSITIVE." —NICOLE

Jensen would have been happy to do nothing the rest of the day after her morning swim in the lake. She needed time to process everything that had happened with her mom the day before. But, when she pulled herself out of the water onto the dock, Grayson was already waiting for her.

"What's up?" she asked, wringing out her hair.

"We still need to get you on a dirtbike," he said, "you up for it today?"

"What exactly is a dirtbike?" She asked, "It's like a motorcycle right?"

"That's not a no," Grayson smiled widely. "Meet me on the back deck in twenty minutes. You need long pants and long sleeves." He jogged back to the house before she could refuse.

Twenty minutes later they stood at the padlocked door under the back deck, Grayson pulled a key out of the woodpile and unlocked it. Inside, there were skateboards, bikes, tubes, wakeboards, and a pile of kid's toys. He walked past all of it to the back. It was too dark for Jensen to see what he was doing but when he emerged pushing a large motorcycle Jensen's eyes became saucers.

"Normally, I'd start you off with a smaller bike," Grayson chuckled, "but Nicole's riding the eighty today."

"There's no way I'm getting on that thing," she refused. "It's way too big for me."

"First of all, you're as tall as I am and this is my bike so I know you'll be fine. Second of all, this isn't going to go well if you don't loosen up a bit. Why don't you just take a seat and get a feel for it," he encouraged.

"What if I crash into the side of the house or ride into the lake?" Her mind immediately went to worst case scenarios.

"Despite how hilarious it would be to see you ride into the lake, I think you'd be more likely to topple over."

She gulped audibly, "Don't let me fall."

"Never." He grabbed her hips and guided her onto the bike, "I've got you."

Grayson leaned in and released the kickstand. Jensen's heart momentarily dropped into her stomach and she gasped, causing Grayson to tighten his grip. His fists clenched the fabric of her shirt, and a wave of goosebumps covered her arms. She hoped he wouldn't notice. She planted her feet on the ground and leaned the bike back and forth in both directions. It was heavy, but she felt in control.

"Okay, I think I've got it now," she told him. He heard her, but he didn't release her. Her voice was wispy and not her own when she repeated, "I think you can let go now. I've got it."

"Oh shit, sorry." He needed to chill out. *Just friends,* he thought, kicking himself for potentially making her uncomfortable. He hadn't meant to keep his hands on her for so long. Letting go, he stepped back, his neck slightly pink as he asked, "You think you're ready to kick-start it?"

"Turn it on? What? Here?" She looked around and calculated all the things that could go wrong. "Aren't we going to the meadow? Shouldn't I learn how to ride there, in the open space?"

"That's a good idea in theory, but you don't want to learn at the meadow. The ground is unpredictable there. Also, there are other people there. I think everything is harder when people are watching." He walked over and grabbed two full-face helmets from the shed, offering her one.

She didn't reach for it. Instead, she nodded to him, "You first."

"Together?"

She nodded hesitantly, not entirely sure what she was getting herself into. He threw a helmet on and slid onto the seat in front of her. She strapped on the second helmet as Grayson explained each step. Then, with a kick of his foot he started the bike.

Jensen gripped her thighs tight and Grayson chuckled. He guided her arms around his stomach and when her hands found each other he called out, "Hold tight," over his shoulder.

She felt like she was holding on sufficiently until the bike moved. Then her grip really tightened. She glued herself to him. After the first two turns, she was comfortable enough to loosen her grip and open her eyes. It wasn't nearly as scary as she thought it would be. It was exhilarating and they weren't even going that fast.

Grayson rode around the house once before unexpectedly pulling out of the driveway and soon they were on the highway. They only stayed on the street for a minute before crossing to a trail on the opposite side of the road.

The path was clear, but Grayson kept veering a few feet into the trees, playing with her nerves. Each time he did, she held onto him tighter, grinning from ear to ear.

They made their way to an empty campground where

Grayson parked his bike. When Jensen climbed off, she gushed, "That was incredible. How have I never done that before?"

Grayson smiled brightly and motioned to the bike, "Glad you like it because you're up."

This time, she didn't look for an excuse. She sat on the bike and asked, "Walk me through it one more time?"

Grayson patiently coached her through how to control the bike. After a half hour of riding in circles she scooted back and let him take over driving again. She'd felt good on the bike but not good enough to ride on the highway. She held on tight as he steered them to the meadow.

The field was huge and just as bumpy as Grayson warned. They pulled up next to two trucks with a few guys milling around them. Grayson hopped off and walked over to his neighbor, Davis, who was clearly the oldest in the group. Jensen made her way to Andrew, who was standing with a group of friends. The only one she recognized was Reed who smiled and nodded at her when she walked up. They were all watching two riders hit jumps.

After the first rider finished, he pulled up beside her. "Hey, Jensen. About time you joined us out here." She recognized his voice but didn't realize it was Brent until he removed his helmet.

She nodded in acknowledgement but didn't reply, she was too focused on the jumps as the other rider launched into the air. There was nothing fancy about the jump except the sheer height of it. Their air-time was impressive, but the landing was sloppy. The bike landed on the back tire first before the front tire came down and skidded out. The rider released the bike just as it tipped over. Somehow, they stayed upright, running off their momentum before turning to gather the bike, entirely unscathed.

When they joined the rest of the riders by the truck, Brent ran over. As soon as the rider removed their helmet, Jensen saw why. It was Nicole, and from the looks of it, Brent was checking that she was okay after her sketchy landing. There was a crease between his brow and concern written across his face.

Nicole rolled her eyes at his worried expression and looked at Davis. "I almost had it that time. I got the bike in position, but I just can't seem to get past my mental block to get my legs to come off the bike."

"You'll get there, just keep working at it," Davis shrugged. "It looked good from here."

Jensen tried to hide from Nicole but was unsuccessful. She caught sight of her right away and shot a glare over Davis's shoulder. Davis turned to see who Nicole was looking at and nearly ran into her. "Oh hey, it's Jensen, right? We met a few nights ago at dinner. I think you dipped out because you were sick or something. Are you feeling better?" His politeness threw her off. It was so at odds with his appearance.

"I am, thank you," she said.

After he re-introduced himself he reached out a hand and said, "Well, it's nice to meet you again. Lydia and Joe speak very highly of you."

"She wasn't sick," Nicole cut in, "she was avoiding you. Princesses can't be seen talking to peasants."

Jensen turned beet red at Nicole's accusation but Davis was unfazed. He turned a glare on Nicole. "Don't be mean."

She laughed it off. "Come on, Davis, don't be so sensitive."

"I'm not the one you were being mean to. You're bullying her. You're clearly trying to embarrass her. It's childish."

Nicole blanched. But Davis moved his attention back to Jensen, "Don't worry about it. I'm used to people being nervous around me. I have that effect on people," he smiled and climbed on his bike. Then he nodded toward Graysons bike and asked, "You any good on that thing?"

"Not yet but I will be," she said with a level of confidence only a professional athlete could pull off.

Grayson and Jensen took turns on his dirt bike. Riding in the meadow took some adjusting but he was patient as he guided her over every bump and dip of the uneven ground. The terrain forced her to keep shifting her body on the bike. It took constant adjustments to stay upright. Everyone else made it look easy.

Grayson pointed out an easy loop, and she took off slowly, following his directions. She heard an engine come up behind her and the next thing she knew, Nicole was riding beside her. Jensen needed to make a left, but she couldn't or she would crash into Nicole. She tried to call out to her to ask her to move out of the way, but she knew she couldn't hear her.

She was guided off the route Grayson gave her. Nicole sped up, cutting in front of her and into the trees on their right. The maneuver forced Jensen into a rocky, muddy creek. She slowed down but her loss of momentum caused the tires to sink into the muddy earth, kicking up brown water. She lost her balance and the bike fell on top of her. It hurt, but she was more focused on the fact that she was on her ass in a creek, soaking wet.

Grayson had to have already been running after them because he got to her quickly and lifted the bike off her then helped her up. As he did, he yelled at Nicole, who Jensen now realized had popped out of the trees and was laughing. "What the hell was that about?" he bellowed, but he didn't wait for an answer. Instead, he turned back to Jensen.

"You said I needed to treat her like one of us," Nicole answered. "Fair is fair."

"You knew it was her first time." Andrew said, pulling up beside her. "You knew exactly what you were doing."

"So what if I did? You guys knocked my ass in the creek last week and thought it was hilarious. Is Little-Miss-Princess above a bit of mud?"

"You could have hurt her," Andrew argued.

"Would you relax?" Nicole snapped, "It was a joke. She's fine!"

"It wasn't funny. Do you even realize how much damage you could've done? She's an Olympian, for fuck sake. You could have jeopardized her entire future with your stupid joke." Andrew was fuming.

Nicole glared at him. "Would you quit freaking out at me? I can't believe you are taking her side?"

"Of course we're taking her side," Grayson joined the argument. "Just because you still hold a grudge against her from the past doesn't give you an excuse to be a bully. You need to grow up and let it go." He knew as the words were coming out that it was the wrong thing to say. Yes, it needed to be said, but Nicole had never taken kindly to being called out in front of people, especially by him.

"Grow up? Let it go?" she mimicked. "Maybe *you* need to grow up. You're the one who's stuck in the past. You're still as obsessed with her as ever." Grayson cringed at her overly honest words. But he couldn't deny that she was right, he was stuck in the past. He had been up all night thinking about the guy Jensen had introduced as her boyfriend. That guy was Grayson's complete opposite. If that was who she was into, maybe he didn't know her as well as he thought he did. Clearly, a lot had changed, but when he spent time with her, it still felt like she was the same old girl he used to love. Maybe she was something in between. Whoever she was now, he wanted to know her and if the only thing she could offer was friendship, he'd take it.

Nicole was still talking. "You're delusional. You've been following her around since she got here. When are you going to wake up and realize that perfect little rich girl Jensen doesn't belong in our world anymore?" She restarted her bike and rode off in a rage.

Nicole's words hit their mark. *Maybe she was right*, Jensen thought, *and she didn't belong there.* To be honest, she wasn't sure where she belonged. The only place she truly felt like herself was in the water. She looked at Grayson for reassurance or some sign that he disagreed, but he was watching Nicole ride away.

"I'll go after her," Brent said, throwing on his helmet.

Quiet fell over them after he left.

Jensen broke the silence with a pathetic whimper as she tried to move her arm. All eyes shot in her direction. "I think something's wrong with my left elbow," she whispered, hoping the admission wouldn't make the situation worse. She turned her arm, trying to get a good look at it, but it was hard to see anything through the mud.

The guys must have seen something she didn't because one of them let out an audible hiss. Grayson knelt down next to her and pulled off his flannel.

"We should get her to the hospital," Andrew announced, and after a second she realized he was talking about her. Reaching her opposite hand around and cradling her elbow, she felt the wound. Her touch stung. She pulled her hand away and it came back wet and bright red.

Not water as she'd originally thought.

Blood.

So much blood.

She began hyperventilating. Grayson tried to keep her calm, talking to her the whole time as he wrapped his flannel around her arm, putting pressure on the wound. She felt faint and nauseous. The pain was bearable, but the moment she saw the blood, she'd panicked.

"Just a few stitches and you'll be fine," Davis assured her.

"She doesn't do needles," Grayson explained. "Could you give us a ride to the hospital?"

Jensen didn't hear Davis' response, but she watched as

everyone but her and Grayson ran over to Davis and Andrew's trucks and drove them back to where she was. They loaded the bikes into the back and Andrew and Reed headed back to the house to tell Lydia what happened. Meanwhile, Grayson bent down and removed Jensen's helmet. Grabbing her face in his hands, he forced her to look up. "Keep your eyes on me," he instructed. "You're gonna be fine. The only lasting damage is going to be to your pride."

It helped until the throbbing started in her elbow. She spiraled into another round of panic when she peeked under the flannel. Blood covered her arm and her eyes instantly filled with tears.

"It's just a scrape," Grayson said, still holding her face in his hands. "Don't look at it, look at me. Don't think about it. Think about something else."

Grayson helped her into Davis' truck. There was a towel laid across the passenger seat, but she still squirmed, trying to keep blood and mud off his seat but Davis didn't seem concerned by the mess. In her world, people treated their cars better than their children. As she fidgeted, her anxiety got worse. She asked how many stitches she was going to need, if it was going to hurt, and how long it would be until she could get back in the water. Neither Davis nor Grayson had any answers for her. They just kept encouraging her to stay calm.

Finally, after five minutes, Grayson demanded a change of subject. Jensen took a few deep breaths and tried to think of anything besides the blood. The argument between Grayson and Nicole came to the forefront of her mind. Something Nicole had said confused her.

"Why did Nicole say that you were obsessed with me?" she asked.

Grayson shifted uncomfortably. He looked at Davis for help, but he just laughed. "Dude, you told her to change the subject."

He let out a long, exasperated breath. "Come on, everyone knew I had a crush on you when we were kids. It was a long time ago."

"I never knew that."

"Really? I think I made it pretty clear. I guess you were crushing too hard on Andrew to ever notice me."

She cringed and Grayson laughed. "Don't worry about it, everyone always loves Andrew. It used to bother me, but I'm over it. And, don't worry, I'm over you, too," he lied, repeating *just friends* in his head. "Like I said, it was a long time ago."

She hated to admit it, but he was right. When they were younger she had always been too wrapped up in Andrew to even notice Grayson. Had she made him feel invisible? She wanted to tell him she saw him now, but that felt like such a personal thing to say with Davis in the car. Plus, that was a door she shouldn't open. After considering it for a second, the only thing she could think to say was, "You know, I don't like him like that anymore."

"I would hope not for your boyfriend's sake," Grayson laughed. "I was jealous of him when we were kids but we're fine now," he said. "It hasn't felt like everything's a competition between us in a long time. Him going to a different high school really helped. Around here, no one expected me to be a football star and I'm not made fun of for knowing the difference between a reptile and an amphibian. I used to be resentful because girls tend to have a thing for athletes, but–"

"I don't think you're exactly having a hard time in that department," Davis interjected with a snicker.

At the same time, Jensen said, "I'm not *into* athletes." Then she had to force herself not to react to Davis' comment.

"You just told me a few hours ago that your perfect boyfriend was the lacrosse and golf captain," Grayson responded. "Hate to break it to you, but that's the definition of a jock."

"That's not a jock," Davis scoffed. "Lacrosse is just wannabe hockey and golf isn't a real sport."

Jensen glanced at Davis and tried not to laugh. "Who said Eric's my type?"

"Um, maybe the fact that you're dating him?"

"Yeah but that's just because we were friends for a long time. Being together just sort of happened."

"Are you saying you're not into your boyfriend?" Davis asked.

"That's not what I'm saying at all," she argued, but she didn't know how to describe Eric. He was undeniably attractive but it rubbed her the wrong way how he cared so much about his appearance. There was never a hair out of place or a single spec of dirt under his fingernails. He was almost too perfect. After spending a week with the Reeses she was realizing how hard she'd been trying to measure up. It was exhausting. Instead of defending her boyfriend, she leaned her forehead against the window and whined, "My elbow hurts."

She thought about her relationship with Eric. She didn't know if she'd ever known attraction until recently. The way she couldn't stop her body's reaction when she was around Grayson was completely new to her. She'd never felt that kind of pull to Eric. Even the first time they slept together, it took her time to warm up to the idea and convince her body that she was into it. Meanwhile, there she sat, covered in mud and blood, and when Grayson's arm brushed up against hers, she could feel his touch everywhere. From the tingling in her fingertips, to the tightening of her nipples.

The only sound in the cab was a fuzzy folk song on the radio. Davis reached over and adjusted the dial flipping from one static station to the next until he gave up and turned it off.

Grayson finally broke the silence. "I seriously can't believe Nicole," he blurted out. "I can't believe how she's been acting toward you. Obviously, she's upset about you being here, but she won't even talk to me. I didn't realize how deep her spite was. I never thought she would pull something like this."

"You know, my getting hurt wasn't entirely her fault," Jensen tried to be a voice of reason. "She had no way of knowing I'd fall on that rock or that I'd get hurt."

"That's nice of you to say, but I know my sister. She might not have been trying to physically hurt you, but she was trying to knock you down a peg. It was mean."

They got to Evergreen Hospital, and Jensen was thankful there was only a short wait in the ER. While she and Grayson sat and waited for her name to be called, Davis talked to a nurse. She was an older woman with hair graying at the roots and deep bags under her eyes.

"What's the deal with her?" Jensen asked, nodding towards Davis and the nurse who had just embraced him.

"You mean Tasha? They go way back. She was Davis' nurse after the accident," he shrugged. "I guess it's normal to become close to someone after they save your life."

She knew Davis' parents were dead, but it was her first time hearing about an accident. She wanted to ask about it, but she didn't want to pry. It made her wonder again about his scars.

The more time that passed, the more she stressed about what was coming next. When her name was finally called she was going to be brought into a back room lit with harsh hospital lights and sterile walls. She would sit on an uncomfortably cushioned platform, likely covered by a thin piece of paper where the doctor would then repeatedly jab a needle into her elbow. She fidgeted just thinking about it.

"I can't do this. I can't do this," she mumbled under her breath.

Her knee bounced rapidly and her eyes darted around the room. Grayson saw her panic. He slid his hand from his lap and casually rested it on her knee. She stopped tapping her leg and her eyes bore into the back of his hand. He could feel her stare, but he refused to look. Eye contact would make the gesture too intimate. He was just trying to comfort his friend.

He moved his hand slowly up her leg and rubbed his thumb back and forth across her thigh. The sensation quickly found its way up her leg to the apex of her thighs. She had to hold in her gasp at her body's reaction to him. She squeezed her knees together, trapping Grayson's fingertips between her legs.

He couldn't help himself, he leaned in and whispered directly in her ear, "You okay?"

His lips were so close, his warm breath hit her earlobe, triggering an equally visceral reaction, her nipples tightened again.

Oh God, what was wrong with her?

She nodded, unable to find words. Her full attention on her body's sudden ache for him to move his hand north. He didn't move his hand, but when she finally pulled her eyes away from his hand on her leg, she looked up and saw that he was watching her closely. Their eyes met and the second they did, his grip just above her knee tightened.

He tightened his grip to maintain control and not let his hand explore her body like it so badly wanted to. But the way she was looking at him, it was almost as if she wanted that, too.

The way he was looking at her made her feel lightheaded. It crossed her mind that he probably knew exactly what he was doing to her right then. He was nothing like the Grayson she remembered all those years ago. Once a dorky tagalong, always following her and Nicole around. But this new Grayson knew how to look at her in just the right way. He had to know what he was doing to her.

It was about time she admitted to herself that Grayson was hot and there was no way she was the first girl to notice. Her mind rushed back to the first moment she'd seen him again in the driveway of his house. He'd made a comment about her panties not being the first he'd ever seen. And then there was Davis' comment about him not struggling with the ladies. Her mind was racing with the new version of Grayson. She thought about what he was like at college and the number of girls who must've thrown themselves at him and was overcome with a rush of possessiveness she had no right to feel.

She should've pulled away from him. Eric crossed her mind and she felt guilty for her reaction to Grayson's touch. Still, she didn't remove his hand from her leg. She decided she needed it there to keep her from panicking. He was the only thing keeping her grounded.

Eyes locked on each other, Grayson slowly moved closer. The way he was fully leaning into her caused her to stop breathing for what felt like the longest second of her life. She could see him searching her eyes as if in them he would find the answer to an unasked question. But she never figured out what he was looking for because a nurse called her name and they sprung apart.

She looked up and saw a petite Hispanic woman in scrubs waiting for her. Turning back to Grayson, with panic written across her face, she was prepared to beg, but he was already standing up.

"I'll come with you," he reassured her. "You'll do great."

Grayson followed behind Jensen and the nurse, thankful that her name was called before he did something he'd regret. He had to be more careful, he couldn't lose himself in her and do something he couldn't take back. He was better than that.

The nurse checked Jensen's vitals, and briefly asked a few questions, then she deposited them into a room and informed them the doctor would be in shortly.

As soon as the door clicked closed, Jensen's breathing became ragged and her chest hurt. She wrapped her arms tightly around herself. "Shit. Shit. Shit," she hissed, trying to take a deep breath.

"Jen?" Grayson asked. He stepped up and placed a hand on her arm, guiding her over to the cushioned medical table covered with a thin sheet of paper. The room was exactly how she'd pictured it would be. Sterile.

"Jensen?" Grayson asked again, louder. "What's happening?"

"I think ..." she gulped in another breath. "I'm having ... *Apanicattack.*" The last three words come out as one since she was unable to find enough air to break the syllables apart.

Grayson jumped into action. He climbed onto the medical table next to her, swung one leg around, and pulled her into his body so she was cocooned between his legs. Then he wrapped his considerable arm span around her and held her tight. She melted into him, feeling right at home in his arms. They were still there when the doctor came in and introduced himself.

After the long process of cleaning her wound, he prepared the orange numbing ointment and laid out instruments. Jensen couldn't watch and she turned her face into Grayson's neck. When she inhaled deeply, gooseflesh formed up his neck and he adjusted slightly away from her. She hid there in the crook of his neck, breathing in his intoxicating scent, memorizing it while his pulse hammered rapidly in his throat.

Grayson had to do everything in his power to remind himself that she was just looking for comfort. They were just friends. It became a mantra he chanted in his head; *just friends, just friends, just friends,* as he held her until the doctor announced he was finished.

When they re-entered the waiting area, Davis was still there, but instead of the nurse, he was now talking to Lydia. As soon as she glanced up at them, Jensen took a step away from Grayson. They weren't physically touching, but the centimeter of space between them suddenly felt far from innocent.

Lydia rushed over and pulled Jensen into her arms, not caring in the slightest that she was still soaking wet and covered in mud. "Honey, how are you? I'm so sorry I wasn't here sooner."

"I'm fine. I just want to go home."

"I'll take you back to the house," she said, leading her out to the car and motioning for Grayson to go with Davis.

"No, I want to leave. I want to go to my *real* home." Jensen said getting into the car. She had decided right then, and there, that it was time for her to go. Being around Grayson was proving to be impossible without her mind drifting. Cheating was not something she would ever do, so why stay when she knew it was a risk? What if Grayson had kissed her? He looked like he wanted to. She wasn't sure she'd have had the fortitude to refuse him. She definitely needed to go home.

Sobbing, she realized she didn't know where home was. Huge crocodile tears poured out of her eyes. Her dorm was the closest thing she had to a home, and it was no longer an option. Her grandparents' house used to feel like home, but that was before she found out about their lies. She had so much money at her disposal and could easily buy a house on a whim, but that wasn't what she needed right then. In that moment, she needed the comforting feeling that only a home could provide. She cried harder with the realization that she didn't have one.

"Honey, I don't think you should drive in this condition," Lydia said once they were both in the car. "Besides, emotions are running high right now. You may decide you want to stay after a good night's sleep."

"No, I don't want to do that. I just want to leave," Jensen argued stubbornly.

Pulling out of the parking lot, Lydia took a deep breath. "I'm afraid I'm not giving you the choice. I won't be letting you drive tonight."

It was the first time in years an adult had parented Jensen

and she wasn't sure how she felt about it. Even Eric's mom, Katrina, would only offer parental advice when Jensen sought it out. Lydia, on the contrary, wasn't asking permission to step in and lay down the law. She did it naturally, as if Jensen was one of her own children.

Normally she wouldn't have minded Lydia parenting her, she might even take comfort in it. But after the ordeal with the stitches and the intensity with Grayson, she couldn't hide her frustration. "You can't tell me what I can or can't do," she argued. "You don't even know me anymore." The response just slipped out and she regretted it immediately.

Lydia looked crushed.

The problem was, Jensen didn't remember what having a real family felt like. Lucy and Eric were the only support she needed. She'd spent the last seven years becoming an independent, self-sufficient person who was content on her own. She didn't suddenly need a parent. It was time to get back to her real life.

They drove in silence for a while. Once she was calm, she felt guilty for what she said. Lydia meant well and had shown Jensen more compassion in the past ten minutes than her own mother ever had. "I'm sorry," she mumbled. "I shouldn't have said that."

Lydia opened her mouth to reply but thought better of it. She took a few seconds before deciding what to say. "I know it probably feels like we're strangers to each other now. I promise you, I'm still the same person I was seven years ago when you used to call me mom." She had hit a nerve, and she knew it. "I hope we get the chance this summer to consider each other family again."

The rest of the car ride was silent and Jensen was relieved when they got back and Nicole wasn't home. She wasn't ready to see her after what she did.

Lydia looked like she wanted to say something. Thankfully, Grayson walked in and pulled her attention, giving Jensen an opportunity to slip upstairs.

"Is she okay?" he asked his mom. "She was pretty rattled at the hospital."

"She's still pretty rattled," Lydia replied. "What exactly happened?"

Grayson explained how she fell into the creek and hit her elbow on a rock. It was the same story Andrew had given, both of them left out the part where Nicole was the mastermind behind it.

"I know there's more to the story that I'm not being told," Lydia said. "Why is she so adamant about going home if it was just an accident?"

"She wants to leave?" It was because of him and he knew it. He had been too forward. She was probably uncomfortable with the amount of attention he'd been giving her. He needed to take a step back and start seriously thinking of her as a friend and only a friend. Starting tomorrow, he'd make the change. Whatever it took to get her to stay. Jensen belonged in his life, period.

Showering, careful not to get her stitches wet, Jensen got the rest of the mud off her body, then plopped down on the trundle in Nicole's room and hugged her pillow to her chest. She called Lucy. Her friend hadn't picked up when she called her from the hospital. Now, she answered on the first ring. Before Jensen could say anything, Lucy was ranting, "Do you know how insane my mother is?" She didn't wait for an answer. "The woman is psychotic. She's got it in her head that I need a man. Like a forever man. She's set me up on a ton of dates, like one a week all summer, with all these high society boys. Gentlemen suitors, she calls them. More like filthy rich Asians." Lucy scoffed. "She is seriously delusional. When is she going to get it through her

Botoxed head that I'm never going to be her perfect Chinese daughter?"

When Lucy's mother, Annie, was younger, she was supposed to go through with an arranged marriage set up by her parents. She didn't. Instead, she went against their wishes and dishonored her family by falling in love and moving to America. She was an up-and-coming designer and her romance with actor Vincent St. Clare put her on the map. Annie and Vincent were the '*it*' couple in New York until they started getting more publicity for Vincent's affairs than their romance. Ever since the divorce, Annie had regretted the choice she made in her twenties and now she'd decided that Lucy mustn't follow in her footsteps.

Jensen laughed, glad for the distraction that was Lucy. "You never know," she said, playing devil's advocate, "you could meet a great guy. Why not stay open-minded?"

"Ugh," Lucy groaned. "If this guy, Nathaniel Chung, is what I have to look forward to, I'm in for a long, boring summer."

"Are you on a date right now?"

"I don't know if you can really call it that. He spent ten minutes talking about his house in The Hamptons during which I almost fell asleep. Thankfully, he caught on pretty quickly that I'm not interested. He's just here to appease his mother as well. So, we put an end to the date and now we're at a bar."

"I can call you tomorrow if you need to go?" Jensen offered.

"Are you kidding? No way, you called me. What's up? How was your first day of work?"

"It was good," Jensen said honestly. So much had happened since work yesterday. She quickly tried to summarize the past thirty-six hours for Lucy. She'd thought about quitting multiple times but didn't. She upset Eric because she totally forgot about his flight. Her mom tried to break into her house and set off the alarm. Grayson and Andrew went with her to Atherton. Andrew got into a fight with his dad, who still lived next door. She went dirt bike riding for the first time and crashed. And, she got eight stitches in her elbow.

"What!" Lucy choked on her drink as Jensen finished summarizing her story, which made her laugh. "Oh my God, Jensen, are you okay?"

"I'm fine."

"Okay, then start from the beginning." Lucy prompted, "This time with details."

Jensen spent the next two hours telling Lucy about everything that happened.

Lucy got hung up on the letters from Laurel. She couldn't believe she hadn't opened them yet. "If it was me, I would have torn all of them open the moment I found them in that damn closet."

After they hung up, Jensen couldn't get Laurel's letters out of her head. Maybe she should rip it off like a bandaid, like Lucy said. She'd open them all, have a good cry, then never worry about them again.

She pulled the shoebox out and found the first letter. Without giving herself a chance to second guess her decision, she ripped it open.

Jenny Bee,

That was it. That was as far as she read. She quickly folded the letter back up and shoved it into its envelope. The nickname triggered a memory so deep in hibernation that awakening it sent a full-body shudder through her. It was a song Laurel used to sing to her when she was really young. She couldn't remember the words, but out of the recesses of her mind, she pulled out a simple melody. She hummed it out loud and then she cried until she'd cried herself to sleep. The letter sat unread on the bedroom floor.

8

"SORRY NOT SORRY." —NICOLE

J ensen planned to leave the morning after getting hurt, but when she woke up her resolve had vanished. She still felt like things with Grayson were starting to cross a line and trying to mend things with Nicole felt like a lost cause but it was Lydia's words that kept her from bolting. Not words of advice, but stern words of a mother who cared for her and wanted what was best for her. Lydia was offering her an opportunity to be a part of their family again and she wasn't about to let Nicole or Grayson ruin it for her.

Thankfully, Nicole was giving her a large berth, and she hadn't found herself alone with Grayson at all.

A few days later, Nicole walked into her room while Jensen was lying on the trundle bed reading. "Sorry, I didn't know you were in here," she said, "I'll leave."

"No, don't." Jensen stopped her before she pulled the door shut.

Nicole pushed the door open but lingered in the doorway, unsure of what to do or say. She had been strategically avoiding Jensen for the past three days but she couldn't keep crashing on Davis's couch. He was right, she needed to apologize but that was easier said than done. Why did Jensen have to go and get hurt anyway? It was so annoying.

"It's your room," Jensen said. "Don't stay away on my account. I'm not mad, I know it was an accident."

"It wasn't," Nicole said. "I mean obviously I didn't mean for you to end up in the hospital but Grayson was right, I knocked you on your ass on purpose, and I would do it again. Sorry, not sorry for treating you like one of us." In hindsight that was probably not the apology Davis was encouraging but what the hell, she did say sorry in there somewhere, so it counted.

"I get it," Jensen replied. "And honestly, I might have found it funny if I hadn't busted my elbow."

"Yeah, sorry about that." There. She said it. Nicole let out a relieved breath, thankful to get that burden off her shoulders.

"It's okay," Jensen said. Then, "Did you need something in here or—"

"Shit, yes." Nicole stepped into her room and started shuffling through drawers and digging in her laundry hamper. "Have you seen my bikini?"

"Are you going swimming?" Jensen asked, enviously.

"Wakeboarding with the guys." She hesitated before adding, "Do you want to come?"

Jensen jumped at the offer despite not being able to go in the water. "Do you want to borrow a suit?" She dragged Lucy's suitcases out from under the bed. Pulling out four suits, she offered them to Nicole, who was preoccupied, staring at the sheer amount of designer clothes. "There's some cute stuff in here." Nicole held up a black velvet mini dress. "Why don't you wear any of this stuff?"

"Someone pointed out on my first day here that designer dresses aren't appropriate attire for the lake." She thought back to the white Vineyard Vines sundress she showed up in.

"Besides, a lot of it doesn't fit," she explained. "It's all from my friend Lucy. Her mom is a designer."

"Yeah I know who Annie St. Claire is," Nicole said. "Just because I live in a small town doesn't mean I live under a rock."

"Well these are all sample sizes. You can take whatever you want."

Nicole pulled out a few articles, admiring each piece. "You should wear this." She tossed Jensen a green two-piece halter that she never would have picked out for herself.

Even if the only reason Nicole was being nice to her was because she felt bad about her elbow, Jensen decided to take what she could get. Nicole picked out a red suit for herself and Jensen told her to keep it. Then, she put on the suit that Nicole picked out.

Grayson did a double take when he saw Jensen. Not just because she looked incredible but because of who she was with. They climbed aboard the boat together, and Grayson shot Jensen a flabbergasted look. He didn't need to say anything, she knew exactly what he was thinking. He was basically screaming, 'since when do you and Nicole get along?' with his eyes. Jensen just smiled and shrugged.

But it wasn't like Jensen and Nicole were suddenly friends again. As soon as they pulled away from the dock, Nicole went back to ignoring her. At least she wasn't shooting daggers her way like she did the last time. It was progress.

Jensen lingered by Andrew, who was at the wheel. She watched Grayson glide across the water, making it look easy. He jumped one wake, then the next, effortlessly. Lining up in the middle, he spun across the surface.

"He's amazing," she whispered under her breath.

"You wanna see something funny?" Andrew asked. He didn't give her a chance to answer before he made a sharp turn, accelerating at the same time. Grayson's whole body jerked to the side, then they were pulling nothing but rope. They circled back around to pick him up and when Andrew reached down to help him into the boat Grayson swatted his hand away, opting to climb in on his own.

"Are you okay?" Jensen asked him.

"His ego's just bruised. He'll be fine." Andrew tousled his brother's hair, getting a glare out of Grayson. "He wanted to show off for you," Andrew laughed.

Grayson didn't respond, annoyed with his brother. He was not mad about getting thrown from the board. Andrew was always doing shit like that, but his comments were unnecessary. Maybe he was showing off a little, but Andrew drawing attention to it made it seem like he was desperate for Jen's attention. The past few days, he'd been trying to make sure she knew he only saw her as a friend. An impossible feat if his siblings kept hinting at his deeper feelings.

Grayson pulled a length of rope out of the bench seat next to him and started fiddling with it, tying and untying different knots from memory. Jensen sidled up next to him while Andrew took his turn on the water. "Is that a Carrick Bend?" she asked as she watched his fingers intricately tie the rope.

He looked up at her in surprise. "How'd you know that?"

"It's on one of my flashcards," she admitted, embarrassed.

"Your flashcards?" He looked confused before it dawned on him and he choked on a laugh. "The boat word flashcards? I totally forgot about those."

Jensen spent the rest of the time on the boat sitting with Grayson. He was trying to teach her how to tie the beautiful knot, but she never figured it out. To be fair, she was having a hard time focusing on his directions. She was highly distracted watching him work. His fingers were long, yet so precise in their movements. She wondered how those calluses would feel on her body, rough against her soft skin.

She shouldn't let her mind go there, but she couldn't help it. She felt warm all over, desperate to dive into the lake to cool down. But Grayson seemed oblivious to the way her body was humming for him.

That night at dinner, she made a conscious effort not to sit next to him. When he was too close, she was sure it was obvious to everyone that she couldn't get a handle on herself.

At The Marina, she was assigned to work in the gift shop. Phil said he was more comfortable with her staying away from the lake while she healed. He didn't want her to risk getting her stitches wet. Miserably, she stood behind a counter for eight hours. Occasionally, the bell on the door rang and a customer meandered around. Rarely did anyone buy anything. She went the entire shift without talking to a single person besides the formality of, "Hello, how are you today?" and, "Thank you, come again."

After work Brent hitched a ride with Grayson back to the house. He sat in the backseat since Jensen was already in the front and brainstormed what new things they could try. Jensen vetoed all his ideas, which included but weren't limited to: mountain boarding, rock climbing, skeet shooting, and bull running, (which, she found out, meant chasing the bulls in the meadow on dirt bikes until they got pissed off and turned on you, at which point you'd have to outrun them back to the perimeter). Grayson assured her that no one had ever been seriously injured, but she was still horrified at the idea of it. Brent thought she was overreacting, but she reminded him that the last time she went out on a limb and tried something new, she'd ended up in the hospital.

They were arguing about whether she could shoot a shotgun with her elbow messed up when they pulled up to the house.

Everything went still as she processed what she was seeing.

Laurel was on the front porch, knocking on the door. Thank goodness Joe and Lydia had taken the kids out for the day.

Grayson elbowed her softly and she realized he was talking to her.

"What?" She tried to shake away the uneasy feeling that arose at the sight of her mother.

"Are you okay?" he asked. "Do you want me to go with you to talk to her?"

"What's going on?" Brent looked between them and then back at the porch. "Who is that?"

Neither Grayson nor Jensen answered him. Jensen considered running before Laurel saw them. It would be easy to back out of the driveway before she looked up. "Can we get out of here?" she asked Grayson.

He wanted to oblige, but her mom wasn't a problem that was going to go away. "Jen, at some point, you need to face her," he said, hoping he wasn't overstepping. "Clearly, she's figured out you're staying here. What's going to stop her from coming back if you avoid her now?"

She knew he was right. Running wasn't a sustainable solution, but it was how she's always dealt with things. Even in her relationship with Eric, when things started moving faster than she could deal with, what did she do? She ran away to California for the summer rather than acknowledge her doubts.

"That's my mom, Laurel," she finally answered Brent's question. "And Grayson's right. It's probably time I stop avoiding her." She climbed out of the car.

"Mom," she called as she walked up the driveway, leaving Grayson and Brent watching from the car. "What are you doing here?"

"I thought you might want to talk about the letters. I'm sure you have a lot of questions and I thought we could work through them together," Laurel said, pulling Jensen into a tentative hug.

Jensen knew that if she told her mom she hadn't read a single one, the thin rope that held Laurel's emotions together would snap. "Why don't we go around back and talk by the water," Jensen offered. She always did her best thinking in the water, on the shore was the next best thing.

She brought Laurel around the back of the house and they sat on logs around an empty fire pit near the lake shore. Laurel looked out over the lake for a while, gathering her words. When she finally spoke, her voice was calm. "This lake is beautiful," she admired. "I can't believe I've lived in California my entire life and I've never been here."

Jensen had little patience for her mother's wistful commentary. She was on edge, eager for Laurel to get to the point.

"I know you didn't drive all this way just to stare at the lake. What do you want? And how did you know where I was?"

"The same thing I wanted back in Atherton," Laurel said, taken aback by Jensen's harsh tone. "I just wanted to talk to you but you disappeared. I found this address on the counter and I took a chance." She handed Jensen the scratch paper she'd scribbled Lydia's address on weeks ago.

"Something came up. We had to leave early. It had nothing to do with you."

"Is everything okay? Whatever it was, it must have been serious if it was more important than keeping your promise?"

Jensen looked up from the paper she was staring at. "What promise?"

Laurel looked at Jensen in disbelief. "You promised you would come back in the morning to talk to me and you never showed up." Pitiful tears pooled at the corners of Laurel's eyes.

"Is that really why you came here?" Jensen asked. "To lecture me?"

"No, of course not. I wanted to talk about the letters. I'm sure you have lots of questions. You never came back the next morning. You said you were going to and you didn't." Laurel said, now worked up. "You lied. My daughter isn't a liar."

"How would you know, you don't even know me."

"That's not my fault," Laurel argued. "Haven't you read my letters?"

She hesitated before admitting, "No."

Laurel looked appalled. "What do you mean? You promised you would!"

"And I still plan too."

"I thought you would want to read them." Laurel's shoulders shook as she cried. "Please try to understand how important this is to me. You were supposed to get them forever ago. Writing them made me feel close to you all these years. Finding out you didn't even know they existed hurt. It feels like you don't even know me."

"You're right, I don't know you," Jensen agreed. And even though she knew it was harsh, she added, "And I'm not entirely sure if I want to." She refused to tiptoe anymore around Laurel's instability.

Laurel gasped dramatically, "I can't believe you would say that to me. I'm your mother."

"I'm just trying to be honest. I need time to think about things. You can't just thrust a pile of letters at me and expect everything to change between us. That's not how this works."

"All I want is a relationship with you. That's it. I didn't realize I was asking too much. Most daughters would wish they had a mother willing to admit their flaws and apologize."

Except Laurel hadn't apologized. She'd jumped straight into complaining, followed by accusing and then crying, but not once had she apologized for anything. Always playing the victim left little room for self-reflection and apologies.

She rambled on about how Jensen was all she had left. Seeking sympathy for losing both her parents, not even acknowledging that Jensen lost them, too. Jensen knew the conversation would lead to their deaths and how they didn't leave Laurel anything in their will. But, to her surprise, Laurel didn't mention the money. She wondered if that was purposeful. Her gran always warned her how manipulative Laurel could be.

"I'll make you a deal," Jensen offered. "I need you to give me time. The letters are right inside and I promise I will read them by the end of summer. Can you please just give me space until then?" She laid it all out for Laurel so there were no miscommunications. "The lake is my place. You can't show up here again."

"You're staying here all summer? What's happening with the house?" She pulled her long sleeves over her hands in a nervous gesture. It was hot to be wearing long sleeves, but, Jensen thought, she probably wore them to hide track marks.

"I don't know about the house. I need time to figure that out too."

Laurel fidgeted and she cast her eyes at the ground as she asked, "Can I still stay there?"

"Why would you even want to?" But Jensen already knew the answer. Laurel had nowhere else to go.

"It's my home," her mother whispered.

Jensen took an exaggerated deep breath, not fully believing what she's about to say. "Just for the summer."

"Really?" Laurel smiled through her tears. "Thank you so much."

"Don't thank me yet. I have some stipulations."

In the end, Jensen gave Laurel the new alarm code so she could turn it on when she left the house. And she got Laurel to agree that while she was staying at the house, she'd take on the responsibilities of sorting through Gran and Gramps' stuff. At least that took one big thing off Jensen's to-do list. Laurel also promised not to bother Jensen again until she reached out first. After Laurel wrote her phone number on a scrap of paper she had in her purse, she handed it to Jensen who promised to call before school started in the fall.

When Laurel got in her car to leave, she rolled down her window. "I just want you to know that I'm really getting my shit together this time. I'm serious. I have a job and I don't need gas money from you or anything."

Jensen looked at her, perplexed. Was she supposed to congratulate her for being able to pay for her own gas? She gave her a half-hearted wave as she pulled out of the driveway, calling out the window that she loved her and she'd see her soon.

When Jensen walked into the house, Lydia, Joe, and Grayson were all sitting in the living room waiting for her. Obviously Grayson told them what was going on when they got home and she knew she was about to be ambushed. Her eyes skipped right past Lydia and Joe's worried gazes to Grayson's. "Take me somewhere."

He jumped up without hesitation, keys already in hand. Lydia started to protest but Joe gently grabbed her arm pulling her back into her chair and subtly shook his head.

Jensen followed Grayson but stopped before getting to the door. He waited for her in the car while she ran upstairs and grabbed the box of letters still on the floor. It was time she got it over with. She didn't want to spend her entire summer with them looming over her.

9

"THERE'S BEAUTY IN BROKEN THINGS." — GRAYSON

Grayson eyed the box Jensen was holding as she climbed into his car, but he didn't say a word about it. They sat in silence as he pulled onto the highway but Jensen was fidgety, and Grayson's mind was spinning with questions.

She was so tense, she jumped at the sound of her phone ringing. It was Lydia. She declined it but less than ten seconds later, Grayson's phone rang. He picked up, told his mom where they were going, then hung up quickly.

"We need to be home before dark." He repeated his mom's warning. "The woods can be dangerous at night."

Jensen nodded in acknowledgment and thirty minutes later, they pulled into the small dirt parking lot of a campground. Water rushed nearby, but the river wasn't visible from where they were. They walked to the edge of the parking lot, and looked down. Water rushed over rocks so powerfully it was kicking up spray and forming rapids.

Grayson led the way down a dirt path to the river's edge. The path was short but steep and he helped guide her, putting her letters in his backpack so she didn't have to carry them.

When they got to the riverbank, they walked along the water. Grayson stopped occasionally to pick up rocks, he put a few in his pockets, then kept walking without a word. She followed him, not entirely sure where their end goal was. Finally, when her feet hurt and Grayson's pockets were weighed down with stones, he stopped, dropped his backpack, and announced, "We're here."

Jensen looked out at the water, no longer rushing over rocks; it pooled wide in a slow flowing current. She glanced at the massive evergreen trees surrounding them on all sides and looked up, letting herself soak in the wonder. The area Grayson led her to was so heavily forested that besides a few patches of blue sky, they were almost completely tucked under a canopy of branches. And, although the road wasn't far off, she felt secluded from the world.

"This is Deer Creek. It's my favorite place to think." He picked up a rock and tossed it. It skipped across the surface of the water four times before sinking. "This spot isn't accessible from the road. You can only get here by hiking along the shore, so no one's ever here."

Jensen found a large stump and sat while he continued skipping rocks. He offered one to her, but she shook her head. Grayson talked to fill the silence. He told her about each rock as he threw it. Spewing out scientific names for each rock and mineral and pointing them out to her on the shore. "Did you know that Deer Creek is one of the last streams in California that provides habitat for migrating salmon?" He asked. He knew she probably didn't care about rocks or salmon but he'd never tried to hold a one sided conversation before and it was easiest to fall back on what he knew. A part of him wanted to invite her to come back in the winter to watch the migration because it was one of the most extraordinary sights he'd ever seen, but Jensen already had plans for the winter holiday. She'd be in Aspen with her perfect boyfriend and his perfect family. He doubted she'd be willing to skip that to watch fish swim upstream. The thought bummed him out and he went quiet.

Jensen wanted to talk to him about Laurel, but she didn't know where to start. She'd always resented her mother for not being in her life and now she was annoyed that she was trying to be. It was impossible to sort out. No matter how she looked at it, nothing positive could come out of a relationship with Laurel.

What if she forwent reading the letters and just gave her a share of the money? That would at least keep Laurel out of her life.

"Do you think I should read it?" she asked, taking out the first letter.

Grayson shrugged. "That's not up to me."

"Okay, but I could use a little encouragement here," she pleaded.

Grayson dropped the rest of the rocks he was holding and walked over to her. He squatted directly in front of her and placed a hand on each of her knees. "You got this," he told her. "I'm right here with you."

She twisted the first envelope in her hands, going over everything she thought it might say and psyching herself out.

"Jen, look at me," Grayson demanded. "I can't imagine what you're going through. I don't know what's in those letters, but no matter what they say, it's not your job to fix her and it's your choice whether to forgive her."

"I'm all she has," Jensen whispered.

"Why do you think that is?"

"Because she drives everyone away." Jensen felt guilty for resenting her mom for her addiction but she couldn't help it. Maybe her grandparents were right to have sheltered her from Laurel all those years. "Now that she knows where I am, what if she keeps seeking me out? I'll never be free of her again."

"Maybe running away isn't the answer this time." Grayson could see her panic and tried to put her at ease. "You asked her to stay away, didn't you? Maybe she'll listen until you're ready."

"That's not the way she works. Gran always said that Laurel only does what's best for her. She's playing nice right now, but that's only because she wants the money."

"Don't worry about that right now. From what I can tell, your grandparents left a lot of unanswered questions. Don't you wonder if those letters might hold the answers you're looking for?"

"Of course I wonder about that. But what if they only leave me with more questions."

He tapped the letter in her hand. "I think you need to open it."

With shaking hands, she slid the paper out of the envelope. Then, she read–

Jenny Bee,

I know it's been years. I'm sorry I didn't write to you sooner. At first I put off writing because I needed time to process. Then, every time I'd sit down to write to you, I couldn't. How do you explain to a three-year-old that her mommy is in jail? I couldn't admit to myself what I'd done, let alone admit it to you. I thought it would be better for you if I just disappeared. I hoped that if you never knew the truth, you could avoid the trauma.

But I feel like I need to explain myself now. I'm getting out soon and I want us to have a fresh start. That can't happen with so many secrets between us. I know your Gran hasn't told you the whole truth, so I will, but I need you to keep an open mind and an open heart. Can you do that for me, Jenny Bee?

The night of the accident I was upset, and I made some bad choices. I don't even remember that night. I woke up in the morning and my world turned upside down. I ran a quick errand and when I left the store, there were police everywhere.

I was brought in for questioning. The night before, there had been a hit-and-run, and a girl was seriously injured. They found my car's side mirror at the scene. I hadn't even noticed that my mirror was missing. They told me that the girl I hit was nineteen. She was thirty weeks pregnant.

Those hours in the precinct were the lowest moments of my life. I felt horrible. I still feel horrible. I pleaded guilty to all charges. I will always be sorry for the pain I've caused in that woman's life and in yours. I regret every choice I made that took me away from you. I'll have to live with that regret for the rest of my life.

I promise you, Jenny Bee, I'm going to make a better life for us. I'm done making bad choices. I'm ready to be the mom you deserve.

I love you. I'm sorry. You are my everything.
Love,
Mom

Her letter said everything Jensen used to wish for. But with the words in front of her, they only made her angry. She couldn't believe Laurel had the audacity to give her a hard time about breaking a promise. It was total bullshit.

When Laurel got out of jail, nothing changed. Her mom had lived in a halfway house nearby for a year but she never even tried to see her. Except once in fifth grade when she tried to pick her up from school and the campus police had to intervene. Laurel screamed for all the school to hear, "That's my daughter! I just want to see her. Please, just let me see her," she'd sobbed, "just once. Please." Rumors followed Jensen around after that. Everyone wanted to know what was wrong with her crazy mother. That was the last time she saw Laurel until the reading of the will.

By the time Jensen left for St. Timothy's, she'd lost the illusion that her mom would be part of her life. When she came home for a week that first summer, Gran told her that Laurel was in rehab. Jensen knew that you couldn't make someone change. You have to accept them for who they are or walk away, and she'd chosen to walk away years ago. Despite the letter saying all the right things, it didn't change anything. Actions spoke louder than words and Laurel had proven time and time again that she wasn't trustworthy or dependable. It didn't matter whether her heart was in the right place. She was still a manipulative liar and Jensen knew that she was never going to change.

"It's okay if you need to cry or get mad," Grayson said as she stared blankly at the letter.

"No, it's not," she whispered, barely loud enough for him to hear. "When I cry, I feel out of control, just like Laurel. When I feel bad for myself, I'm playing the victim, just like Laurel. When I get angry, I'm a loose cannon, just like Laurel. I hold it all in because I don't want to be like her."

She'd already shown too much emotion to Grayson. She'd opened up faster to him than she did with anyone in her life. Even with Lucy, it took her months before she felt comfortable talking to her about anything real. But with Grayson, it came easily.

"I would never think you're anything like her," he promised. "I don't want you to hold anything back with me." He reached out and placed his fingertips under her chin, lifting her gaze from the letter.

"I'm not sure you understand what you're in for," she challenged, trying to lighten the mood.

"I think I do," he challenged back, not falling for her attempt at distraction. He placed a large rock in her hand. "I think you should throw this as hard as you can." He pointed at a large boulder. "At that rock."

"Why?" She turned the rock over in her hands.

"Because it's okay to be angry."

She must have had a lot more anger in her than either of them realized, because, on her first throw, she shattered the large rock into several pieces. Grayson picked up a broken shard and brought it over to her. He placed it in her open palm. "This is Fire Agate," he explained. "It's a mineral in the quartz family, look."

He turned the rock over in her hand. The broken side was rust-colored and speckled with green and gold. It was beautiful and unexpected. "You shouldn't be scared to fall apart," Grayson told her. "There is beauty in broken things."

With his words, a crack formed in the dam she'd built to hold back her emotions.

Jensen continued breaking the fire agate, collecting her favorite pieces and saving them. They stayed at the river far longer than they'd planned. It wasn't until her arm was aching from breaking the quartz and the sun was dipping behind the mountain, casting darkness over their already shady spot, that they agreed it was time to leave.

Grayson filled his backpack with the rocks and Jensen carried the box of letters on their way back to the car. She had only read the first one.

The sky was black and speckled with stars. They had to use the flashlights on their phones to navigate the rocks, causing both their batteries to die by the time they got back to the car. Jensen was glad she was with Grayson. Normally she would have been terrified of the dark forest and sounds of nature around them. They didn't phase him and he guided them back to the campground effortlessly.

On the way back to the house, they stopped for pizza. Sitting at the bar, they watched Reed slinging dough while they ate. As soon as they climbed back into the car, Jensen's exhaustion hit. She didn't let herself fall asleep, but she leaned her head against the window and zoned out, counting the stars.

"Where have you two been?" Lydia scolded the moment they walked in the door.

"I told you where we were," Grayson answered calmly.

"Jensen, you can head upstairs and get ready for bed. I need to talk to my son," Lydia directed.

Jensen looked at Grayson, who nodded that it was fine. Instead of going up to her room, she perched on the stairs, listening to their conversation.

"Do you know how worried we've been? I told you to be home before dark. You know what can happen in the woods at night! And, since when do you ignore your phone?"

"Sorry," Grayson started, "but I could see it in her eyes, Mom. She was going to run. She needed to get away to work through everything going on with her mom. I figured she was better off if I went with her."

"Did she talk to you about Laurel?"

"Some."

"What did she say? Is she okay?"

"She's angry," he answered. "I told her that was okay and we broke some stuff."

"Grayson, the last thing she needs is for you to fuel the fire. Whatever is going on between Jensen and Laurel, it isn't your place. I don't like you in the middle of it. They need to figure out their differences without you encouraging her anger."

"I'm already in the middle of it," he argued. "And I wasn't encouraging her anger. I was helping her get it out. You're the one who always said how important it was to embrace my emotions. When I used to get angry at dad, you told me it was okay, good even. You taught me to channel my feelings into something productive."

"I'd hardly call breaking things productive," Lydia countered. She took a deep breath and calmly added, "I suppose I just wish she would come to me with her troubles like she used to. I feel like she's put up a wall between us."

"She's not the little kid we knew seven years ago. She's changed a lot and sometimes it feels like I'm the only one who realizes that. If you want a relationship with her, accept that it's gonna be different."

"You're right, she has changed a lot," Lydia responded. "She's a young woman now. Don't think I haven't noticed the way you look at her."

Jensen was straining to hear Lydia's words as Andrew slid onto the stair next to her. "What are you doing?" he whispered.

She shushed him, "I'm eavesdropping. Grayson is in there with your mom."

"Is he in trouble? What'd he do?" Andrew pried.

"I don't know if he's in trouble," Jensen said through her teeth, "I can't hear with you in my ear."

He stopped talking and leaned toward the hall trying to hear what was being said. They both jumped at the sound of footsteps approaching, and turned to run upstairs not wanting to get caught. But Grayson was already turning the corner, and he crashed into Jensen.

"Wow," he laughed as he grabbed hold of her so neither of them would fall over. "Eavesdrop much?"

Andrew was already halfway up the stairs, having taken them two at a time. When he made it to the top, he called out in a whisper, "I was just coming down for a snack, but if Mom's on a rampage, I'm staying in my room."

"You shouldn't have taken all the blame," Jensen said to Grayson once they were alone.

"Don't worry about it," he shrugged.

Once upstairs, she went into Nicole's room, exhausted. She didn't even bother to change, just pulled off her jeans and slipped her bra off before collapsing onto her mattress. She got the best night's sleep of her life.

10

"WHAT'S GOING ON WITH YOU?" —ERIC

Grayson had to drag Jensen out of bed the next morning. "Get up. We're gonna be late."

He tried again five minutes later. "Jen, wake up. We both slept through our alarms."

"Jen, not kidding. Get your ass out of bed," he demanded on his third attempt.

The next thing she knew, she was drenched and gagging on water. She jumped up, glaring at Grayson, who was holding an empty pitcher.

Only he didn't notice her death glare because he was preoccupied, looking at her chest. She looked down and saw that her shirt was soaking wet and clinging to her, not to mention her lack of pants. She yanked a blanket off the bed and covered herself up.

He averted his gaze, offered a halfhearted, "Sorry for that," and told her again that they were going to be late before leaving the room.

She dressed quickly, brushed her teeth, and threw her hair in a ponytail. Grayson handed her a steaming cup of coffee when she got into his car.

"Good morning," he smiled as she absorbed the caffeine and glared at him, still mad over the way he woke her up. Before long she rolled her eyes and decided to let it go. "Thanks for making sure I wasn't late."

He sent her a shit-eating smile. "Sorry 'bout that, but I did kind of owe you one. You got me grounded for the first time in my life."

"You're grounded? Are you allowed to be grounded when you're an adult?"

He laughed. "I asked the same question. But, in the words of my mother, while I live under her roof, I follow her rules."

"Sorry."

He shrugged, "It's only a week. Plus, I think it's a right of passage. Everyone should be grounded at least once."

Lydia's plan of putting Grayson on house arrest backfired. On the third day, while everyone was hanging around the living room, she entered the room with Julia on her hip and her apron splattered with dirt.

"I have had enough of this," she announced. "What are you all doing here? Grayson is supposed to be bearing his punishment ALONE."

"I'm just here to pick up Avery," Davis said before shuffling Avery out the door.

"I'm here with Jensen," Brent said.

"Same," Reed added.

She looked at Jensen, who timidly asked, "Am I not allowed to have friends over?"

Lydia's face softened considerably when she answered, "Of course you can, Honey." Then she turned to Grayson, who was smiling, and shook a trowel at him. "Don't think I don't know you're getting away with something," she admonished before heading back into the garden.

As soon as she left the room, Brent picked up the remote and asked, "So, what are we gonna watch?"

They'd spent the past two days playing video games, which Jensen was horrible at. She was a highly competitive person and she'd come in last place or was the first to die in every game. Which was why, when it was her turn to pick, she requested they watch a show instead.

Brent left the choice up to her, since she was the one who'd asked.

"Anything's fine," she said. "My school had strict rules. Televisions weren't allowed in dorms, so I've hardly seen anything."

"What kind of college doesn't allow TVs in dorms?" Reed asked, appalled.

"It wasn't college. I went to a boarding school in Connecticut for the past seven years," she explained.

"You went seven years without a TV?" Brent gasped.

"It wasn't so bad. I got used to it."

"Get comfortable," Brent instructed. "We have so many shows to binge."

They were four episodes into a zombie show when her phone rang. Digging it out of her back pocket, she saw that it was Eric calling. Cringing at her phone, she knew she had to answer it. They hadn't talked in almost a week. Grayson, seeing her dilemma, paused the episode they were on and everyone in the room let out exasperated groans.

"Jensen, what the hell are you doing?" Brent admonished. "Let it go to voicemail."

"Sorry, it's my boyfriend," she apologized. "I have to talk to him." Begrudgingly, she swiped to answer the call.

"Hi Eric," she said, trying to feign excitement. Before she could ask how his trip was, or tell him she missed him, three couch pillows hit her in the face.

Throwing them back at Brent and Reed, whom she knew

were the culprits, she tried to say something to Eric but the next thing she knew, she was being fully attacked with pillows and cushions. She searched for shelter, yanking Grayson in front of her to act as a barrier between her and the onslaught. Squealing with laughter, she forgot about the phone still pressed against her ear.

"Jensen, what is going on over there?" Eric asked, his voice laced with concern.

"Sorry," she said as she threw another pillow at Brent before ducking behind Grayson again. "Just an impromptu pillow fight," she explained. But suddenly Grayson was turning on her with a pillow in hand and she had to run for it.

She dove behind the couch where she found Andrew. "Teammates?" she asked him. He nodded and together they threw pillows aimlessly over the back of the couch.

Putting her phone on speaker, she called out, "One second, Eric." Reaching her hands up over the back of the couch, she gestured for a timeout. She was out of breath and smiling widely.

When her phone was back in hand, Eric was requesting a video call. She answered it and Eric's face appeared on the screen. Andrew and Jensen both leaned their backs against the back of the couch, laughing and catching their breath. Catching sight of herself in the reverse camera, she quickly ran her fingers through her knotted hair. Behind them, poking their heads over the back of the couch, Grayson, Reed, and Brent were all equally disheveled.

"Hey there, Doctor Boy," Grayson said.

Brent jumped in with impeccable timing. "Jensen, you can't have a boyfriend. You're my dream girl." He winked at her.

"Hey, I had her heart first," Andrew argued.

"Pretty sure you'd both lose out to Grayson if we're being real with ourselves," Reed piped up.

"Ignore them," she told Eric, rolling her eyes. "They're all idiots. All of them are single and there's a reason for it."

"Wow, harsh burn," Brent laughed at his own expense.

"Jensen, can we talk in private?" Eric asked, finally speaking up. He was cold and unwavering. It was opposite to the fun, playful words floating around the living room.

"Sure." Her reply was robotic and all the humor had drained out of her voice. She stood and walked out to the front porch.

As soon as the door shut behind her, Brent was talking. "That's the boyfriend? She can't honestly be happy with that guy."

Grayson was trying not to read too much into Jensen's body language, but Brent was right. When she talked to Eric, the vibrant girl he knew completely deflated. He'd had the sudden urge to grab the phone and hang up on him. No one should make her dim her light for them.

Sitting on the top step, Jensen told Eric, "I'm alone now. What's up?"

"What's up? That's all you have to say? We haven't talked in a week! I've called you so many times and it keeps going to voice-mail. What's going on with you?"

"Sorry, I've been working a lot," she apologized lamely. If he knew that every day after work, instead of calling him back, she'd been going out with her new friends, it would only hurt him.

"You have a job?" he asked, and she realized she hadn't even told him about The Marina. But instead of asking her anything about her job like Lucy did, he just asked "Why?"

"Working is what everyone does at the lake in the summer."

"But you weren't supposed to be at the lake all summer," he said accusingly. "And surely you don't need to work."

"I like it. It's been fun," she said, ignoring the first part of his statement.

"That still doesn't explain why I haven't heard from you in over a week. I thought I was more important to you than some job you don't even need."

"You are important to me." She tried to dig her way out of the hole she'd found herself in.

"Are you sure? Because lately, it feels like I'm not much of a priority to you."

"I'm sorry I've made you feel that way. You are a priority to me. You know I care about you."

"Really? Because we don't even talk anymore. It barely feels like we're in a relationship. Is that what you want?"

"I don't know what I want," she admitted, more to herself.

"Do you want to take a break?"

"That doesn't sound like the worst idea while I figure things out," she conceded. A break could solve her worries about how fast their relationship was moving and relieve the guilt about having so much fun without him.

Eric immediately looked wrecked by her words, making her backtrack. "I'm not saying that's what I want. There's just so much on my plate. I can't make you the priority you deserve to be right now."

"So I'm the easiest thing for you to cut?" He was clearly hurt. "That's what every guy wants to hear from the girl he loves."

He'd never said that to her before, that he loved her. And what was worse, he said it sarcastically, only meant to make her feel bad. The thing was—she didn't feel bad. As soon as she let herself consider the option of taking a break from their relationship, she knew it was what she wanted. She just didn't know how to explain to Eric that they were moving too fast without derailing all their plans.

"Don't say you love me right now," she said. "I'm still on board for Stanford and we can revisit the idea of being together once school starts. It just doesn't feel like it's working right now."

"What, so you want to hook up with all your hillbilly friends and then just get back together in a month like nothing happened?" he barked. "I'm not an idiot Jensen. I've noticed that you are always hanging around those guys. Please tell me you haven't already hooked up with one of them. Am I just the idiot sitting around waiting for you to call while you're off with another guy?"

"No, Eric I–"

He didn't let her get a word in. "If you want to throw away the last seven years of friendship and the future we have planned over some summer fling, then just do it. Don't coddle me and make it out to be a break when we both know that what you really mean is a breakup."

"I don't want to break up!" she yelled, finally making her voice heard. "Absolutely nothing is going on with any of those guys and I can't believe you'd think I'd do that. I'd never cheat on you."

"I don't like you staying there," he replied. "If you want to stay together, I want you to leave."

"Are you giving me an ultimatum?"

"I don't like the way I feel when you're there. It always used to be easy between us, and now I'm second guessing everything and doubting you. I hate feeling this way. I need you to leave because I can't keep feeling like this."

"You're the one throwing away seven years of friendship because of your own insecurities. I'm sorry for how you're feeling, but that's on you. I'm happy here, and I'm staying."

"Even if it means we're over?"

"Yes."

"Fine." He hung up and she stared at her phone for a while, waiting for him to call back. He never did. Finally, she headed inside.

Jensen entered the living room in a daze, too stunned to even know how to react. She kept going back to what he said about throwing away their friendship. Did that mean they weren't even friends anymore? She didn't know how to respond to such a monumental statement. Eric and his family were so important to her, always taking her in when she had nowhere else to go. She thought about him telling Katrina they broke up and she felt her heart break.

She looked up to find the guys staring at her. "I think we just broke up."

"You're not sure?" Andrew asked.

"No, I'm sure we just broke up. I'm just not sure how to feel about it."

Grayson jumped up and pulled her into a tight hug. "You're going to be okay."

His mind was racing with possibilities, but he knew that her being single didn't change anything. They were just friends, and he was determined to respect that. Then she wrapped her arms around him and that thought went out the window.

Her hands tightly gripped the back of his t-shirt. His palm cupped the back of her head where it was cradled in the crook of his neck, before running down the length of her hair. He turned toward her and pressed his face into her golden hair. He breathed in her tropical, summer-time smell of passionfruit and a hint of sunscreen.

"You're going to be okay," he said again, this time directly into her ear for only her to hear.

Someone behind him coughed, and after a few more seconds, he released her.

Brent asked her if she needed to blow off some steam, but all she could think to do when she was feeling unsteady was to take to the water. That wasn't an option with her stitches.

"I think I just want to be alone," she answered Brent, but she was looking at Grayson. He was still standing so close and watching her.

She broke eye contact with him and rushed upstairs. Once in Nicole's room, she threw herself down on her bed dramatically.

"What's up with you?" Nicole asked from her spot at her desk.

"I just got dumped," she grumbled into her pillow.

"That sucks."

Jensen sat up, hugging the pillow to her chest and said, "It does. And it was for a stupid reason. He's feeling jealous and insecure, which is annoying because there's nothing for him to be jealous of. It's not my fault all the people I've met here so far are guys. It's not like I'm attracted to any of them."

Nicole was just staring at her, her eyebrows raised as Jensen groaned, threw herself back down, and screamed into the pillow before grumbling out, "That's a lie. They're all hot and it's impossible not to notice, but I would never have acted on that attraction. Never."

Nicole didn't respond to her meltdown. She put her shoes on, grabbed her purse, and walked out. But, before she closed the door behind her, Jensen heard her mumble, "Well, I guess it's good to know you're not a bitch *and* a cheater." Then she slammed the door.

Jensen needed to talk to someone who would understand. She needed Lucy.

Her friend answered on the first ring. Jensen told her about the breakup and gave her a play-by-play of the entire conversation. Lucy agreed that Eric was being unfair, but then she asked Jensen why she didn't just appease him and leave.

"I'm not saying you should do what he wants," Lucy clarified. "It's just not like you. You're always the one to bend. I like that you're not letting yourself get walked over anymore. Eric will like it too. It probably just threw him off. You guys will be back together in no time."

11

"WHAT'S WITH THE STARING?" —ANDREW

Jensen intended to spend her entire day off in her pajamas. She didn't even plan to leave her bed. Her plans are thwarted when Andrew barged in just after noon and told her he'd volunteered them to babysit the kids for Lydia.

She reluctantly moved her pity party to the couch and watched Andrew play with Dustin, Julia and Avery. She paid attention to Andrew as he rough housed with the boys, wrestling them both at once. The game moved on to a high stakes version of hot lava monster where they were jumping across the furniture. All the while, Jensen kept her eyes fixed on Andrew. He sent questioning glances her way a few times when he caught her staring. When he and Avery dragged stools in from the kitchen to build a pillow fort, he caught her watching him again and he finally snapped, "What's with the staring?"

"Sorry." She jumped up and got to work, draping a blanket over the stools. Andrew eyed her suspiciously and when he turned back to what he was doing, her gaze wandered back over to him.

He whipped around to look at her. "God, Fish, would you stop? I can feel you watching me. What's up?"

"It's nothing, it's just, your knee doesn't look hurt," she observed.

"That's what this is about? Grayson told you about my knee?" Andrew asked.

"Actually, your mom did, a while ago. I've been curious about it. Specifically, what the doctors said. It has to be pretty bad if there were no rehab options. Plus, there's no scarring from surgery and you're using it just fine."

"You've been spending a lot of time thinking about this, haven't you?"

She swallowed and nodded.

"She gave you the entire sob story about how my dreams were destroyed and I'll never be able to play again, huh?" He seemed so nonchalant talking about it but she recognized it as a well-rehearsed line.

"It's been really hard." He flipped his emotions over on a dime and suddenly looked so broken. "Everything I worked for, gone in a moment." But then he broke into a conniving grin. "Do you know how hard girls fall for that sensitive shit? You wouldn't believe how much tail I've gotten because of my bum knee." He shot her a cocky smile. She didn't allow her response to show on her face. He was hiding behind that smile and they both knew it.

"If something were to prevent me from swimming, I don't know what I would do. If football is as important for you as swimming is for me, I can only imagine what you're going through. Maybe you need to deal with it by hooking up with tons of girls. I won't judge you if that's your way of coping."

"Or maybe I really am fine," he countered.

"I wouldn't be. I haven't been able to swim for ten days and it's been miserable waiting for these stitches to come out tomorrow."

"You know, I could do that for you." Andrew offered. He had all the confidence in the world and he promised he'd done it before. After some convincing, she agreed. Anything to not have to go back to the hospital.

Andrew ran upstairs while Jensen waited on the couch. She was feeling pretty uneasy by the time he returned with rubbing alcohol and fingernail clippers.

"What are those for?" she asked.

"Don't worry, I know what I'm doing," he reassured her.

"You know what," she pulled her arm away, "I think it can wait until tomorrow. I'm not in a rush. Swimming in the lake is teaching me some bad habits, anyway. I am less focused on form and speed and more focused on adjusting to the wind and current." She was looking for excuses.

"I know of an Olympic sized pool you can practice in if you let me help you."

"Are you serious?" She asked, her fear melting away, replaced with excitement.

Andrew poured the rubbing alcohol over the clippers and she offered him her elbow. As he cut out each of her stitches, he talked to her to keep her distracted from what he was doing.

He told her that all summer, while she and Grayson have been at The Marina, he was working at the high school in Tanglewood, coaching the football team through their summer conditioning. So many boys had asked for extra help that it was becoming a full-time job. They had daily conditioning, but he also met up with a group of kids for one-on-one drills and weight training. Because he was there so often, he had a set of keys to the athletic facility, which included a pool.

"I thought it would be fun," he opened up to her. "Coaching kids. I didn't realize how hard it would be." His voice was quiet and grave. "Watching all these kids play a game I love while I'm stuck on the sidelines. Watching them take for granted the fact that they can play. I want to scream at them sometimes. They're letting these days slip by, not understanding how lucky they are. In adulthood, there aren't many opportunities to be a part of a team. I miss it."

Nicole walked in just as Andrew clipped the last stitch. He called out to her and asked her to take over with the kids. At first, Nicole refused, but Andrew challenged her. "You owe me."

"I do not," Nicole snapped back at him.

"You do, because I know who you've been sneaking out with every night this summer and I've kept my mouth shut. If you want me to continue to keep my mouth shut, then you'll do this for me." Nicole's eyes shifted nervously over to Jensen. "She doesn't know," Andrew told her.

"You're blackmailing me?"

"You could look at it that way, or you could look at it like we're doing each other a favor."

Nicole threw herself down on the couch and pulled out her phone. "Whatever, just go," she huffed.

Tanglewood was forty minutes away, but Andrew cut ten minutes off that time. He knew the roads well, a product of driving the route every day. When they arrived, the parking lot was mostly empty. Andrew parked in a back lot behind a gym and led her through a locker room and then down a long hall.

"Just promise me," he pleaded, "promise you won't let it slip through your fingers."

"You mean my swimming?" she asked. "Swimming isn't my dream. It's just something I do. I don't plan to turn it into a career. I'm going to medical school."

He shook his head at her, disappointed. "You closed your eyes the entire time I removed your stitches and you hate needles. Tell me one thing, why do you want to be a doctor?"

"You're not really one to talk. Aren't you planning to be an accountant or something?"

Walking away from him, toward the doors at the end of the hall, she pushed them open, and right in front of her was an enormous pool. Breathing in the chlorine, she finally felt at home.

She stripped down to her swimsuit and Andrew grabbed a stopwatch. After a few warm up laps, she asked him to time her.

It was her first time in weeks swimming a 200 meter free. After the fourth lap, she stopped at the wall and looked up at Andrew. He was staring at the stopwatch in his hand. "I don't know much about swimming, so I don't know what's considered fast, but you're fast. I don't care what you say, you're a swimmer. Jensen, if you want them to, someday people will know your name." He was so confident. She rolled her eyes at him and he tossed her the stopwatch.

She stared at the number then looked at Andrew. "You started it too late, or stopped it too early," she criticized. "Make sure you start it as soon as my feet leave the platform, not once I'm in the water."

"I did."

"You couldn't have. This number isn't realistic. I haven't been under two minutes since The Olympic Trials. This is nine seconds shy of the world record. Maybe the clock's broken. Try using your phone for the next one." Her mind was spinning with the possibilities. Maybe she still had the potential to reach all the goals she had made for herself over the years. But she quickly suppressed those thoughts remembering that her goals had changed.

"Would you stop doubting yourself?" he lectured. "I'm telling you, the time is right. You're meant to be a swimmer, and we both know it. Medical school won't satisfy you. You don't have time for organic chemistry and two math classes. You need to be focused on swimming. I know it's what you want and you're good enough."

"That's rich. You want me to follow my dreams, but you aren't following yours."

"My dreams are dead, crushed," he argued. "Yours are still very much alive."

"That's bullshit and you know it." She lifted herself out of the pool, sitting on the edge next to him. In a gentler voice she added, "If you can't play football anymore, then find a new dream. Don't settle for being an accountant for the rest of your life. Do you really think working for your father is going to make you happy?"

She dove back into the water, leaving him there to think. Andrew continued to time her for another hour. She'd gotten faster than she was a few months ago. Every swim was consistently under two, but none of her times beat the first one.

On their way home, Andrew finally admitted, "I hate it," and to clarify, he added, "the job my dad has lined up for me."

"Then why are you planning to do it for the rest of your life?"

"What I want and what's required of me are not the same thing. That's life. You still have time, but for me, it's time to grow up. I may hate it, but my dad's given me an opportunity I can't pass up. He's offering me a good job right out of college. I would be stupid to turn him down."

"You know what's stupid? Spending the rest of your life as miserable as your father. Is that the life you want, Andrew, a life like his?"

When they arrived back at the house, Nicole was out front playing with Dustin, Julia, Davis, and Avery. Davis had Dustin on his shoulders and Nicole was holding Julia. They were playing basketball. The hoop was on the lowest setting. Avery passed the ball to Dustin, who laughed hysterically as Davis raised him above his head so he could dunk the ball. Nicole raised Julia up to block the shot, but they were unsuccessful.

Noticing the car, Nicole walked over to the window and Andrew rolled it down. "You guys need to clean up the living room." She talked over Jensen to her brother. "I'll keep taking care of the little monsters." She tickled her little sister as she called her a monster, and Julia shrieked. "But the mess inside is on you."

Andrew and Jensen cleaned up the fort together. As they folded blankets, he asked, "What do you recommend I do?"

"Start by figuring out what you want. Apparently, you used to be motivated and have goals. Try being that guy again. Be someone you would be proud of, and Andrew, stop whoring around. You're better than that."

Andrew threw a pillow at her and they both laughed. "I'm serious!" She tossed the pillow back at him. "Have you ever considered letting a girl get to know you past all the physical stuff? Because you're actually pretty great."

12

"THE BEST THING I'VE EVER SMELLED." —JENSEN

Climbing on the dock after a rigorous distance swim, Jensen saw her friends sitting at the picnic table on the shore. She'd been MIA since the break-up with Eric.

Brent stood and made his way across the wobbly dock. "We're heading out to go windsurfing," he took a seat beside her. "I think you should come. It might help get you out of your head."

She appreciated his offer, but her arms were gassed. "There's no way I'll have the strength today." Emphasizing her aching muscles, she rubbed her arms.

"Okay, but you can't keep avoiding us," he nudged her shoulder.

"I have an idea," Reed called out from behind them, where he was running up the dock, causing it to sway. "Why don't we head out to the meadow tonight after dark?"

"I'll get the beers," Brent volunteered even though he was only nineteen. It would make more sense for Andrew or Reed to supply alcohol since they were legal, but no one questioned Brent's offer.

"I'm not really much of a drinker," Jensen said.

"You don't have to drink, just come," Andrew said, making his way towards them. She turned and saw Grayson, Nicole, and Davis still sitting at the picnic table. "Brent's right, a meadow party is exactly what you need. It will be fun."

At dinner, Andrew mentioned the party to Lydia, but instead of telling her it'd be in the meadow, he told her it was going to be at a girl named Jamie's house. They all knew how Lydia felt about them being outside past dark.

Lydia seemingly had no problem with them going, her only response was, "Keep an eye on Jensen," which made her feel like a child. She was the same age as Brent, but no one thought he needed a babysitter.

"Don't worry, we will," Grayson promised.

"I wasn't talking to you." Lydia shoveled food into Julia's mouth as she continued, "You're not going. Today's your last day of punishment."

"Are you being serious right now, Mom?" Nicole tried to argue on Grayson's behalf, but Lydia wasn't having it.

"You be careful," she warned Nicole, "Or you'll be staying home with him."

Jensen called Lucy after dinner, looking for advice on what to wear to a meadow party.

After the phone rang for a full minute, Lucy finally answered in a whisper. "Hey girl, one sec." There was a shuffling sound on her end before she was back, her voice still hushed. "Sorry, I had to find a hiding spot."

"Who are you hiding from?" Jensen asked.

"Just my date. No biggie." She brushed off Jensen's concern. "I'm behind a dumpster in an alley on 41st street," she whispered.

"Is that safe?" Jensen asked, her mind now completely focused on Lucy's situation.

"It's a heavily populated area, don't worry," Lucy whispered.

"Are you okay?

"Oh yeah," she laughed, "but apparently my date, this guy, Daniel Long, thought this setup was like an arranged marriage sort of thing. He seriously pulled out a ring in the middle of our dinner."

"What?" Jensen choked on her laugh. "No way!" That could only happen to Lucy.

"Way!" Lucy giggled. "I thought it was a joke, but he was like, down on one knee. There were all these people staring, and someone started taking pictures! I don't want that shit on the internet, so I just ran. I was going to get a cab, but he chased me before I could. So, I hid behind this dumpster. I'm waiting for my driver to get here. Oh, I think he just pulled up. Can I call you later?"

When she got off the phone, Nicole was shuffling through her closet, looking for an outfit. Meanwhile, Jensen was pulling out clothes from Lucy's bags. Trying to send her an olive branch, she asked Nicole if she wanted to borrow something.

They spent the next forty-five minutes trying on clothes. When Andrew poked his head in the room and neither of them were ready he asked Nicole if she could bring Jensen and he would catch a ride with Brent.

Finally, after digging through all of her drawers and Lucy's bags, Nicole threw a top at Jensen. It was a light tan cable knit with long sleeves and it looked cozy. Jensen pulled it on and then realized it was a crop top. It fit loosely, hanging off one shoulder. She pulled her arms across her front to cover her midriff.

Nicole rolled her eyes. "Why work so hard to look like that if you won't flaunt it?"

Jensen looked in the mirror again while Nicole got dressed. She hated to admit it, but Nicole was right. The top looked good and with her high-waisted jeans, it only showed a small sliver of her stomach. It was nothing all the guys hadn't seen before. She spent half her life in a swimsuit after all.

"Okay, I'm good with this one," she said.

By the time they got to the party, it was already in full swing. They parked near a bunch of other cars, some with their headlights on and people lingering around them. They walked towards a large circle of trucks surrounding a bonfire. Andrew immediately called Jensen over. She found him across the field. Nicole joined a group of people sitting in the bed of a red truck. Brent scooted over to make room. Some of Jensen's coworkers were sitting with them, laughing. She wanted to join them. Instead, she forced herself through the crowd until she was at Andrew's side. "Wow, you look hot." He gave her a one armed hug before going back to his game.

The truck bed was open with a piece of plywood laid atop it, acting as a table, set up for beer-pong. Andrew tossed a ball and it landed in one of the two cups on the opposite end of the table. He draped an arm over Jensen's shoulder and announced, "See, I knew she'd be good luck."

She slunk out from under his arm and took a step away. There was a case of water bottles against the tire next to her and she pulled one out and was about to open it when one of Andrew's friends handed her a pink wine cooler. She looked at the two drinks she was holding, contemplating which one to drink. She's only ever been drunk once.

Normally she never attended parties but it was hard to avoid one that was thrown in her honor. When Jensen broke the Junior World Record, her swim team had surprised her when she got back to school with a party. As soon as she walked in the door, a drink was thrust into her hand and someone called out, "To Jensen, for her record-breaking 200 meter free!" The girl raised her glass and so did everyone else in the room. All eyes were on Jensen as she tried her first taste of alcohol. It was delicious. It tasted the way she imagined the Caribbean would taste. As soon as she took her first sip, she decided she needed to try every flavor. She drank the wine coolers like they were water. It didn't even occur to her that she was drunk until she was throwing up in the hall plant an hour later and Lucy was holding her hair back.

"Never let me drink alcohol again," she moaned as Lucy guided her down the hall and back to their room. Thank goodness Lucy was there, because there was no way Jensen could walk upright without her help. Her head was spinning.

Less than ten minutes after Lucy tucked her into bed, they heard the party get broken up. A faculty member knocked on their door. "Keep your eyes shut and pretend to be asleep," Lucy hissed at her. Then her best friend answered the door.

"Hello Ms. St. Clare," the woman said to Lucy, "is Ms. Fisher here?"

"Of course. Where else would she be?" Lucy responded innocently. "She was tired after the swim meet, so she went to bed early, but I can wake her if you need me to," Lucy offered helpfully.

"No need," the woman said. "I was just making sure you're both in your room. She is captain of the swim team, after all."

"Oh? Is there some sort of party going on?" Lucy asked, obliviously.

"You didn't hear it?"

"I keep my headphones in when I study," Lucy explained. "Did anyone get in trouble?"

"Don't worry about it. You just get back to your studying. I'm sorry for disturbing you."

The moment the door closed, Jensen puked all over her bed. Lucy spent the rest of the night taking care of her.

In the morning, she had a pounding headache. She also found out half of her teammates were suspended.

The incident ended up being pretty major, resulting in more than *half the seniors on the swim team getting community service. It was bad timing because everyone was hearing from colleges. Each time someone received a rejection letter, there was speculation that they'd been denied because of the misconduct on their record.*

Despite not getting caught and nothing officially going on her record, Jensen made herself do the same amount of community service as the other girls on the team.

"You don't drink at all?" Andrew asked, walking over to her. She was lost in thought and staring at the drink in her hand.

"I had a bad experience last time. I think I'm gonna stick with water tonight." She put down the pink drink.

Andrew shrugged, "You're prerogative."

As Andrew introduced Jensen to each of his friends, he draped his arm across her shoulder again. Each guy gave her an approving nod while Andrew tossed the ball he was holding and landed it in the last cup, ending the game. After Andrew was challenged to another round he pulled Jensen into him and said, "Only if I can have Fish as my partner."

Then to her, he whispered, "Don't worry, I'll drink for you."

It seemed to Jensen that Andrew kept finding excuses to touch her. When she missed her second shot, he offered to show her, but she pulled away from him. "I think I've got it," she told him, annoyed. While she lined up the ball, Andrew stood back with his friends. She heard them talking about her and she tried to ignore them, but it was impossible.

"You never said she was such a babe," one guy said in what could barely pass as a whisper.

"And look at that ass, man. I can't believe you never mentioned that ass," she heard another one say. She fought the urge to turn and glare at them.

She landed the ball in the cup, causing them all to roar with cheers and she missed what Andrew said in response. Whatever he said, it shut them up.

After that game, she stood off to the side by herself as she waited for her next turn and Andrew came and leaned up against her. "Your friends are tools," she whispered.

"They won't say shit like that anymore. I let them know you're off limits," Andrew reassured her. She wondered what he said to shut them up. Andrew draped an arm around her again and she felt like he was claiming her. Standing right in the middle of her childhood fantasy didn't feel as amazing as she thought it would. The thought of being stuck under Andrew's arm all night just made her feel trapped. She looked longingly at the truck where her friends were laughing together. Peeling Andrew off her, she readied herself for what she needed to say.

"Can you please stop hitting on me?" she whispered. "You keep putting your arm around me and finding reasons to touch me. I'm not cool with it."

Andrew looked confused and slightly embarrassed that she was confronting him in front of his boys. He leaned forward and whispered back, "I wasn't hitting on you, Fish. I'm just looking out for you, making sure no one else tries anything."

"But, all the winking and the flirting?" she accused him.

"What flirting?" Andrew asked.

"You called me," she brought her voice down to a whisper again, "hot stuff and babe."

"God, Jensen!" Andrew let out a bellowing laugh. "Sorry to burst your bubble, but I say shit like that to everyone. I called Grayson hot stuff yesterday."

"So you were never flirting with me?"

"Not once," he confirmed. "That would be weird. It would be like hitting on my sister."

"You think of me as a sister?"

He shrugged, "Sorry."

"Don't be. That's actually kind of great." She draped her arm over his shoulder. "But I think we fit better like this."

"You did not just call me short." He glared up at her.

"Of course I did. That's what sisters are for," she shot him a wink.

He laughed and bumped her shoulder. "You know, it's kinda a bummer that you're finally over me."

"I'm walking away now." Before he teased her anymore, she went to find her friends. At least now she knew where they stood and she was glad he thought of her as family.

Nicole wasn't with the rest of the group when she wandered over to them. So, instead of sitting down, she weaved through the party looking for her. They had been getting along earlier and she hoped that would continue. If she could use the party as a chance to make amends, it would make being there worth it.

After wandering around for a while, Jensen made her way to the opposite end of the meadow where all the cars were parked. She accidentally interrupted Reed with a girl horizontal on the hood of a car. When they saw her they broke apart and sheepishly climbed into the car. As Reed started the engine, his headlights lit up the rest of the area and Jensen caught a glimpse of Nicole. She wasn't alone. Jensen tried to turn around and run, but the headlights caught Nicole's attention and she turned toward them, right to where Jensen stood. Backlit by the headlights, Jensen stood frozen as her and Nicole's eyes met. It was like a car crash—she knew she should look away but she couldn't. Because in the backseat of a car, with her skirt hiked up and her top missing, Nicole was straddling a guy. And not just any guy, she was with Brent. Nicole was going to kill her.

Jensen turned to hightail it out of there but before she even took two steps Nicole was swinging the car door open, shouting "Wait!" She sounded panicked. "It's not what you think."

It wasn't a big deal, Jensen told herself. Lots of people hooked up at parties and Nicole could do whatever the hell she wanted. Then again, he was Grayson's best friend. Brent ran to

Nicole's side in the next second and Jensen looked between them, mouth gaping. Her mind was racing. What was Brent thinking? Nothing good came out of hooking up with his best friend's twin sister.

"Grayson doesn't know," he whispered. He glanced around like he was scared someone would overhear them. "I was going to tell him but–"

"I wouldn't let him," Nicole finished. "Please, keep this between us, Jensen. My brother doesn't need to know. He'll want an explanation. He won't understand."

Brent scoffed at her words, and before Jensen could say anything, they were arguing. "Don't you think enough people know at this point?" he challenged Nicole. "Can we finally drop the sneaky shit? First Davis, then Andrew, and now Jensen knows. Eventually, Grayson's going to find out."

"We're not together. There's nothing to find out," she hissed.

"Funny, because from where I was sitting, it sure as hell felt like we're together. Nicole, It's been weeks. I can't believe you're still denying how you feel. We're together, whether you're willing to admit it or not. We have to tell Grayson, I hate keeping this from him and I don't want him finding out from someone else."

"Jensen won't say anything, will you?" Nicole shot her a withering stare. Jensen shook her head, no. Even though she knew that if they didn't tell him, she would. "And I already talked to Andrew and Davis and they're going to keep their mouths shut, too. Besides, we've gone over this, and we're not together. I'm leaving at the end of the summer. Without a boyfriend waiting around for me, hoping I come back."

"Can we not get into this again?" He looked over at Jensen uncomfortably.

"We wouldn't have to if you'd finally hear me. You and I are NOT anything. We won't ever be anything. I was perfectly clear when this started. I'm leaving. I'm flying to the opposite end of the country in September. A relationship would be pointless."

"How can you call it nothing and pointless? Don't forget that I've been there for every moment we've shared. You're just trying to be mean."

Nicole's ferocity intensified. "Well, that's me, a cold, heartless bitch. I've never pretended to be anything else. Why are you with me if that's not what you want?"

"I'm not with you. You've made that perfectly clear," he shot back and before she could respond, he stormed away.

Nicole hustled after him. She stopped and turned back to Jensen. "Please don't say anything," she begged, looking desperate. Jensen couldn't seem to form words. Her mind was still processing everything that played out in front of her. She nodded, and Nicole turned and ran after Brent.

Jensen stayed in the parking lot until Brent's truck pulled away. Then she went looking for Andrew so she could tell him she was ready to go.

"Jensen!" Andrew's friend hollered, and the rest of them chorused, "Jensen!" excitedly.

"Have you guys seen Andrew?" she asked.

"He left with some chick. Why do you need him?"

"You don't need him. You can chill with us. Be my good luck charm this time," another guy said.

She declined his offer and went searching for Nicole. When she found her, Nicole was drowning her sorrows. "Maybe you should chill out," Jensen said, "You're supposed to be my ride."

"Change of plans." Nicole threw back a shot. "Andrew took my car."

"How are we getting home?" Jensen asked.

"Don't worry about it. We're here now and we'll get home eventually. I've got it covered. Can you please just be cool and not be a total buzzkill."

Jensen was stuck, and she could freak out about it, or enjoy herself like everyone else seemed to be doing. It was crazy and irresponsible and in that moment it also felt right so she smiled and asked Nicole, "What are we playing?"

Sometime later, she was throwing up behind a tree and regretting her choices. Someone was holding her hair back, whispering that it's going to be okay and she'd feel better soon. It was a guy's voice that was comforting her and she thought it was Grayson. She said his name, and the guy corrected her, "No, Jensen, it's me, Davis."

"Davis?" She leaned on the tree so she could look up at him. "Oh yeah, tattoo face."

"Well, that's a lovely nickname," he laughed.

"Where's Grayson?" she asked, looking around. She was sure she heard his voice.

"He's back at home. He didn't come tonight, but don't worry, I'm here to bring Nicole home and I can take you, too."

Davis helped her up, and somehow they made it to his truck before she hurled again. He helped her onto his bench seat where Nicole was already inside waiting for them. "She's still crying," Jensen felt compelled to acknowledge, telling Davis as if he couldn't see Nicole for himself. "Her and Brent got into a fight. I think it was my fault."

"I don't want to tell you what to do," Davis offered. "But if you want to survive this drive home, it might be best if you don't talk to Nicole."

"Gotcha," Jensen winked and whispered, "I think she hates me." Which made Davis laugh.

Nicole surprised them both by answering. "I don't hate you, but I'm not about to let you back into my life just for you to leave again. I'm not going through that shit again."

"I'm never going to leave like that again." Jensen rolled down her window, desperate for fresh air.

"And don't break my brother's heart," Nicole demanded in a mumble.

"I won't," Jensen promised.

When they pulled up to the house, Nicole asked Davis if she could crash on his couch. It was not even midnight, and her mom would still be awake. Davis agreed and offered Jensen, "You want the other couch?"

Remembering when Lucy had to take care of her the last time she got drunk, she refused. She didn't want to be a burden to Davis. He'd already have his hands full with Nicole.

"Are you going to be okay on your own?" he asked.

She hiccuped and nodded. The hiccups were disgusting. Each one tasted like puke and made her regret all her choices. Davis parked in his driveway. As she walked next door, she focused on keeping a straight line. She had almost convinced herself that she was sober enough to hold a conversation with Lydia when bile rose in her throat. She rushed to the planter next to the door and released the remaining contents of her stomach.

"Nicole, is that you?" Lydia's voice came from inside and Jensen heard her footsteps approaching. She stumbled down the front steps and ran around the side of the house.

On the side of the house in Lydia's garden, she called Grayson in a panic. The phone rang four times before he finally answered in a grumbly, sleepy voice, "Hello?"

"Grayson," she tried to whisper but ended up shouting his name, "it's Jensen. Can you help me?"

"Jen?" His voice instantly became more aware, "are you okay?"

"I'm outside in the garden, but your mom is downstairs. '*Hic.*' I don't know how to get in. '*Hic.*' Can you help me?"

"Are you drunk?" His voice was disbelieving.

"I was drunk. I don't think I am anymore. I think I extricated all the alcohol from my body. Is there a word for that period between being drunk and being hungover because I think that's where I'm at?"

"How did you get home?" he asked.

"Davis."

"Can you make it around the house? Meet me on the grass outside my room."

"Yeah, and Grayson, can you bring me some mouthwash?" she pleaded, getting him to laugh.

Crouching down, she made her way around the back of the house. It was covered with windows, offering views of the lake from every room. The windows were normally one of her favorite features, but at that moment she despised them. She lost her balance as she snuck past the living room and fell face-first into the dirt. In order to avoid falling again, she crawled the rest of the way. When she made it to the grassy area in front of Grayson's room, he was already there, waiting. He laughed when he saw her crawling. There was dirt caked on her pants, on her palms, on her face and in her hair.

"You can stop crawling now," he told her and pointed at the closed blinds on the windows next to her. Grayson offered her a hand, and she let him help her up.

Grayson's original plan, for them to scale the side of the house and climb into his bedroom window, was no longer an option. Jensen was too drunk. Instead, they walked out to the dock and she nearly fell into the water as it swayed back and forth with the waves. Grayson steadied her. With his help, she made it to the end. They sat and Grayson handed her the mouthwash. She swished for a full minute, the minty taste a relief to her taste buds.

After she spit into the lake, he took off his sweatshirt and handed it to her.

She thanked him as she pulled her arms through the holes.

Instead of pulling it over her head, she laid it across her body like a blanket. The water hitting the dock sprayed them, shooting a chill down her spine. She pulled the sweatshirt up over her cheeks and nose and took in a deep breath of spearmint, coconut shampoo, and woody aftershave. "This is the best thing I've ever smelled."

Grayson laughed and then asked, "Why did Davis give you a ride instead of Andrew?"

"Andrew left with some girl. He didn't have his car there, so he took Nicole's. I guess he was assuming we would get a ride home with Brent because that's who brought him. Then Brent left and Nicole and I were stranded, so she called Davis."

"I thought you didn't drink much. Were you upset about the breakup?"

"I don't drink when I'm sad. I'm not my mother," she bit out at him. "And no, I wasn't upset. Why would I be upset about that?"

"I don't know," he bumped his foot against hers, teasingly, "he was your boyfriend, Jen. It would make sense for you to be sad."

"We shouldn't have been together in the first place. Do you know it took him months to convince me to give him a chance? I never really thought of him as more than a friend. There was never this constant need, you know, like there is with you." She looked over at him to see if he was following and he looked back at her, stunned. Maybe she said something wrong, but the word vomit was still coming. "Besides, the sex wasn't very good. We never clicked in that department. You know what I mean? I used to think I just didn't like sex but I don't think that's the case anymore. It was just boring. Nothing like it would be with you."

Grayson nearly choked on his tongue. She was saying the words he'd been wanting to hear all summer. But they came out slurred, and he knew she was only saying them because she was drunk. Also, she kept comparing him to her ex and he didn't want to be a rebound.

"Sometimes I wonder what it would be like to have your hands on me," Jensen was still rambling. "I could never finish with Eric."

Desperately trying to steer the conversation in a different direction, Grayson asked, "So, is the breakup going to change things? I'm just asking because it seems like this whole doctor plan was more his idea than yours."

"I could be a doctor," she answered stubbornly. Then, she hiccuped again, making her resolve much less convincing.

"Of course you could," he agreed. "But do you want to?"

"I don't know what I want," she whined, and it was true. "I'm the one who picked Stanford and I think I still want to go. But the reason I picked it was for their swim team and now that I'm retired I'm not sure if it's where I want to be. Everything is so undecided."

"Then be undecided," Grayson encouraged.

"That's the opposite of what Eric would say," she giggled. "He put me in a cage. When I'm with you, I don't feel like that. I feel like I can do anything."

He liked that he made her feel free, but he couldn't get past the comparison to her ex *again*. Was the only reason she liked him because he was the opposite of Eric?

Once her hiccups had subsided and Grayson was confident in her ability to climb the trellis, they walked up to the house. The trellis was covered in vines spotted with yellow flowers and she stopped to admire them. Grayson stayed behind her in case she fell, but she made it without his help. She did, however, damage a good amount of the vines. When she got to the over-hang outside his window, she waited for him there.

He popped open his window and climbed in first instructing her, "Try to be quiet and careful of the lamp."

Jensen followed after him, disregarding both his instructions and falling ass first into his room. It wasn't some romantic fall either, like you see in the movies. She wished she could simply fall into him, stare into his eyes and share a perfect kiss. Unfortunately, she wasn't nearly that graceful. Her ass hit the floor, her feet found the lamp that he'd just warned her about, knocking it over, and her head collided with his bedside table

"Ouch!" she shouted, rubbing her forehead as she stood up on wobbly legs.

"Here, let me see." Grayson moved her hand aside and used his fingertips to brush the hair out of her eyes. There was a small red mark on her forehead, and he carefully ran his thumb across the inflamed skin. "Does this hurt?" he asked as his fingertips grazed her temple. She shook her head, and Grayson's hand slipped down her cheek. His hand was so large it covered her entire cheek and jaw. His fingers curled into the hair at the nape of her neck and he pulled her towards him.

Jensen's heart raced and her eyes fluttered closed. It was finally happening. He was going to kiss her.

With purpose in his eyes, Grayson leaned down and his lips met her forehead. "There. All better."

When he pulled away, Jensen slowly opened her eyes, lifting them to meet his. But Grayson's eyes were hooded, staring unabashedly at her lips which had parted. She didn't dare move while he lingered there, entranced. He let out a long, rattled breath then leaned in again and softly pressed his forehead against hers. "You should get to bed."

With shaking hands she reached out and wove her fingers through his belt loops. She pulled him along with her as she stepped back until her calves hit his bed frame. Then she lowered herself onto his mattress and tugged him toward her. Grayson took a step closer and his breath hitched as Jensen's fingers unhooked from his pants and slunk under the hem of his shirt.

"I have this thing about your abs …" she said, leaning in and kissing his stomach.

"Jen," He said her name as a frustrated moan, "We can't"

"Can't what?" she challenged, "You said to go to bed and I'm in bed."

"You're in my bed."

"Do you want me to leave?" she asked, terrified that he was about to reject her.

He knew the right thing to do was to send her to her own bed but he read the self-consciousness on her face and he couldn't send her away. After a long, drawn out breath he said, "Scoot over."

She did as she was told and moved over, making room for him. When Grayson crawled in next to her she rolled to face him. "Hi," she whispered with a goofy smile on her face.

"Hi," he whispered back, shaking his head. His mouth crooked up at the corner. Lying on his back, he crossed his arms over his chest and didn't let himself turn to her. His bed was small and he already knew how close she was. If he turned toward her and their breath mingled between them, he'd lose his damn mind. He was already hanging on by a thread.

"So, we're in bed." Jensen said, her voice huskier than it was a moment ago. Against his better judgement he glanced over. She was propped up on one hand and as soon as their eyes met she beamed. She wet her bottom lip with the tip of her tongue, and his eyes darted there, hungrily. Intrigued by his reaction, Jensen unabashedly bit her bottom lip.

He groaned. "You're killing me, Jen."

Between his words and the tortured look on his face, Jensen was filled with a boost of confidence. It was exactly what she needed in order to do what she'd been wanting to do since the first time their eyes met that summer. She leaned in, waiting for him to come the last inch, and to her mortification, he turned away.

She looked so hurt, he felt the need to explain himself. "It's not that I don't want to. I do. Badly, but–"

She didn't let him finish his sentence because that reassurance was all she needed. It urged her on, and before she could overthink it, she sat up and crawled on top of him. She kissed his stomach again as she crawled her way up his body, throwing a knee over each side of his waist until he was trapped beneath her. When she started to lower herself down on his lap she looked at him, searching for a sign that she was out of line, but instead his eyes were staring at her hungrily and his hands gripped the sides of her thighs, hard. She pushed into him until there was no space between them, then she rocked her hips against his length.

He lined up with her perfectly.

She whimpered at the feel of him even through her jeans, and the noise triggered a deep guttural sound from Grayson. She was pretty sure that groan was one of euphoria and the pipe she felt pressed up against her was a clear sign that he was enjoying himself. But not a second later, he was sliding her off his lap and standing up.

He wiped a hand across his face. "We can't do this now." He looked apologetic. "Not like this."

He left the room, giving some bullshit excuse that he was going to grab her water and Advil. She knew he was just trying to put distance between them.

Grayson walked out and fell back against his bedroom door, running both hands across his face. "Fuck," he said, stopping himself from turning around and going back to her.

He wanted to spend the rest of the night kissing her. It didn't feel like she was too drunk but he wasn't willing to risk it. The things she'd confessed in her drunken ramblings made him hopeful that his feelings weren't as one sided as he initially thought. From the way she was talking, it was possible that she wanted him just as desperately. He was right to walk away, there was no way any of those confessions would have slipped out if she were sober.

He walked downstairs to get her water, his mind spinning. There was no rush, there were still several weeks of summer. She just ended a relationship that was moving too fast and he didn't want to make the same mistake as her ex. But if she really felt that way about him too, they could make this work. Their schools weren't too far apart, an hour at most. They could see each other on weekends.

He had to force himself to slow down. She might not even remember this in the morning.

Grayson headed back upstairs with water and meds in hand, resolved to act like nothing had happened. She'd be embarrassed if she knew some of the shit she said to him. Jensen was a runner and he couldn't risk her running scared before he got a real chance. No, he'd keep being her friend and let things play out naturally.

As he climbed back into his bed, Jensen stirred. She should get up and go to Nicole's room but she couldn't talk herself into moving. She rolled to the side and Grayson's intoxicating scent hit her again. A wave of tiredness overcame her, and she snuggled into his sheets and pulled his comforter over herself. After burying her face deep into his pillow and taking a deep breath, she drifted off to sleep feeling completely relaxed.

Grayson, however, wasn't able to relax at all. He stayed awake the rest of the night, thinking about their almost kiss as he watched her sleep. It was okay to stare, he decided, since she'd been the one to crawl into his bed. She looked adorable and hilarious as she slept, dead to the world, with dirt on her face and leaves still in her hair. At one point, he tried to untangle a leaf, but she swatted him away, so he left it there and let her sleep undisturbed. Around 6:00 a.m., he climbed out of bed and busied himself cleaning his room.

Grayson was the first thing Jensen saw when she opened her eyes. He was sitting on the floor next to the bed, folding a t-shirt. When he saw that she was awake, he smiled and handed her two Advil. It wasn't until she saw the two bright blue pills that she realized how badly her head hurt.

"What time is it?" she asked as she sat up and rubbed her eyes, thankful that he had the lights dimmed.

"Almost 8:00," he told her and she groaned.

He folded the last two shirts and put the pile of clothes away. She watched him move around his room, not saying anything. When he finished, he sat down next to her on the bed. She had to pull her legs into her body so he wouldn't sit on them.

"Nicole's not in her room," Grayson said. "I thought you guys came home together."

"We did." She rubbed her eyes again, trying to silence the pounding behind them.

"So, she didn't go home with Brent?" he asked.

Her eyes went wide, causing her head to throb further. "You know about them?"

"Of course I know," he chuckled. "I know the two of them better than anyone. Suddenly, they're spending all this time together. I'm not an idiot. It's not like they've been particularly subtle."

"Thank God. I'm so glad you know. I found out last night and Nicole begged me not to tell but I knew I couldn't keep it a secret from you."

"I would have broken you if you'd tried," he laughed and shoved her playfully. "You're terrible at keeping secrets. You wear your emotions all over your face."

"I totally would have broken," she admitted. "But to answer your question, no. She didn't go home with Brent, I think she crashed on Davis' couch last night."

Without even knocking, Lydia peeked her head in. "Jensen, are you in here?"

Grayson and Jensen both whipped their heads around to face her. "Would you mind coming downstairs? We need to have a little chat about last night."

"Last night?" she asked nervously.

"Andrew and Nicole texted to tell me they were both staying at their friend's houses last night. You're the only one who made it home. Since you're covered in dirt, I'm assuming you know something about what happened to my garden? Before you try to make up an excuse, you should know we have cameras."

"Yes, ma'am." Jensen looked down at her hands, embarrassed.

"Do we also need to discuss why you're in my son's bed?" Lydia stared at Grayson.

"Nothing happened, Mom," he said so nonchalantly that Jensen almost believed him. Did she just imagine throwing herself at him? There was no way. She could still feel the memory of their almost kiss.

"You're still an accomplice." Lydia placed a hand on her hip. "Don't pretend you're innocent." She directed her focus back to Jensen. "I'll see you downstairs," she said, leaving the door open behind her.

13

"I CAN'T HELP BUT BE A BITCH, IT'S MY DEFAULT SETTING." —NICOLE

L ydia was waiting for Jensen when she got downstairs. She sat on the couch and Lydia passed her a cup of coffee. Putting the mug to her lips, she hoped the caffeine would help nurse her hangover, but after swallowing a large sip, she grimaced. The coffee was too warm to qualify as iced coffee and too cold to warm her up. She set the mug down and fidgeted under Lydia's scrutiny, searching for her voice. "I'm sorry."

But Lydia waved her apology off, shaking her head. "I've raised three teenagers. I know these things happen. A few trampled flowers aren't the end of the world. I'm glad you all got home safely." She took a sip of her coffee and Jensen slumped in relief. "That being said, you will make it right before our 4th of July barbecue. I expect you to replant my flowers and you will purchase them yourself."

"I think that's reasonable," Jensen said, trying to sound responsible despite her behavior last night.

Hours later, after a large, hot coffee and another round of Advil, Jensen headed out to the dock and stretched. She bent to touch her toes, and with her head upside down, between her knees, she heard someone step onto the dock behind her. She opened her eyes and saw Grayson walking towards her. He had an awkward smile on his face and a towel in his hand. She stood up quickly and turned around.

"I think I'm ready for that race," he said, dropping the towel he was holding.

"I'm not up for it today." Jensen said. "I'm just doing a few laps."

"So, what you're saying is I might actually stand a chance?" he teased.

"In your dreams." She waited for him to say something about last night, but he just started stretching. She couldn't look at his body without thinking about the way it felt snuggled up against her in bed less than twenty-four hours ago.

He'd hinted a few times that he was into her, but maybe he was just a big flirt because last night when she'd thrown herself at him with all her inhibitions out the window, he'd shut it down. And now he was acting like nothing happened.

Without warning, Grayson quickly counted down "three, two, one. Go!" Then dove into the water. Even with the head start, it wasn't close. Jensen outswam him in three separate strokes.

As they laid on the edge of the dock afterward, catching their breath, Jensen got lost in her thoughts. She was so desperate for him to reach across the sliver of space between them and touch her. She thought about his lips, wishing they would explore her body. She wanted to feel his teeth on her inner thighs and his warm breath between her legs. Last night was fuzzy but she was pretty sure she had begged at one point.

She looked over at Grayson and he looked back. Yearning, that was what he must've seen in her eyes.

He desperately wanted to reach out and touch her. The need

overwhelmed him. Their eyes held each other and he smiled crookedly. "What are you thinking?" he whispered.

She couldn't divulge the whole truth without being sure he felt the same. So, looking up at the blue sky, she told him a small truth. "I want to stay here forever."

"I don't know about forever," he laughed, "but at least until school starts."

She flushed, glad he misunderstood. Thankfully, he didn't know what she really wanted was to stay right there, on that dock, in that moment, with him forever. It was a moment of desire, sunshine, and the spray from the lake. It was perfect and if she could, she would bask in it for the rest of her life.

Over the next few days Grayson swam with her whenever he could. On days he got home late, she'd already be in the water and he'd wait for her on the dock until she finished. They talked about everything under the sun. Sometimes their conversations got deep, like how she was coping with the loss of her grandparents, or how Grayson was struggling to find common ground with Nicole, which used to come so easily. Other times they'd be in tears from laughing so hard at the most ridiculous stories, most of which revolved around Lucy's antics. Mostly they talked about what they'd taken to calling 'the lost years'. Through all their conversations, Grayson didn't make a move. He didn't even try, despite her constantly staring at his lips. Some days she felt like she was going to combust because of how badly she wanted him.

As they lay out on the dock one afternoon, she wondered aloud, "How did you get so into boats?" This had become their new normal. Every afternoon they'd lay out in the sun and talk for hours.

She realized in the past month working at The Marina with Grayson and Brent, that they were the ones everyone went to with their questions. There wasn't a tier system at The Marina, but if there was, they'd be at the top.

"It was Brent who got me interested in them," Grayson explained. "When we first moved here, I was looking for a job. No one would give me one because I was too young. Brent and his Grandpa Doug overheard me asking around town. Doug came right up to me and handed me a business card with his name and phone number on it. The card was for his plumbing company 'Sierra Plumbing', so I thought I was getting a job fixing toilets or something. He wrote his home address across the bottom of the card and told me to have one of my parents call him that night and to be at his house at 7:00 a.m. the next morning."

"Turns out, he had hired me to help repair his old yacht. He was too old to do it on his own so he hired me and Brent to help. We spent the entire summer together learning about boats from Doug. The next summer I applied at The Marina and Phil hired me on the spot. He told me he couldn't ignore a recommendation from Doug. I've worked there every summer since."

After their conversation about Grandpa Doug, Grayson realized he hadn't spent any time over there since getting home from school. So, the following day after work, he and Brent headed over for a few hours giving Jensen a free afternoon to work on Lydia's garden like she'd promised.

Lydia wrote a list of all the plants she needed to purchase and gave her directions to the nursery in town. Luckily, Reed was working there and with his help she found everything on her list easily.

She carried her purchases around the side of the house to the garden and found Lydia waiting. She was wearing one of her signature aprons and had an extra one for Jensen. While they knelt in the sod together, Lydia talked about her family. Jensen asked her how she met Joe and she told her how she backed into his car in a parking lot in Chico. That was where they lived after they left Atherton and before they moved to Evergreen. She told her all about meeting Joe and how everything moved quickly between them. Lydia and Joe knew what they wanted, and they weren't willing to wait once they found it. The kids got a new stepdad, a new home, and a year later, a new brother.

Nicole wouldn't even give Joe a chance at first. She thought the only reason Lydia married him was because she was pregnant. Nicole was so jaded that she threatened to move back to live with her father.

"It wasn't the wedding or the fact that I got pregnant right away that upset her. I think the move to Evergreen is what did it," Lydia told her. "She hates living so secluded from the rest of the world. She plans to travel and live in an iconic city like New York, or maybe even Paris someday, surrounded by art and culture. It's where she feels like she belongs."

While on the topic of Nicole, Lydia encouraged Jensen to try to work things out with her. Jensen wasn't sure they'd ever be able to fully work through their differences: she and Nicole were complete opposites, but she promised Lydia she'd at least try.

She hadn't talked to Nicole since the night of the party. She wasn't even sure where she went every day. Did she work? Did she have friends outside of the regular group of guys that hung around the house? Jensen hadn't really put any effort into getting to know her. So, after finishing the garden, she sought her out.

Lydia gave her the address of the coffee shop where Nicole worked in town. She said if she wasn't there, she should check with Andrew or Grayson because they usually knew where she was.

When Jensen pulled up to the coffee shop, it was already closed. It had small town hours, only open five hours a day on weekdays.

Nicole's car was still in the parking lot, so she pulled up next to it and waited.

Ten minutes later, Nicole exited the building with another girl who made her way to a cute convertible across the parking lot. "See you tomorrow, Jaime," Nicole hollered at the girl. Then, she froze when she saw Jensen leaning against her car. "What do you want?"

"I was hoping you'd be free to hang out," she said lamely.

"I have plans with Brent," Nicole said. "Why aren't you following Grayson around like usual?"

"He and Brent went to Doug's house after work," Jensen explained and she saw the moment Nicole realized her plan to use Brent as an excuse no longer worked.

"Great, so you're basically only here because Grayson's busy." She rolled her eyes and got into her car.

"Where are you going?" Jensen raised her voice over the car's engine.

Nicole rolled down her window. "What?"

"Where are you going?" she repeated. "Can I come?"

Nicole didn't look thrilled, but she eventually agreed they could hang out back at the house.

Jensen pulled out of the driveway behind her and when Nicole turned into the gas station, she continued on to the house to wait for her. After she parked in the driveway, she lingered on the porch until it was clear that Nicole wasn't coming. She made her way up to Nicole's room, disappointed that her efforts were useless. She was just going to have to try harder. Was she really expecting her to accept her offer of friendship on her first try? No.

She was reading when she heard a car pull up to the house. Looking out Nicole's bedroom window that looked at Davis' house, she saw Nicole going into his garage.

She closed her book, worked herself up to try one more

time, and headed downstairs. When she stepped onto the front porch, she could hear Nicole and Davis talking in his garage. She stepped closer to listen.

"She's just so fucking perfect now. It pisses me off. And the way everyone is falling all over themselves to get her to like them. I mean, Grayson and I used to be inseparable over the summers. I don't get to see him or Andrew when they're away at school. The summers are supposed to be ours. She shows up out of the blue and now everything's changed."

"I don't think you're being very fair." Jensen heard Davis respond from inside the garage. "Didn't you say she doesn't have any family? Take it from someone who knows what that's like; she needs you guys. This world isn't meant to be navigated alone. And as far as her being perfect, I can't believe you of all people would judge her based on her appearance. I thought you were better than that."

"You're right, I know you're right," she said, her voice laced with emotion. "I tell myself that I'm being irrational and I'm not being fair, but then when I'm around her, I can't help but be a bitch. It's my default setting."

Davis laughed, breaking up some of the intensity.

Jensen turned and went back into the house. She didn't want to be caught eavesdropping. At least that explained why Nicole was always mad at her.

A short while later, Nicole came into her room while Jensen was reading. Usually, they didn't hang in there, but to her surprise, Nicole sat down at her easel and started pulling out paints. She put a few strokes on her canvas before clearing her throat. "Sorry for blowing you off this afternoon."

"That's okay," Jensen responded. She wasn't sure she would have forgiven her so quickly if she hadn't overheard the conversation with Davis. But, admittedly, she wouldn't like it if someone showed up and monopolized all of Grayson's time, either.

"If you still want to hang out, we're going cliff jumping at Shelby Falls tomorrow," Nicole said. "You could come."

"That sounds fun," Jensen said, trying not to sound too excited. "Count me in."

The next day, they drove over to the trailhead together. They didn't fit in one car, so everyone hopped in the bed of Davis' truck. Reed climbed in and introduced a local girl he brought with him. It was the same girl that Jensen had seen leaving the coffee shop with Nicole the day before.

"Hey, where's Andrew?" Reed asked, and the girl next to him scoffed. Reed gave her a funny look and then texted him. A second later Andrew replied.

Go without me.

Grayson reached out a hand, helping Jensen climb into the back of the truck. Nicole rolled her eyes, probably thinking Jensen was too prissy to climb into a truck on her own. No matter what she did, Nicole seemed to have a negative reaction. Jensen ignored her and turned to thank Grayson. She asked if they were going to get in trouble for sitting in the truck bed, but everyone assured her that the sheriff was chill. He was an ancient man who didn't care what they did, as long as no one complained and no one got hurt.

They parked in a turnout along the Feather River. Jensen wondered how they were going to manage the hike with all the stuff they'd packed. Thankfully, the trail was short and even carrying a cooler, towels, and other supplies, they got to the falls in less than ten minutes. They hiked down a steep trail and when they crested the last turn they emerged next to a perfect little swimming hole. There was a set of small, wide waterfalls pouring into the sparkling, blue water. There were a few people already on the sand. They made their way past them to set their stuff down.

Reed and his friend immediately stripped off their over clothes, and ran for the water. Davis was busy unfolding the chairs he'd carried, leaving Grayson, Nicole, Brent, and Jensen on the sand putting on sunscreen. Brent rubbed sunscreen over Nicole's back and shoulders, leaning in and kissing her on the neck once while he did it.

Brent had finally told Grayson what was going on between him and Nicole earlier that week, while the two of them were at Grandpa Doug's house. Brent said it was a strategic move on his part because there was no way Grayson would punch him in front of Doug.

"You want me to do your back?" Grayson asked, coming up behind Jensen, his mouth millimeters from her ear.

"Sure," she squeaked out, the hair-raising on her arms and the back of her neck, nervous but also excited for him to touch her. They swam together daily and she always put her own sunscreen on so she was pretty sure he was looking for a reason to touch her.

Grayson picked up the bottle of lotion and Jensen slid off the straps of her cover up dress and let it pool around her ankles. She was wearing a bikini for the first time all summer instead of her normal sporty two piece. She heard Grayson's intake of breath when he saw it.

He put his hands on her lower back first and she felt a shiver roll up her spine. "Is it cold?" he asked, his warm breath still right in her ear.

"It's fine," she replied. The temperature had nothing to do with the sensation flowing through her body.

His hands ran up the length of her spine and dipped momentarily under the tie on her bathing suit. She put all her effort into not letting on what his touch was doing to her. His hands slid low again, his finger massaging the lotion into her skin. Ever so slightly, he dipped his fingertips under the ties at her hips. "Just want to be thorough. Is that okay?" he asked.

Words evaded her, so she was forced to answer with a nod. She was so hot she could melt into a puddle in his hands. How badly she wished she could press against him and find out if he was feeling what she was, but they weren't alone.

She forced herself to step away from him. "I think I need to cool down," she murmured and she heard him chuckling as she ran for refuge, not stopping until she was completely submerged in the cold water.

14

"DON'T FORGET TO USE PROTECTION" —
ANDREW

Chaos ensued in the days leading up to the 4th of July. Lydia was doing everything in her power to keep the house clean, snapping at anyone who left so much as a sock on the ground. Grayson and Jensen had been working double shifts at The Marina because of the holiday. Nicole was feverishly working on framing her prints and putting the finishing touches on her newest piece. It was her first time getting a spot at the Art and Wine Festival in town and she was overwhelmed getting ready for it. Andrew and Joe spent most of their time readying the trucks and dirt bikes for the town parade. Not knowing what to do after work, Jensen occupied the time keeping Avery, Dustin, and Julia entertained.

On the 4th, Phil scheduled short four-hour shifts, giving Grayson and Jensen just enough time to make it to town for the parade.

Andrew's truck was decked out with flags, bows, ribbons and Avery's dog, Oreo-Hotdog, who was in the bed sporting a new look. He was entirely covered in red, white, and blue. "What happened to you?" Jensen scratched him behind his ear. "Did somebody paint you?"

"It's just sidewalk chalk," Avery held up a bucket of the stuff. "I drew stripes on the driveway and then had him roll over on top of them. Doesn't it look cool?"

"Very cool." She stopped petting the dog, realizing a good amount of the chalk has transferred to her hands. She dusted them off on her legs, leaving smeared chalk handprints on her thighs.

"You want me to get that off?" Avery picked up a water gun and Jensen backed away, laughing.

"I think I'm good."

"Parade's starting soon," Andrew hollered from the driver's seat. "Hop in."

Grayson helped her into the bed of the truck, which was full of super soakers and large buckets of water. There were towels laid out, so the bed didn't get too slippery, but they were already soaked.

"I probably shouldn't have worn white," Jensen stated as she looked down at her plain white tee and denim shorts that Nicole helped her pick out that morning. She also helped her with her hair, pulling it into two French braids and then topping off the look with a red white and blue bandana rolled to act as a headband. Nicole also lent her a tiny American Flag bikini that she said she wore last summer. Jensen put it on to appease her, but she had no intention of letting anyone see it.

They drove at a snail's pace down Main Street. Some people threw candy out to the crowd, others launched confetti. They hosed people down with water. It was a hot day in the high nineties and the crowd welcomed the refreshing spray. The kids in the crowd loved it. Some even called out to them asking to get sprayed and others ran alongside the truck.

By the time the parade ended, Jensen was drenched. Grayson, seeing her predicament, ran over to his jeep and pulled out his Marina Staff t-shirt. "I wore it this morning, so it's not exactly clean, but it is dry." He held it out to her. She pulled it over her head, inhaling deeply as she did.

As soon as the parade was over, they found Nicole in the park under a white pop up at the Art and Wine Festival looking entirely overwhelmed. She was trying to talk to three different customers at once. She directed one woman over to Grayson and he jumped in to help without hesitation. When an entire family entered the tent right behind them, Nicole turned to Jensen and asked, "Where's Andrew?"

"He left right away," she replied. "He said he had plans."

"What about my dad?" she asked. It took Jensen a second to realize she was talking about Joe. It was the first time she'd heard one of them refer to him as 'Dad' and it threw her off.

"He went back to the house with Lydia to help set up for the barbecue. But I can help."

Nicole looked at her like she wanted to refuse, but they both knew Jensen was her only option. Plus, she was already there.

Nicole's tent was exploding with art. She was selling hyper-realistic charcoal portraits. There was an entire wall of example pieces she'd done. She handed out business cards and relayed commission prices. There was a table of shirts and hats with the same watercolor mountain range and her handle @Nicole-ReesesPieces. She was so professional when she talked to customers.

Jensen didn't know what to say to the customers, but thankfully Nicole's art sold itself. She just had to keep customers interested long enough for Nicole to swoop in and take over. They kept it up until the crowd from the parade started to disperse and they were finally able to breathe.

Grayson and Jensen were sitting in the folding chairs and Nicole was talking to the lady working the booth next to them when Davis walked in.

"Hey man, what are you doing here?" Grayson waved him over.

"I just got off work. Avery is running around here somewhere. I came to pick him up. I knew Nicole had a booth, so I thought I'd check it out while I'm here." He wandered into the tent.

Davis walked up to the wall of charcoal portraits. He wasn't looking around at all the faces, he was transfixed on one. It was a portrait of a woman with long hair blowing in her face. The woman had her head tilted down and her mouth open like she was laughing. It was a great, raw, piece of art. The woman looked gentle and beautiful. There were laugh lines on her forehead and crow's feet by the sides of her eyes.

Nicole walked over to see what Davis was looking at. "I love this picture." She nodded at the woman's portrait. "When we moved into the house, I used to paint in the garage. I was seriously lacking inspiration, and I knocked all my paints over in frustration. This was before I had a job, so I couldn't just go out and buy more on a whim. So anyway, I was crawling under the workbench, trying to pick up all my shit, and I found this picture taped to the underside of the counter. Something about it spoke to me and I knew I had to draw her. My paints were all ruined and the only material I had left in my supply was some charcoal."

"She is the first portrait I did. I spent weeks perfecting it. Ever since then, I've considered her my muse."

"How much?" Davis asked.

"Excuse me?" Nicole asked in a shaky voice. "Didn't you just hear my story? She's special, and not for sale."

"I'd like to buy it." He'd already pulled out his wallet.

"Why would you want it? I promise you it means a hell of a lot more to me than it will to you."

"I highly doubt that," he said, his voice stoic and his eyes watery as he whispered, "because that's my mom."

"W- What?" Nicole's voice was more like a gasp. She reached out and removed the piece from the wall. She stared at it, noticing the resemblance for the first time, then she handed it to him.

A slight smile appeared on his lips as he whispered, "It's incredible. It looks just like her." A tear fell down his cheek, but he didn't care that they were all watching him. He pulled out a stack of cash and held it out to Nicole. "I know it's not enough for something that's so important to you."

"No Davis, I can't take your money, not for that."

"I know how hard you've been saving for New York. Just take it." He continued holding out the cash.

"Why don't you work it off?" she offered. "I could use some help here and that way I can let these guys leave." She nodded toward Jensen and Grayson.

"Deal," Davis agreed. "Avery will want to stay longer anyway."

Grayson offered to stay in case they needed help cleaning up, but Nicole told them Brent would be off work before the fair ended and he'd help. This gave Grayson and Jensen two hours to walk around before they had to get back. As they checked out the other booths, Grayson kept finding reasons to touch her.

One booth was selling Lake Evergreen hats. Jensen tried on about ten before deciding which one she wanted. She'd never been a baseball hat wearer, but maybe she could be. She picked out her favorite one and turned to ask Grayson what he thought. He reached out and pinched the bottom of one of her braids where it was tied right at her collarbone. "You always look cute." He twirled her braid, making his fingertips graze over her skin. His eyes scanned down her body, from her flip-flops up to her denim shorts, to his oversized Marina shirt she'd borrowed, and finally to the hat. He tugged her braid teasingly before adding, "You know, you sort of look like a local."

He didn't know it but that had been one of the best compliments she'd ever received. She smiled the entire time he paid for the hat, and wore it proudly for the rest of the day.

As soon as they got back to the house, Lydia shoved plastic table cloths at Jensen and told her to cover all the tables. She directed Grayson to help Joe with the fire. An hour later, the tables were all festive. There was a bubble machine going, patriotic music playing, and red, white, and blue adorned everything just in time for guests to arrive.

The guys jumped right into a game of cornhole, leaving Nicole and Jensen sitting at a picnic table together.

Jensen asked her how many paintings she'd sold. But Nicole only answered with a shrug and a single word, "some."

"That was cool of Davis to stay and help so we could walk around. I'd never been to an Art and Wine Festival before. It was fun."

Again, a one word response, "cool."

She kept trying, desperate to find some common ground. "Grayson bought me this hat. He says it makes me look like a local," she laughed. "I guess I've come a long way from the Vineyard Vines dress I showed up in five weeks ago."

Nicole turned to her. She stared at her hat and then rolled her eyes. "You don't look like a local, you look like a rich girl trying too hard to fit in, which you still don't." Then she crossed her arms across her chest and turned back to watch the cornhole match. But she mumbled, "Why are you even talking to me?"

"I thought maybe we could try to be friends again," Jensen tried not to let her voice tremble.

"I have plenty of friends. I don't need more. Especially not ones who have a track record of disappearing from my life. I haven't heard from you in seven years and then suddenly you're staying with us for the summer and you want to be friends? It's weird, and it's messing with my head. I don't even get why you're here?"

"I thought you guys invited me. I thought because you missed me?"

"Missed. Past tense. After a year without even one phone call, I got over it."

"You didn't want me to come?"

"I didn't exactly get a vote," Nicole huffed. "I didn't even know you were coming till you were already here."

"Do you want me to leave?"

"I want you to stop acting like everything's gonna go back to how it used to be. I don't even know you anymore."

"That's what I'm trying to do, get to know you."

"Sorry, but you missed your chance." She picked at something under one of her nails, acting like the conversation wasn't affecting her.

"That's bullshit," Jensen bit out.

"Excuse me?" Nicole froze, finally giving Jensen her full attention.

Jensen stood in response, full of rage. "You heard me, that's bullshit. I couldn't have missed my chance because you never gave me one. From the moment I got here, you've had a chip on your shoulder. Well, you need to get over it. When are you going to get that it wasn't my fault? I didn't want to leave. I would have done anything to stay. I was eleven! It was out of my control. I was sent away and I'm sorry that it hurt you. But have you ever stopped for a second to think about what it was like for me to have you ripped out of my life? I didn't just lose my best friend, I lost everything I loved. I'm trying so hard to find my way back to that person. Why won't you let me?" Looking up, she was unsurprised to find all four boys staring at them. She turned around just as the first tear fell, thankful that Nicole didn't see it. She stormed into the house and went straight upstairs. It felt wrong to go into Nicole's room. Instead, she opened the next door and entered the room, not even hesitating, throwing herself down on Grayson's bed.

He came in shortly after and laid down next to her. He pulled her into a hug and she curled into him, fitting perfectly in his arms. She had always hated being held, not knowing what to do with her long limbs, but with Grayson, it felt natural. Their legs tangled together and she folded into him, seeking comfort.

"She hates me," she mumbled into his chest.

"She doesn't hate you." He sounded so sure. The soothing circles he drew on her back didn't slow for a second.

"She just told me she doesn't want to be friends."

"Jen, listen. She doesn't hate you," he repeated. "You being here is confusing for her. She took it really hard when we lost you. She hasn't had a best friend since we lived in Atherton. It's been hard for her to let anyone else get close after that. Even in relationships, she always ends things quickly. See how she is with Brent, never giving it a real shot. She's scared. She's used to people leaving and so she doesn't let herself get attached so she won't get hurt. You being here brings up a lot of old feelings for her. She felt like you abandoned her."

"I abandoned her? It was the other way around. You guys moved away while I was at school without even telling me. I got home for summer break expecting you to be there. Your dad had to tell me you moved."

"What do you mean? Your gran said she told you. She said lowerclassmen were only allowed personal phone calls once a week to family members. Nicole asked to call you so many times. We all did."

"That was a lie and she didn't tell me anything," Jensen cried. "I asked for your new address and phone number, but she said she never heard from you again. You can't imagine the time I've spent missing you guys over the last seven years and wondering why you didn't keep in touch. I thought you forgot about me until I saw the cards."

"Jen, I'm so sorry." He held her until she stopped crying, all the while rubbing circles across her back. It felt like it took forever for her to calm down, but even once she had, she wasn't ready for him to let her go.

After a while he sat up with his back against the headboard. He pulled her up, positioning her between his knees, her back pressed against his chest.

He turned on his tv to a news station that was airing a 4th of July parade. They both agreed that the one in Evergreen was better. It may have been small, but it was perfect. As they watched, Grayson's fingers traced gentle, barely there shapes along her arms, making her baby hairs raise.

"Shit, did you see that?" He laughed about something on the tv but she had stopped paying attention to it the moment his skin was on hers.

"What?" she asked.

"The baton twirler just hit herself in the face," he laughed, but she was still distracted. Her mind was busy following the movement of his fingers. They were wandering down her arms, leaving a trail of goosebumps in their wake. His breath tickled her ear when he whispered, "Are you even listening to me?"

"I'm distracted." She blushed and she was glad he couldn't see her face from his angle.

"Do you want me to leave you alone?" He breathed into her ear, momentarily halting his hands.

She shook her head, swallowed roughly, and whispered, "No. Stay."

After a split second of consideration he lowered his head and burrowed into her neck. She felt him smile against her skin.

Then, fleetingly, the faintest touch of his lips just below her ear. "Jen ..." He spoke her name with such adoration it made her feel angelic.

She wanted him to say her name like that all the time, like a praise. She turned to look at him and he was right there. "Grayson ..." But she had nothing else to say. She didn't know how to form sentences with him so close. She turned her entire body around so she was facing him and he cupped the back of her thighs and pulled her onto his lap so she was straddling him just like before. Only this time Grayson didn't look unsure at all. He reached up and tugged her braid softly like he had earlier. "I like your hair like this."

The move was like a dose of cold water being poured over her. It reminded her of what he said right after tugging her braid at the fair. He'd told her she looked like a local, something that elated her until Nicole ruined it. She was suddenly brought back to how it felt to have Nicole tell her she'd never belong there. Was Grayson just being nice when he said that? Was he just being nice now because she was sad and throwing herself at him?

Worry lines formed across his forehead and his eyebrows scrunched as he examined her emotions changing before his eyes. "What's wrong?" One hand was still on her arm, but now it was tense. "Did I do something?"

"No," she answered so quickly she nearly cut off the end of his question. "I was just thinking about something Nicole said, and maybe this isn't the best idea?"

He pressed his forehead to hers. His fingers slipped off her arm and wrapped around her, his other hand found her hip. "Don't listen to her, listen to me," he pleaded with her. "How can it be a bad idea when it feels so right?"

His hand ran up her body until he was cupping her cheek. He leaned in and stopped a breath away from her lips. "Jen, I've been wanting to do this all summer." She felt the faintest touch of his lips against hers as he talked. "Tell me now if you don't want this because once I taste your mouth, I won't be able to stop. I've been waiting for weeks to make sure you feel the same and to not feel like a rebound. But I'm tired of waiting. I want you so bad. It's all I can think about–"

She didn't wait to hear more. She closed the gap between them.

Grayson kissed her softly, but with so much assurance. Sliding his hand behind her neck, he guided her one way and her lips parted in response. She was surprised by how much she liked him taking charge. His tongue teased at her lower lip tentatively before pulling back. Then he came back, kissing her harder, causing her to open for him again, and this time he was even more sure as he entered her mouth, the tip of his tongue meeting hers. The hand on her back wrapped around her and gripped the fabric of her shirt, making it ride up. She didn't know how he was able to do anything with his hands when she couldn't even think straight. Finally, she wrapped one arm around Grayson and slid her hand into the back of his shirt. He groaned at her touch, urging her on. Slowly, she slid her short nails down his back. Her other hand slid into his hair as he rolled her, so she was flat on his bed and he was on top of her.

He broke their kiss, "Is this okay?" his hand dipped under her shirt as he asked.

She nodded, and it was all he needed before he was diving in to kiss her again. Their lips found an exquisite, if not slightly frantic, rhythm as their tongues tangled together while they let their hands explore. She could feel the evidence of her need slick between her legs, but Grayson never ventured there.

He moved to kissing her neck as his hands snaked around her, grabbing her perfectly toned ass. He pulled her into him. As he ground into her, his mouth explored her neck and she let out a soft whimper when he whispered into her ear, "God, Jen, your body was made to be worshiped." He trailed kisses along her collarbone and in the hollow of her throat. His hands slid up her body, over her ribs then down her stomach to the top of her waistband. His lips trailed down her chest between her small breasts. Then he slid down until he was kneeling between her legs. He ran his hands up the long length of them. "From the first moment I saw you this summer, I haven't been able to stop thinking about these legs." He placed one of her legs on his shoulder and kissed her inner thigh. "So strong, and capable, and so fucking sexy." He kissed her a bit higher. "Did you know I have to stop myself from punching every guy that looks at you?" He nipped at her skin and she squealed out a giggle. "And of course, everyone looks at you because it's impossible not to." He kissed right at the inside seam of her shorts. "You're so fucking beautiful." He looked up at her with hooded eyes. "Surely you know how beautiful you are." She dropped her leg from his shoulder as he turned his attention to the other one, and as he kissed his way up it, his hands kneaded at her thighs, the motion loosening her always tight muscles. Every touch of his lips sent bolts of electricity straight to her core.

He moved up and kissed along the waistband of her shorts. He pulled on the button with his teeth and she lifted off the bed, pushing into him, encouraging him to keep going. She never wanted him to stop. He was driving her crazy. But he didn't undo her shorts. Instead, he made his way back up her body.

He kissed her lips tenderly once, tamer than before, she wanted him to be rougher. She needed him to be. Biting gently at his bottom lip, she pushed her hips up into him. He responded by grinding against her, his length rubbing against her shorts in just the right place. He pushed against her one more time, hard, so hard, and matched the roughness of her kiss, but then he broke away and rolled off of her.

They were both panting and had to catch their breath. Once she had, she looked at Grayson. He must have sensed her eyes on him because he turned a second later. She wasn't sure what to say, so she just smiled timidly. Grayson's grin wasn't nearly as shy, but broad and playful.

"Wow," he laughed.

"Yeah, wow," she agreed, giggling along with him.

Grayson wrapped an arm around her shoulder and pulled her into his side. The TV was still on and he went back to watching it, but he wasn't paying attention. He wondered if her mind was spinning as quickly as his.

Finally, Jensen asked, "Why'd you stop?"

"I didn't intend to take it so far in the first place," he admitted sheepishly. "I think we should take it slow." Grayson played with the hair at the end of her braid. "I want to be sure neither of us has any regrets."

The word lingered in the air between them. Regrets. It ate at her.

They watched an episode of a mindless sitcom. She wanted to ask him what he meant by having regrets, but somehow, she ended up on his lap again. He held her against him and rested his chin on her shoulder. Occasionally he speckled her neck with kisses while his hand traced a roadmap of every freckle on her thigh. His touch eased her worries. She'd never regret something that felt so right.

When the sky was fully dark, the crowd outside quieted and moved down to the water's edge to watch the fireworks. Andrew poked his head in the room and Jensen instinctively tried to climb out of Grayson's lap, but he held her there—one arm wrapped around her and the other planted high on her thigh, teasing the inseam of her shorts.

Andrew didn't look the slightest bit surprised by their position. He just said, "Fireworks are starting in ten minutes. A bunch of us are going out on the boat. You wanna come?"

Jensen looked at him questionably and he clarified. "There's a firework show on the lake that launches off the Peninsula. You can see the fireworks from all the lakefront houses, but the best view is from a boat."

"I don't think Nicole wants me there," Jensen answered.

"Who cares what she wants," Grayson retorted. "I want you there."

"I'm not feeling exceptionally social," she said as an excuse. "I don't want to be a downer while everyone's trying to enjoy themselves." She turned to Grayson, "You should go. I don't want you to miss out because of me."

"I've seen the fireworks from the boat plenty of times. I won't be missing anything. I want to stay with you."

Andrew backed out of the room. Jensen let out a small sigh, relieved that he didn't say anything embarrassing. Then he turned around, "Alright well, you kids stay safe," he chuckled. "Don't forget to use protection. If you need a condom, there's a box in my bedside table." He barely got the last words out before Grayson threw a pillow at him.

To her surprise, they didn't stay in their snuggled up position on the bed. Grayson slid out from behind her. "Come on," he walked across his room and popped open his window. "Just because we aren't going out on the boat doesn't mean we're missing the show."

Grayson tossed pillows and his comforter onto the roof before guiding Jensen out after them. They sat against the back of the house, snuggled against the pillows and wrapped together in the comforter. Something swooped down in front of Jensen's face and she shrieked, pulling the comforter over her head and moving as close as she could to Grayson.

He joined her under the blanket. Her eyes took a second to

adjust, but once they did, she saw the huge smile split across his face. He leaned in and kissed her softly.

When they broke apart, he didn't pull away, leaving their noses touching. "What was that?" she whispered.

"Just a few bats," he chuckled. "They're fairly harmless. I'm surprised this is the first time you've seen them. They come out every night."

"I always assumed they were birds," she whispered and her voice cracked, making him laugh harder.

He was trying to coax her out from under the comforter when they heard the first firework. Together they slid the blanket off their eyes, keeping it pulled up to their throats. Grayson held her tight the entire time and even after they saw the boat return to the dock, he didn't let her go.

Andrew was heading into the house when he caught sight of them on the roof. "Quit being antisocial and get your asses down to the fire," he called up to them. "It's my last night."

Andrew was leaving the next morning to work for his dad. It was the first dose of real life creeping into their summer and the thought sent a shudder down Jensen's spine. She wasn't ready to go back to reality.

15

"THIS IS NOT GOODBYE FOREVER" —ANDREW

J ensen woke up to her alarm far too early the next morning. She dragged herself out of bed, her wet hair a tangled mess atop her head. Ignoring it, she rushed downstairs, hoping she wasn't too late. When she got downstairs, the house was dark and silent. What else would she expect at 4:00 a.m.?

As she stepped onto the porch, Andrew and Davis looked up from where they were standing at the bed of Andrew's truck. They looked like they should've been strangers instead of the close friends she knew them to be. Davis was in his work boots, jeans, and a Sierra Plumbing T-shirt, a stark contrast to Andrew next to him in a pristine black suit.

"Fish, what are you doing?" Andrew walked toward her, offering a nod to Davis, which he took as his cue to leave. He climbed into his truck and pulled out of the driveway, leaving them alone.

"I came to say goodbye," she told him and he pulled her into a tight hug.

"We said goodbye last night," he reminded her.

They had stayed up late, sitting around the fire listening to

Davis play guitar for hours. Despite Andrew having to be up early to be at his new job by 9:00 a.m., they stayed until the fire was nothing but embers and Andrew still wasn't ready to call it a night. Nicole and Jensen put their differences aside and after Davis headed home everyone else walked out to the dock to stargaze. Laying on their backs, looking up at the stars, Nicole cuddled up to Brent, and Jensen cuddled up to Grayson. Reed tried to cuddle up to Andrew (so he wouldn't feel left out) and Andrew pushed him away, laughing. Brent stood up first, stripped down to his boxers and jumped in the lake. The rest of them followed. They stayed out until they were all shivering and desperate for warmth. Then, they sprinted up to the house in their underwear, laughing the entire way. When they got to the porch, Grayson grabbed Jensen and kissed her right in front of everyone. They all hooted and cheered as he deepened the kiss, making her smile against his mouth.

Jensen finally fell into bed around 2:00 but she knew Andrew had to leave at 4:00 and as fun as the night was, she didn't feel like she got a proper goodbye, so she set her alarm and fell asleep, her hair still soaked with lake water and a smile still on her face.

"You know you could still change your mind," she said.

Andrew laughed without any humor, "It's time I start being realistic about my future, Fish. I need to start taking my life seriously."

"I'm really going to miss you," she said and when she felt her eyes well up, she didn't hold back the tears like she used to. She just let them fall.

He grabbed her face in both hands and wiped away her tears. "Listen to me," he commanded. "This is not goodbye forever. You and me, we're not letting anything come between us again. You hear me? I'll see you soon." He kissed her cheek which was salty from her tears, and gave her a long hug, trying to convey how much he'd miss her.

After watching Andrew leave, she sat in the dark for another minute and was about to go back to bed when she heard someone crying. Walking toward the sound, she made her way to the side of the house where she found a pretty brunette, her hair tied up in a messy bun and freckles splattered across her cheeks and nose. Jensen's eyes went straight to the sweatshirt the girl was drowning in. The hoodie hung low on her petite body, covering her shorts, and the orange letters across her chest read: Boise State Football. She recognized it immediately as Andrew's, but the girl was a mystery.

"Are you okay?" Jensen asked. "He just left. I could call him and–"

"No!" The girl cut her off. "No. Don't call him," she said looking at Jensen with a strange mix of sadness and disbelief. "It was stupid of me to come. Don't mention this to him. Please?"

Her desperation made Jensen agree. The girl walked out to the Reese's dock and climbed aboard a small boat that was idling there, she glanced back at Jensen one last time before disappearing around the peninsula.

Jensen headed back up to her room and fell into a restless sleep.

The next day she was scheduled to work in the gift shop and although The Marina was busy for the holiday, as usual, the shop remained empty. Jensen cleaned the counter, swept the floor, and wiped down all the windows. She was tempted to pull out her phone even though Phil had a strict no phone policy. According to him, rule number one of boat safety was 'don't be distracted by your phone.' But, surely that didn't apply to her in the gift shop.

Instead, she played with one of the souvenir Yo-Yos on display. After a few failed attempts, she decided it was useless.

The Yo-Yo and her were never going to get along. Every time she was confident that it would come back up, it didn't. A few times she got it to return but she couldn't figure out what she did to make the damn thing listen to her. It was dangling at the bottom of the string and she couldn't get it to cooperate, so she swung her wrist around in a melodramatic fit just as Grayson walked through the door. He had to duck to avoid being hit.

"Sorry. Sorry. I'm so sorry." She gathered up the evil toy and the string. Grayson just laughed. "Is this how you greet all your customers?" he asked as he walked behind the counter and took a seat on her stool. "No wonder no one comes in here. You attack people at the door."

"Ha ha, very funny," she said unenthusiastically. "What do you want anyway?"

"I could sense that you needed my Yo-Yoing expertise."

"Are you an expert at Yo-Yoing?" she asked in disbelief.

"I have a Boy Scout merit badge for it."

She laughed at such a ridiculous statement, but stopped when she realized he was serious. "I can't believe you bought one of these." He fiddled with the light up toy, untangling the string.

"I had time to kill, so I decided to learn a trade."

"In what world is Yo-Yoing considered a trade?" He rolled up the string. Then, he effortlessly began to Yo-Yo. He did one trick and as the Yo-Yo swung back and forth between his fingers, he looked over at her. "What?"

"Nothing, I can see it ... You, as a Boy Scout."

"Don't make fun." He shot her a warning look.

"Oh, I wasn't going to. It kind of excites me. I like that you know how to tie a good knot," she grinned deviously at him, putting all kinds of imaginative thoughts in his head. The toy whipped around mid trick and he hit himself in the face. Cringing, he dropped it on the floor.

Grayson took two long strides toward her, crowding her space. He backed her into the wall until his entire body was pressing against her. His hands found hers and he guided them up above her head where he held them there. "Do you like being tied up, Jen?" His eyes were glowing mischievously and they followed the movement of her tongue as she wet her bottom lip.

She shrugged and let out a nervous giggle. "I don't know if I like it. I've never tried it." Her words came out timid.

He kissed her once, hard, his hands sliding down her arms and cupping her face.

The bell on the door rang, and they spring apart. Caught.

"What's going on in here?" Brent asked as he leaned on the doorframe.

"Nothing," Grayson answered nonchalantly. "Just checking Jen's teeth for cavities ... with my tongue."

"That's an odd talent," Brent laughed.

"You're both children." She glared at them, trying with all her might to not let her smile escape.

Grayson laughed and reached out, wrapping an arm around her waist, pulling her into him.

"Brent, get him out of here. I have ten minutes left of my shift, and it's impossible to get anything done with him hanging around."

Brent laughed and tugged at the back of Grayson's collar. He fell backward out the door and they both laughed at him. As they walked away, she heard Brent say, "It's about time, man."

Summer was halfway over, and Jensen never wanted it to end. She swam every morning before work and sometimes, if she was off early enough, she'd swim again before the wind picked up.

After swimming, most days she went to the meadow or out on the boat. She'd gotten pretty good at wakeboarding. After two tries, she stood up and since then she'd also tried knee boarding and tubing. They'd gone paddle boarding, kayaking, hiking, and even shooting.

For the most part she was down with anything the guys wanted to do after work except mountain boarding, that was a hard pass. Sitting on the picnic table, she watched as they rode mountain boards down the sloped lawn, across the dock, and jumped off a ramp at the end. They tried to convince her to join, but she was content on the sidelines. She was justified in her decision twenty minutes later when Reed emerged from the water with a split knee and a huge grin on his face.

Jensen couldn't fathom how he could smile with so much blood gushing from his knee. "Is he going to need stitches?" she asked Grayson, her face draining of color.

"Nah," Reed answered. "I'm sure Davis has some super glue."

"Excuse me? What?" She followed him as he walked up and around the house, blood now dripping down his shin. They all entered Davis' garage and he looked up from where he was working on a mountain bike, his hands coated in grease.

"What's up?" he asked.

"Busted knee," Reed answered and Jensen saw Davis's eyes flick down to the cut.

He walked over and grabbed a bottle of dish soap from a large plastic sink and tossed it to Reed, who caught it effortlessly. "Use the outside shower on the side of the house to clean up," he directed, then he washed his hands roughly.

Reed came back with a clean but still bloody cut. Davis tossed him a towel right out of the dryer. "Put pressure on it," he directed. "Get the blood to stop as best you can."

Reed showed Davis the wound after a few minutes and Davis nodded and pulled out a tube of superglue.

"Is this really the best idea?" Jensen asked Grayson. "You were a Boy Scout. Don't you ... like, know first aid?"

"Yeah, I do, but Davis has always been better at this kind of stuff. Trust me, he knows what he's doing."

She was watching Davis squeeze the superglue onto Reed's knee when her phone rang. It was Lucy and she hadn't talked to her in over a week, so she took a few steps away and answered.

"You'll never believe what I'm doing right now," she answered in lieu of a hello.

"You mean besides ignoring Eric's phone calls?" Lucy asked.

Jensen rolled her eyes and ignored her comment entirely. "I'm watching one of my friends super glue one of my other friends' knees back together."

"Excuse me? What?"

Jensen laughed. "That's exactly what I said. Apparently, it's a pretty common thing to do in place of stitches."

"Maybe *there* it is," Lucy argued. "But I'd go straight to Dr. Abby." She named her mom's plastic surgeon. "Now, what's going on with you and Eric?"

Jensen glanced around. She wasn't going to talk about Eric in front of Grayson, so she muted her phone and told him that she was going up to Nicole's room to talk to Lucy. He nodded, and she dashed into the house next door.

She didn't take Lucy off mute until she was upstairs, laying on her stomach on the trundle bed. There was so much to tell her. She wanted to fill Lucy in about Grayson, but felt compelled to downplay her feelings. She didn't want it to get back to Eric that she had moved on so quickly. But Lucy knew her too well and called her out on it.

"That's great that you're so into him. But have you really thought this through?"

"No, I haven't thought it through at all. That's what's so great about it. We don't have any plans, we haven't even talked about the future. It's the first time in years I've let myself live in the moment and embrace how I'm feeling right now."

"Yeah, I get that, but it's so not you. I mean, what happens in September when school starts? I'm just telling you what you'd tell me. You're always the practical one and I'm worried about you. You and Eric had so many plans. Are you sure you want to throw them all away? Have you and Grayson even talked about what happens at the end of summer? Are you guys staying together? Is this just a summer fling?" She let out a long exhale. "Look, I don't want to be a downer, but I feel like you're setting yourself up to get hurt. This thing with Grayson seems like fun, but it's not something to change your life over. It's not like you to be so impulsive or ignore your responsibilities. I mean, you haven't dealt with the house, or with your mom. Isn't that why you're in California? And what about Eric? What do you plan to do, never answer his calls? You've been friends for years and it feels like you're throwing that all away. I'm so happy that you're happy, I really am, but maybe just try to hold on to some semblance of reality. Eric knows he made a mistake, and he wants you back. You should at least hear him out."

Between Lucy's uncertainty and Andrew leaving, Jensen couldn't help but let a seed of doubt plant in her mind. Andrew clearly left some girl behind and Nicole seemed totally fine leaving Brent when she went to New York in a few weeks. Was that what Grayson thought this was?

Trying not to dwell on her newfound worries, she busied herself by opening her email. Lucy was right about one thing. She had been pushing too many responsibilities aside. Scrolling through over a hundred unread messages, she found multiple from the Stanford swim coach and some from Eric too, but she scrolls past them. She agreed with Lucy that she owed him a conversation, but she wasn't ready to face that yet. Even thinking about him felt like welcoming a gray cloud to block out the summer sun. It felt wrong. As she clicked through her emails she noticed some from her financial advisor and a few from the property management company but she scrolled past them as well. Her plate was beginning to feel very full.

Grayson knocked on the open door and she looked up at him and smiled. He told her they were all going to the meadow. She wanted to go, but she turned him down, showing him her inbox. Grayson offered to stay, but she encouraged him to go. "What are you going to do? Just lay here and stare at me while I read?"

"I like staring at you." He leaned down and kissed her casually.

Replying to emails made her feel productive. Lucy knew her so well and she was right, she needed to check things off her internal list. Next was the box of letters from Laurel, still sitting on the dresser. She'd only read the first one, and it was time she got to the rest. After Grayson left with their friends, she pulled out the box.

The letters were all addressed properly to her, but never mailed. They were all desperate pleas for Jensen to write her back and a few empty promises about how she would never repeat her mistakes. Jensen fought the urge to roll her eyes as she kept going, wondering why Laurel was so desperate for her to read them.

She got halfway through when she couldn't read anymore. They all said the same thing; Laurel was sorry, and she loved her. However, Gran was right, Laurel was manipulative, and she has a knack for playing the victim.

When she went to put the letters away, her eye caught something. She pulled the thin paper out from the bottom of the stack of remaining letters. It was a cut-out of a news article.

Hit-and-Run Atherton, C.A.—Authorities detained the motorist responsible for hitting 17 y.o. Black, female, Mercy Jackson in a hit-

and-run accident. The victim was struck head
on at approximately 1:35 a.m. on Sept. 2nd and
suffered extensive injuries. Officers received
an anonymous tip at 8:00 a.m. on Sept. 3rd,
which led to an arrest and confession.

She already knew the details from Laurel's first letter but it
was different seeing it in black and white. She tucked the article
back into the box and wondered how many lives Laurel would
ruin before someone put their foot down and stopped enabling
her.

She was no better than the next person. She was giving her a
place to stay and she couldn't even convince herself to regret
allowing it, because it was keeping Laurel away from her.

The following day, Grayson asked Jensen if she wanted to go
swimming and she refused. It wasn't that she didn't want to
swim. Usually the lake was her therapy, but maybe being alone
with Grayson was a bad idea. August was quickly approaching,
and she was already in so deep. Trying to guard her heart, she
said, "I'm actually feeling a bit lazy today. " She curled up in a
camping chair on the lakeshore with a book. After reading the
same paragraph three times and not comprehending a single
word, she looked up at Grayson, who was staring at her.

"What?" she asked, defensiveness creeping into her tone.

"Stanford doesn't excuse you from practice for being lazy,"
he challenged. "So neither do I." He scooped her up and flung
her over his shoulder, managing her weight easily. She wasn't
exactly small or easy to throw around, but he carried her like it
was nothing.

"Put me down," she laughed as she squirmed and playfully
hit his back. She wrapped her dangling legs around his waist as
he jogged down the dock to the water and threatened to drop
her in the lake. She was laughing, thighs gripping him tight, her

arms around his neck. "If I go in, you're coming with me." She squeezed her strong thighs even tighter. Grayson shrugged, pulled his phone out of his pocket, and dropped it on the dock. He kicked off his shoes.

"What are you doing?" she shrieked.

"Throwing you in the water," Grayson kissed her quickly, biting playfully at her bottom lip. When he pulled back, grinning widely, he stepped off the dock with her in his arms and they freefell. She was screaming and laughing as they crashed into the lake. They broke apart underwater and she popped up, still laughing and ready to enact her payback when a shadow was cast over her. She looked up just as Grayson surfaced behind her, wrapping his arms around her stomach. To her surprise and horror, someone was standing on the dock, staring down at them.

"Hey." Grayson let her go and swam over to the dock, pulling himself up. His clothes were drenched. He flipped his wet hair out of his eyes and gave the newcomer the once over. He looked familiar, but Grayson couldn't place him. "Are you looking for Joe?"

"Jensen, actually." He answered, watching her climb out of the water.

"What are you doing here, Eric?" she asked.

"Eric?" Grayson asked, stunned.

"Yes, Eric," he stepped between them possessively. "As in her boyfriend."

Grayson tried not to let his panic show but the guy standing in front of him bled wealth and confidence. He didn't just show up to talk to Jensen, he was there to get her back. And by the looks of him, Eric usually got what he wanted.

For the past two months Jensen had lived with Grayson's family, worked with him at The Marina and surrounded herself with his friends. He wasn't ready for that to end. He'd *never* be ready for that to end. But it was just occurring to him that while he had shown her every part of himself, Jensen hadn't done the same. She had an entire other life that he knew nothing about. A life she might be planning to go back to.

"Well, shit." Grayson grabbed a fist full of his own wet hair. He didn't introduce himself or say anything else. Before Jensen could process what was happening or deny that Eric was still her boyfriend, Grayson was shaking his head and walking away.

"I'll catch up with you in a sec," she called out to him. He didn't respond, he just waved a hand in the air in acknowledgment that he heard her and kept walking to the house.

16

"HARRY STYLES?" —LUCY

"You shouldn't be here," Jensen snapped at Eric as Grayson walked away.

"Clearly I should," he reached for her hand but Jensen recoiled. The silence grew uncomfortable between them. She wanted him to leave so she could go after Grayson, but Lucy's words came back to her. She owed him a conversation. If she walked away, she didn't know if they'd ever recover. Their friendship, all their history ... she'd be giving up everything.

As if he was reading her mind, Eric said, "My mom is here too. She's up at the house."

She couldn't imagine what Katrina must've thought of her. "But I still don't understand what you guys are doing here?"

"We came to bring you home," he said. "My mom came because she didn't want me to run into Laurel on my own. We went by your house because I thought you'd be there. Laurel told us where to find you. She looked good, Jensen, healthy. She apologized to my mom and asked us to tell you that she hopes to hear from you soon. My mom said she looked entirely different from the person she met in February."

Even through the awkwardness, there was a level of comfort

and familiarity with Eric. She could see it, the future they'd mapped out: graduating from med-school, getting married, living in the city until they started a family, then moving to the suburbs, but not too far from his parents. It was a plan they'd talked about at length, but now there was another option. A winding path veering into the unknown.

"I can't just pick up and leave," she said. "I have a job here and friends."

"We have a flight out of Sacramento tomorrow. We got you a ticket."

"You can't just buy me a ticket without talking to me first," she said indignantly. She wanted to jump back into the lake and swim until she cleared her thoughts and calmed her emotions. But she couldn't do that, she needed to talk to Grayson. He was probably waiting for an explanation.

She stepped away, but Eric reached out and caught her wrist. "Have dinner with me tonight?"

She cringed. "Eric, we broke up–"

He cut her off. "As friends. Have dinner with me and my mom. Please?"

"Maybe," she said, thinking of Katrina. "I'll text you and let you know." Then she jogged up to the house, leaving him staring after her.

She barged into the back door on a mission. "Where's Grayson?" she asked the first person she saw who happened to be Joe.

"He went upstairs," he answered.

She was desperate to get to him, but when she turned to thank Joe, she froze. Katrina was in the kitchen, sitting on the bench in the breakfast nook with Lydia.

"Jensen," Katrina only said her name, and Jensen was already crying. She rushed to her. As soon as Katrina stood,

Jensen wrapped her in a hug. Katrina squeezed her tight, only cringing slightly at the lake water soaking her Chanel blouse.

"I've missed you so much," Jensen mumbled into her hair.

"My girl, we've missed you, too. The distance has been hard on all of us. That's why we came."

Jensen didn't respond, unsure of what to say.

When she got upstairs, she changed into dry clothes. Quickly throwing on the first thing she found, a small crop top and yoga pants, before knocking on Grayson's door.

"Come in," he called.

She opened the door timidly, ready to find him fuming. But Grayson was just sitting on his bed in sweats and a t-shirt looking at his phone. He raised his eyebrows at her. "What's up?" he asked, like Eric showing up had no effect on him.

"I'm sorry," she started but she couldn't think of anything else to say so she just repeated, "I'm so sorry."

"So, are you guys back together?" he asked.

"What? No!" She stared at him, shocked. "Of course not."

"But he wants you back." It wasn't a question.

"He wants me to go to dinner with them tonight. But I won't if you don't want me to."

"You should go."

"What? Why?" Was it too much to ask for him to fight for her?

"You said you guys have been friends for years. I don't want you to have any regrets. I don't want to be your consolation prize and I really don't want you to resent me someday for being the reason you lost someone important in your life."

She nodded, tears at the corners of her eyes, but she didn't let them fall. "You're right," she said numbly. "I guess I should go."

She searched her luggage for something appropriate to wear. The cut-offs and t-shirts she'd worn all summer would stand out next to Eric and Katrina, who always dressed exquisitely. Even on the dock, Eric was in a nice polo and khakis. She settled on a black velvet mini, the same one Nicole had admired only weeks ago. It was hard to believe she used to wear that type of thing casually. The dress was tight around her waist but loose around her thighs. She couldn't wear a bra with it so she went without, thankful her chest didn't require one.

After drying and straightening her hair, she added a light coat of makeup and stepped into a pair of nude heels before heading downstairs where Katrina and Eric were waiting for her.

Grayson glanced up when she walked into the living room and his face slackened. She didn't even try to hide her blush as he looked at her. His eyes burned into hers, setting fireworks off in her belly. She had to look away. Eric swiftly leaned in and kissed her on the cheek, which was closer to her jaw since he was shorter than her, especially in heels. When she looked back at Grayson, he'd turned his attention back to his phone.

"You look beautiful as ever, Darling," Katrina said as she planted a kiss on Jensen's other cheek. "Is this the Channel dress you got at fashion week? It's adorable."

"No, this is Lucy's. It's from last season. Just a Chloe she picked up in Paris," she answered easily, falling back into the lingo she knew well. The dress fit in perfectly with Katrina's outfit, which was clearly expensive, and Eric's gray slacks and dark blue button-down shirt. His hair was parted loosely, the way he used to wear it. It made her nostalgic for a time when things were much less complicated.

They ate at a restaurant on the West Shore. Their dinner was delicious, and the conversation flowed easily. Eric and Katrina talked about their trip to Barcelona and Jensen filled them in on all the adventures she'd had that summer. She left Grayson out of her stories, out of respect, but she told them about her job and all the new things she'd tried.

She was having a good time until Katrina excused herself to take a call.

Eric saw his opening, and took it. "I miss you." He reached out and placed his hand over hers. "I miss us."

She slid her hand out from under his. "Eric, a lot has happened in the past month."

"You mean you and that guy?" he asked. "Look, I obviously don't like it, but I forgive you."

"There's nothing to forgive," she argued in a hushed voice so it wouldn't carry in the crowded restaurant.

"How about we just agree to put it behind us?" Eric offered, a bit taken aback by her newfound confidence. "We don't need to talk about him again after we leave."

"I don't think you're getting it—"

But he interrupted, "I'm in love with you."

While simultaneously, she finished with, "I don't want to get back together."

It was silent between them. One second, two, three. Eric fidgeted in his seat, the only sign that he was uncomfortable. Finally, he said, "I still think you should come home. Maybe we'll figure this thing out between us and maybe we won't, but you don't belong here." It was the same thing Nicole had said on the 4th of July and her stomach dropped. "Come home with us?" he pleaded.

When they got back to the house, Eric opened Jensen's car door for her. She stepped out and Eric closed the door behind her. He swiftly placed a small jewelry box in her hand. She looked down at the gift. "What's this?"

"Something I got for you in Barcelona," he explained. "I thought of you everyday I was there. Now, I need to say something and I need you to let me say it. I told you once on the phone and I know it was bad timing. I told you again tonight, but I don't think you really heard me. I love you. I'm in love with you. I have been since we were eleven years old. I'll wait for you if that's what you need. Please come with us tomorrow. Please give me a chance." He wrapped his arms around her, holding her tight. At first she just stood there awkwardly, her arms limp at her sides, but eventually she gave in and hugged him back. He was still one of her best friends. When they broke apart, he looked like he wanted to kiss her but decided against it. He just nodded once at someone over her shoulder before getting into the car with his mom.

"We'll be back at 8:00 a.m. to pick you up for the airport," Katrina said with a bright smile as they drove away, leaving Jensen frozen in the spot.

"What is it?" someone asked from behind her and she nearly jumped out of her skin. She thought she was alone.

She turned and saw Davis leaning against his garage-door frame.

"I don't know," she said. She walked toward Davis with shaking hands and opened the box.

There was a thick, white, glossy paper inside with fancy writing on it.

> *So you can carry the water with you, and it will wash*
> *your worries away. Love, Eric.*

The necklace inside was stunning. A diamond encrusted wave on a silver chain. She pulled it out and started crying. It was the most incredible gift she'd ever received. Eric knew her so well and loved her so much. He was off buying her the most thoughtful gift while she was falling for someone else. Guilt ate at her.

Davis peered over her shoulder. "Damn. Nice."

"He told me he loves me," she said. Not sure why she was telling Davis. "I don't know what to do."

"I think you do," he said. "You know, Jensen, you've changed a lot since the beginning of the summer. At some point, you have to make a choice. You can't be two different people. Either way, it's gonna suck and you're gonna lose someone. Just make sure that whatever you choose you can live with it."

"You think I should stay?" she asked for clarification.

Davis shrugged. "I'm not here to tell you what you should or shouldn't do. You need to make the choice that works best for you, not the one that makes the most people happy."

She hugged Davis and said goodnight, then walked out to the dock and sat there, contemplating his words. He was right, she had changed. She thought about all the new things she'd done. At school, she was stuck in a routine, never doing anything new or adventurous. She got perfect grades; she volunteered weekly, and she was responsible. The new Jensen was incredibly irresponsible. She hadn't responded to her emails, prepared for school, dealt with Laurel, or the house. Instead, she'd been kissing Grayson at work, going to parties and getting hurt doing stupid stunts. She wanted to be a responsible, good student, but she also wanted to experience life to the fullest. Those two versions of her felt like they were worlds apart. How did she choose between them?

When she finally went up to the house, it was late. She knocked lightly on Grayson's door, hoping he was still awake so they could talk. There was no reply. She pushed open his door and found his room dark and empty. She texted him: *Where are you?* But got no response.

She didn't sleep that night, tossing and turning and listening for Grayson to come home. As soon as the sun rose she got up, eager to find him so they could talk. She threw on her yoga pants, Uggs, and a sweatshirt and ran out to her car, speeding around the lake to The Marina. He was scheduled to open.

When she got there, she found Brent in the parking lot. "Where's Grayson?"

"Jensen, what the fuck is going on?" Brent took her in. Her hair was unbrushed, piled on top of her head, and there were dark circles under her eyes.

"He called out ... said he needed a personal day. What happened between you guys? He came over last night and said it's over."

"Damn it." She pushed the pads of her palms into her eyes. Trying to alleviate some of the headache that was creeping in. "Things are all messed up."

After filling him in on what happened over the last sixteen hours, she begged him for advice, knowing that Brent would be straight with her. She really needed that right then. "I'll give you my advice, but it's important to remember that I don't know shit about relationships. Just look at me and Nicole. We're a wreck. But I know Grayson, and he doesn't do 'messy'. You need to figure your shit out. Don't drag Grayson into it unless you're sure."

Eric and Katrina were at the house when she got back from The Marina.

Nicole came out the front door, dragging two of Jensen's suitcases onto the front porch. She had already piled the rest in the driveway. Eric and Joe are loading them into the car.

"Nicole, I–"

"Save it Jensen," she said. "We've all known you've had one foot out the door all summer. It's been just a matter of time. I mean, you never even unpacked. You were always going back to your real life."

"But Grayson–"

"Grayson's known all along," Nicole explained. "He knew it

was going to end. It's just happening a few weeks earlier than he thought it would. You don't take the summer girl with you into your real life."

Jensen felt her face drain of color. On the drive home from The Marina, she had decided to stay. Nicole's words left her questioning everything again. She tried one more time.

"I shouldn't leave things the way they are," she said. "I shouldn't leave without at least talking to him."

"Well, he clearly doesn't feel the same. He knows you're leaving, and he's not even here. Believe me, he doesn't care. You should just go. We're not eleven anymore, if he wants to reach you, he knows how." Nicole was shoving her out the door. Jensen was overtired, overemotional, and desperate for someone to talk to. For her, that person was in New York. She needed her best friend, so she let herself be guided into the car.

She called Lucy from the airport. "Guess who's going to be in New York tonight?"

"Harry Styles?" Lucy guessed, naming one of her favorite artists. "I know. I already have tickets."

"No," Jensen replied, "me."

"You? Why are you coming to New York? What happened?" Lucy asked.

"Why does something have to have happened for me to visit my best friend?"

"It doesn't, but I can tell that something did. Seriously, Jensen, what's going on?"

"I'll explain when I get there," she promised.

She didn't focus on everything she was leaving behind until she was seven thousand feet in the air.

17

"DAMMIT NICOLE" —GRAYSON

Brent called his best friend repeatedly after Jensen left The Marina. Grayson had been stressed the night before, and in his panic he'd told Brent that things with Jensen were over. But, by the way she'd responded when he told her that, he doubted it was true. Grayson was making something out of nothing and he had to tell him before she did something drastic, like leave. Unfortunately, with Grayson calling out, his workload was falling on Brent's shoulders. So, all he could do was hope that eventually one of his calls would go through.

The sun was high in the sky by the time Brent got off work and was finally able to track down his friend. It didn't take long. There were only a few places Grayson went that didn't get service. He spotted his Jeep and parked beside it in the small riverside campground. Then, he hiked down toward the spot he often heard Grayson talk about. He walked for so long that he wondered if maybe he was supposed to go upriver instead of down. But, just as he was considering turning around he heard the soft *clickclickclickclick* of a fishing rod reeling in.

Grayson had been fishing for a few hours. He'd needed to clear his head but he was confident that Jensen would find him when she was ready to talk. He just couldn't be in the same space as her ex any longer. When he finally heard footsteps approaching he let out a relieved sigh before realizing it wasn't her.

"Catch anything good?" Brent asked as he rounded the bend and found Grayson.

"What are you doing here?" Grayson bypassed his question, knowing Brent wouldn't have tracked his ass down for no reason.

"I think the real question is what are *you* doing here?"

Grayson shrugged and tossed a new line. "Just needed some time to think."

"Are you an idiot? Think about what? You and I both know you're crazy about her. Don't roll over and let the other guy win."

"That's not what I'm doing."

"That's what it looks like. Grow some balls and go get her."

"It's not that simple. She has this whole other side of her that I don't even know," Grayson said defensively. "What if this whole summer has just been some sort of escape for her? What if the girl I'm falling for isn't even the real her?"

"Sounds like you're making shit up because you're scared."

"I'm fucking terrified," Grayson confirmed.

"Of getting hurt?" Brent asked.

"Of her destroying me." Grayson dropped his head in defeat and as he did, his eyes caught on a shard of fire agate. He bent and picked it up, remembering the last time he'd been in that exact spot. He'd been with her. Jensen had been vulnerable with him, showing him every side of herself. She'd been angry, sad, happy, excited, hurt, and scared with him. It didn't matter if he didn't know every piece of her past, he knew her at her core.

"You'll never know if you just let her slip through your fingers." Brent was saying. "Take it from someone who has to watch the girl getaway. You don't want to go through it man, it fuckin' sucks."

"That's different, Nicole's leaving. Jensen isn't going anywhere."

"According to Nicole, she left for the airport a few hours ago."

"What?" Grayson pulled out his phone but he already knew what he'd find–he had no service.

"That's why I'm here man, to tell you she's gone."

Grayson dropped his fishing rod and ran back to his car. He couldn't believe she had actually gone with Eric. Yes, he had panicked and had been frustrated at the whole situation, but at no point did he actually consider that she would leave. It was his own damn fault too, he should have fought for her. Regrets overwhelmed him as he raced up the path. If he could go back in time he would do the last forty-eight hours differently.

As soon as he got back into service range he opened his favorite list and clicked the name at the very top. It rang and rang but she didn't answer. He didn't bother leaving a message, he knew she didn't check them. Instead, he hung up and called again, and again, and again as he drove towards town. Call it a hunch or call it twin intuition, but Grayson knew she had something to do with it.

He pulled into the coffee shop's small parking lot, slammed the door of his Jeep as he climbed out and stormed inside. "Where is she, Jamie?" he demanded of the girl behind the counter.

"It's for you," Jamie called into the back.

Grayson didn't wait for Nicole to respond, he made his way around the counter and pushed through the door that said employees only. His sister was sitting at the desk scrolling through her phone. He knew she'd been screening his calls.

"What did you say to her?" he asked as the door swung shut behind him.

"What are you talking about?" Nicole side eyed him, then quickly turned her attention back to her phone.

She was lying. He could tell by her lack of eye contact. "What did you say to Jen? I know her and I know she wouldn't have just left. You did something."

"First of all," Nicole sat up, finally giving him her full attention, "how dare you? Second of all, she was going to leave eventually anyway. You and I both know she was slumming it with us. She was always going to go back to her real life."

"So, what? You shoved her in that direction?"

"I was trying to protect you," Nicole countered, standing. "You were getting too attached."

"You weren't trying to protect me, you were trying to hurt her. You've had it out for her since she got here."

"Believe it or not, you're wrong. Everything I've done has been for you. From the moment she got here, you've been falling at her feet and I knew she would inevitably hurt you. And besides, Jensen's world goes beyond this tiny shithole town we're stuck in. She's got a famous best friend, a boyfriend who's a fucking Vanderbilt, and a swim career that's going to take her all over the world. She is bigger than this town and bigger than us and she was always going to leave us in her dust.

You're my favorite person in the whole world Grayson, and I couldn't just sit back and watch her hurt you."

"So *you* decided to hurt me instead?"

"I didn't mean to," her eyes welled, a vulnerability she only allowed in front of him. "You have to believe me when I tell you, that was not my intention."

He pulled his baseball hat off and ran a hand through his hair before putting it back on. Shaking his head, he breathed deep and dropped the tension in his shoulders. "You don't know her. You never took the time to get to know her. She wasn't slumming it with us, she was learning that there's something else out there besides the life she was stuck in. You of all people should get that since you feel stuck in the circumstances life dealt you."

There was a long pause between them during which Nicole contemplated her options: keep arguing her point, or concede and support her brother. A part of her still felt justified in what she'd done, but a bigger part of her just wanted his forgiveness. It was out of character but for Grayson she'd do just about anything. All she ever wanted was his happiness. So, she swallowed her pride and apologized.

"I'm sorry," she said barely loud enough for him to hear. "I shouldn't have said it."

"Said what?" Grayson asked. "What exactly did you tell her?"

"I told her something like, you knew she was leaving and you didn't care because she was only ever a summer-timer."

"Dammit Nicole," he huffed.

"I really am sorry," she whispered. "I'm sure you guys will figure it out. She'd be stupid to choose that tool over you."

"What? You think I should just call her up and beg her to come back. She's probably halfway to New York by now."

"Well, if this is really what you want, then go get her." She sat down and pulled her phone back out while Grayson thought. He could do it, there was nothing stopping him.

"Damn, not a lot of options," she said as she scrolled, "are you okay with two layovers?"

"What are you doing?" He looked over her shoulder at the travel site she had pulled up.

"Buying you a ticket of course." She rolled her eyes. "Can I just say how annoying it is that you're gonna make it to New York before me."

Grayson went straight to the airport, in his rush he didn't

even stop at home. But hurrying turned out to be unnecessary. His flight was delayed.

Jensen woke up in the guest bedroom at Eric's apartment the next morning to her phone buzzing under her pillow. It was Lucy. They hadn't seen each other yet because Jensen got in late. Lucy offered to bail on her plans, but Jensen knew she had been looking forward to that concert for months. "Hello?" she answered groggily.

"I'm coming to pick you up," Lucy announced. "We're going to breakfast."

"It's like 5:00 a.m.," Jensen complained.

"It's actually 8:00." She could practically hear Lucy rolling her eyes through the phone. "There's a time difference, remember? Anyway, I'm already on my way. Be ready in ten. I'll call you when I'm downstairs."

Jensen was used to getting ready quickly. She'd been doing it all summer for work, but that morning was particularly hard. Despite her exhaustion, she barely slept, second guessing her choice to leave and missing Grayson desperately.

She'd never second guessed her instinct to run before, but this time it felt wrong.

She was scared of Grayson getting too close, close enough to break her. It was easier to leave before that could happen. She knew she wouldn't be able to handle him leaving her at the end of summer. So, she went with the safe option. It wasn't until there was no turning back that she saw her mistake. She had been breaking off tiny pieces of her heart all summer and giving them to him bit by bit without even realizing it. Until she was on the opposite side of the country and she felt empty.

Putting on a pair of denim shorts and a tank top, she threw her hair in a messy bun and was in the middle of brushing her teeth when her phone rang again. It was Lucy. She was in the lobby waiting for her.

As Jensen rushed to meet her, she passed Eric's parents having breakfast in the dining room. John looked up from The Times and asked, "Going for a run?"

"No, I'm meeting Lucy for breakfast," she said.

"Hmm," Katrina crinkled her brows together. "What an interesting outfit choice for breakfast. I suppose you only have your lake clothes with you? Would you like to borrow something?"

Jensen looked down at her shorts. "I'm fine in this," she smiled and rushed out before she could second guess her decision. Self conscious, she examined her outfit in the elevator's mirrored door, but she looked how she always did. Sure, her shorts were too short, but what was so wrong with legs? And maybe her tank top showed a bit of a stomach but she didn't care about that anymore.

She saw Lucy across the lobby the moment the doors opened. Lucy was in an army green jumpsuit with a cinched waist and black strappy stilettos. Her makeup was flawless, and she styled her hair to perfection. She was holding a clutch and a tray with two coffees.

She rushed to Jensen and wrapped her in a one-armed hug, careful not to drop the coffees. It had been years since they'd spent so long apart. When Lucy finally released Jensen, she handed her a hot coffee.

"You're a lifesaver," Jensen mumbled between sips.

They linked arms and walked out of the building. "So, seriously, what are you doing here?" Lucy wasted no time in asking.

"Don't I get five minutes to wake up first?" Jensen pleaded.

"No, I've been waiting for the scoop since yesterday. Spill."

"I think, *maybe,* I'm in love with him," Jensen said into her coffee. It was the first time she'd said the words out loud, but she said them without hesitation.

Lucy gagged on her coffee. Then she spent twenty seconds

coughing, "Excuse me? Love? As in '*grow old together, I want to have your babies'* Love?" she asked.

"I'm not ready to have any babies," Jensen smiled, "but yeah, that kind of love."

"Wait, with who? Eric or Grayson?"

"Grayson, of course."

"Okay, I'm confused." Lucy fiddled with her necklace. "If you're in love with Grayson, then why did you just get on a plane with Eric?"

"I panicked."

"Oh my God, Jensen," she snorted, "I cannot believe you. You know, sometimes I really think you need therapy."

"Believe me, I've known that for years," Jensen laughed at her own expense.

"I didn't even know you liked this guy until a week ago and now you're in love with him? Wait, is he the reason you broke up with Eric? And I still don't understand what the hell you're doing here? What do you mean 'you panicked'?"

"Eric and Katrina just showed up. I was already in my head about Grayson and I freaked out. I couldn't think past the possibility of never seeing Eric or Katrina again. Eric was so understanding. You know how he is. He always knows exactly what to say. I felt guilty and then he gave me that ridiculous necklace and told me he loved me."

"Oh yeah, the necklace," Lucy lit up. "I helped pick it out. Isn't it to die for? If you're not into it, I'll gladly take it off your hands."

"It's stunning." Jensen admitted. "But don't get too excited. I'm giving it back to him."

Lucy pouted but moved on quickly. "So, back to your boy. *Grayson.*" She said his name like it was a dirty secret. "Tell me about him."

And so she did. She couldn't seem to stop talking about him

once she started. "... so yeah, now I'm all excited to see a salmon migration which I never thought I would care about before, but he makes it sound so exciting. He whips out the most random, fascinating facts all the time. He knows so much about the mountains and forests, it's really cool. And he's seriously good at everything. He's taught me how to do so many things and he's so patient with me when he's teaching me something new. But the thing is, even when he's not the best at something, he still makes it fun. Like, his sister is such a better wakeboarder than him and he never complains or gets frustrated. He still goes boarding all the time and cheers on Nicole. But then, when it is time to be competitive, he totally is. We race in the water all the time and he's determined to beat me one day. No matter what we're doing together, I always end up laughing and having fun. Even at work, I wanted to quit my job halfway through my first shift, but then I worked a couple of hours with him and I loved it. And now I love my job, even when it's boring, I'm able to enjoy it because Grayson showed me how. The other day I was totally bored while working in the gift shop, which is the worst position. Nobody ever goes in there. Anyway, I decided to learn how to Yo-Yo, which I know sounds ridiculous, but then Grayson came in and ... what?" Lucy was beaming at her, the biggest smile Jensen had ever seen on her face.

"You're seriously in love with this boy," she couldn't stop smiling. "Oh my God, Jensen, I've never seen you like this."

"It's bad Lucy, I can't stop thinking about him and I feel like I need to bring him up in every conversation which isn't cool since I'm staying at Eric's place and I don't think that would go over well."

"Have you talked to Eric about any of this, or is he still under the impression that he stands a chance?"

"I told him in California that I don't want to get back together. I reminded him at the airport that we're just friends.

But, he said he'll wait for me. I don't want him waiting around for something that's never going to happen. But I also don't want to lose him from my life completely."

"Well, what *did* you talk about?" she asked.

"I told him about my job and my new friends. He just kept saying that I've changed a lot."

"I don't think you've changed," Lucy interjected.

"You don't?" Jensen asked.

"Well, I mean, you're much more sure of yourself, and you seem like you're more comfortable in your own skin," she winked. "But you're still you. And I don't think those are bad things."

Lucy had always seen her for who she really was. It made her feel even more confident in their friendship and in herself. She thought back to sitting on the dock only two nights ago, trying to figure out which version of herself she wanted to be. Was Lucy saying she could be both?

The rest of the walk consisted of Jensen giving Lucy a play-by-play of her entire summer. After another block, they stopped and grabbed bagels.

"So, I still don't get what happened with Grayson?" Lucy asked.

"I came here."

"You mean you guys were making out one second all hot and heavy and totally into each other, and the next your ex shows up and Grayson is being totally cool about it, and then you just leave without any explanation?"

Jensen shrugged, and Lucy smacked her on the back of her head. "What was that for?" She rubbed the spot where Lucy hit her.

"You need some sense knocked into you." She took a huge bite of bagel then continued with her mouth full. "If you're in love with the guy, you tell him. Don't run off with someone else.

God, Jensen, you're like the smartest person I know, but you can be such an idiot sometimes."

"I can't tell him when I'm pretty sure he doesn't feel the same way."

Lucy stopped in her tracks. "What do you mean? You literally just talked for ten minutes about what a great kisser he is. I would say that's a pretty clear sign that he's into you."

"Yeah, for now." Jensen shrugged. "It's just what the locals do. They hook up with the summer-timers and when summer ends, they go back to their real lives and leave it all at the lake. I couldn't handle the thought of him leaving me. I watched it happen after Andrew left. A girl showed up looking for him and she'd clearly been crying and he didn't even wait around for her to say goodbye. And then there's Nicole and Brent. She's leaving him at the end of summer like it's no big deal. I got scared."

Lucy pulled Jensen into a hug right in the middle of the sidewalk. They got bumped by multiple people and sworn at twice before she released her.

Jensen thought she missed New York, but she hated how she couldn't even hug her friend without nearly getting knocked over. She was no longer used to the constant hustle and the insane amount of people.

"Get out of the sidewalk, fuckin' bitches," someone yelled from the crowd of pedestrians. Lucy threw up a middle finger before tugging Jensen along so they weren't blocking the sidewalk.

Jensen suddenly felt like the city was suffocating. "Can we go to the park?" she asked and Lucy obliged quickly.

Sitting in the park, they watched a guy play fetch with his dog. A group of elderly ladies showed up and rolled out yoga mats. They completed a series of impressive yoga positions but had to stop abruptly when the dog took notice and wouldn't stop humping one of the women. Lucy and Jensen found it hilarious and had to fight to contain their giggles. The ladies packed up and left and when they walked past, they overheard one of them saying, "That dog had such impressive persistence. It reminded me of my first husband, Byron," which sent them rolling with laughter.

Sitting in the park laughing with Lucy reminded Jensen why she used to love the city. Where else could you see a seventy-year-old woman get molested by a terrier while in child's pose, then compare it to her ex husband?

Once their laughter subsided, Lucy asked if she wanted to grab lunch. Jensen agreed and Lucy hesitated before adding, "Would it be cool if we meet Eric at the club?" She looked apologetic for even asking. "He just texted and I haven't seen him since he got home from Spain. He went straight to California to get you."

"That's fine," Jensen agreed, but a part of her didn't want to see him. Reluctance that she'd never felt before crept in. She'd been trying so hard to hold on to what they used to be, that she'd been ignoring the fact that things would never be the same.

At the country club, the manager stopped Jensen at the door. He pulled her aside and told her in a very professional voice that her attire was not in line with the dress code. He handed her a page of the club's dress policy and informed her she needed to dress accordingly in order to be permitted onto the premises.

Jensen started walking back towards the town car but Lucy stopped her. "Wait," she exclaimed. "I got this." She pulled out her phone and shot off a text.

Five minutes later, they were being led around the back and through the employee entrance by a cute, boyish waiter. He led them through the kitchens and they entered the restaurant from behind the bar. "Keep your legs under the table and you'll be fine," he told Jensen as they walked towards where Eric is sitting with three other guys.

Lucy tried to follow Jensen, but the waiter caught her around the waist and pulled her back. "So have I earned that date yet?" Jensen heard him ask.

"Fletch ..." she whined his name. She wanted him to beg. Lucy played with guys like they were mice and she was a lioness. This guy didn't stand a chance.

"Come on, Luce. Just one chance?"

"Tonight. I'll text you," she said, strutting away.

They quickly made their way across the room to where Eric was sitting with some school friends. Jensen rolled her eyes when she saw Brayden, he had always rubbed her the wrong way.

"Jensen ..." Eric's eyes went wide as he scanned her outfit. She wasn't sure how to act. She hadn't expected him to be with friends. Did they know about their breakup? "Baby, what are you wearing?" he asked, answering her internal question before she could ask it.

She slid into the seat next to him and shrugged. "Clothes."

"You better watch your girl, Eric," Brayden said, "people see her dressed like that and they're going to think you picked her up in one of the *special members'* rooms."

"Excuse me?" She crossed her arms over her chest and glared at him.

"I mean, your ass is practically hanging out of your shorts," he continued. "Eric, you let her dress like that in front of people?"

"Eric doesn't *let* me do anything. I have my own mind, thank you very much."

"You should've seen the place I dragged her out of," Eric laughed. "We went out to dinner one night and the nicest restaurant had plastic tablecloths. Nobody in that town had any perception of class. Her neighbor had tattoos on his face and he was literally covered in dirt and grime. You know what Jensen did? She made friends with him. I wouldn't be surprised if someday he murders his entire family. He looked the type."

"Davis is one of the kindest people I've ever met," she interjected. "How dare you talk about him that way! You don't know him or anything about him. He's had a hard life, both his parents died and–"

"There you go. He's already done away with them," Brayden laughed.

She stood so fast she knocked her chair over. "You guys are assholes," she announced loudly.

"Excuse me, Miss," she felt a hand touch her arm, and she turned to see the manager standing there with a frown on his face.

"Yeah, yeah," she shrugged him off. "I'm leaving anyway." She stormed out of the club with Lucy following hot on her heels.

"I hate that guy," Jensen ranted. "I don't know why you guys hang out with him."

"Better the devil you know," Lucy shrugged. "Braydon's an absolute dickbag, but Jensen, have you seen him? I know he was a total asshole to you and he's always brought out the worst in Eric, but I'd still totally use him for his body."

Jensen scoffed, "And you think I'm the one who needs therapy?"

Lucy laughed, but quickly sobered. "Sorry they said that about your friend." She thought for a second, then added, "And about your shorts. I don't think you look like a hoe."

Jensen laughed, "Hey, at least he called me an expensive whore. I'm sure the girls that service the members here make bank."

This made Lucy crack up, and Jensen's mood swiftly

improved. She refused to let those idiots get to her. They were ignorant. What really upset her was that she used to laugh alongside them. When she first met Davis, she was nervous, and she had avoided him. She wasn't any better than Eric and his idiot friends.

"I can't go back to Eric's house," she told Lucy an hour later when they were at her mom's place. Lucy was digging through her closet trying to pick an outfit for her date that night and Jensen was sitting on her bed, giving her opinion.

"You could always stay here," she called from deep inside her closet. "I don't think my mom's in town. What about this one?" She stepped out in a green gown. Jensen shook her head at it. Lucy nodded in agreement and dove back into her racks of clothes.

"I don't know why you're changing. The jumpsuit you're wearing earlier was perfect."

"Yeah, but he already saw me in that." She came out in a red strapless dress. "Too much?" she asked.

"Definitely," Jensen laughed. Not only was the dress comically long on Lucy, it was also a cocktail dress. "Do you even know where he's taking you? Try to remember he's a waiter. I doubt he's about to wine and dine you at Per Se."

"Oh, Per Se sounds so good right now," Lucy said, referring to her favorite French restaurant, even though it cost your first-born to get a table. "We should go before you leave."

"I don't think we'll have time," Jensen said. "I'm leaving tomorrow."

Lucy pouted. "So soon?"

"I shouldn't have come in the first place."

"Okay, well, if you're seriously leaving tomorrow, then we're not about to spend the evening apart. You're coming with me tonight."

"On your date? No way!" Jensen tried to refuse, but Lucy was adamant. "It's actually perfect," she smiled as an idea formed in her mind. "My mom's been trying to set me up with this guy named Peter for weeks. I'll have him meet us and he can be your date. You'd be doing me a huge favor and anyway, what else are you gonna do? Sit around here and mope? I don't think so!"

She unzipped the red dress and stepped out of it. They'd shared a dorm for seven years, so this wasn't the first time Lucy changed in front of Jensen. But when Jensen looked up, she gasped, "Lucy, what is that?" she asked, pointing. Tattooed high on her ribs was the word *Saucy* in loopy scrawl with a tiny bottle of hot sauce next to it.

"Oh, you know, just your typical act of teenage rebellion," she winked and shot Jensen her best saucy smile. Then she picked up the red dress that was pooled around her feet and tossed it at Jensen. "Put that on. It'll look better on you anyway."

They spent the next two hours pampering themselves. Lucy did Jensen's hair and makeup, just like old times. Jensen remembered her first day at the lake and how she let Nicole kill her confidence. She doubted herself, but as Lucy curled her hair into some intricate updo, she had to admit she liked getting dressed up. It was never going to be a regular part of her life, but it was fun occasionally. She shouldn't have let Nicole get to her.

When Jensen told Lucy what kind of date she could expect from Fletcher, Lucy took matters into her own hands. She asked him to meet them at one of her favorite restaurants instead of risking letting him choose. Heaven forbid she ended up eating diner food or found herself in a bowling alley having to wear rental shoes.

After meeting Peter, Jensen was quick to confirm that it was not an actual date. Lucy said not to worry about it, but Jensen wanted to make sure. Thankfully, Peter just laughed at her comment. He shrugged and said, "You're not really my type.

Don't get me wrong, you're gorgeous. But, I have a thing for hunky blonds. Think Chris Hemsworth or Brad Pit."

He had a boyfriend, but his parents didn't know yet. He was pretty sure they suspected, hence the reason for this date. She relaxed, enjoying talking to Peter. He told her all about his boyfriend and she gave him a full recap of the past few weeks and how crazy she was about Grayson.

"What the hell are you doing here? Girl, you need to go get your man," Peter said.

Jensen agreed, laughing and telling him she was catching the first flight out in the morning. He offered to let her charter his family's plane, but she refused. She'd already bought a plane ticket earlier that day. Fourteen hours wasn't going to change anything. Grayson was either going to forgive her for leaving or he wasn't. She couldn't even consider that it might be the latter.

Lucy's date was awkward. Fletcher had clearly never been inside such a nice restaurant before. He seemed uncomfortable and fidgety most of the night. Lucy seemed to get bored with their conversation, realizing quickly that they had nothing in common. She kept jumping into Jensen and Peter's conversation, ignoring Fletcher entirely. Jensen's phone rang and she was about to ignore it when she looked down and saw Andrew Reese's name on her screen. She excused herself from the table quickly and rushed outside.

"Hi, Hello?" She fumbled with her phone, trying to answer before it went to voicemail.

"Fish, what the fuck is going on?"

"Andrew," she said, relieved to hear his voice, "I'm such an idiot –"

"I'd say ... Where are you?"

"Manhattan," she answered, hugging her arms around herself when she got catcalled by a cabbie.

"Damn, you certainly know how to make an exit," he chuckled, then asked, "You're not staying with your ex, are you? I know you have better sense than to get back together with that guy."

"No, we're not back together. I'm staying at Lucy's."

"Where does she live? Not somewhere sketchy I hope."

"Andrew, her parents have an apartment on Fifth Avenue, across from The Met."

He laughed. "You say that like I'm supposed to know what you're talking about."

"Sorry, I forgot you've never been here. It's nice." A coat was draped over her shoulders and she turned and saw Fletcher next to her in a white button down tucked into faded slacks. His thrift store jacket was wrapped around her.

"Hey Fish, I have to go," Andrew said through the phone. "I'll call you later."

She agreed, and hung up the call. "Thank you," she said to Fletcher as she pulled the coat closed around herself. Her shoulders loosened as she unwrapped her arms from around her waist.

Fletcher put his hands in his pockets and replied with a shrug, "No problem."

"What are you doing out here?" Jensen asked.

Another shrug, "I should've known she was out of my league when she bribed the hostess with a handful of Benjamins just to get a table, huh?"

Jensen cringed. "Lucy is my best friend, but she has only ever known a life of privilege. Don't judge her too hard for being a product of her environment."

He let out a long, exaggerated exhale. "I think I'm gonna head out. I've got a long trip back to Brooklyn. You goin' back inside?"

She nodded and slid his coat off her shoulders. "Thanks again," she said, handing it back to him.

Fletcher nodded and started walking away down the street.

As Jensen stared after him she had the strangest feeling that she should join him, leave the high society frauds in her dust and walk away from it all. But, she turned and looked through the window of the restaurant and saw Lucy. She'd never abandon her friend but she wished Lucy would open her eyes to the new way she saw the world.

They were already walking the tightrope of a long distance friendship. If Jensen turned her back on the world of old money and country clubs, she worried their friendship would become collateral damage. It happened after high school – she heard about it all the time. People changed and even the best of friends lost touch. She was already losing Eric, she couldn't lose Lucy too. So, she walked back into the posh restaurant and pretended she still belonged.

18

"I MIGHT HAVE A SLIGHT TENDENCY TO RUN."
—JENSEN

Grayson was sitting on the steps of The Met, wondering if Andrew's directions had led him astray when a luxurious car with dark tinted windows pulled up in front of the building across the street.

Jensen and Lucy thanked the driver before climbing out of the car. As soon as they entered the lobby of the building, Lucy plopped down on a chaise and started unbuckling the straps of her heels. "Ugh," she groaned as she yanked them off. "I've been in heels for like fourteen hours and my feet feel like they're going to fall off." She tossed them on the floor and curled her toes, groaning.

Jensen bent down to pick them up and when she stood, she came face to face with Grayson.

Her eyes widened in disbelief before asking, "What are you doing here?"

"You didn't say goodbye," he answered with a crooked smile.

"You followed me to *New York* because I didn't say goodbye?"

"I wasn't about to let you disappear again."

He stepped towards her, the air between them growing thick.

It felt like an invisible cord held her there, entranced. She needed to find words but none came.

Dropping her clutch and Lucy's shoes, Jensen closed the short distance between them. Grayson's hands went up to her face, cupping it gently. Jensen wrapped her arms around him while he gazed at her like she was something precious and fragile before pulling her mouth to his. The world around them could have melted away during that kiss and neither of them would have noticed. Grayson pulled back fractionally and met her eyes. He kissed her once more, quickly, then wrapped her in his arms and pulled her into the most tender hug of her life. It said, *I missed you*, and *don't ever leave me again.*

"Grayson," she whispered into his chest as he squeezed her like he never wanted to let go, "I'm sorry. I never should've left."

"Especially without talking to me," he agreed. "What were you thinking listening to Nicole?"

"I panicked. There was so much happening and I needed my best friend," she explained.

"Well, at some point this summer you became *my* best friend," he whispered. "And I needed you."

She didn't know how to respond without word vomiting that she was in love with him, so instead she kissed him again, harder, hoping it expressed everything she didn't say. He sucked on her bottom lip making her gasp, then smothered that gasp with his mouth. His tongue caressed hers in a hungry, possessive way. It was a side of Grayson she'd only experienced glimpses of and the way he took control made a whimper slip out.

"Do you know what that sound does to me?" he growled against her mouth.

Somewhere outside their embrace, someone cleared their throat. Grayson pulled away, but he didn't let go. Fused together, they looked over at Lucy. She was holding her keys out to them, hooked on a perfectly manicured finger. "Take them. I'll take a walk around the city, maybe get a hotel."

"Lucy, you don't have to do that," Jensen said.

Lucy rolled her eyes. "Jensen, that boy just flew three thousand miles to tell you he loves you. I'm not an idiot. I know what happens next." She tried to pass the keys off to Jensen but she wouldn't take them.

"We could take a walk," Grayson said to Jensen. "I've always wanted to see Central Park. It'll give us a chance to talk, if you aren't too tired?"

"You want to go into Central Park after midnight?" Lucy laughed. "That's a good way to get murdered."

"You are such a tourist," Jensen chuckled. "We can go tomorrow. Where are you staying?"

"I hadn't gotten that far," he shrugged. "I don't even have a change of clothes with me. After Brent told me you left, I practically drove straight to the airport. I would have been here yesterday but my flight was delayed. Then I missed my connecting flight and I had to sit on standby all day."

"Why didn't you just call me?"

"Nicole said something about grand gestures."

"What happened to not listening to Nicole?" Jensen asked.

"Don't worry about a place to stay," Lucy interjected, placing her keys in Grayson's hand. "You'll stay here." She glanced down at her phone as it lit up. "I already have a place to crash and I'll come back in the morning with clothes for you from my mom's studio. I'm sure I'll be able to find something for you. You've got the right build for a model, would you ever–"

"No," Jensen cut her off. Then she slid her hand into his and pulled him toward the elevator, calling over her shoulder, "Thanks Luce."

"This is not what I expected when you said apartment," Grayson said when they stepped into the penthouse. He walked over to the grand piano and tapped out a simple five note melody. Then, he stepped up to the massive window that looked out over The Met.

Jensen stepped up behind him and wrapped her arms around his waist. She placed her chin on his shoulder and took in the view with him. "It's beautiful, isn't it?"

He took a few deep breaths. Her hands moved up and down with his chest as it expanded and contracted.

"What are you thinking?" she asked in a hushed voice.

He let out a long exhale before answering. "I flew three thousand miles to be here, and I would do it again to prove what you mean to me." He turned and pulled her against him. "But I need to know if *this* is what you want? I can't give you *this*." He motioned around them,"The lavish apartment, designer gowns, and the American Express black card. It's not who I am."

He looked down at her dress and took a step back. "You look gorgeous. This dress is dangerous." He ran his hands up either side of her waist, his thumbs brushing the undersides of her breasts, making them heavy. "But is this the life you see for yourself? I want you, but I'll never belong in this world."

"I've never felt like I belonged here either," she whispered, putting her head on his chest. "I forced myself to fit in to survive," she explained, "but I don't really belong here. I belong with you. My place will always be with you."

Grayson pulled her against him, his lips crashing into hers, roughly. His tongue plunged into her mouth and she opened for him, desperate for him to fill her again. Their kisses were urgent and needy, she'd never felt so out of control. As their kisses grew more frantic, her mind relaxed, and her body began to respond instinctively. She pressed herself into him as his hands explored her body. The thin, silk fabric of her dress left little to the imagination. His hand cupped one of her breasts before slipping around to her backside. His fingers dug into that firm muscle and he lifted her, swiftly turning them, then pushing her up against the enormous glass window. The long slit on her dress tore, completely exposing her up to her hip as she wrapped her legs around his waist.

Grayson pushed his hips into her, trapping her between him and the window. His erection pressed against her and she writhed against him. She could tell his size was impressive despite the denim cage confining it. Rubbing the apex of her thighs against the rough denim, she had to break away from their kiss to catch her breath. As Jensen panted, Grayson's lips found her neck. He bit her collarbone, then he bit at her puckered nipple through her dress. She grabbed his biceps tightly, her nails digging in as she threw her head back and whimpered his name. "Grayson, please."

He covered her mouth with his again.

His hand slid down until he found the exposed skin on the back of her thighs. Palming the skin possessively, his large hands covered a large expanse of her leg before roaming back up to her ass without the fabric of her dress as a barrier. She was obsessed with the feel of his rough hands on her soft skin. "Are you not wearing underwear?" he asked, cupping her bare ass.

"I am," she replied in a breathy, barely audible whisper.

His hand ventured higher until he connected with the thin string of her thong. "Holy fuck," he panted, sounding just as out of breath as she was. He massaged her high on her cheek, then snapped the elastic string against her skin teasingly. She bit at his bottom lip in response.

One hand released her ass, and he slid it between her legs. He rubbed her over her panties then pulled back, his eyes glazed over as he asked, "Are you bare for me?"

A second passed before she realized what he was asking, and when she did, she swallowed roughly and nodded. She'd gotten all her body hair permanently removed two years ago for The

Olympics. Grayson rubbed over her panties again and again until she was begging, "Please."

That one word was all he needed. The next time his fingers rubbed over her, he pushed the fabric aside, and slid one digit in. He went slowly, letting her adjust to his large hand and the sheer length of the finger inside her. When she moaned, he was tempted to add another, but she was so tight and he didn't want to hurt her. Instead his other finger found the ball of nerves at her center and he stroked it. As she rode his hand, a knot tightened low in her belly, and when he adjusted the angle, the knot unraveled.

She whimpered his name until the sensation was so much that she cried out, releasing her pleasure onto his hand. "Oh my God," she mumbled, holding on to him as she caught her breath. Then she slid down his body until her feet hit the ground. "That ... Wow."

"Yeah," he chuckled, "I know."

"I never knew it could be like that," she admitted, staring at him reverently.

His hair was a mess from her frantic grip, his flannel was wrinkled from the hours he'd spent on a plane, and his jeans sported a massive bulge, confining his still hard cock, straining against his zipper.

She reached for his belt and he stopped her before she could undo it. "Don't worry about it," he said.

When her face fell, he amended, "Believe me, I want you. There's nothing I want more. But I've been in airports for the past two days and I need a shower."

Twenty minutes later, after Grayson had showered and Jensen had borrowed a satin pajama set from Lucy's closet the two of them curled up in bed in one of the guest rooms. Jensen lay on his bicep, while Grayson mindlessly played with her hair.

"I talked to Nicole before I left," Grayson said.

"About grand gestures?" she asked.

"Yeah, but also about how she was the one who told you to leave. She said she tried to convince you that you were only a summer fling. I can't believe you bought that."

"Well, it made sense, Andrew left some girl behind, and Nicole has no problem leaving Brent. I guess a part of me just figured that's what you guys do."

"At what point did I ever give you the impression that I'm anything like my siblings?" he admonished, slightly annoyed to be lumped in with their dysfunctional relationships.

"It's not that you've ever given that impression," she admitted. "It's that we've never even talked about the future."

"I didn't know you wanted to. From where I stood, you'd already been in a relationship that had your whole future planned out and it put you in a box. I didn't ever want you to feel trapped with me."

"So, it's not that you don't see a future with me?" she asked, letting her insecurities show.

"All I ever do is think about a future with you. But I didn't want to scare you."

"I might have a slight tendency to run," she admitted sheepishly.

"And I'll always come after you. But maybe next time, you could choose somewhere a little closer than the opposite side of the country."

"Sorry," she whispered, leaning in to kiss him. She slipped the tips of her fingers into the waistband of his boxers but he stopped her just like he had earlier, causing her to pull back, with a curious look.

"There's no rush," he explained. "I don't want you to think that's why I came here. I'm not expecting anything."

She sat up, speaking with a newfound confidence, "Let me make this clear. I don't feel rushed, or pressured, or coerced. The opposite actually. I've been waiting for this and I don't want to wait any longer. If I don't get to touch you soon, I might explode." There was endless desire in her eyes. "I want you Grayson. I've wanted you for weeks, and I know you want me, too. Don't be respectful. Don't say what you think you're supposed to say. Just take what's yours. Because that's what I am. Yours."

Done hesitating, he rolled on top of her. "Okay, but me first."

"No fair, you already–" He kissed away her objection as he snaked a hand down her body and between her legs. She was ready for him, wet and pliable. He brought her right to the edge but just before she went over, he stopped, slowly pulled his finger from her folds and slid it into his mouth.

"You taste delicious," he practically growled.

"I want to taste you too," she pleaded. Grayson didn't need to be asked twice. He rolled onto his back and guided her between his legs. She was hesitant at first, staring at his briefs which looked like they were confining a monster of a dick. Jensen's hands shook slightly as she reached for his waistband. He could tell she was nervous but he didn't say anything, trusting that if it was too much for her she'd say so. Fingers hooked into the elastic band, Jensen slid his boxers down until he sprang free. She got her first look at him–pink and swollen. His shaft was long and graceful, topped with a round purpling head, and rooted with a small patch of hair.

Dare she say, it was–pretty.

She'd never thought too hard about penises before, it was just another body part. Not Grayson's though. His looked like it had been chiseled by a craftsman, custom made for her. After admiring it for longer than she'd like to admit, Jensen ran her hand down his hard length and gripped him tightly. Her touch constituted a loud groan from him, and not for the first time she was grateful that they were alone.

"Is this okay?" she asked as she pumped her fist up and down. He was big, so big that she wondered if it would hurt the first time. She'd only had sex a handful of times, and Grayson's length was substantial.

"Perfect," he whispered. Need written across his face as he watched her fist his cock. She licked her lips, contemplating her next move before she bent down and flattened her tongue at his base, licking up the long vein. She wrapped her lips around his head tasting a burst of saltiness. With a hand around his base, she continued pumping.

Worried that her inexperience would show, she looked up at Grayson to see if she was doing it right. He was watching her and when their eyes met he let out a long groan. Satisfied, she dropped her gaze but his hand quickly found her cheek. "Look at me," he instructed.

She released his head with a pop of her lips and looked up, "Sorry, I've never done this before."

Her admission seemed to agonize him. "You're perfect," he whispered.

"I want you to show me what you like," she encouraged.

Then, with a devious smile, she lowered her mouth back onto him. She worked her mouth over him, watching his reactions to see what he liked. Grayson reached his hand out and grabbed a handful of her hair. He hesitated a moment making sure she wouldn't reject his guidance, and when she didn't, his grip tightened and he thrusted into her. Slowly at first, but when she didn't pull away, he thrusted harder. She felt him all the way in the back of her throat. He was close, she could tell by the way his movements became erratic and his legs tightened up.

"I want to get there together," he tried to object but there was no stopping the momentum.

"We will," Jensen said, popping him out of her mouth, still

pumping him with her hand. "But right now, I want to taste you."

She barely had time to wrap her mouth back around him before he was pouring himself down her throat. "Fuck," he groaned as he watched her swallow every drop of him. Throwing his head back, his heart racing, he tried to come back down to earth.

Jensen crawled up the bed and snuggled into him, a proud smile on her face, and a light sheen of sweat coating her skin.

He kissed her forehead, her jaw, her neck, making his way to the thin satin strap on her shoulder. He slid it off. Undressing her slowly, admiring every inch of skin he uncovered until she was completely bare before him. He licked the tip of one of her rosy nipples, then took the other in his mouth entirely. When he breathed across her wet peak, goosebumps pebbled across her skin. He ran his hand down her tingling skin to the apex of her thighs. She propped herself up on her elbows, watching curiously as he slid down her body. "What are you doing?" she asked.

"Returning the favor," he said, kissing her hip and running his lips across the smooth surface of her pelvis.

"You don't have to," she said, her voice quivering with nerves and anticipation.

He kissed her inner thigh and then just above her opening, igniting a spark. "I've been thinking about this since the moment you stepped back into my life." He licked slowly up her folds until he found her little ball of nerves. He sucked gently, turning the sparks in her core into a full-fledged flame. She let out an uncontrolled moan and fell back, basking in the pleasure as he lapped and flicked at her sex. He slid a finger inside her and that flame became a raging inferno.

"Jen, I need to add another finger. You're so tight and I need you ready for me, okay?"

She nodded vigorously, then groaned at the sensation of his second digit sliding into her. She was already on the edge of combustion, and when Grayson slipped that second finger in she let out a yell of pleasure. He hooked his fingers, his mouth still worshiping her sex until she erupted. He lapped at her center, consuming all of her like she did him.

Climbing up her body, his lips found hers, and she could taste herself on his mouth. They kissed lazily for a moment before Grayson's kisses turned hungry and Jensen felt every part of him line up perfectly with every part of her. He grinded against her, desperate for friction.

"Jen, I need to be inside you."

"Yes," she said, reaching between them and guiding him to her entrance.

He grimaced as his head rubbed against her slick opening. "I don't have a condom," he realized out loud, hating himself for not planning for this exact moment.

"I guess you're not a very good Boy Scout, after all. Aren't you supposed to 'always be prepared'?" she teased.

"Jen," he moaned.

She had mercy on him, "I'm on birth control. I get the shot." Then, as an afterthought, she added, "And I'm clean."

"So am I," he responded. "But, are you sure–"

"Yes," she didn't let him finish. "Grayson, I need you." She pumped her fist over him and brought him back to her entrance. "Please."

He pushed inside her partially, giving her body a chance to adjust to his size. He pulled back, then thrust in further. The stretch was both painful and euphoric. When he entered her a third time, she took all of him and the fullness was overwhelming.

He paused, "Are you okay?"

Jensen nodded and whispered, "Grayson, I need you to move right fucking now. I feel like I'm going to combust."

He chuckled and kissed her deeply as he slowly began moving inside her.

"Faster," she begged after his slow thrusts brought her close to the edge again and again. "I need more."

"I want this to be good for both of us. If I move any faster, I'm going to cum. I'm barely holding it together as it is. You're so tight," he whispered directly into her ear, but he sped up, groaning into her neck as he thrust harder and harder, bringing her back to that edge.

"I'm close," he told her.

"Go ahead," she said, doubting she'd be able to get there again anyway.

But Grayson refused to leave her wanting. As if he knew her body better than she did, he slowed his thrusts, went up on his knees and slid a hand between her legs where they remained connected. With his other hand, he palmed her breast. Rubbing at her core and her nipple simultaneously, he built her up, until he finally took her nipple into his mouth as his long fingers worked their magic, releasing a cry from her. Her inner muscles contracted around his shaft as he worshiped her, and a moment later he followed her over that edge, pouring every drop of himself into her.

When Jensen woke up the next morning, she was turned away from Grayson, but she felt his morning wood pressed up against her and she backed into it. His breath caught, and he groaned. "Don't do that if you don't intend to finish what you start," he grumbled sleepily into her ear.

"I have every intention of *you* finishing," she said. But her plans for them were interrupted by a knock on the bedroom door.

"I'm coming in, so I sincerely hope everyone's decent," Lucy called as she cracked open the door. She entered the room carrying multiple bags with her mom's label on them. She dumped them on the floor. Then, climbed onto the bed, snuggling up to Jensen, the same way she used to when they lived together. She laid on top of the comforter. Grayson cleared his throat awkwardly, thinking about the fact that he still has a raging hard on and they were no longer alone.

Lucy's eyes trailed down the comforter. "Nice tent," she said. "Jensen said you were a Boy Scout."

"Oh my God," Jensen groaned and pulled the blanket over her head, mortified.

Grayson just laughed. Jensen peeked out of her hiding place and saw he'd put a pillow across his lap, other than that, he didn't show any sign of embarrassment. To her surprise, he nodded and said, "It's Lucy, right?" She nodded too, and he went on, "It's nice to meet you. Sorry, I didn't introduce myself last night."

"Oh, it's cool, I get it. You were a bit busy professing your love," she winked at Jensen.

"Can you please explain to me why you're in bed with us?" Jensen asked. "We were kind of in the middle of something."

Lucy snorted out a laugh. "Oh, I bet you were." Her eyes strayed down to the pillow on Grayson's lap.

"Hey," Jensen snapped her fingers in Lucy's face, "eyes up here."

This made Lucy laugh hysterically, and as always, when Lucy laughed, Jensen did too. She was such a tiny person to have such a boisterous laugh. Once they'd finally calmed down, she told them, "Get your asses up. I'm not letting you sleep the entire day away."

Jensen checked the clock, sure enough what she'd thought was morning was actually late afternoon. Grayson thanked Lucy for the wake-up call even though he would have been fine to spend the entire day in bed. And as soon as Lucy left, he pulled clothes out of the bags she brought him. His face fell.

"What's wrong?" Jensen asked.

"Does she seriously expect me to wear this?" He pulled out a shiny bomber jacket and held it up for Jensen to see. "Twenty-five-hundred dollars," he croaked, reading the tag. "You could buy a car for that much money."

She laughed and scooted across the bed to help him dig through the bags. Buried at the bottom was a plain white tee and a pair of gray slacks that fit him perfectly.

When they entered the main room, Lucy was waiting for them. She cringed when she saw Grayson. "Did none of it fit?" she asked. "I thought I was pretty close with the sizes."

"You were spot on," he said. "It was impressive. This was just the most, me."

"It's an undershirt," she deadpanned.

"People spend over a hundred dollars on an undershirt?" he asked under his breath, bewildered.

In the kitchen, there was a huge breakfast spread. "So, what's the plan?" Lucy asked as they all filled their plates. "Jensen already missed her flight, so are you guys staying in the city for a while?"

"I have to get back to work." Grayson said. "I only got my shifts covered for three days."

Lucy looked at Jensen. "If you're leaving soon, I think you need to talk to Eric. You can't leave things how they are."

"Lucy ..." She wanted to disagree with her, but she knew she was right. She glanced between her and Grayson, trying to convey to Lucy with her eyes, *'but what about Grayson? He came all the way here. I can't just leave him alone in a new city!'*

"I agree with Lucy," Grayson said, to her surprise. "It's what I was trying to encourage you to do back at home. I think you need closure and you won't get it unless you talk to him."

19

"DON'T TELL ME HOW I FEEL" —ERIC

Lucy volunteered to show Grayson around Central Park while Jensen made her way two blocks south, to Eric's. When she got to his parent's apartment, she knocked timidly. She'd texted him earlier, so he knew she was coming, but it still felt weird to let herself in like she used to.

Eric looked wrecked when he opened the door. His eyes were red rimmed and his hair was unkempt. As soon as Jensen stepped inside, he wrapped her in a tight hug. "I'm so sorry for what I said about your friend," he said into her shoulder. "I didn't know he was important to you. I never would've said anything if I'd known."

She reached behind her, grabbed his arms, and guided them away from her body. Then, walking past him into the living room, she took a seat on the leather couch. "It wasn't just what you said that upset me," she admitted. "It was the fact that I used to find that funny. I used to sit around and judge people like they were below me. That's not who I am anymore."

"You're pretty tall, a lot of people are below you." He nudged her playfully trying to remind her of the friendship they used to have. She offered him a courtesy grin, thankful that he was trying to keep the mood light, but not finding him funny. "Is that all you wanted to talk about? If so, noted. I will try my best not to talk about people like they're below me. Done!" He smiled and placed a hand on her knee. "Now, can we talk about us?"

She stood and walked across the room to the chair, taking a seat. "Eric, I told you in California, there is no *us*."

"Jensen, come on ..." He looked exasperated. "I get that you've had a fun summer, but summer's almost over. Things can go back to normal now."

"No, they can't." She looked down at her lap. "You were right when you said I've changed."

"Great, then give me a chance to show you I can love the new you. Don't I at least deserve a chance?"

"It's not about what you deserve, Eric. I know you deserve better than this. Of course I know that." He wasn't hearing her. "You're a great person, but you and I don't work."

"But at school–"

"At school?" she scoffed. "At school, I was in a cage. A uniform, a curfew, and a strict set of rules trapped me and I lost who I was. But this is me, Eric. I grew up playing outside, bare-foot, picking up bugs, and climbing trees. I was thrown into a school full of girls who turned their noses up at me. It was easier to blend in than be labeled the outcast."

"I love dirt bike riding and wakeboarding and jet skiing. My body craves adrenaline. I've felt more alive the past two months than I have in my entire life. Why can't you see that?"

"So, what you're saying ..." he stood and started pacing, his face aggravated, "is that the girl I'm in love with doesn't exist?"

"Please stop saying you're in love with. You don't love me."

"Don't tell me how I feel, Jensen," he snapped. "I have loved you since I was eleven years old. Since the day we met."

"You couldn't have." She felt tears coming and began tapping her leg, trying to release some of her nervous energy. "Because you didn't even know the real me." She was trying to keep her voice down, but it kept involuntarily rising.

"Whose fault is that?" he was yelling now. "I've always been real with you."

"God, Eric, please try to understand. I didn't do this on purpose. I tried so hard to be the person who the school, and my gran, and you expected me to be that I forgot who I was. It's not like I planned for this to happen. I know how unfair this is to you. I should've told you I was changing, but I didn't even realize it at first."

Eric put both hands on the back of the couch and squeezed the fabric tightly. "You think I didn't notice you were changing? You've been pulling away for weeks. We hardly talked all summer. I said we should take a break because I thought it would make you miss me. I could tell you needed space. It wasn't supposed to be forever. I thought once we got to school, you'd start acting like yourself again. Then I talked to Lucy, and she said you were moving on. I knew I had to come get you. I had to remind you how good we are together."

"I'm sorry it didn't work out that way," Jensen said as a tear rolled down her cheek. "I wanted to be the girl in your plan so badly. I'm sorry I came back here with you and led you on. That was never my intention. I just missed my friend. I told you in California that I don't want to get back together and that hasn't changed."

After a long, tense silence Eric finally relented. "At least we tried." He dragged a hand through his hair and added, "Don't get me wrong, this sucks. But I knew something was wrong between us when you didn't ask me to come to California. Every time I invited you to Spain, I kept waiting for you to ask me to come with you instead. I would've said yes. You said you needed to deal with the house, but that didn't stop you from spending the entire summer at the lake. That's when I realized the truth. It wasn't about the house. You just didn't want to spend your summer with me. I think I was clinging on so hard because you're the first girl I've ever loved."

"You still think you loved me, even after everything?" she asked.

"You'll always be my first love." Eric walked over. "Can I hug you?"

She nodded and stood, and he wrapped his arms around her waist. "At least we'll always be friends." He whispered and she cringed.

"Eric, I don't think that's a good idea." She tried to make her voice sound as gentle as possible.

"You've been my best friend for the past seven years. Why would that change?" She wouldn't meet his eyes. "This is because of that guy I saw you with, isn't it? I should have known. All this crap about how you've changed is bullshit. It's about him. It's *all* about him." He started pacing again.

"I didn't come here to talk about Grayson."

"I'm right, aren't I? You've fallen for some small town hick and you're going to throw away everything for him. Is he really worth it, Jensen? Is he worth throwing away all our plans and everyone who cares about you?"

"Yes. He's worth everything."

He opened his mouth like he was going to argue, but then shut it. A look of confusion crossed his face, followed by sorrow.

Finally, he asked, "So, this is really it?"

She nodded, "I'm sorry."

"I can't believe this is goodbye." He shook his head in denial and when she didn't backtrack he turned on his heels and exited down the hall toward his bedroom.

"Goodbye Eric," Jensen whispered under her breath before going to gather her bags. She stacked the luggage by the front door, then called the lobby for a baggage cart. They told her they would send someone up shortly. While she waited, she pulled out the jewelry box that held the necklace from Eric and placed it on the coffee table.

Katrina came out of her office. "Jensen? Is everything okay? I was on a call and I thought I heard yelling." Eyeing the pile of luggage by the door, her face fell. She sat next to Jensen on the couch, reaching out for her hand and asking, "What happened?"

Jensen hadn't let herself dwell on how hard it would be to lose Katrina until then.

For seven years, Katrina's presence had been a constant in her life. How was she supposed to say goodbye? Katrina was the one who stood outside the bathroom after Jensen locked herself in the first time she got her period. She'd welcomed Jensen into her home for every holiday. She bought Jensen her first bra and her prom dress, despite the fact that Jensen could afford it. She said that it was a mother's privilege to get to do those things. Not to mention the fact that she came with her to California after her grandparents died. She had been a pillar in her life, holding her up. Without her, Jensen felt like she might crumble.

"I'm so s-s-sorry," she said through her sobs. "I never wanted to hurt him or lose any of you."

"Shh, shh, shh," Katrina tried to soothe her, but she was beyond comforting.

"I wish none of this had happened," Jensen cried. "I wish I had listened to my gut and we had just stayed friends. I knew I loved him, but I knew it wasn't in the same way he loved me. I thought my feelings would catch up to his. Now, we can't go back."

She knew the best thing for everyone was a clean break. But letting go of Eric also meant letting go of Katrina. It wasn't fair to him to continue a relationship with his mom. She knew that, but it didn't make it any easier.

"Jensen, listen to me," Katrina gripped her hand tightly. "You were never obligated to stay with my son in order for me to love you. Of course, I hoped it would work out. I wanted you to be my daughter so badly that I put an unfair amount of pressure on you and I'm sorry."

There was a knock at the door. It was the baggage cart she requested. Katrina pulled her into a hug and said, "I love you."

"Thank you for everything." Jensen stood with tears streaming down her cheeks and made her way to the door. She wouldn't let herself regret her choice, but it was still hard to walk away.

"I hope you get everything you want out of life," Katrina said as Jensen pulled the door closed.

And Jensen knew as she rode the elevator and made her way back to Grayson that she was making the choice that would lead her to exactly that—everything she wanted out of life.

They woke up early the following morning to get to the airport. Lucy had breakfast waiting again. She looked up when Jensen and Grayson walked into the kitchen. "I still cannot believe you bought one of those t-shirts," Lucy grimaced at Grayson's *I heart NY* shirt. "I literally threw thousands of dollars worth of clothes at you, and that is what you're wearing?"

"I like it," Jensen said, smiling at him.

"No, you don't. You can't possibly like it," Lucy said. "You are just blinded by love. It's kind of gross, if I'm being honest."

Her comment made Grayson light up with a smile. He pulled Jensen in for a kiss and Lucy groaned and threw a piece of her bagel at them before announcing, "You two are disgusting." But when they broke apart, she had a wide smile across her face. Jensen picked up the bagel scrap and threw it back at her.

"Are you seriously going to wear that in public?" Lucy asked Grayson, back to focusing on his shirt.

"That's why I bought it," he shrugged.

"And you won't keep any of the stuff I got you?" she asked in confusion.

"I'm not trying to be rude, it's just not my style."

"No, no offense taken," she said. "I'm just trying to understand. Most people beg me for free clothes. You're different than I expected, but I admire your self awareness."

"Someday, you should come to the lake. Then you'll get it," Jensen told her.

"Nah, my place will always be in the city. But, speaking of the lake, you guys need to hurry. You don't want to miss your flight."

They gathered all five of Jensen's suitcases and called for the cart. Grayson helped load it despite the bellhop's insistence that it was his job. Lucy rode down to the lobby with them and Jensen pulled her into a tight hug. She didn't know when she was going to see her again. Lucy hugged Grayson, too, then she stood by the elevator watching them walk away. "Bye. I love you!" Lucy yelled.

When they got to the large glass doors, she called out to them, "Oh, and don't worry about the ass print on my window. I'll go ahead and clean that for you." Jensen glanced at the concierge and the doorman, both of whom were pretending they heard nothing.

She and Grayson rushed to the street and climbed into the waiting car. Lucy stepped onto the sidewalk just as they pulled away from the curb, and Jensen rolled down the window and called out, "I love you, too."

Once Lucy was out of sight she turned to Grayson and burst out laughing. "I hate her, but I'm going to miss her so much," she told him.

20

"K-I-S-S-I-N-G" —DUSTIN (AND BRENT)

They got back to the house with all Jensen's luggage in tow and were met with a chorus of, "Grayson and Jensen sitting in a tree, K-I-S-S-I-N-G," from both Dustin and Brent.

"Very mature," Grayson said, looking at Brent.

Grayson and Jensen headed for the kitchen, famished after traveling all day. They'd had layovers in Dallas and LA before finally flying into Reno where Grayson had left his car. Then they had to drive two hours home.

While Joe and Brent brought the suitcases upstairs Lydia instructed, "Take them to Andrew's room," She looked at Jensen, "Now that he's gone, it would be silly to make you and Nicole share."

Jensen relaxed, glad she wouldn't have to invade Nicole's space again. But, if she was being honest, she'd hoped she'd be staying with Grayson. As if Lydia read her mind, she announced. "Ground rules." Raising a finger like they were unruly kids. "You're sleeping in separate bedrooms and I expect you to remember there are impressionable children in this house. Do you understand me?"

Jensen nodded and Grayson answered, "Yes, ma'am."

"I know I can trust you," she said, laying it on thick.

When they headed upstairs for bed, Grayson kissed Jensen softly in the hall before they went into their separate rooms. She changed into her silky summer pajamas and pulled Andrew's blanket up over herself. She was watching a video on her phone that Lucy posted about her latest date, when there was a soft knock on her door. Grayson didn't wait for her to answer, instead he just pushed it open. He was shirtless, with the waistband of black boxer briefs peeking out over the top of his low hung gray sweats. He leaned casually against the door frame and crossed his arms over his chest. Jensen's ovaries clenched at the sight of him.

"So, am I coming in here, or are you coming with me?" he asked with a devious grin on his face.

"Your mom just said it's not allowed."

"What she doesn't know won't kill her," he shrugged. "Besides, Andrew's been sneaking girls up here for years. Several this summer alone, and I'm pretty sure he didn't wash his sheets before he left." He scanned the bed she was in.

"Ew!" She flung the covers off and jumped up.

Grayson laughed. "That was too easy." He took her hand and led her to his bedroom.

As soon as he closed the door, his hands explored her. He grabbed a fist full of her silk cami at her hip and yanked it low, kissing the upper exposed part of her breast. "I like your pajamas," he grumbled into her skin.

"I like yours, too," she whispered as she wrapped her arms around him and slipped her hands into the back of his sweats. He guided her backward across the room until the backs of her knees hit his bed and she fell onto it. He climbed on top of her and she could feel him hard against her. He kissed her passionately and when he grinded against her, it was in a slow, rhythmic motion.

After long meaningful kisses and a few soft whispered words, the rhythm of his hips stopped as he began to undress her. It wasn't feverish and rushed like it was last time. They took their time, memorizing each other in a quiet, adoring way. And when Jensen could no longer stay quiet, she turned her face into his pillow to muffle her moans.

They fell asleep quickly, exhausted from their long day of travel.

The next morning Jensen went with Grayson to The Marina, knowing she'd have to grovel to get her job back. She'd never had a job before, but even she knew it was frowned upon to leave the state without notifying anyone. She left her friends scrambling to cover for her and didn't even give it a second thought. It was a sign of her privilege and she was embarrassed by it.

"Phil, please," she begged, following him down the dock. "I'll work in the gift shop every day," she said. "I feel awful."

He crossed his arms, but he wasn't very intimidating. She probably had more muscle mass in her ass than he had in his entire body. "Jensen, I can't just rehire you after three no call-no shows in a row. People will say I'm giving you special treatment." She cringed, it sounded bad when he said it like that. His phone rang and he held up a finger, walking away to answer.

"Damn it. Fine." He yelled, and it took her a second to realize he was talking to her again. "Nadia is sick and Hawk's already called out this morning."

"So, I can have my job back?" She clenched her fists in excitement, waiting for him to confirm.

"Fine, but I'm not paying you," he said.

To his surprise, she said, "That's fine."

"What? No, Jensen, I have to pay you. I was kidding."

After covering for Nadia who was only scheduled to work a morning shift, Jensen caught a ride back to the house with Brent because Grayson was scheduled to work all day. As soon as they got to the house Brent asked her if she wanted to go wakeboarding. She'd been planning to swim but she was getting pretty decent at wakeboarding and Brent was always good company.

Unfortunately, when she and Brent walked down to the boat ten minutes later, it was to find Nicole waiting for them. Jensen hadn't seen Nicole yet and she wasn't sure the middle of the lake was the right place to hash things out.

"Are you one hundred percent positive she's not bringing me out there to hide my body at the bottom of the lake?" she whispered to Brent.

"Eighty-Twenty," he answered with a chuckle.

"Those are not good odds," she hissed as he climbed aboard.

Thankfully, Nicole didn't seem particularly murdery that day. Surprisingly, she looked remorseful.

"I get it, you know," Jensen said, walking right up to her.

"You get what?"

"Why you sent me away … I've monopolized all his time this summer. I'm sorry."

"Don't be nice to me right now," Nicole said. "I don't deserve it."

"Well, I'm not yelling at you. I already tried that on the 4th of July and it didn't work."

"You were right, you know," Nicole admitted. "When you said I never gave you a chance. I don't give anyone a chance. I expect the worst out of everyone so no one can hurt me. Grayson's the only person who's never let me down, and now I've betrayed his trust."

"If you knew you were going to hurt him, why'd you do it?"

"I knew you leaving would break him, and I figured it would be easier if you left before he got any more attached."

"I wouldn't have left at all if it wasn't for you," Jensen said.

"People always leave." Nicole countered.

"You're judging me pretty harshly for someone who's about to do the same thing. Are you still planning on running off to New York?" Jensen glanced over at Brent, who was behind the wheel, giving them space. "Look, I'm sorry I got on that plane. I knew it was a mistake even as I was doing it. But you better get used to me because I'm not going anywhere."

"It won't work. You guys are too different," Nicole argued. "I watched it happen to my mom and dad. They loved each other, had a happy marriage, kids, a house, the whole thing. But they couldn't get past the fact that they were too different. Dad's all about image and Mom's all about substance. They couldn't find common ground."

"Just to be clear, I'm like your dad in this scenario?"

"Do you even know what Grayson's going to school for?" Nicole challenged.

"Of course, environmental science," Jensen answered.

"Do you know what that means? There's no money in it. It's not glamorous work. He'll be in the trenches in underprivileged areas, helping people. It couldn't be more different from the life you've lived up till now."

She let Nicole say her piece, but Jensen already knew all this. Grayson and her had spent hours every day talking on the dock after her long swims during those perfect moments together. He'd told her about his plans, his dreams, his hopes, and his regrets, and she'd shared the same with him.

"Not that it's any of your business, but I've given up a lot to be with him. I don't take this relationship lightly. I know what I'm getting myself into, and I know he's worth it. You haven't said anything that I don't already know. Despite what you think, you are not the only one who cares about him. I know it will be hard to navigate his career and my schedule. But we'll face those hurdles together. I'm not about to give up on him because it might get hard." As she said it, she followed Nicole's eyes as they landed on Brent.

Changing the subject abruptly, Jensen said, "Brent risked his relationship with his best friend to be with you. I'd say that's a pretty big declaration, wouldn't you?"

"He asked me if we could try to make it work long distance," Nicole admitted. "I haven't given him an answer yet."

"Sounds like I should give you guys some space to talk," Jensen said. Then louder for Brent to hear, she added, "You know what, I think I'm going to hang back and get some swimming in."

After the boat pulled away, she sat on the dock with her feet dangling in the water, waiting for Grayson. He knew to find her there. Sure enough, not long after, she felt the familiar sway of someone running on the dock.

He took a seat beside her and wrapped her in a hug. "I talked to Nicole," she said into his chest.

Grayson pulled back, "How did that go?" He reached out and held her hand, and she tangled her ankles around his as she recalled their conversation for him.

Hours later, they were still sitting on the dock, the sun was setting and they were talking about all the places they wanted to travel. They both had extensive lists.

"I've always wanted to go to Hungary," he added to the list they were compiling.

"Oh, Hungary's awesome! Worlds were in Budapest last year and I loved it. It's such an underrated country."

"Okay, that's the third place I've listed that you've already been to because of swimming. I need to catch up," he joked.

"We could plan a trip when our school breaks line up," she offered. "It'll have to wait until after swim season, though." Grayson reared back and looked at her with wide eyes. "Jen, are you planning on swimming at Stanford? When did you decide?"

"In New York. It was something Katrina said. She said, 'I hope you get everything you want out of life.' I thought of you first, but I also thought of swimming. I'll regret it for the rest of my life if I don't go for it. I wanted to talk to you about it first because it's a big commitment. I already turned down the scholarship so I'm going to have to walk on. It obviously depends on if I make it, but–"

"But nothing. Of course you'll make it. Have you called the coach yet? You need to call right now."

She laughed and pulled her phone out of her back pocket. It lit up with several notifications. There were six missed calls from Stuart Paulson, her financial advisor. She clicked the most recent voicemail and listened to it.

"Hello Ms. Fisher, this is Stuart Paulson, from Paulson & Paulson Asset Management. I'm calling regarding a series of discrepancies we've discovered in one of your accounts. Please return my call at your earliest convenience. Thank you."

Instinctively, she knew it had something to do with Laurel. She never should have trusted her in that house alone.

21

"NO SHIT 007." —ANDREW

Jensen put her phone on speaker so they could both hear the voicemail. Her financial advisor, Stuart, didn't go into detail in his message, but there was an email from him that briefly explained the problem. Money was being wired out of one of her accounts and it was raising red flags.

"We need to go." Grayson jumped up, reaching out his hand to Jensen. "I know dealing with your mom is gonna be hard, but it's time."

"I know," she agreed. Then, the word '*we*' computed in her brain. "Wait, you're coming with me?"

"Of course," Grayson said. "I just have to call Phil and get my shifts covered for a couple of days."

"Oh, shit," she smacked a hand over her eyes in a classic facepalm. "I forgot about work. There's no way Phil's going to forgive me for bailing again. I just got my job back today."

"You want me to talk to him?" Grayson offered.

"No, I should do it." She let out a long groan. "Soon I'll be able to add getting fired to the list of new things I did this summer."

"On the bright side, there's only a couple weeks left of

summer." He tried cheering her up. "I think you've gotten the full first job experience you were looking for."

They walked up to the house together and headed straight upstairs to pack. In Grayson's room, Jensen dumped out one of Lucy's bags and together they filled it with a mix of their stuff.

Downstairs, they told Lydia what was going on. She hugged Grayson and whispered in his ear, "Take care of her." He nodded and picked up their bag, bringing it out to the car. After she hugged Jensen, Lydia said, "I love you, and your mother loves you too in her own way."

Jensen huffed audibly. "She has a weird way of showing it."

"Try to remember that forgiveness is never easy, but it's often the answer."

"Yeah, I'll keep that in mind." She tried not to let the sarcasm bleed into her voice.

On the drive, Jensen tried to call Stuart Paulson, but it went straight to voicemail. It was after work hours and he must have gone home for the evening. She didn't need him to confirm what she already knew.

Somehow, Laurel had gotten her hands on her bank information and had transferred the money to herself. Jensen should have seen it coming. Laurel thought she had a right to the inheritance. Clearly, she'd figured out how to get it.

Jensen spent the entire drive fueling her anger. By the time they arrived at the house, she was fuming. She marched up to the door and keyed in her code and without hesitating stepped into an empty foyer. Laurel had taken down all the art, wrapped the pieces in brown paper and set them against a wall. The entry table was gone, and the rug was rolled up. Grayson caught up with Jensen and they walked into the living room together. It was completely empty.

"Laurel, it's me, Jensen," she called out and her voice echoed through the empty space.

"Jenny-Bee!" They heard her voice from the top of the stairs. As soon as they reentered the foyer Laurel saw them. "I'm so glad you're finally here," she said, "why didn't you call? I would have made dinner."

She stopped a few steps from the bottom when she saw the looks on their faces. "Jenny, what's wrong?"

"Have you been stealing money from me?" she asked.

Laurel's face went white. "What?" Her voice was barely a whisper. She shook her head feverishly. "No. No, I would never ..."

Jensen climbed the stairs, walking right past her. "Where are you going?" Laurel asked, stepping in front of Grayson to follow her daughter.

"To Gramps' study to see if you've been in the safe." Jensen stated as she reached the upstairs landing.

Laurel grabbed her around her upper arm and tried to stop her progress. "Jenny, wait–"

But Grayson was right behind her, and he stepped between them. He glared down at Laurel forcing her to take a step back to look up at him.

"Don't touch her." His voice was full of warning. Jensen had told him what happened at the will reading; he knew what Laurel was capable of.

He turned and followed Jensen down the hall, leaving Laurel at the top of the stairs. When they reached for a door, Laurel said, "Let me explain."

Grayson looked over his shoulder at her, but Jensen didn't wait for Laurel's explanation. The room they stepped into was empty of furniture. The floor, however, was littered with documents. There was a pile of checkbooks and bank statements in the corner. Laurel must've used them to set up the wire transfer. There were stacks of cash and opened ledgers all over the floor, along with pens and highlighters.

The painting that used to hide the safe was leaning against the wall. The safe was sitting open with nothing except a gun inside. The weapon worried Jensen, and she reached behind her for Grayson. He grabbed for her hand immediately and stepped up so his chest pressed against her back reassuringly. "Grayson," she whispered his name. "There's a gun in the safe."

Grayson walked across the room and removed the weapon. He was no stranger to holding a gun, but this weapon differed from the ones he'd shot before. He'd held shotguns and rifles for recreation, but never a handgun. It was unnerving how heavy it was despite its size. He removed the safety and held it at his side.

"I don't think we'll need it but ..." She let her sentence fall off, but Grayson knew what she was thinking. Stay armed and ready, Laurel was unpredictable.

"Jenny-Bee," Laurel had caught up with them and her voice came out broken, "Tell him to put it down." She kept looking back and forth between her daughter and the gun in Grayson's hand. "I swear I'll explain."

Jensen took a few steps back towards Grayson, the papers on the floor crinkling with each step. "I don't want an explanation from you," Jensen announced. "I just want you to leave. I read your letters and all they told me is that you're exactly who I thought you were. A liar and a flake and someone who doesn't deserve to be in my life."

"Please don't say that," Laurel cried.

"I need you to leave. Grab your stuff and get out. You're not welcome in this house anymore."

"Jenny–"

"She said leave." Grayson raised his voice and Laurel jumped, looking back at the gun nervously. She nodded and slowly backed out of the room. Grayson followed her and stood in the hall while she gathered her things. He walked her downstairs and made sure she left. Once she was gone, Jensen keyed in a new alarm code and together they did a full sweep of the house, making sure the windows and doors were all locked.

A few minutes later, while tension was still running high, someone knocked on the door. Grayson palmed the gun again, just in case, and Jensen checked the doorbell camera. When she saw who it was, she rushed forward and flung the door open.

Andrew was standing on the porch, in a nice navy suit with a gray tie. He smiled broadly. "I just got home, and I saw the car," he explained.

Jensen reached forward and pulled him in for a hug. In all the chaos, she'd forgotten that Andrew was staying at his dad's next door. After saying hi to Jensen, he went to hug his brother but stopped short when he saw the gun in his hand. "Woah, what the fuck dude? Why do you have a gun?"

"It's a long story," Jensen said. "Come inside. I need to lock the door."

Andrew looked over his shoulder into the front yard and then back at them with his brows scrunched together in confusion. "Wait, where's Laurel?" he asked.

"She left and she won't be coming back," Jensen told him. "She's been stealing money from me."

"What?" he still looked confused. "No, she's the one who caught the discrepancy."

"What are you talking about?" Jensen asked.

"She didn't know what she was seeing, but when she was cleaning out the office, she found some documents that confused her. She brought them next door to show my dad, knowing he works with numbers. She thought he could help. Unfortunately, for her, he's been away on business for the past week, so she's been stuck with me. I've been helping her every day after work. We haven't gotten very far. All we know is someone's been wiring $120,000 a year to the same foreign account. The money is being sent to a charity that doesn't exist."

"You've known about this for a week?" Grayson asked. "Why didn't you tell us?"

"I told her to tell you guys," Andrew said. "But Laurel was nervous about being the one to give you the bad news. She wanted to wait until we had some answers. She asked me to give her time. Plus, you just got back from New York yesterday. I kind of agreed with Laurel that we should wait to tell you."

"But why help her in the first place?" Jensen asked.

Andrew took a deep breath, and on his exhale he said, "I don't know. When she was showing me the initial documents she found, she was so panicky. At first, I just wanted her to calm down. But once she stopped crying and showed me what she discovered, everything she was saying made sense. I get the feeling that no one's really helped her or listened to her or taken her seriously. I wondered what would happen if I did? I offered to help her, and to my surprise, she's actually pretty damn smart."

"Is she clean?" Grayson asked.

"I haven't asked, but I haven't seen a single trace of drugs or alcohol in the entire house," Andrew answered. "Even the medicine cabinets are empty. And she has been totally sober every time I've seen her."

"So, you're saying I just wrongfully accused my mom of stealing from me when she was just trying to help?"

"I'm sorry, Fish." He turned his attention to Grayson, who was still holding the pistol. "You didn't have the gun on you when you talked to Laurel, did you?"

Grayson cringed and Jensen whispered under her breath, "Shit."

"She probably thought we were threatening her," Grayson confirmed.

"No shit 007," Andrew replied. "We have to find her. You just sent a recovering addict out on the street while she's upset and alone. Jensen, didn't she give you her phone number?" he asked. "She always keeps her phone charged. She checks it every five minutes to see if you've called."

Jensen was already feeling bad enough without that added bit of information. "She wrote it down, but I didn't save it," she admitted. "I might've stuck it in that box of letters that's at the lake, but I'm not sure."

Andrew called Nicole to see if she could find the phone number, but she wasn't at home and it was too late to call anyone else. Lydia, Joe, and the kids would all be asleep.

They tried to figure out where she'd go, but they knew nothing about Laurel. They didn't know where she worked, where she'd go, or if she had friends. They had no way of finding her.

"It won't do us any good to drive around town looking aimlessly," Grayson said reasonably, so they called it a night.

Jensen woke up the next morning to her phone ringing. Her cheek was pressed into Grayson's bare chest and her body was curled into his side. She peppered kisses across his chest as she reached across his body for her phone on the bedside table. He didn't let her get to it, wrapping his arms around her and trapping her on top of him. He went to pull her in for a kiss, but she turned away. "I have morning breath," she admitted, embarrassed.

Grayson turned her toward him anyway and planted a soft, closed mouth kiss on her lips. "I don't care," he whispered against her mouth. She leaned in and kissed him again, but her phone ringing for the second time interrupted the moment.

"You better check it," Grayson said, disappointed.

She grabbed the phone and saw Stuart Paulson's name on her screen. Climbing off Grayson, she answered.

Stuart was quick and to the point, asking if they could meet with him that morning.

Jensen looked longingly at Grayson stretched out on the large, white bed. She wanted to crawl back under the covers and get lost in him again. Unfortunately, real life was waiting.

Outside Stuart's office, she couldn't stop tapping her leg nervously as they waited. When he finally called them in, he didn't give them much new information. The red flags he'd found were the same ones that Laurel had shown Andrew. He was, however, able to narrow down the timeline. The transfers started fifteen years ago and had been paid in monthly installments of ten thousand dollars, equaling nearly two million in potential money laundering. He requested permission to put a freeze on the account in question, which Jensen immediately approved. There was an open investigation to track down where the money was going. Once it entered foreign banks, it was hard to pinpoint a destination. He told Jensen he was required to report the transgression within ninety days of discovering it, and by then they should know more. He talked about leaning on the bridge accounts, and he offered some investment updates, but she wasn't listening anymore.

Two million dollars over fifteen years in illegal money transfers was going to cost an exorbitant amount in back taxes, especially in California. She couldn't wrap her head around how much it was going to cost.

When they got home, they went into the study to look for answers. Unfortunately, neither Grayson nor Jensen were well versed in reading financial documents. They decided their efforts would be better spent looking for Laurel.

Jensen was still not sure she could trust Laurel, but she felt incredibly guilty for kicking her out the way she did. Her words were harsh and unnecessary and for that, she knew Laurel deserved an apology.

Grayson came up with an idea, they should contact the rehab center she went to. They had to rack their brains to remember that her sponsor's name was Wendy. When they got a hold of her, Wendy told them to look for Laurel at her job. She gave them the address for a pet store in San Carlos.

Jensen had been so focused on finding Laurel that she hadn't considered what she'd say once she did. She needed to apologize; she knew that, but then what?

She regretted the way she spoke to Laurel, but she had meant what she said. Between all her bad choices and broken promises, Jensen was scared to risk giving her a chance.

They pulled into the parking lot and spotted her immediately. Grayson parked and they watched Laurel lean against the building less than ten feet away. She pulled out a pack of cigarettes from her bag and her hands trembled as she lit one. She inhaled deeply, then looked up to the sky as she let out a long exhale of smoke. It was while she was standing there with her head leaned back against the wall and her eyes closed to the sun that Jensen saw what Andrew was talking about. Her mother looked so hopeless and broken, and nothing like the manipulative villain her gran made her out to be.

Jensen stepped out of the car without a plan. "I talked to Andrew," she called across the parking lot and Laurel's head snapped in her direction. "He said you didn't do it. I'm sorry for not letting you explain yourself and for what I said."

Laurel didn't say anything. She looked stunned. "We'll be staying at the house for a few days while we try to figure things out," Jensen added. "If you need a place to stay, I'll change the alarm code back." She climbed back in the car, not giving Laurel a chance to respond. "We can go," she told Grayson.

Andrew went over when he got off work. The three of them were in the study when Laurel knocked on the front door. Jensen changed the alarm code back, but she appreciated that she was knocking. She stood to answer the door and Grayson asked, "You want me to come with you?"

"I've got it," Jensen said as she checked the doorbell camera on her phone to confirm it was her. Then she went downstairs and opened the door.

"Hi Mom," she said. It was the first time she'd addressed her that way without animosity, nerves, or annoyance coating her tone. "Come in."

Laurel looked nervous as she stepped into the house. "The guys are upstairs in the study," Jensen said, leading the way up the stairs. "Do you want to drop your stuff off in your room?"

Laurel agreed and followed her. When she joined them in the study a few minutes later, Andrew immediately told her, "Laurel, we have a new development. Grayson and Jensen met with a financial advisor today and he says the transfers started almost fifteen years ago."

She paused where she was standing just inside the doorway. "Do you know what month they started?" she asked, her voice quiet and shaky.

"September," Jensen answered, "Why?"

Tears filled her mother's eyes. "Because fifteen years ago in September, I hit Mercy Jackson."

The room went silent. No one knew what to say until Jensen finally asked, "Will you tell us about it?"

"I wouldn't even know where to start," Laurel responded.

"Start from the beginning," Andrew suggested, sitting on the floor and waiting patiently for her to begin.

22

"JENNY-BEE" —LAUREL

L aurel was eleven the first time she realized her parents didn't want her. She was nothing more than a box to check.

- *Date for x amount of years, check.*
- *Get engaged, check.*
- *Get married, check.*
- *Buy a house, check.*
- *Start a family, check.*

That was her, the final checkmark on their carefully thought out list.

She was raised by an endless stream of nannies and when she was old enough, they sent her away to a school where she would live for the next seven years. She thought she was lucky. Like Harry Potter, she'd make lifelong friends and form bonds stronger than family, but that's not how her story went.

It surprised her to learn that many of her classmates still lived at home with their families. Her school was in Woodside, only twenty minutes away from her house. However, the option to live at home was never presented to her. Her parents chose this school for its boarding option. The few students who took part in the boarding program were an odd mix; a couple of child geniuses, some foreign diplomats children who spoke choppy English, and a boy who, in Laurel's opinion, was troubled.

Laurel was lumped in with the freaks and found it hard to make friends. She started acting out, purposely breaking rules, and trying to get her parents" attention. They couldn't justify boarding school being the best place for her if she kept getting in trouble there. Surely they would let her come home.

That wasn't the case.

Instead, all Laurel got was a letter from her mother, threatening her. According to her mother, if she were to get expelled, there were other options. Her mother included a pamphlet to a girl's Catholic school in Connecticut. Uniforms were required, there was a strict curfew, and a dress code on weekends. She read through that pamphlet and knew her mother wasn't bluffing. She would send her away without a second thought.

Laurel tried to clean up her act. She started paying attention in class, and actually raising her hand. But her good behavior didn't erase her past, which haunted her in the form of a pile of detention slips that she had to cash in. It was there, in detention, where she finally found her people.

Laurel's new friends were thrill seekers, free-thinkers, and rule breakers. As kids, this equated to harmless pranks, some questionable outfit choices, and a few more detention slips, but as they got older, their vices shifted.

Laurel wasn't a fan of the party scene, but she didn't want to fade into the background. So, she went to the parties and when she was offered that first hit when she was fourteen and all eyes were on her, she couldn't say no. What would her friends think?

As they got older, the parties got bigger, and the drugs got stronger. She was surrounded by people who had more money than *they knew what to do with, more access than anyone should have, and no sense of self-preservation.*

It was at one of those parties in her senior year that Laurel spread her legs for the first time. She didn't even know the guy's name, and she was too high to bother asking. She was acting solely on feeling, and he had felt good. It wasn't until she missed her next period that she was even sure she had lost her virginity; she had been so out of it that night.

She kept the pregnancy hidden from everyone for months. But when she'd lay in bed each night, she'd pull up her shirt and talk to her stomach. She called the baby Jensen because instead of parties she had spent the last month binging the show Supernatural. She figured it could work for a boy or a girl. If it was a girl, she'd just call her Jenny.

Her friends were fed up with her for always skipping out on them, but she didn't care. She had a new best friend. In bed every night, she'd talk to her stomach.

When she felt that first flutter low in her abdomen, the feeling like a bumble-bee buzzing around, she whispered into her dark dorm room, "Hi there, Jenny-Bee." She didn't know why, but she was sure it was a girl. "I'm your mama. We're family, just you and me. I promise I'll never let you feel invisible like I do. I love you, my sweet, sweet Jenny-Bee."

By graduation, Laurel was thankful for the loose fit of the robes. She was showing and her mother would definitely notice. Laurel knew she'd have to tell people soon. She'd need a doctor and a delivery plan. She couldn't deliver on her own.

A week after school got out, after she'd moved back into her parents house, she told them. They sat around the table together. They didn't even do that for Thanksgiving or Christmas.

The reason for the meal, she quickly learned, was to ambush her with her college acceptance letters. She was running out of time to make a choice, and many deadlines had already passed. Her father was yelling and her mother was crying. What would people think if their daughter didn't go to an Ivy?

"I'm not going to an Ivy! I'm not going to college at all." Laurel stood from her chair and unzipped her hoodie. She had been wearing them all week despite the balmy California summer. She threw the sweatshirt down on her chair and placed a hand over her stomach. "I'm pregnant." She spoke calmly now, not wanting to scare Jenny-Bee, who was buzzing away. "And I'm going to defer for a year so I can stay at home with my baby."

Her father slammed an open hand down on top of the stack of college acceptance letters. He stared at her for three long beats, stood and left the room without a word.

"Jesus Christ, Lord Almighty," her mother stared up at the ceiling, doing the sign of the cross. Then her eyes fell on Laurel and she asked, "Have you lost your damn mind?"

Her mother wanted her to abort the child, but she refused to even consider it. She respected a woman's right to choose, but this was her choice. Jenny-Bee was hers.

Her mother kept her in the house all the time, ashamed of her daughter's condition.

At the end of August, she gave birth to an eight-pound five ounce perfect baby girl. Jensen Megan Fisher, the middle name chosen for the nurse that held her hand the entire time. No one else showed up.

Parenthood was harder than Laurel ever imagined it would be. She was exhausted all the time, but she loved her daughter. However, she was lonely, and she missed being around other people. When Jenny started walking, Laurel started taking her to playgroups and park meet-ups, but the other moms were so much older than her. They turned up their noses to her and most thought she was the nanny.

She had Jenny-Bee, but she decided it was time to get her life back on track. She would miss spending all day with her daughter and leaving Jenny with a nanny would be hard, but she couldn't wait for *school to start. She'd accepted a place at Menlo College for the fall. It was nothing fancy, but at least she'd be around people her own age.*

Except, when school started, and she met people her age, they gaped at her when she told them she was a mom. Some flat-out stared, and others whispered behind her back.

She was walking through campus one day; her head down, trying to hide in her curtain of golden hair, when someone called out her name. "Laurel! Hey, Laurel, is that you?" She looked over and recognized T.J., a guy from the parties she used to go to in high school.

"Shit, it is you." He jumped up from the group he was sitting with and jogged over. "Hey, you went hella far off grid, huh? I heard you had a kid and shit."

"Jensen," Laurel said defensively.

"Like that actor from Supernatural?" He smiled at her. "I love that show." He looked back at his friends, then back at her. "What are you doing now? You wanna hang?"

Laurel could see them passing a blunt around the circle. She should have said no, she was a parent. She was supposed to be responsible. But it was the first offer of friendship she'd had in a while, so she took him up on it.

When they approached the circle, T.J. introduced her to his friends. "Guys, this is my friend Laurel. She has a kid."

"Damn, that's tight. How old?" another guy asked.

"She just turned one," Laurel answered. To her surprise, no one made her feel bad for being a teen mom.

The girl next to her just passed her the joint. "Here," she said. "One-year-olds are tough. You need this more than I do."

Laurel held the joint, torn. "She named her kid after the actor on that show, Supernatural." T.J. announced.

"Awesome," they all said and Laurel smiled. Then she took the hit.

She continued meeting her new friends every day after class. She often found herself the object of T.J. 's attention and after a while, a situation-ship formed between them. Laurel was hesitant to let him in, but it was nice to have someone. T.J. was still a kid himself. He had no responsibilities, nor did he want any. Laurel was drawn to the care-free way he viewed the world. Unfortunately, she couldn't afford to have the same mentality. She had Jenny to think about. T.J. would invite her to parties, ask her to go home with him after class, or hang out longer each day, but Laurel always refused. She didn't want Jenny with the nanny any longer than necessary.

After a year, Laurel finally admitted that what she and T.J. had was a relationship, but it wasn't a healthy one. They broke up constantly. They were crazy about each other, but their priorities were in such different places. She knew it wasn't going anywhere, so she never introduced him to Jenny. But she kept seeing him because it felt good to be wanted.

Just after Jenny turned three, Laurel started her third year of college. She had a heavy course load, but she was happy. She had finally settled on a major, biochemistry. Maybe she'd work in a lab, or go to pharmacy school, or even go for her doctorate. She had a world of opportunities before her.

When her professor asked her if she'd be interested in assisting on a research project, she jumped at the opportunity. They were working on developing affordable at-home genetic testing kits. She asked her mother for a sample explaining the science behind why she needed it. They were testing their own families to get a foundation for their research. She was so excited to work with her professor, a woman who was passionate about women in STEM.

"What are you babbling about, darling?" her mother asked, clearly not having heard a word she said. "What on God's green earth could you need my spit for?"

Laurel simplified her answer. "For a science project."

She gathered her father's sample as well, and then one from Jenny. The next day, she isolated her samples with the solution provided by her professor. She examined each one under the microscope, comparing each genome to the next. She matched the Single Nucleotide Polymorphisms in her and Jenny's genomes first. Then, from there, she found the match with her mother's. When her father's sample was under the microscope, she was stumped. She couldn't find any obvious similarities. She asked her professor to look. Maybe she didn't know what she was looking for after all.

Her professor looked at the samples and came back with the same result. She asked if she could keep them overnight for further tests. Laurel agreed, but she already knew what was wrong. It was the way her teacher wouldn't look her in the eye.

She was supposed to meet T.J. after class, but she went straight to the parking lot instead. After speeding home and slamming the front door open when she barged in, she found her mother in the sitting room. "Why didn't you tell me?" she yelled.

"Laurel, what on earth..." Her mother looked up, startled.

"Why didn't you tell me that Dad isn't my real father?"

Her mother's face went white. She looked around, making sure they weren't overheard. Then she walked across the room and closed the French doors, giving them privacy. When she turned back to face Laurel, her expression had darkened. "Who told you that?"

"So it's true?"

"Keep your voice down," her mother hissed. "Who told you such nonsense?"

"No one told me. I tested all of our DNA at school today. I saw it with my own eyes."

"Well, that settles it," her mother sighed in relief. "You're just a child. You must have done something wrong."

"I didn't. I did everything by the book and when I couldn't find the connection, I had my professor check. Does Dad know?"

Her mother was backed into a corner, and she knew it. "No," she admitted, "And he's never going to. When we got married, there was a strict prenup in his favor. If he finds out about the affair, he'll leave me with nothing. You won't fare any better. Do you think he's going to keep taking care of you, or Jensen, after he finds out you're illegitimate? He will leave us with nothing. That expensive college you go to, the nannies who care for Jensen, not to mention the roof over our head, it will all be gone if you don't keep your mouth shut."

Laurel couldn't believe what she was hearing. "You don't think he deserves to know?"

Just then, her father's voice rang out from the foyer. "Off to golf, Dear."

"Do not say a word," her mother said through her teeth. Then she swung open the French doors and put on a fake smile. "You're out of the office early," she observed.

"Ah, well, you know how it goes. We'll end up talking business on the course." He checked his watch. "I must be off. I have a 3:30 tee time with Greg." He kissed her on the cheek before departing.

After the door closed behind him, Laurel couldn't hold back her words. "You've been lying to him for years. Do you even know who my father is?"

"That's rich coming from a child who got herself knocked up in high school. Don't you dare point fingers at me. I did what I had to, to provide the best life for you."

"Are you fucking delusional? You haven't provided the best life for me. You've done the bare minimum as a parent and thrown money at every problem that's come your way. The only good thing I have is Jenny. She is the only reason I haven't already told Dad. She's why I didn't go to him first."

"If you tell him, Jensen will have to live with the consequences. Can you live with that?"

Laurel didn't know what to say. There was no right answer, so she turned and walked out. She went upstairs and sat in the rocker in the corner of Jenny's room while her daughter napped. She watched *her sleeping so peacefully, so innocent and oblivious to the bad in the world. Laurel let silent tears fall down her cheeks.*

That night when T.J. called and invited her to a party, she went. As soon as she walked in the door, she pulled the red cup out of her boyfriend's hand and took a huge gulp. "What is this?" she asked, downing it.

"Um, Hennessy," he answered hesitantly. "Hey, are you good?" He hadn't seen Laurel so completely reckless since high school.

"Fan-fucking-tastic," she answered as she surveyed the bottles on the counter. "Is it this one?" she asked, pointing to the amber liquid labeled Hennessy.

T.J. nodded, and Laurel uncapped the bottle and took a huge swig. "I need something tonight. What's circling?" she asked.

"Um, the girl in the black dress has coke." He pointed at her through the crowd. "I have half a tab of Molly left that I was gonna take, but if you need it, it's yours. There's plenty of weed, of course. What exactly are you looking for?"

"Who has Benzos?" she asked. Benzodiazepine was an antidepressant, used for anxiety. Laurel just wanted to feel numb.

"Shit, I don't know. Maybe hit up Tre? He usually has a pharmacy in his backpack." Before she could walk away, he caught her around the wrist. "You want to tell me what's going on?"

She slid out of his grip, answering, "No." Then she made her way to Tre.

He had exactly what she needed. He pulled a canister out of his backpack, asking, "How many do you want?"

She handed him a stack of cash. "However much this buys me."

She walked away with the entire canister of pills and a warning from Tre. "The comedown can be pretty rough on those. Don't take them all at once."

She waved over her shoulder that she heard him. Then she popped two pills with a swig from her bottle. Twenty minutes later, she took another, then later one more. She kept this up, snacking on the anti-anxiety meds like they were candy. Benzos are less toxic than most drugs and rarely result in overdose, so she wasn't worried. But they were also known for causing intense blackouts when used in heavy doses. She only remembered that fact after she woke up in her living room the next morning, still in last night's clothes, wondering how she got home.

When she went into the kitchen, her mother was sitting at the breakfast nook. She looked as exhausted as Laurel felt. She was probably up all night panicking that Laurel would say something to her father. "We're out of milk," her mother announced. "The nanny's upstairs getting Jensen dressed for the day, but they'll be down for breakfast soon. She'll want her milk."

"I don't feel like going to the store. She can go without for one day." Laurel placed a mug under the espresso machine.

"You are the one who chose to become a mother at eighteen. You kept the child against my better judgment, so you need to care for that child. If she needs milk, you'll get her milk. This is what you signed up for." Laurel rolled her eyes. Her mother lectured her like that all the time. She wasn't in the mood to argue with her.

She grabbed her keys off the counter and asked, "Do you need anything else while I'm out?"

Her mother shook her head.

Laurel went to the closest place that sold milk. A small corner market down the street. She grabbed a half gallon of organic vitamin D milk, paid, leaving her change in the tip jar, and walked back to her car. Except, police cars blocked her car in on both sides with their lights flashing. She watched the officers curiously, her heart rate kicking into high gear as a third cop turned into the parking lot.

They were there for her. She knew it before the first officer stepped out of his car and addressed her. "Laurel Fisher, put your hands up where we can see them."

She didn't know why they were reading her a list of rights or sliding handcuffs around her wrists. But she did everything she was told. An officer guided her into the back of his vehicle and when she looked out her window, she noticed that her left side mirror was missing. One of the other officers was taking a picture of it. It had been torn from the car completely and she hadn't even noticed it. What had happened last night? What did she do? None of the scenarios she came up with in the back of the police car were as bad as the truth.

23

"A FLAW IN YOUR STORY" —ANDREW

T he girl Laurel hit had been pregnant, and according to the officers, the accident caused her to go into preterm labor. The baby was born ten weeks early and was in critical condition. Laurel would never forgive herself if that child didn't make it.

She told the police everything she could remember about the night before. From the alcohol she had consumed to the drugs. They tested her, but she already knew what they'd find. The drugs were definitely still in her system and the alcohol likely was too. She apologized profusely, but she knew her words were meaningless. They couldn't change what she had done—nothing could.

They set her bail at $75,000.

She called her mom to come get her.

Mercy Jackson's baby died later that same day.

Laurel was sentenced to six years for a DUI and felony hit-and-run resulting in a fatality. She knew she deserved every one of those minutes she'd spend in prison.

Every second was spent with her daughter before she went away. She soaked in everything about her, from her wispy golden hair to her sing-song voice. She slept with Jenny every night, whispering promises and apologies.

A new family had moved in next door a few months prior. The mom stayed home with her three young kids and though Laurel had never introduced herself, the woman always smiled at her when she saw her. The day before she had to turn herself over to the state, she took Jenny to the plant store and together they picked out a plant bursting with yellow flowers.

With the plant in hand, they knocked on the door. The woman, Lydia, was not like the other moms Laurel had met. She wore a floral wrap dress with a mismatched floral apron over the top of it. She was barefoot, and her brown curls were tied in a knot atop her head. Lydia recognized Laurel immediately and didn't hesitate to welcome her and Jenny into her home. Jenny darted off to play with the three kids, leaving Laurel alone with Lydia. She was still awkwardly holding the plant. She extended it out to the woman. "We brought this for you."

Lydia recognized the plant instantly despite the lack of a tag on it. "Honeysuckle," she said. "How lovely."

"I have a favor to ask of you," Laurel said abruptly. She wouldn't waste time with small talk. Time was the one thing she didn't have. She explained everything to the stranger about how she had hated her childhood and how, because of her mistake, her child was going to suffer a similar fate. Jenny deserved better; she didn't want her to feel alone in the world. "Can you keep an eye on her, please? Make sure she knows someone in the world cares what happens to her. She's my everything, and I need to know she's going to be okay while I'm gone."

The woman moved to sit on the couch beside Laurel and wrapped her in a tight hug. "It's rare to find anyone as open and vulnerable as you have been with me. Thank you for trusting me. I promise to love her as if she were my own."

Laurel hoped the woman was genuine. She had no way of making sure she kept her word, but she trusted her nonetheless.

The next morning Laurel walked out her front door, knowing she wouldn't be back for several years.

The day she was released, all she could think about was seeing her daughter. It's all she'd thought about for years. She got a ride with the prison transport to the halfway house she was assigned to live in for the following year. She had tried to arrange a pickup with her mom, but she hadn't answered the phone in months.

Laurel's hope was that Jenny could stay with her. It would be a big change from the privileged life she'd led, but at least they'd be together.

She got to her parent's house just after noon and it was her mother who answered the door. The blood drained from her face when she saw Laurel standing on her porch. "What are you doing here?" She looked at Laurel like she was mud on the bottom of her shoes. "You have no right to be here."

"No right?" Laurel didn't understand. "My daughter lives here."

"She's not your daughter anymore." Her mother stepped out onto the porch and closed the door behind her. "Your father and I have legal custody, and you have not been granted visitation."

"What?" Laurel shrieked the question. "Why not?" She barged past her mother, pushing the door open. "Jenny?" she called into the empty foyer. Then louder, "Jenny-Bee."

"It's Tuesday at noon. She's at school. Any good parent would know that." Her mother tried to belittle her, something that came naturally. Laurel hadn't even known what day of the week it was. She hadn't even considered school. Jenny was already in fifth grade.

She stormed down the driveway and started walking down the street toward the elementary school. If her guess was right, Jenny likely attended the same private school Laurel had gone to. It wasn't too far.

She sat on the lawn outside of the community tennis courts across the street from the school and cried. Kids started lining up at cones, *waiting for their parents to pull up. She scanned the area. Then, she saw that golden hair. It had darkened some, but it was unmistakably her. And before she even knew what she was doing, Laurel was moving toward her daughter.*

"Jenny-Bee," she called out to her when she was on the sidewalk, only ten feet away. She crossed the street toward her daughter. But Jenny wasn't smiling. Did she not recognize her? "Jenny-Bee it's me, Mommy. I came to bring you home today. Do you want to walk home with Mommy?"

Before she could reach her, a teacher was stepping between them, blocking her view of Jenny. She tried to look past the rather large woman, but Jenny was hiding.

'Was she scared? What lies had her mother been telling her? Was it the letter she sent about the accident that scared her? What did she expect? She had killed someone, after all.'

Then the campus police were there, and they were pulling Laurel away. She started panicking. What if they sent her back to jail? She couldn't go back, not without seeing her daughter. As they pulled her into a building, she shouted, "That's my daughter!" Then she begged, "I just want to see her." Then she sobbed. "Please, just let me see her, just once." Jenny peeked out from behind the woman. She looked terrified. Laurel cried, "Please."

She wasn't arrested but was required to meet with her probation officer, who informed her that her little stunt had cost her any chance at visitation. He told her she needed to prove herself worthy to the judge and then maybe, in a year, they could revisit visitation.

Laurel sobbed for days. She was entirely inconsolable. Until one day she woke up and decided to clean up her act. She'd get a job, maybe even finish college. She would prove she was not just fit for visitation but fit to regain custody. There was just one problem: the panic attacks. They'd been happening every day since she'd been out and she didn't know what was causing them.

She started a job as a receptionist. The women at the halfway house helped line it up for her. As soon as she could afford it, she went to the doctor. She was diagnosed with situational anxiety and given a prescription for anti anxiety meds. When she picked up the bottle at the pharmacy the following day and read the label, Benzodiazepine, she refused to take them. She would have to suffer through the panic attacks. She wouldn't take those pills again.

Exactly a year and a day after the incident at the school, Laurel marched down to the public defender's office and pleaded her case. She needed someone, anyone, to hear her out. She sat down with a kind man who agreed to look over her case. In less than five minutes, he shook his head and gave her an apologetic look. "Your parents are powerful people, Ms. Fisher," He told her like she didn't already know that. "They have an entire team of lawyers on retainer. I'm afraid that with your history and their legal team, there's not much I can do for you. Unfortunately, that's the way the world works. The rich are untouchable. My advice to you is to make nice, get in their good graces, and perhaps if you're lucky, they'll agree to a compromise."

Laurel left the meeting with all her hopes plummeting. That man had clearly never met her mother. The thought that she was capable of compromise was laughable. But she had to try. Otherwise, what had Laurel done it all for? The job, the night classes, fighting through the panic attacks every day. It had all been for Jenny.

She arrived at her parent's house the following day ready to beg. But, as soon as she stepped onto the front walk, she felt that all too familiar tightening in her chest. Then, shortness of breath followed before she began gasping. She pulled the prescription bottle she'd been carrying around for over a year and held it in her shaking hands.

This panic attack was worse than ever. She decided that one pill wouldn't make her an addict. She needed it. She'd never abuse them like she had that night. She'd learned her lesson.

Her parents were expecting her at noon and she couldn't show up late, but she also couldn't show up like that. She opened the bottle and tipped one pill into her palm. Before she could talk herself out of it, she threw it into the back of her throat and swallowed it dry.

She paced and waited for the fast-acting medication to work its magic and after a few stressful minutes; it did. She relaxed and knocked on the door.

Her mother answered the door with a bright smile and welcomed her into the sitting room. The reception was odd, Laurel expected hostility.

"Where's Dad?" she asked.

"He won't be joining us," her mother answered. "Now, what is this about Laurel?"

"I want to see Jenny," she stated calmly.

"Impossible, I'm afraid," her mother replied.

"But why is it impossible? I'm better now. I have a job and I'm going to school. I'm moving out of the halfway house this month and I already have an apartment lined up. All I want is to see her."

"Well, I'm glad to hear you've finally outgrown your rebellious stage, but that doesn't change the fact that seeing Jensen is impossible. She doesn't live here anymore."

"What?" Laurel wasn't expecting that.

"She attends and lives at a Catholic boarding school on the East Coast. She's really thriving there."

"You sent her away?" Laurel knew it was important to keep her cool at that moment, but she felt like she was going to burst. She couldn't hold back her words. They forced themselves out of her like vomit. "What, you don't think boarding school fucked me up enough, so you thought you'd go for round two with my daughter?" She felt physically ill. "How could you? If you didn't want her, then why not give her back to me? I can love her and care for her better than any school."

"Doubtful," her mother laughed. "She's thriving there. I see no *reason why she'll need to come back here. She'll be attending a rigorous swim camp during the summers and I don't believe she has plans to return for holidays, either. So, as I said, it'll be impossible to see her. Besides, Jensen has no interest in seeing you. She told us before she left how excited she was for a clean slate, where rumors won't follow her around about her deplorable mother."*

Laurel left her mother's house feeling lost. Then she saw a man pull into the driveway of the house next door. When he got out of his car, she called out, "Excuse me," and he whipped his head around. When he spotted her, he waited expectantly, but didn't offer a smile. "Do you know if Lydia's home?" she asked.

"Lydia doesn't live here anymore," he answered, as he walked up to his door and pulled out his keys.

So the woman hadn't followed through with her promise. She'd abandoned Jenny the same way Laurel had. Maybe she'd never shown her kindness again after that day. Laurel had really thought she would. She started crying. The man looked at her uncomfortably. Then he stepped into his house without another word and closed his door.

Laurel pulled the pills out of her purse. She dumped four into her hand and threw them back. Nothing mattered anymore besides numbing her pain.

Two weeks later, when Laurel had an episode at work, she found she was out of her trusty pills. How had she gone through sixty so quickly? She could no longer manage her anxiety without them, so she filled the prescription. Then she filled it again the following week.

When the pharmacist told her that he couldn't fill her bottle without a new prescription, she dumped an entire display of multivitamins on the floor in the drugstore. Then she asked around until she found an alternative source for her needs.

Laurel stopped attending classes and stopped showing up for work. Three eviction notices got stapled to her door. She owed money to people she shouldn't owe money to. She had entirely lost herself and it had only taken eight months.

She showed up on her parent's doorstep with her trusty yellow suitcase and an ultimatum for her mother. Either she let Laurel move in and give her a monthly allowance or she would go public about the paternity results she'd found. She didn't care anymore who it would hurt, because she couldn't possibly fall any further. Her mother didn't have a choice but to agree. Laurel had nothing, and that made her willing to risk everything.

Laurel lived there comfortably for years, becoming more dependent on her parents as time passed. Her parents acted as if she wasn't there. It didn't bother her as long as she got her monthly allowance so she could take care of her needs. But Laurel wasn't taking care of her own needs at all. All her money went towards those pills she desperately needed to get through her days. Her hygiene, her goals, her relationships, and even her spirit all took a backseat to the one thing that became the sole focus of her attention, getting rid of the pain.

Benzodiazepines didn't cut it for long, her body grew too used to them, and they weren't giving her what she craved. So, she sought stimulants to lift her up.

She was a shell of a person. The only time she felt like herself was when she'd write to Jenny. Her mom promised to include the letters in the care packages she sent. That was part of their deal. She wrote Jenny endless lies and empty promises about how good she was doing. Her daughter was already ashamed of her, she didn't want to give her more reason to be. It didn't matter anyway, Jenny never wrote back. But writing the letters kept Laurel sane. They were the last remaining sliver of the real her.

When her mother got sick, she declined rapidly and was hospitalized. Laurel didn't know how to feel. She hated her mother, but she depended on her. She gave Laurel the roof over her head and food to eat. She was the reason Jenny was thriving, and she was, in fact, thriving. She was smart, strong, hardworking, and beautiful. As much *as Laurel hated to admit it, she knew the boarding school her mother paid for was the reason.*

She tried to work up the nerve to visit her mother in the hospital. How was she supposed to say goodbye? She had such conflicting feelings. When she finally found the courage to go to the hospital, it was too late.

When her father called and told her that her mother had passed, laurel spiraled. She didn't know she could feel any lower. She shut everyone out and let the grief consume her. Days later, the maid arrived after her weekend off and knocked on Laurel's door. The woman was shaken. She had found Laurel's father's body; he had collapsed in the foyer and Laurel hadn't noticed. She hadn't left her room in days. How long had he been lying there? Did he suffer? If she had found him sooner, might he have survived?

Days after her father's death, Laurel realized she was almost out of money. She didn't have a bank account; she'd been receiving cash from her parents all that time. The cash flow was gone. She called Gregory to find out when she would get access to their accounts. She left a long series of messages but he never called back.

She went to Gregory's office in Palo Alto. He was her father's best friend, and she knew he would handle her parent's will. His law office was immaculate. Everything from the fresh flowers to the bleached grout between the tiles made the space look classy. As soon as she walked through the main doors, she felt out of place.

She begged Gregory to make time to see her. He finally agreed, so she wouldn't make a scene. Gregory told her he couldn't tell her anything until after the reading of the will.

"When is that happening?" she asked.

"I'm leaving here in a few minutes. Isn't that why you're here?"

"Why wasn't I invited?" she challenged.

"Laurel, I don't have time for this conversation. When Jensen arranged this, I assumed you were in the loop since you're still living at the house. You are still living at their house, aren't you?"

"Of course."

"My advice is, stay away for a few hours. Let me speak with Jensen and then, after we get through all the legal talk, I'll answer your questions."

"Jensen's going to be here?" Laurel couldn't believe what she was hearing. "My daughter is going to be at my house? Today?"

"Laurel, you know your parents wouldn't want you near her. You need to keep your distance during the proceedings," he warned her. "Now," he stood and buttoned his sports coat, "I must be off or I'll be late for our meeting."

Laurel flew out of that office as fast as she could. She'd be damned if she was going to miss seeing her daughter. But as soon as she got in the car, her hands started sweating and her chest felt tight. She realized that if she wasn't invited to the reading of the will, that meant she was likely left out of it.

Panic set in. She had to calm down, but her last bottle of pills was empty. She needed something; Jenny couldn't see her like that.

On her way, she stopped at a friend's house. She couldn't go to her dealer's because she already owed him money. But Leah, a friend from prison, would take care of her. She always had something. Laurel pulled up to the tiny, run-down house in East Palo Alto and banged on the door. When Leah finally answered, it was with a growl. "What the fuck do you want?"

"I need an upper now," Laurel begged. "Please tell me you have something."

"I don't got shit. I'm broke as fuck," Leah replied. She gave Laurel a once over and huffed. "Get your ass in here. You look like shit."

"I can't stay," Laurel explained. "I'm supposed to go see my daughter right now."

"No shit, Jenny's in town?" Leah asked. Then she rolled her eyes. "Fine, I'll take pity on you just this once." She disappeared into the house and returned a minute later with a paper plate with a few *brownies on it. "Someone left these here after we partied last night. I don't know what's in them, but shit was strong as fuck."*

"Thank you." Laurel took one off the plate and wrapped Leah in a quick hug. "I owe you one."

"Damn right you do," Leah called after her and she ran back to her car, taking a large bite.

Laurel knew eating the brownies was a mistake. They started to kick in before she even arrived at the house. It was one of the worst highs she'd ever had and the comedown was even worse.

When she woke up in jail the next morning, she sobbed. After all the waiting, once she finally got to see her daughter, she'd ruined it. She proved she was exactly who Jensen feared she was, a monster.

She knew she wouldn't be able to make bail. She'd be locked up again. But days later, an officer sat her down and gave her a choice. Jenny offered to pay for her to attend a rehab center instead of pressing charges. It was rehab or jail.

Laurel didn't understand why Jenny gave her the option. Did she think she was redeemable? Her flaws were on full display, but her daughter still believed in her. She was afraid to hope, but a tear fell down her cheek as she told the officer she would attend the program. She felt a spark ignite inside her for the first time in years. If she got clean, she might find her way back to the person she used to be. Someone who was worthy of Jenny.

Jensen needed time to process after Laurel finished telling her story, but Andrew didn't. As soon as Laurel was done he said, "Wait, there's a flaw in your story."

"What?" Laurel asked.

"You said the woman next door, Lydia, you said she never followed through on her promise, but she did."

Laurel looked curiously between the two boys and her daughter before asking Andrew, "how do you know that?"

But it was Grayson who answered, "Because Lydia is our mom."

Laurel sat stunned at that realization while the others thought about her story. There was no way to know if Laurel was telling the truth, but at some point, while she'd been talking, Jensen wondered if everything she'd been told about her mother was a lie. Maybe it was time she stopped telling herself that Laurel was playing the victim and accepted she actually was one.

24

"I'M SORRY" —JENSEN

"So, you're telling me you weren't an addict before I was born?" Jensen finally asked. If she were to believe it, and she was tempted to, that meant her grandparents were guilty of innumerable lies. Her grandfather wasn't her grandfather at all. Laurel wasn't an addict until after Jensen went away to St. Timothy's. Her mother wasn't in rehab that first summer, but rather was working hard to get custody. It was too much to take in. But one thing was for sure, Laurel knew the exact date of the accident. September 2nd was a date she'd never forget and the money transfers started less than a week later.

"I think we need to find Mercy Jackson," Laurel announced. "I killed that woman's child. If my mother was helping her, she probably didn't have insurance to cover the medical bills. We can't leave her to shoulder that debt alone."

Andrew Googled the name Mercy Jackson and came back with nothing within a fifty-mile radius. She might have moved away, but he tried again, searching for anyone named Mercy in the area. He found several results where Mercy was the surname, but only one where it was the first name. Mercy

McMillon was located less than ten miles away, in Mountain View.

"It's worth a shot," Grayson said, copying down the address.

"I can't face her after what I did," Laurel admitted. She tried not to put herself in stressful situations. If she let her anxiety take over, she needed the pills. That pull was always there, but usually it was manageable. During an anxiety attack, it wasn't. "I'll stay here."

Jensen could see that just talking about it was making her mother jittery. "Andrew," she asked, "can you stay with her? Grayson and I will go find Mercy."

Jensen tried not to worry on their way to the house. It might not even be the same Mercy. But if it was, Jensen would have to explain that it was her mother who had ruined her life.

The woman who opened the door of the small, one-story house didn't look like her life was ruined. She had a baby on her breast and a toddler pulling on her leg. She offered them a bright smile made even brighter by her dark skin. "Can I help you?"

"We're looking for Mercy Jackson," Jensen said. She could hear the nerves in her own voice.

"It's McMillon now. It has been for about ten years," the woman said, "but I'm Mercy."

"I'm Jensen Fisher," she introduced herself. She was about to introduce Grayson, but Mercy let out a long sigh.

"I knew the day would come when a Fisher would come knocking on my door."

Jensen and Grayson shoot each other curious looks, then Jensen continued, "My grandparents passed away a few months ago. We recently discovered some money transfers, and we thought you might know something about them?"

"Why don't you come in," she offered, pulling open the door.

Two more kids ran down the hall behind her and the toddler that was attached to her leg let go and chased after them.

Mercy led them down a hall cluttered with toys to a sliding glass door. She exited onto the back porch and called out, "Come on, you hooligans. Let's get some fresh air." All three kids came running, along with another child they hadn't seen yet. The four kids didn't bother with shoes; they just darted outside, sprinting to the play structure on the lawn.

Mercy took a seat at the table on the patio and gestured for Grayson and Jensen to sit. As they took their seats, she effortlessly covered herself up as she slid the baby off her breast and began burping him over her shoulder. No one said anything as she patted the baby. Jensen watched the kids play, their wildness reminding her of her own childhood with the Reeses. Was Laurel the reason Lydia invited Jensen into their family? If so, Laurel was protecting Jensen, even as her own life was falling apart.

"I'm sure you have a lot of questions," Mercy interrupted Jensen's thoughts. "Let me start by saying how sorry I am for my part in it."

"What could you possibly have to be sorry for?" Grayson asked.

"When Carol visited me in the hospital, I should have turned her in immediately. But I heard her out instead. I was distraught. I was just a teenager, and I had just lost my child. I had a terrible home life and I couldn't pass up the money. All she needed me to do was keep my mouth shut. She said there was already a confession. I wouldn't be required to lie on the stand or do anything illegal. She asked me to keep quiet, so that's what I've done."

"Hold on a second, who's Carol?" Grayson asked.

"Carol is my grandmother," Jensen explained. Then she asked Mercy, "What did she need you to keep quiet about? I think you need to spell it out for us. Do you remember the accident? Because Laurel doesn't remember anything about it."

"Well, she wouldn't, would she?" Mercy nodded like this made perfect sense. "She wasn't even there. It was Carol Fisher who hit me that night. I don't know why Laurel volunteered to take the fall for her mother. It wasn't my business. Like I said, all she asked me to do was keep quiet."

"Except Laurel didn't volunteer to take the fall," Grayson spoke on Jensen's behalf, knowing she wouldn't be able to. Her mind was reeling. All the lies she'd been told about her mother came crashing down.

Grayson reached over and squeezed Jensen's shaking hand. Then he turned and looked into Mercy's wide eyes. "Laurel thinks she's been guilty all these years."

"That's not possible," Mercy whispered, obviously rattled by the revelation. She didn't want to believe what they were saying. Laurel must've known she wasn't there. "She had to have known," she pleaded, fighting back tears.

They all took a moment to process. The air around them was stagnant. Finally Jensen said, "I think my mom needs to hear this. If I invite her over, would you be willing to tell us the whole story?"

When Mercy agreed, Jensen called Andrew and asked him to bring Laurel over.

While they waited, Mercy put the baby down for a nap and called her neighbor, Dominique, to take the other kids to her house then she made Jensen a cup of tea. "To calm your nerves," she said when she placed it on the patio table in front of her. Mercy sipped on tea too, trying to steady her breathing. She jumped at the sound of the doorbell, then rushed to answer it.

A moment later, she guided Andrew and Laurel into the backyard where Jensen and Grayson were waiting. She offered them both tea as well, but they declined. Laurel took the empty seat next to Jensen and without second guessing the urge, she reached out and grabbed hold of her mother's hand. Laurel was so anxious about meeting Mercy and yet she was there, because Jensen asked her to be.

"Can you tell us exactly what happened that night?" Grayson asked.

Mercy nodded. "I was nineteen and thirty weeks pregnant. I was living in East Palo Alto, but that night I went to a party in Atherton with my boyfriend. Tre used to hit up all the private school parties back then. I hated that he was dealing, but it was the fastest way for us to make money. We were young with a baby on the way and we were desperate."

Tre had mistakenly over sold some pills to Laurel at the party. He felt awful. He told her not to take too many, but she ignored his warning. She was belligerent, yelling at her boyfriend for trying to take care of her, then breaking up with him in front of everyone. The guy stormed out, abandoning her there. Tre was worried about her. She was clearly unstable, and he felt responsible.

Mercy helped him find Laurel's purse, thrown haphazardly on the counter. They dug out Laurel's ID and were relieved to see that she only lived five blocks away. Tre pulled out her keys and dragged her out front, clicking the key-fob until he found her car. He deposited Laurel into her passenger seat, then took the wheel.

Mercy wanted to stay at the party a bit longer, but she agreed to meet Tre at the bus stop later.

Tre brought Laurel home. He pulled into the rounded driveway and parked right in front of the garage. Then he hauled Laurel to the front door and rang the doorbell. It was late, but her mom answered the door. Her eyes were bloodshot, and she had the stench of gin on her breath. "What is going on?" she asked, eyeing her daughter. "What's wrong with her?"

"She took some pills," he said. Laurel wasn't completely uncon-

scious, but by the way she was leaning all her weight on him, she was awfully close. "She'll be fine. She just needs to sleep it off."

He went to pass her to her mother, but the woman stepped aside, cringing at him. "Just put her on the couch," she directed.

He laid Laurel on her side so she wouldn't choke on her own vomit when she inevitably threw up. Then he left, hoping she'd be fine after a good night's sleep.

As he walked out front, Carol said, "I need you to move the car." Tre ignored her and kept walking. She yelled, "My husband put a lock on the liquor cabinet so unless you plan to go buy me a bottle of Gin, you'll move the damn car." He had parked right in front of the garage and it was blocking her in.

"Probably a good thing," he said, tossing her Laurel's keys. They landed at her feet in the driveway. "You shouldn't be driving anyway."

He walked down the long driveway, heading for the bus stop. Before he reached the street, he heard the roar of an engine behind him. He turned and saw Carol behind the wheel of Laurel's car. She tore out of the driveway, nearly hitting him as she did.

Meanwhile, Mercy had just left the party and was headed toward the bus stop. She wanted to stay at the party, but got bored quickly after Tre left. Everyone was intoxicated and being pregnant, she couldn't partake, so she'd bailed early.

The accident happened so quickly. Mercy was approaching the bus stop, looking down at her phone, sending a text to Tre. She looked up when she heard the tires screech. A car swerved off the road, the mirror hitting the corner of the bus stop getting yanked free. Then the car careened into her.

It was Tre who found her lying on the ground, unconscious. He checked her pulse, then picked up her phone off the ground next to her. His hands shook as he wiped her blood off the screen. The phone was open to their text thread. She had been in the middle of texting him. Her message said–

Just got here. Me & Baby are hungry been
craving ch

He closed the text, never discovering what she was craving, and
dialed 911. He explained their location to the operator, leaving out his
name or his relationship to Mercy. Once the ambulance was on its
way, he squeezed her hand tight. He placed his other hand on her
stomach and prayed for the first time in his life. If there was a God, he
hoped he was listening. Then he left the scene. He couldn't linger once
the cops arrived. He was already on probation. He couldn't be caught
with a backpack full of drugs and cash.

Mercy didn't remember the accident. The police questioned her
and she couldn't even recall the color of the car. She was in shock.

Carol showed up at the hospital the following day. Mercy didn't
recognize her and thought she might be a lawyer. She was dressed
pristinely. Carol sat down at her bedside and handed Mercy a check
for one hundred thousand dollars. Mercy gaped at it. She had never
seen so much money in her life.

Before she could process what was happening, Tre entered the
room. He froze at the sight of Carol, and his demeanor shifted. "What
the fuck are you doing here? You should be in jail."

Carol stood and calmly ran her hand down her blouse, making
sure it wasn't wrinkled. She met Tre's eyes and replied, "I thought we
could work something out."

Tre eyed the check in Mercy's hand and put two and two
together. He couldn't see the amount, but nothing could make up for
what he suspected she'd done. "Whatever she's offering, don't take it,"
he instructed Mercy. "This is Laurel's mother, she's the one who hit
you."

Mercy looked back at Carol, seeing her in a new light. Less than
twenty-four hours ago, this woman had hit her and left her for dead.
Now she was sitting there, completely calm, worried about the wrin-
kles in her shirt instead of about her baby currently in the ICU. She

would not let her buy her way out of it. Mercy ripped up the check and threw it on the woman's expensive shoes.

Carol's composure momentarily fell, but then she took a deep breath and smiled. "Here's how it's going to work," she said, pulling out her checkbook. She wasn't taking no for an answer. "My daughter has offered to take responsibility for this unfortunate incident," she said. "Laurel is already at the precinct confessing. All you need to do is stay quiet."

She told them she could set them up for life and then she offered a deal they couldn't refuse. Five thousand dollars a month for the rest of their lives and she would pay all their medical bills.

*That kind of money would change everything. Mercy could go to college and put her kids through college someday. She could live comfortably. It was a future she'd never thought she would be granted. Her life had always been a struggle. She considered saying yes, but Tre answered first. "Five thousand dollars **each**," he countered. "You'll wire it to each of our accounts every month."*

"Deal," Carol agreed easily, like that kind of money barely fazed her.

Life comes down to choices and Mercy often wondered if they had made the right choice that day. Tre took the money and let it ruin his life. He expanded his dealing operation and eventually found himself in jail. But that money had bought Mercy a way out. Her house, her education, her kids, their college funds—it was all because of that money. She even adopted her sister's kids when the state took them. None of it made up for the child they lost, but it felt like everything happened the way God intended. But God couldn't have intended this.

"Laurel, I am so sorry that your life was ruined because of my selfishness." Mercy apologized sincerely.

They all turned to Laurel, waiting with bated breath for her response. She'd been uncharacteristically quiet the entire time Mercy spoke. She looked stunned, not even shedding the tears Jensen had assumed were coming. "You aren't selfish," she finally said. "My mother manipulated all of us. We're all better off without her."

Jensen nodded in agreement. She knew that everything her grandmother had ever told her was a lie. Laurel showed Mercy such grace and understanding. She was the complete opposite of the woman her grandmother had described. At that moment, she was proud to be her daughter.

Before they left, Jensen pulled Grayson aside and asked, "Do you mind getting a ride with Andrew? I want to drive with my mom. We have a lot to talk about."

"Sure," he agreed easily, kissing her and rubbing his arms up and down over her biceps. "Are you okay?"

"I will be," Jensen said, looking toward Laurel. "I'm more worried about her."

He nodded and kissed her once more on the forehead before pulling her in for a quick hug. From the passenger seat, he watched Jensen walk up to Laurel and ask if she could give her a ride home. They walked to the car together as Andrew slid into the driver's seat.

Andrew followed Grayson's gaze. "They're going to be fine, man," Andrew said.

"How can you be sure?" Grayson asked. "She's already been through so much. What if Laurel hurts her?"

"Laurel's not a bad person, Grayson. She's just been dealt a shit hand," Andrew said. "I've spent the past week with her and I believe her when she says she just wants Jensen to be happy. They need to figure this out."

"You're right, I know you're right."

"So, you really love her?" his brother asked with a goofy smile.

Grayson shoved his shoulder and laughed. "Shut up and drive." But, as they pulled out of the driveway, he answered, "Yeah, I really do."

Andrew nodded, "Good."

Jensen and Laurel drove for a few minutes in silence. They were both processing the bomb that was just dropped on them. Laurel was innocent. Holy shit! It was just sinking in. Jensen thought back to that photo album she found on Laurel's bed all those weeks ago. They'd been happy. Their lives were entirely uprooted because of Gran and her lies. Tears fell rapidly and Jensen had to pull to the side of the road. She couldn't catch her breath. Her life could have been so different. She sobbed, wrecked by the life she lost.

Laurel unbuckled her seatbelt and leaned over to wrap her arms around Jensen. She held her and whispered, "Shhh Jenny-Bee, everything's going to be okay." And for the first time, hearing her mother's nickname for her was a comfort.

"I'm sorry," Jensen finally said through her tears. There was so much she was sorry for. For never seeing through Gran's lies. For not reading the letters when Laurel asked her to. For holding onto doubt even after Laurel told her story. Worst of all, she was sorry for not seeing her mother for who she truly was. She let Gran cast a shadow so dark she wasn't able to see through it to the light.

"I'm so angry," Jensen yelled. "Why aren't you more angry?"

"I'm sure when it sinks in, I'll be royally pissed, but right now I'm so relieved that I didn't kill that baby. I feel like a weight has been lifted off me," Laurel said. "We know the truth. Now we can start to heal."

They got back to the house and Jensen started the conversion they should've had months ago. "About the will–"

Laurel cut her off. "Don't worry about the money. It was never about the money. It was always about you."

25. "HONEYSUCKLE THRIVES WHEN IT CAN GROW WILD" —LYDIA

The phone rang and rang. He was probably sleeping, it was nearly midnight on the East Coast after all, but Jensen was relentless. She had no problem messing with his sleep schedule when he'd been the one to make all those 4:00 a.m. wake up calls.

"What?" The man screamed into his phone. It was a tone she was so familiar with that it brought a smile to her face.

"Leon, it's me, Jensen. I'm coming out of retirement, I thought you'd want to know," she said to her private coach of the past seven years.

"Ah," he said, his voice still gruff but no longer angry. "What took you so long?"

"I had to do a little self discovery," she said.

"Did you find her? Is she a gold medalist?" he asked.

"I think she might be," she answered.

"Where are you? I'll be on the first flight out."

Jensen gave Leon instructions to fly into Reno airport and get a car into Tanglewood, the closest town to Evergreen with an Olympic sized pool. Then, she asked Andrew what kind of strings he could pull to get her some private training time there.

He wouldn't be returning with them to the lake but by the next morning he had booked her a three hour training block from 4:00 until 7:00 every morning.

Suddenly Jensen wasn't as upset about the text she'd received from Phil letting her know she'd been taken off the work schedule. She wouldn't have time for work anymore. Everything had to go into swimming if she was going to walk on to Stanford's team.

While Grayson loaded their suitcase into the car, Jensen ran up to her room and grabbed her bag of swim gear that she'd saved which included kneeskin suits, swim caps, and goggles. Then she ran downstairs, threw the bag in the trunk and looked back at the empty house. She didn't need to say goodbye, she wouldn't miss it. It had never been her home. She would, however, miss Andrew but they'd said their goodbyes the night before, knowing he'd already be at work when it came time for them to leave.

"Got everything?" Grayson asked.

"Yep, lets go," she nodded and kicked her feet up on the dash.

Grayson drove and Jensen was glad to be putting that house and its memories in her past. When they pulled into the parking lot of the pet store, Laurel was already waiting for them out front. She smiled when she saw their car pull in and jogged over and opened the back door.

"Are you sure this is okay?" she asked as she slid in.

"Absolutely," said Grayson. "We talked to my mom last night and she's excited you're coming."

"Your boss was okay with you taking the time off?" Jensen asked.

"Just for the week," Laurel confirmed. "Andrew said he'd bring me home. He'll be there next weekend for his sister's going away dinner."

When they arrived at the lake, Dustin barreled out of the house, jumping on the first person to exit the car. Grayson tossed his brother in the air twice, then plopped him on his shoulders.

"How's it going, Little Man?" Grayson asked, giving Dustin a fist bump.

"Davis taught me how to use a screwdriver and I learned righty tighty and lefty loosey," Dustin said, "It's cool because it rhymes."

"Very cool," Grayson nodded in agreement. "Hey Buddy, I want you to meet someone." He turned and gestured to Laurel as she climbed out of the car. "Dustin, this is Laurel. She's Jen's mom."

"I like you. You have a cool name," Dustin said without hesitation. "It rhymes with Coral."

"It does." Laurel smiled at Dustin's immediate acceptance of her.

They were just walking up the porch steps when Lydia stepped out with Julia on her hip. She swept them each into her arms one by one.

When Lydia hugged Jensen she whispered, "I'm so proud of you." But she didn't elaborate further. Was she proud of her for discovering the truth, for coming out of retirement, for forgiving her mother, or maybe a mix of all three?

Whatever she was proud of, Jensen accepted it with a gracious, "thank you," and realized she was pretty damn proud of herself too. The past few days had been a whirlwind of emotions and instead of running away from it all, she'd leaned on Grayson. She'd trusted him to navigate the storm with her and together they'd come out of it stronger. That first night after finding out the truth, she had been angry. No, pissed. She'd ranted and yelled and it hadn't scared Grayson away. The opposite–he'd gathered her up in his arms and held her tight.

Then, he brought her down to the garage, opened a box of her grandmother's fine china and began throwing it at the walls. The noise drew Laurel and Andrew to them, wondering what was going on. When they found them in the garage surrounded by broken china, instead of freaking out, they'd joined them. The whole experience had been cathartic, and bonding.

And when the dishes were all shattered and Jensen was done fuming, she let herself cry.

Lydia released Jensen and turned to Laurel, who wasn't expecting a hug. Lydia pulled her in as casually as she did the others. She hugged her tightly and said, "I did my best to look after our girl."

Laurel cried and offered a sincere, "Thank you."

When they broke apart, Lydia nodded to the house, "Did you notice the Honeysuckle?"

"It's the same one?" Laurel asked, dumbfounded.

"It is," Lydia confirmed. "I dug it out of the ground myself when I left Atherton. I was worried it wouldn't survive, but I wasn't about to leave without it. It barely bloomed when we first moved away, but when we moved here, it came back to life. Honeysuckle thrives when it can grow wild." She caught Jensen's eye and they both smiled.

After inviting them in, Lydia spent a long time sitting with Laurel, showing her pictures of Jensen's childhood. She had an entire photo album dedicated to her. Jensen wished she had seen the album sooner. The photos dug up so many memories. She stood behind the couch, leaning over the back to see them. There was one in particular of her and Grayson that she asked to keep. Lydia slipped it out of the plastic sleeve and handed it to her.

She was eight years old, and she was begging Andrew to marry her. "Please, please, please," she kept saying.

"Fish, don't you think you're getting too old to be playing pretend?" A twelve-year-old Andrew asked.

"If you play with us today, I promise I'll never ask you again. Cross my heart and hope to die."

"No. I don't want to play," he said.

"But it's just pretend."

"I don't even want to pretend to marry you," he said.

"But your mom told us to play something together. This is what me and Nicole want to play."

"Then you guys can have a wedding and I'll ride bikes with Grayson," Andrew said.

"But we rode bikes all morning, and besides, Grayson already agreed to play with us. Come on, please?"

"Do you know how much my friends would make fun of me if they found out? Everyone would think I liked an eight-year-old," he scoffed.

"You don't have to be so mean, Andy," Grayson said, walking over.

Grayson hit his growth spurt late. He was a full inch shorter than Jensen that summer, and three inches shorter than Andrew, but he still defended her.

"I told you it's not Andy anymore. I'm Andrew now."

"You think you're so cool now that you're in middle school, don't you?" Grayson said.

"Yeah, because I am." Andrew shoved his brother as he walked past him.

"Where are you going?" Grayson yelled at him.

"I'm gonna go see what Rachel's doing," Andrew said, walking two doors down and knocking on Rachel Sunday's door.

Rachel Sunday had moved into town a few weeks prior. She was girly and annoying, and Andrew always wanted to invite her to come play with them. Jensen hated her and her evil red hair. She lived on *their street for a couple of years, but during that time it felt like Rachel was ruining her life.*

Andrew came back a few minutes later with Rachel in tow. "Ok, I decided I want to play," Andrew said.

"Really?" Jensen jumped up excitedly.

"Yeah, but I can't marry you. You're too little. I'm gonna marry Rachel instead."

"You're just doing this to be mean," Grayson said to Andrew.

"No, I'm not. Rachel's the one who said we should play with you guys. I just agreed with her."

"You're being a butthead," Nicole said, and Jensen gasped. Andrew didn't even seem fazed by the insult.

They picked all the flower petals off Lydia's roses in her garden and used them to line the sidewalk as their aisle. Rachel took the yellow flower crown from Jensen. She said it looked like something the bride should wear, not the bridesmaid. She walked down the sidewalk and when she got to Andrew; he reached out and held her hands. Jensen was so jealous she thought she might die.

They didn't really know what was said at weddings because none of them had ever been to one. Andrew and Rachel both said, "I do," and then Nicole said, "you may kiss the bride."

Nicole and Jensen always played 'wedding' with pretend boys, so there was never any real kissing. Jensen expected this wedding to be the same. She nearly fainted when she saw Andrew lean forward and kiss Rachel Sunday right on the mouth. Rachel Sunday had to look up to kiss Andrew and when she did, Jensen's flower crown fell off her head and onto the ground. She reached to pick it up, but Rachel took a step back and smashed it under her foot.

Jensen started crying, and she didn't want everyone to make fun of her, so she ran home. She wasn't really upset about her flower crown. She was upset that Rachel had stolen it from her. She was so mean. How could Andrew like someone so mean? Jensen was upset that he kissed her. She was pretty sure that it was his first kiss. That kiss was supposed to belong to her.

An hour later, her doorbell rang, and the maid answered it. "Jensen," she called across the house. "The neighbor boy's here."

She got her hopes up that it was Andrew coming to say he was sorry and he loved her, too. She checked to make sure she didn't look like she had been crying. Then, she ran to get the door. Her eyes were still red-rimmed, but they weren't too bad. She skidded to a halt in front of the open door. When she saw Grayson standing there, her smile fell. "Hi, what's up?" she asked.

"Here," Grayson said, holding out a beautiful flower crown.

"You fixed it?" she asked, taking it from him.

"No. Yours was ruined. I had to make a new one."

"Thanks," she said.

"Anyway, I just didn't want you to be sad," Grayson said, then he stood on his tiptoes and kissed her. It was so quick she almost didn't realize what had happened. Before she could wrap her head around the fact that a boy had just kissed her, he was asking, "So, do you want to come over for dinner? Mom's making spaghetti."

They never talked about the kiss again. Sometimes, Jensen thought she'd made it up. But in her hand was a picture of her and Grayson. A crown of honeysuckle on her head.

Even at eight years old, he had been extraordinary. How had she never noticed? She was so thankful that Lydia had snapped that picture.

Grayson slid up behind her and wrapped his arms around her waist, looking over her shoulder at the photo. He chuckled softly in her ear. "I remember that day," he said, replaying the same memory in his mind. "I had some serious game. I spent an hour making that crown just so I could shoot my shot."

"You're pretty smug, considering it took you ten years to nail it down," Jensen joked and Grayson laughed, squeezing her tight.

Practices with Leon started first thing the following morning. She had picked up some bad habits from swimming in the lake. While she had gotten faster, her starts and turns were a mess.

She arrived back at the house after her fifth day of training, sore and frustrated, but her mood quickly turned around when she saw Andrew's truck in the driveway. She ran into the living room and collapsed onto the couch next to him

"How was practice?" Andrew asked.

"I'll let you know once I regain feeling in my deltoids," she smiled.

Grayson came up behind her and placed his hands on her aching shoulders. He massaged the tight muscles, forcing a groan out of her. "That good, huh?" he asked.

She turned her head, offering a soft kiss to the top of his hand.

"Thanks," she whispered. "That feels amazing."

That night they sat around the table and toasted to Nicole, and all the big adventures that were soon to come her way. Brent hadn't left her side for the past week, clinging on to every moment they had together, he could feel her slipping through his fingers. He'd asked her to stay but Nicole was resolved to leave. She told him she loved him. That he was the best, most unexpected thing to ever happen to her, but none of that was going to change her mind. He was trying to respect her choice but his own trauma led him to believe she'd leave and he'd never find that feeling again. So, after dinner he tried one last time to convince her to stay. It didn't go well and the night ended in tears shed by both of them.

The next day she left for the airport without a goodbye and without looking back.

Andrew left next, taking Laurel with him. She was headed back to the house for a couple weeks. She'd finish packing it up, then put it on the market. Jensen was supportive of her mothers decision to sell, it was after all, Laurel's decision to make. That was one of the first things they'd discussed after the truth came to light–the inheritance.

Jensen knew the only thing to do was give Laurel her rightful share, but when she offered, Laurel turned it down. She didn't yet trust herself to have access to so much money when she was still recovering. Instead, the only thing Jensen could convince her to take was the house.

Laurel accepted on the condition that she be able to sell it and use the profit to pay off the back taxes on the money that had been laundered. The house would easily catch an eight figure sale so she'd still be left with plenty to live comfortably.

When she got back to the house she checked the mail before going inside. She shuffled through it and was about to toss it on the counter when she came to the last envelope in the stack. A piece of handwritten mail addressed to Carol Fisher. She opened it carefully, unsure who would be writing to her mother.

She read the letter twice before picking up the phone and calling Jensen.

"Mom?" She answered on the first ring. "Is everything okay?"

"I just received a letter addressed to my mother, from Tre."

"What does it say?" Jensen asked, putting her phone on speaker so Grayson could hear, too.

"It says he hasn't gotten his money this month and if he doesn't he's going to expose the truth about who really hit Mercy." Laurel summarized. "What do I do?"

"Do you know what that is?" Grayson asked.

"It sounds like a threat," Laurel answered.

"No, it's a chance to clear your name."

The thought of clearing her name had never even crossed her mind. But if she had a clean record she could truly get a fresh start. She was only thirty-six, there was still so much life to be lived and for the first time in a long time she was excited for what the future held for her.

After Jensen got off the phone she turned back to Grayson, "Okay, let's go, Brent and Reed are waiting for us." They were going parasailing that afternoon, something Leon had lectured her about endlessly that morning.

"What if you get hurt?" He yelled.

Jensen shrugged. "I'll be careful, but if I get hurt then I get hurt. I'm done living my life scared." There were only two weeks left of summer and she planned to spend every minute she had left soaking up all Evergreen had to offer.

On the last day, Jensen and Grayson met out on the dock as soon as she was done training. Tomorrow they would have to leave the lake and get ready to go their separate ways. The early morning air was crisp, reminding them that fall was right around the corner.

The past few days had been full of logistic conversations about how they would make the distance work. They went over Stanford's swim schedule, Grayson's workload as a junior, how long the commute was between their schools and when they'd be able to see each other. It was going to be tough but Jensen wasn't worried about it. She had learned how important it was to make time for the people who really mattered and there was no way she'd ever let Grayson slip through the cracks.

They sat on the dock for the last time that summer and Jensen put her head on his shoulder. "I'm really going to miss it here," she whispered both to the lake and to Grayson.

"I always hate leaving at the end of summer," he agreed. "This summer more than most."

"Are you going to be okay with the fact that this might be our last full summer here?" They'd already talked about it at length, but she couldn't wrap her head around everything he was willing to give up for her. Summer was a big season for swimming and if she was serious about going back to the Olympics in two years there was no way she'd be able to play hooky again for an entire summer. And if she was lucky and her swim career continued it could be years before she had the luxury of a whole summer at the lake. She refused to let swimming take over her entire world like it had before, but she wasn't the kind of person to half ass anything. If she was going for it, then she was going for gold.

"I told you before and I'll tell you as many times as you need to hear it." He squeezed her hand. "I'm with you, no matter where you go, I'll always be by your side."

"But Evergreen is your home," she countered.

"No," he said, "you are. Someday we can come back here and make a home in Evergreen if that's what you want, but until then I want you to follow your dreams and I want to follow mine and we'll cheer each other on as we do it."

Tears came to her eyes and the only words she could come up with were the three she had yet to say. "I love you."

Grayson chuckled and wrapped his arms around her, "I'm glad because I can't imagine my life without you. I'm so in love with you. I love the piece of you that's driven and hardworking, that's about to take the swimming world by storm. I love the piece of you that's gracious, that's willing to start fresh with your mom and include her in your life. I love the piece of you that's adventurous, that's always down to try something new. And I love the piece of you that's emotional, that gets sad and angry and isn't holding back anymore. And when you put all those pieces together, they form an incredible soul that I think might have been put on this earth just for me to love."

Never in her wildest dreams did Jensen think anyone would see her so clearly, but Grayson did. He loved her, not despite her flaws, but for them. "You know, a home here someday isn't the worst idea. I think a piece of my heart will forever be in Evergreen."

"As long as I can have the rest of it," Grayson said.

"It's already yours."

ACKNOWLEDGMENTS

I have been writing books for as long as I can remember. My writing has always been for me—a hobby. I didn't begin taking it seriously until my family moved out of California and I was missing my home desperately. And so, I wrote this book first and foremost as a love letter to California and all the beauty it has to offer.

The place I missed most was the lake where I spent the summers of my youth. If you read my dedication you know that this book was written for my Grandparents, "for all the memories at the lake." Well, while Lake Evergreen is fictional, it is based heavily off of the real lake I grew up going to, Lake Almanor, and the home my grandparents own on the East Shore. Summers spent there are some of my fondest memories.

And while writing this book certainly helped with the homesickness, nothing ever cured it. My husband saw my need for mountains, lakes, and fresh (non humid) air. He knew how much I loved to be outside and even though we had just bought our dream house two years prior, he knew I wasn't happy. So, we moved to a small town of 2,024 people in Northern California, three minutes away from a beautiful lake in the Sierra Foothills. It's everything I've ever dreamed of. I am thankful for him every day for recognizing what I needed and giving me the life I've always wanted. I now get to write in a place that truly inspires me.

But, this story didn't just come to me out of the blue. It was one of many stories that I had brainstormed, outlined, then tucked away to be written *someday*. I'm incredibly happy that this book made it out of my scribbled notebook pages. I first started outlining it almost eight years ago while sitting poolside at Burgess Park, in Menlo Atherton watching the kids I nannied practice for swim team. So, to the Chopra family, thank you for welcoming me into your home and as a part of your family for the seven years I worked for you. As you can tell, the Menlo Park, Atherton, and Stanford areas have always stuck with me.

I also need to extend my gratitude to Suzanne Scotten for her incredible editing, and to Lisa Gunatileka for proofreading. I don't pretend to be good at this, I just like to tell stories. It's because of you that the commas and quotation marks are all in the right places.

To my cover artist My Lan Khuc, thank you for seeing my vision and making it a reality. Your art is incredible and you truly captured my characters beautifully.

I also need to acknowledge the endless support I've received from my family. My dad, Paul Boswell, my sister Rebecca Boswell, and my brothers, Nathan Duenas and Frankie Duenas, all of whom have read this book despite my trying to convince them otherwise. But, in my brother Nathan's words (which really sums up how it goes in my family), "You wrote a whole ass book, of course we're going to read it." They really are the most supportive and encouraging family out there.

Finally, for my mom, Alyson Boswell, who's a freaking Saint! She's my alpha reader, first draft editor, brainstorm partner, and all around best friend, she does it all. This book wouldn't be what it is without you. Thank you!

ABOUT THE AUTHOR

E. M. Langston is an emerging author of small town contemporary romances. She's been writing novels since high school, is an avid reader, and is also a teacher, a mom, and a wife. She has two kids, two large dogs, a cat, and an incredible husband who she's known since childhood (It's a real life enemies-to-lovers story.) Together they live in a quaint home in a small town in Northern California.